FRESH HEIR

MICHAEL REILLY

ISBN: 0615445616
ISBN-13: 9780615445618
Library of Congress Control Number: 2011902592

This book is a work of fiction. All characters, places, and events are either invented or used fictitiously. Any resemblances in this book to actual events, places or persons, living or dead, is coincidental.

For Lara

&

In memory of K.F.R.

1

❖ ❖ ❖

BACKSEAT BLUES

I believe my dad decided to go on this trip the day I was born. That was nearly twelve and a half years ago. Not that he's farsighted. If anything, he admits, he likes to focus only on the present under the belief that everything in his future will somehow find a way on its own to slip down the wrong road. But when it comes to the road down *my* future life, he seems to be the grand wizard of great expectations. You know that soft part on top of a baby's head? I think they call it the fontanel. Yes, I think they do. Well, I've had this recurrent dream where I'm an infant and my fontanel throbs like a nervous heart while I sit alone propped in a rocking chair as race cars roar through our backyard and my dad stands naked on our roof shouting: "Slow down! Listen up! My kid's a prodigy! My kid's a prodigy!"

I guess all dreams are just a twist on reality for good or for bad. And the reality is, I've heard versions of these cheers from my dad ever since I can remember. Fortunately, in real life he's always had his clothes on. Unfortunately, he's taken no care to temper these cheers in front of my friends, which lately is a source of wicked embarrassment—for me and my friends. But give the guy credit. So what if he gushes excitement over my future, often at the expense of his own. Sometimes they call that self-lessness. I guess. At least he's not like a lot of my friends' parents who call their kids spoiled, lazy, and ungrateful. Or worse. Like my friend Zach's dad, who calls him spoiled, lazy and ungrateful, while driving him to hockey tournaments all over God's creation with pledges that one day Zach's going to make it to the Big Time. Zach has learned to despise hockey and has confided to me that he's going to do everything in his power *not* to make it to the Big Time, so his dad will never be the next famous father of an unfulfilled superstar. OK, so maybe I put words in his mouth, but the point is, Zach really resents his dad these days. It's scary.

I don't resent mine. Mostly I feel sorry for him. Just look at him now, bobbing and weaving his head on his chicken neck to the sound of Steely Dan he's cranked up way too loud in the car so we can't hear the honking outside. It's a pathetic obsession for New Yorkers to honk madly on the Long Island Expressway in dead-still traffic, as if it might miraculously launch everyone into motion again. A kooky woman in a little red car next to us isn't honking, but tilting over her steering wheel with the sneer of someone who has a better solution in mind. Like maybe the exaggerated slant of her body toward her destination might get her there quicker, despite the five thousand cars ahead of her not going more than two miles per hour. Who knows, maybe it does work, that tilting thing. It does for those ski jumpers in the Olympics when they soar through the air. They're mostly Scandinavians, aren't they? Ingrid over there next to us has soared past at least forty times already in the span of fifty yards. Twice she's picked her nose. I'm sick of seeing her. And I begin to conclude this is going to be one long trip.

"This will break up soon, kiddos," my dad pledges feverishly. He's peering at us with forced glee through the reflective tint of his sunglasses, and I just grit my teeth waiting for my little sister to fart again in the seat next to me. "You doing all right, Jame?" he asks me, as if the Shrek-like pallor of my skin might be indicating otherwise. I nod my head, not too vigorously or it might foment the nausea. I try to steer my gaze away from the bumper sticker on a Hummer the color of bile plodding past on the left for the gazillionth time. *There are 3 kinds of people: Those who can count and those who can't*, the sticker says. Now that's pretty funny, Einstein, but it doesn't atone for your driving that hunk of bile. Einstein's tailed by a BMW that's driving like it's on a yo-yo string: jerking forward, drifting back, jerking forward, drifting back. I can't tell who's driving the BMW since the windows are tinted, just like the Hummer's. My dad would argue it's definitely a woman because they all drive like, well, yo-yos. The tinted windows all around send me into a trance as they repulse the pearly rays lancing through the thick air of an early summer heat wave that seems to carry with it the perpetual hum of cicadas, even though I really can't hear a darn thing above all the honking. And my dad's jarring recital of "Dirty Work."

I began to feel the nausea the moment we descended the driveway under the lurching birch tree, and my dad swerved to miss the speeding UPS truck. It wouldn't have happened if we'd left in the morning, when UPS never makes deliveries. Nine o'clock was our target departure time, but my dad usually operates off a clock that's about five hours behind the rest of the world. So we set off at 2:10, and I was ready to puke at 2:15. It's now 3:15, and we're probably no more than two miles from home. Just think, only 4,600 miles left until San Francisco, when you include all the planned diversions. I *told* my dad this was a bad idea.

It'd help my stomach if I could ride shotgun, but it's been poached by some lady I'd never in my life seen before this morning. Now apparently I will be spending the entire summer in close quarters with her.

she sounds wacky. That's an e-mail I get from my friend Jessica when I describe the lady to her. Jessica's sharp and let's me be myself. That's why I like her. Not *like her,* like her. But like her as a friend. Although I can't help noticing Jessica's chest going nuts these days, and this kid Frank who lives down my street says she's going to be *some* snatch when she gets older. Frank's going into tenth grade. He smokes pot. And he likes to play ring-and-run at two in the morning. My dad says next time he does it he's going to squash the kid. Like a gnat. Which is perfect because that's what Jessica says Frank looks like. She makes me laugh. And, lately, cry a lot when she talks about that thing with her mother.

now i think i know wat the lady smells like, I type back on my smartphone. We stick to e-mail because her mom won't let her do Facebook. And texting is out of the question. Texting, her mom says, promotes salaciousness. OK. Whatever.

cat litter n anchovies, I continue to type. Chastely.

haha...sounds yummy. just like when my dad makes dinner. Jessica totally adores her dad. To this I can relate. But her mom too? I can't deny this double dose of devotion sometimes makes me envious deep down. That's alliteration.

i hate this trip already, I write back.

miss u already :) I leave her hanging. I'm sure she doesn't like that, but I refuse to engage in girly talk.

"Oh, thaaaaaat's it, moron! Cut in front of me like it's going to get you anywhere in this godforsaken traffic!" That's my dad. The thing about his cheerful disposition is it's brittle, like the shell of a candy apple when you first bite it. Other drivers definitely like to bite my dad, which might explain the race cars in my dream. He despises drivers of all sorts, mostly the ones that drive like he does. Which might explain why slowpokes piss him off the most. I'll never forget the time he flipped off the old lady crawling along in front of us who just happened at that time to be my third grade teacher, Mrs. Hanley. She failed me on my next spelling test—not because the words were spelled wrong, but because my writing was "too sloppy," which I found dubious. But I'd rather a failing grade than a shotgun blast to the head from some freak slightly miffed by my dad's impatience on the road. He finds some way to get irked by just about every driver he encounters, which isn't a good habit in New York, or if you're driving across country. By my calculation we may encounter about 5,544,631 cars between New York and California, so I've braced myself for lots of hell-raising from the driver's seat. Yes, this is definitely going to be a long trip. Unless we get shot first.

"Penis breath!" That's my little sister aiming her venom at the moron who just cut in front of us. She's good at imitating my dad's petulance and usually does so with meticulous movie quotes—except that her lisp often distorts the words, so in this case they come out like "peenith breff." She watches lots of really old movies in the car, usually ones she probably shouldn't. *ET*'s been her favorite of late and is fairly tame compared to most. My dad buys them for six bucks a pop at Target. She's five, my sister. In addition to farting a lot—really noxious farts worse than the ones from the old ladies in church—she lies profusely, which I'm not uncertain might be a hereditary trait akin to my father's tendency toward delusional pronouncements about my future. My sister—she does have a name, which is Sara, although we call her Frizzy, which she pronounces *Fwizzy*—also wields a wicked temper. She exhibits it with a violent shriek followed flawlessly by a squint, rendering the victim helplessly mute and making me sort of lament the brow-beatings her future husband will one day suffer from. Oh, and Frizzy has asthma; she hacks constantly. She's allergic to just about everything under the sun: dogs, cats, sheep (don't ask), peanut butter, grass, dust, mold, and most perfumes. In addition to coughing, they—that would be everything under the sun—often make her break out in red blotches all over her body. This in turn makes her feel *fwizzy*, as she declared one time a few years back, subsequently earning herself the nickname Frizzy, which is what we thought she really meant. As if it really meant something. Thought of this last unusual allergy, the perfume one, now makes me wonder if my dad ordered the mysterious woman in the front seat not to wear perfume, which, if she had, might have gone a long way toward extinguishing the cat litter/anchovy scent and thereby appeasing my stomach ache. But it'd just be better if she weren't here altogether and I could ride shotgun.

After rummaging though my sister's Hannah Montana backpack, I finally locate my headphones. This reminds me that you can add stealing to the illustrious set of skills she seems to be developing so precociously. I've often wondered what crooked path her life might one day meander down, but my father insists all girls are that way and not to worry. Who said I was worrying?

I'm just settling into the rhythm of Eminem when I feel the hum of my cell phone in my lap. Besides noticing that the vibration feels kind of good down there, my nausea picks up a notch when I notice it's my mother calling. I'm certain if I ignore it, she'll continue to call until I answer, so I opt for immediate suffering in hopes of mitigating the damage.

"Hi, Mom."

"Where are you, honey?"

"In Dad's car."

"Well, I figured that, dear," she says, with the most artificially syrupy voice. I wonder if it might finally make me barf.

"We're in Canada, Mom. We're fleeing the country."

"Jamie! That's not funny. Where are you?"

"A strip club in Canada. Frizzy loves it. Do you know what they call knockers in French?" I ask as if I were an expert. In response, silence grips the line for several minutes, and I can't tell if my mom is shocked or simply enjoying a quick massage on the shoulders from that gay husband of hers. All I know is I can hear the honking again…and another old lady fart. Then some coughing. Ingrid slides by on the right again, still leaning. Einstein and his hunk of bile on the left. I *reeeally* feel sick.

"Jamie, please, sweetie. I just would like to have a civil conversation about your trip. Now, where are you?"

"You know that house you didn't like? The one with the people in it you didn't like either?" I didn't give her a chance to answer, for fear she might be getting another massage. "Well, we're so close I think once we get up to the next rise in the expressway, sometime within the next forty-five minutes hopefully, I might be able to look back and still see our chimney. I think Dad left a fire burning. You know how he likes a fire in June."

"Did you say you're in New Jersey, honey?" Oh God. The damage is done.

"Listen, Mom," I say, much too civilly, "I'm having trouble with the connection. I'll call you back." I hang up without waiting for an answer and wonder if she wonders if I'll ever call her back.

"Hey, Jame! Hey, Jame!" I can hear my father's squeaky voice above the soothing rap music in my ears, but I continue to stare out the window and ignore him because I know what's coming. He backs off and cranks up his own tunes again. I can feel the heat searing my face through the window, baking off the expressway's black top, off the Hummer's windows, off the empty paint can among the litter on the shoulder of the road. The heat's in stark relief to the cool blast from the air conditioning, which is insufficient enough to prevent my legs from sticking to the leather seat as my shorts ride up and pull my skin taut. Frizzy's eyes are glued to the TV screen and she hacks in a trance. I can hear the sound blasting, because she usually refuses to wear headphones, which she claims are "ear-wa-tating."

Slowly my nausea begins to wane, and I realize it's because we're driving faster. Not fast. Just faster. It's enough to prompt Frizzy to ask if we will be in "Sand Fwan-sicko" soon. My dad says, "Sure, pretty soon." I just snicker and stare out the window. The roadside litter becomes blurred with speed, and I can no longer make out pieces of tire from discarded shoes. How in the world is it that people can lose their shoes on the side of an expressway? I can see my dad pointing out the window in pantomime at the police car parked on the side of the road. I pull the earphone out of my left ear quick enough to hear him say, "That's what did it, kiddos. *That* cop parked right there on the side of the road, just sitting there, doing nothing…just doing nothing, except maybe cleaning the donut crumbs off his lap. It's stopped traffic from here to the moon."

"Y'all a dickwad," my sister mumbles, as she turns her head out the window toward the cop. No problem with the lisp there. And it gives her the chance to rehearse the contrived Southern accent she's been trying to perfect. I think it's because my dad insists we have some southern heritage. Although I believe he's thinking it's aristocratic heritage, not hillbilly. Her bad language falls deafly on my dad's ears but is loud enough to turn the head of the Shotgun Bandit. Actually, bandit's too cool a word. Shotgun Snatcher is better. It's not as bad as being a baby snatcher, I suppose. But almost. The Snatcher can't quite muster a full turn to look at my sister behind her, so she looks at me. She cocks her head so she can let me see her eyes over the tops of her sunglasses, but they're too fat for her bony face. I catch nothing but the extrusion of her nose, which looks like someone wedged a marble up it, giving it a long, hump-like curve groaning under the weight of the ridiculous-looking glasses that are as big as hubcaps.

Quickly I glance back out the window and notice the car veering toward the exit for the Cross Island Expressway, with the Frogs Neck Bridge looming up ahead. My dad's bebopping again like a pigeon that's been drinking from a puddle of Mountain Dew, and he gives a carefree officer's salute to a black sedan that zips by on his left.

"I haff to go pee," my sister declares. But we all pretend not to hear her. Now that we're moving, I decide to put down the window for some fresh air to help my stomach. After a couple of clicks on the button, I realize the window lock is on and yell up to my dad in the front seat. He's deaf against the blare of his music, although I can't tell what it is with the blare of my own music piped directly into my ears. Nor can I tell how loud I'm yelling, so I pull out my earphones and yell again, louder. This must be how it is in a nursing home, and my dad flinches like an old man whose hearing aid just zapped him.

He quickly lowers his music and says, "What's up, Jame?"

"Can you please take off the window lock?"

"Oh, sure thing, kiddo." But he ignores my request and instead seizes the chance he now has with my headphones removed. "Hey, Jame, how 'bout a little quiz work."

"Fine," I say. I resigned myself a long time ago to keeping him amused. The truth is, it usually keeps me more amused than anything when he quizzes me, particularly when he doesn't have the immediate ability to double check my answers on the Internet. But he's come prepared for this trip, with a whole binder of stuff printed out, which he's now trying to flip through with one hand while swerving all over the road.

"OK," he says, once he's figured out a way to steer the car straight. "Tell me about the Battle of Bull Run."

"First or second?"

"Huh?"

"Dad, there were two of them."

"Oh, yeah, right, right. Let's start with the first."

The Civil War's been his thing for the past few weeks. It's because, he says, we're heading through the South, and it's going to be important for me to associate the sights down there with my store of knowledge. We're supposed to be stopping to visit cousins in Virginia, on my mom's side of the family, which should be interesting. I begin spouting some facts about Bull Run, substituting General McDowell's name with General Pershing's to see if my dad has any clue whatsoever. Which he doesn't. He just keeps giving me the thumbs up sign like some dorky politician.

Now might be the time to explain how it is I can recite facts about the Civil War, or World War One, or just about any war, or even the life-time batting averages of the Mets starting line-up from the 1986 World Championship team, the last one I'm sadly sure they'll ever have. The thing is, I can recite just about anything that I've read or heard in the past, even if it's just been once. I've been able to do this ever since I can remember, although my recollection is no doubt biased by my dad's indulgent procla-mations to anyone who will listen that I could recite the entire alphabet—backward and forward—when I was six months old, amazingly after hear-ing it for the first time. My dad's put me through all kinds of intelligence tests, all of which declare me "gifted." I often wonder what good's a gift when it sometimes makes you ill. Like you've eaten too many M&Ms. But who knows, maybe my stomach problems are related to something else, like my sister's gas. Or my gassy mother.

The fact of the matter is, I'll never stop reading so gluttonously because I enjoy it. I always have. Otherwise, I'm pretty normal. I think. History books, biographies, those I do mostly for my dad. It's the novels I love best. I read the last *Harry Potter* in six hours straight. It's mostly adult books I read now. I like funny ones because they don't seem to be too hard on my stomach. I've covered just about all the American classics. And I've read Dickens up the ying-yang. That's my dad's phrase. Reading all this stuff to me is like those guys who do those hundred-mile running races. It must be painful for them at times, masochistic in a way, but adrenaline keeps them going. And once they finish, they feel like they've conquered the world. Although most probably don't have their dads cheering loudly in their ears.

All the reading I do, and the ability to remember all the big words I encounter, might help explain why I can spout off words like *gluttonously* and *masochistic*, although I do confess there might be times I misuse them. Once or twice a year. And there are lots of times I don't use them at all, like with my friends, when I just stick to monosyllables and mostly grunts. The exception of course is with Jessica, whose eyes always light up with genuine fascination when I act like my real self. What a novelty.

I have been silent for several moments, my dad still giving the thumbs up sign, when he finally realizes my lips are no longer moving and asks me, "What about the other one, Jame?"

"What other one?"

"The other Bull Run."

"Oh right, well in 1869..." I begin, which sets him off flipping wildly through his binder, swerving the car into the adjacent lane again and inviting a long honk from a yellow cab definitely being driven by a terrorist-in-training well over ninety miles an hour. With my heart feeling like it's in my stomach, I turn to Frizzy as I now realize she has been hacking away nonstop for several minutes. It's then I notice the blotches on her forearms, which she's rubbing at vigorously.

"Frizzy, are you OK?" I ask.

"I'm weelly itchy."

"Dad..." I say, with the composure of one who has recited the following words far too often in his young life: "Frizzy's having a reaction." My dad turns his head. The car swerves. The driver passing on the left honks, loud and long.

"Have you eaten anything today, Frizzy?" By this question, we all know—except for The Snatcher—that my dad isn't asking if Frizzy has eaten *anything*, which of course she has, but anything with peanut butter, or more realistically, anything possibly processed in a plant that had processed something like peanut butter, or something remotely resembling peanut butter, at any time since the conclusion of the last Ice Age.

"No," Frizzy says.

My dad does a double take to his right. "Gimme that!" he says, reaching over and snaring something out of the hands of The Snatcher. Notice, by the way: It's Snatcher. With an *-er*. Anyway, I digress. It appears he's snared some sort of granola bar she has just opened and taken one bite out of.

"What," she says defensively, not as a question but as a statement. "It doesn't have nuts," she asserts. I believe this is the first full sentence I've heard her utter since we left the house, and I'm not impressed. "I know you told me no nuts," she adds righteously. My dad proceeds to read the label, holding it within inches of his eyes, as I silently plead for him not to ask The Snatcher to steer. Which he probably wouldn't because she's a woman. After a few moments and remarkably no swerving, my father tosses the granola back in The Snatcher's lap and glances again at Frizzy. Now *there's* a swerve!

"We've got to get you some Benadryl," he says. "It's in the back." Please, not the EpiPen, I say to myself.

We pull off the expressway at a sign that says *Bell Blvd*. It's then my dad turns to The Snatcher again with a sharp stare. "You don't happen to have pets, do you?"

"Yes, I do," she says spryly. "Two cats. Noodles and…"

"Damn!" my dad grunts with teeth closed, the butts of his hands pounding the steering wheel.

"What," she says. "It's not like I have them with me…"

"Doesn't matter, doesn't matter," my dad grunts again. "You people with your cats and dogs, you always have pet hair on you wherever you go. I should have thought of that…"

"What," she says again, which I am beginning to find annoying, as if I were not zealously trying to find any annoying things about her. "I wash my clothes, thank you very much."

"Doesn't matter, doesn't matter," my dad says. What's with the repetition? By now, he's pulled the car over into a McDonald's parking lot with sooty arches. He fishes the Benadryl out of the back and feeds Frizzy a cupful. He sits back in the seat and we all stare silently for several moments, as if we are waiting on pins and needles for Frizzy to either clear up or croak. We watch a large man get out of his car and waddle up to the door of McDonald's. He can barely fit through. Frizzy groggily says the guy looks like a sumac fighter. I think I'm the only one who realizes she means sumo wrestler. But everyone nods knowingly nonetheless and stares longer.

Next, it's The Snatcher who breaks the silence. "What if you let her walk around outside a bit and get some fresh air?" My dad doesn't answer. He just shakes his head with a whipping motion that reminds me of a dog shaking off after a swim.

"Frizzy's allergic to pollen, too," I say, amazing myself with this hysterical eruption of benevolence coming from my mouth.

"No, Jame," my dad counters. "There's no pollen here. We're in Queens. It's the petrochemicals I'm worried about." Add that to the list.

"I think she's OK, Dad," I say as I scan Frizzy's complexion and then reach over and pinch her for the hell of it. She gives me "the stare," minus the shriek first, because I think she's feeling too loopy to pull it off. My dad's not convinced Frizzy's OK, so we wait for several more minutes, all gazing at the door to the restaurant, wondering when the sumac fighter's coming out. We'll never know, since it's *now* time to go. My dad has decided this arbitrarily, which I believe is not inconsistent with the way most adults make their decisions. So be it. I'm just happy to get a move on it, seeing as we'll probably have about thirty-five more of these incidents before we get to Sand Fwan-sicko. My dad swings the car back toward the on-ramp for the Cross Island, running a red light and nearly causing a collision, but he's none the wiser. Ignorance is bliss, right? That's a cliche. We turn and descend the ramp toward the expressway, then suddenly jerk to a complete stop. What a surprise: Traffic is at a standstill. My dad grunts like he does when he's in the bathroom. He grips the steering wheel with one hand like he's trying to choke it. Then he swings the other hand up and raps himself three times in quick succession. Right smack on the fontanel.

2

Solecistic Soup

"So what do you think of The Kid?" Doug asked.

"The Kid?"

"Yeah. The Kid. Jamie. What do you think?"

"Oh," Ashley said, pushing the sunglasses up her nose. The fact she was wearing them inside was a habit in people that irritated Doug. "He seems a little sulky," she said.

"Yeah, yeah," Doug muttered. "That's the age you see. Their moods change like the wind on a fall day." He took a sip of his coffee and glanced down the long corridor, where Jamie was waiting outside the door to the women's bathroom for Frizzy, out of earshot. "The Kid's a genius," Doug continued softly, while leaning in toward Ashley as if disclosing information that posed a threat to national security.

"Ahh," she said carelessly, showing much more interest in where next to bite her cranberry scone. They sat in Starbucks, somewhere in a leafy suburb midway down the New Jersey Turnpike. Doug Shoop, father of the wunderkind and the wheezer, stared across the square wood table at Ashley Weiner, putative expert on elite private prep schools and universities.

"How do you think he compares to other kids, you know, who you've seen…whom you've seen?" Doug asked, leaning back, now confident The Kid couldn't hear.

"Who I've seen?" she asked. "I haven't seen many yet, you know…I'm new."

"Oh yeah." Doug watched her take another bite of her scone and a crumb hung on her lip, but she didn't seem to care. Rather, she chewed like she was having an orgasm. "Mr. Hildenberger said you worked admissions at Harvard for several years, though, right?" Doug asked nervously. "And you went to Yale and Andover, right?"

"No, I went to Pomfret."

"Oh yeah, right," he said, scrunching his eyebrows together like people do when they want to appear knowledgeable, but frankly he'd never heard of Pom—whatever. It sounded like a fairy name. No way The Kid's going there. "So?" he finally said.

"So?"

"So, how's The Kid stack up to what you saw when you worked admissions and when, you know, you were in school?"

"Oh." She took the last huge bite and closed her eyes sensuously, then said with her cheeks sticking out like a gerbil's: "He's good. Really good."

Doug took a sip of coffee, blowing on it first, even though it had cooled. His breath was rich with pride as well as an irritant he couldn't quite pinpoint. He glanced at his watch and rubbed his eyes to soothe the sting of fatigue. They hadn't exactly gotten off to a great start yesterday. He was still fuming inside at his decision to take the Throgs Neck Bridge. Or *Frogs Neck,* as the kids call it. When he had seen the backup he'd headed for the Whitestone, but it was at a crawl, worse than the Frogs Neck. So he turned around when he saw traffic that way picking up. He was patting himself on the back just as he decided to pull over and let Frizzy squat on the side of the road, having ignored her several demands to go pee for more than forty-five minutes. It must have been just enough of a delay to allow some maniac to cut another car off up on the bridge and cause a pile-up that took four hours to clear.

They didn't cross the line into New Jersey until 11 p.m. It was another two hours until they got beyond the land of the smokestacks and found a hotel in the suburbs. They awoke the next morning later than Doug hoped, which about summed up every day of his life. They had grabbed breakfast at a Pancake House and set off to find a one-hour dry cleaner. "I can't have you polluting this car with cat hair for the whole trip," he had insisted to Ashley. "Frizzy'll never make it." So they drove. And drove. The handy search program on his stupid smartphone was worthless, like an intellect with no common sense. It indicated a dry cleaner, called Dickie Fong's, 1.3 miles from the Pancake House, but it turned out to be a Chinese restaurant called Dickie Fong's. So they drove on, until Doug lost all patience and

insisted Ashley run into Target and buy a new outfit until they could get
all her clothes cleaned.

"Twenty dollars?" she griped, after he'd handed her two tens with the
pride men feel when they're footing the bill. "This won't get me very far,
even in Target."

But she did all right, as far as he was concerned. That's what he thought
now as he sat across from her in Starbucks and tried to tear his radar gaze
away from her chest, nicely shaped through a tight, stretch-knit white shirt
scooping low in the neck. Her breasts were incredibly round, too small to
be fake, which pleased him. He hated boob jobs only the rich could afford.
But hers could have been enhanced by one of those super-duper wonder
bras that sometimes simulate a succulent navel-orange shape. He could live
with that.

"They cost more than twenty bucks, you know."

"Huh?" Doug said, as he snapped his eyes up toward her face.

"The shirt...and the jeans," Ashley said. He noticed she had finally
finished chewing the cranberry scone. That was about when he decided she
really looked a little like Big Bird, with her beak nose, deep-set dark eyes,
and kinky yellowish hair that hung down just above her shoulders. *Should
be calling* her *Frizzy*, Doug thought. "They cost more than twenty dollars,"
she repeated as he half-listened.

"Oh, OK," he said. He glanced at his watch and cursed to himself as
he realized it was close to noon. They were at Starbucks because, on the
way back to the turnpike from Target, they stumbled upon a one-hour dry
cleaner. Dickie Fong's, if you can believe it. Doug couldn't pass up the opportunity, so they dropped off all Ashley's clothes, went to Starbucks, and
returned an hour later.

"Bad news," the lady said as she peered up at them, her head barely high
enough to see over the counter. She looked like she could have been old
enough to be Mao's lover. "Bad news," she said again. "Machine broke."

"What do you mean the machine broke?" Doug asked.

"Machine broke. Like kablooey," she said, gesticulating wildly with her
hands and blowing a noise out of her mouth to imitate an explosion.

"So what does that mean?" Doug asked.

"Kablooey mean machine broke. Lady clothes stuck in machine."

"Well, how long will it be?"

"Man come fix it, but he at restaurant now fixing wok."

"Restaurant?" Doug asked. "What restaurant?"

"Restaurant. Dickie Fong's. Down street. You like wonton?"

"No, no wonton," Doug said, shaking his head as they left and headed to Starbucks again.

"Dad, I'm hungry. Can we get lunch?" Jamie had returned with Frizzy from the bathroom.

"Lunch? We've just had breakfast three times!" Doug growled, showing unusual irritation toward his son. "We need to go back to the dry cleaner in a few minutes and see if Ashley's clothes are ready."

"Forty more minute," Mao's lover said, when they returned to the dry cleaner. "You go have wonton soup at Dickie Fong's. Bubba take care of you."

"Bubba?" Doug asked.

"He grandson."

"Who's Dickie?" he asked. But she just scrunched up her mouth as if he'd requested some sushi.

"Mmmm...I love Chinese," Ashley announced a short time later, as she engulfed a forkful of lo mein and one of the stray noodles did a dipsy-doodle before sticking to the underside of her chin like a leech. She was the only one who'd ordered anything. Frizzy ate gummy bears in lieu of risking eating something that had been cooked in peanut oil since the waiter didn't seem to understand Doug's probing on the issue.

"Do you use peanut oil?" he'd asked when they'd first sat down.

"Yes, yes, no, no peanut oil," said the waiter.

"Yes, you do use peanut oil?"

"No, no, peanut oil, yes, yes." At that point Doug just threw up his hands in despair. He'd already decided not to order something for himself after he saw the waiter blowing his nose in the corner with no evidence that he'd subsequently washed his hands. Just a superficial wipe on his pants leg. Germs wigged Doug out. He was hoping it wouldn't be their waiter, but turns out he was the only waiter there. *Bubba*, his name tag read.

"What are you going to have, Jame?" Doug asked, turning to his son.

"Nothing, I'm not hungry."

"Not hungry? Ten minutes ago you told me you were hungry and asked if we could have lunch. That's why we came here!"

Jamie shrugged his shoulders, assuming his dad understood it meant he'd changed his mind. "I'll just have a Pop-Tart in the car later," he said. So, they all just sat there watching Ashley eat her lo mein. Slowly. As if she were the only one there and had no desire to leave before the early bird special kicked off. It wasn't that she took small bites. They were big, actually. Too big, in fact, to make anything but the slowest, most methodical, chewing motions effective.

"Dad, are we going to make it to Philadelphia for Zach's game tonight?" Jamie asked.

"Definitely, Jame, we'll get there," Doug mumbled half-heartedly, still mesmerized by Ashley's eating performance.

"Oh, Frizzy! That stinks!" Jamie squawked.

"No, Jame, I think that's the egg drop soup," Doug said, nodding to the half-eaten bowl in front of Ashley. "It is a little foul. I need to step outside to get some air for a few minutes."

He stood in a parking lot and munched a fortune cookie. They'd snared a handful at Dickie Fong's…the dry cleaners. "Life's path shall open up from the woods of darkness," Doug read to himself. He chuckled and tossed the slip of paper in the trash bin. He thought about pulling out a cigarette; that's what he'd seen a lot of men do in these situations, idling on sidewalks. But he didn't smoke, except that one time in high school when the nuns caught him behind the school with that dirtbag named Ripper and his mother made him say fifteen novenas. He'd only taken one drag. Jeez. That was the extent of his smoking. So now he stood there on the sidewalk with his hands in his pockets and one foot kicked back against the wall in an ostrich pose. The heat wave seemed to be lifting. Or maybe it was just cooler in New Jersey. He figured they were somewhere near the turnoff to the Poconos. It always seemed cooler there when he was little. The Poconos was about the farthest he'd ever traveled in his life, with a few exceptions. Every summer they'd go there, at least until his father was found drunk and naked in a room at a nearby motel. He was tied up to a heart-shaped bed spinning under a ceiling mirror with a disco ball hanging overhead. The woman who'd bolted from the room with his father's watch and wallet was *definitely* not Doug's mother.

"Nice," Doug said to himself as he quickly shook the horrid memories from his brain and surveyed his new Expedition out in the parking lot. He was proud of it, even though he really couldn't afford it. But he was used to not being able to afford things. It was just one of those aspects of life feckless men resigned to mediocrity learned to accept without bitterness. Sometimes. He'd first trained himself when he was scraping by after community college. He tended bar for a while at some dive on Long Island, but marriage convinced him he needed a real job. Selling annuities out in Patchogue offered some fine prospects for him, until the long drive every day began to get to him. It was not the forty-five-minute length; it was the fact he was always moving opposite the flow—the pace of life heading into Manhattan, where the real riches were earned. His young bride, Corrine, suggested they move out East, but Doug knew it wasn't a good idea, and so he decided to quit selling annuities altogether when he realized after two years he still didn't know what the hell an annuity was.

So he succumbed to the inevitable: becoming a stockbroker. His father, grandfather, and great-grandfather had all failed as stockbrokers. For years he'd fought the lure as he passed the train station each morning where the button-downed Wall Streeters with their French cuffs and starched white collars boarded the Long Island Railroad. Their eyes always seemed glazed with a mixture of stress over what they faced in the day ahead and relief at the thought of escaping the wife and kids left in the verdant suburbs behind. Doug didn't have any kids, and his wife hadn't started annoying him yet, so he had nothing to escape, except the fear of dying prematurely. That's what happened to his father, grandfather, and great-grandfather. They died. Nasty, tormented, self-inflicted, pre-mature deaths. So Doug thought it best to tiptoe into the stockbroking arena and stay away from Wall Street, taking a job at a small brokerage firm in Manhasset where, his boss liked to joke, he could milk all the Buchanans. Whatever that meant. Surprisingly, he seemed to do all right, which produced enough domestic euphoria to beget a son, Jamie. But before his son had turned two, Doug was randomly fired. When he asked why, his boss just said, "Maybe this isn't your cup of tea." Or coffee, which is what Doug splashed down the guy's ugly lime dress shirt before storming out.

So be it. He tended bar again for a while, before trying his hand at selling real estate. He took a measure of comfort in the fact that he was saved from a premature death. He also found that selling real estate allowed him to settle into a comfortable cocoon, where all pressure to succeed remained locked outside his bright red '79 Mercury Cougar he bought used and drove around all day, cutting the cheese at will and blasting some old eight-track tapes. Except when there were clients in the car, of course, usually women—lonely, gullible, annoying wives whose husbands toiled worlds away in Manhattan so they could buy a bigger house they would rarely see. For Doug, selling real estate beat the hell out of annuities. Everyone knows what a house is, for Pete's sake. He could have been great at it, but soon realized he despised working with the rich people and all the reductions to mediocrity they induced with their Cadillacs and paddle tennis games at the country club and haughty phrases, like "the master's a little tight..." "Tight like your ass," Doug mumbled one time a little too loudly, and he almost came to blows with the stuck-up witch. That was when he decided he would work only with people like himself, the Average Joes relegated in life to the middle strata despite the pleadings of their irrepressible flights of fancy. The result was, he didn't make much money, a fact that he was sure never bothered his wife, until the day she left him for that weasel who works at Goldman Sachs. At least she didn't need their house, or the car, or the kids.

He kept all those, thank you very much, and he decided the car was the first to go. Once Jamie got into the Elite Leadership Exposition for Gifted Youth (otherwise know as ELEGY), and Doug decided they should drive there—to San Francisco—he knew they needed to arrive in style. So he went with the Expedition. Sangria red it was. All his cars had been red. Except the last one, the minivan: the one he'd just gotten rid of. Corrine had made him get Mojave sand. *No more bossing around from her now,* he thought scornfully. And he'd keep this car clean, now that her slovenly paws were dirtying someone else's world. Weasel.

It felt good paying for the Expedition in cash. Plunked it right down on the table in front of the guy's beer gut, just like a bigwig. Who cares if he took out a third mortgage to get the cash. It was worth it. Jamie would arrive at ELEGY in style. Better than all the other kids. It was the first big step, he thought...the first big step. A necessary investment. Ashley was too. She was costing him a bundle, but one day he'd be rich, he knew it, and Jamie was his passport. Whatever it took.

The person he really wanted was Mr. Hildenberger. Juddy M. Hildenberger. He owned the company, Elite Schools R Us, Inc. Once

Doug had heard about these consultants to help kids get into the best prep schools and universities, he knew it was the thing for Jamie. Doug spent weeks researching hundreds of different consultants. He wrote down the names of thirty-two who "guaranteed results or your money back." Thirty-one of them turned Doug down when he tried to hire them to come along on his cross-country trip for the entire summer, although several did give the idea pause when Doug brazenly offered to pay outlandish amounts of money. That he didn't really have.

Hildenberger gave it the most pause. "That's not really what we do…" he'd said hesitantly over the phone to Doug, his raspy New York twang sounding more like one of those guys who graduated from Hofstra and not Harvard, like Hildenberger's bio claimed on the Web site. "Most of our sessions are thirty minutes long. A whole summer is a lot to devote to one child."

"The kid's a genius, though!" Doug argued. "And he's in middle school. It says on your Web site that middle school is *exactly* when they should be focusing on getting into the Ivy Leagues."

"Right," Hildenberger said. "But I'm not sure I can commit my staff to that amount of time. We work with thousands of kids in the greater New York Metropolitan and New England areas who are vying to get into the top prep schools and universities. We can only guarantee results by following our system. We can set your son up on the standard plan…"

"I don't want standard!" Doug cut in. "This kid's not standard." The back and forth went on for twenty minutes, until Hildenberger said, "Well, I do have an idea…"

The idea was Ashley. She was new, and it might be good training for her. She'd take the train down from the Boston office and the next day be ready to go. Doug was a little tentative about the newbie, but felt better after Hildenberger said he would still guarantee results or Doug would get some of his money back, just not all of it, since this was a special case. Doug liked that: *special case.*

He smiled to himself as the door to the restaurant opened and Jamie and Frizzy sauntered out, Frizzy's white shirt stained with a rainbow of gummy-bear goop.

"Where's Ashley?" Doug asked.

"She's ordering dessert," Jamie said.

"Dessert! Chinese restaurants don't serve dessert! They give out fortune cookies!"

"Key lime pie," Jamie said. "She's ordered key lime pie."

Doug shook his head and headed for the Expedition. "Let's just wait in the car. I can still smell the egg drop soup out here."

"That was me," Frizzy said, giggling. Jamie punched her in the arm. She farted again, glowered at her brother, then reached for his hand so he could guide her safely through the parking lot.

"Dad," Jamie asked, as he hurried to catch up with Frizzy in tow. "You sure we're going to make it to Zach's game? It starts at six."

"We'll make it, kiddo," Doug said. "We've got plenty of time. Trust me."

3

HANGMAN

Never trust the intentions of adults. Unless you have a good sense of humor.

hey. where r u? Jessica writes.

somewhere outside philadelphia, I type back. *i hope*

?

my dads lost

ooops

no problem, just the usual. at least we r not in canada. hows things with u?

my moms in the hospital again :)

yikes…sorry

its ok, the chocolate chip cookies there r good. gotta go. tell Zach good luck

yeah. if we ever get there

Dairy Queen…again. We've passed it six times. My dad insists the GPS says to turn on Birch Street, but he can't seem to find it, and I'm beginning to wonder if he thinks it might magically appear if we just keep circling around the block while the annoying mechanical voice continues to berate us to make a "right turn in point-two…miles." I can feel my nausea begin to return. The game starts in twenty minutes. I assured Zach we'd be there, although I know my dad's not happy about the detour. It was good fortune (for me at least) that Zach's ice hockey odyssey around the nation this summer took him to Philadelphia for a tournament just as we were due to be passing though. The way my dad sees it, the game is just an impediment to his desire for my enrichment in the City of Brotherly Love. He quizzed me the whole way here from the dry cleaners on Ben Franklin and the battle at Valley Forge. I tried to tell him there was actually no battle there, but he thought I was yanking his chain. Rather than argue, I conceded that he might be right and subsequently concocted some description based on what I knew about the captures of Trenton and Princeton. I thought this might distract him enough from the Liberty Bell. But no such luck. He insisted we at least squeeze in a visit, and if we hadn't gotten lost, we would have had more time there. Nor would we have been rushed had The Snatcher not lost an earring in the Front-Seat Graveyard. You know that space between the two front seats and the center console, where if you drop something, it never again sees the light of day? She dropped the earring at some point while we were looking for a parking space on the street, since my dad refused to pay for a garage. Surprisingly, he helped The Snatcher try to find her earring, which seemed to me suspiciously chivalrous. But it didn't work They never found the earring. And we barely saw the Liberty Bell.

"Oh, that's it, schmuck, cut right in there without even the slightest thanks. Idiot. How obnoxious!" And that right there is perhaps in the top five of my dad's biggest pet-peeves on the road: When he tries to be courteous and the other driver doesn't acknowledge it. He attempts to compensate for this fairly common absence of civility by offering profuse thanks to those rare drivers who show *him* courtesy. It's not a good idea, this profusion of thanks thing. Last month on our way home from the grocery store, some guy was nice enough to let us cut over into the turn lane when my dad found himself way out of position going into our neighborhood. Rather than making the turn, my dad sped up and tailed the nice guy, who I think thought (perhaps correctly) my dad was a lunatic. So the guy accelerated to give my dad the shake. Finally my dad caught up and started waving like a duck that just burned its ass on a spotlight. "Thank you, thank you, thank you!" he screamed out his window at the man whose eyes were wide with fear. They were both traveling pretty fast by this time, and my dad didn't notice the curve in the road, nor did he listen to my shrieks of alarm. He plowed over three garbage cans and then into a fire hydrant. The car wasn't too smashed up, but it was good and flooded. That's why he was forced to get rid of the minivan.

I stare out the window as I watch Dairy Queen go by again. It looks particularly dirty and bleak now that a mist has begun to glaze the world outside. Ten minutes until game time. Not surprisingly, my dad tries to exude a facade of hope as he likes to do at the most hopeless of times.

"Guess I just don't know Philly too well, kiddos," he says nonchalantly. "All I do know is the Eagles suck and they blew up the Chicken Man here once." He punctuates his joke with a screwy laugh as we all stare numbly in ignorance.

He remains unperturbed for a few more minutes, until he mutters, "Damn, we're going back over this river again. How'd that happen?"

Don't know. *This river* would be the Schuylkill. My dad pronounced it something that sounded like "Snoogall" the first time we passed over it, like we were supposed to do to get to the suburb where the rink is located. Apparently. Passing over it again the opposite way is definitely not good. And I can tell he has no appetite this time to pronounce its name. Going over it a third time is inevitable, I suppose, as we try to make our way back out toward the suburbs for round two. Still no closer to our destination.

Finally, a sigh so big comes from the front seat, I'm noticing the windows steam up. It's from The Snatcher. "Why don't you pull over and ask directions?" she snips. My dad just glances at her like she's insane and somehow forces a smile that quickly begins to leak with pain.

Frizzy farts, and when I lean over to hit her, I see something pink and plastic in her hands. I know just what it is, and dreading what's coming next, I snag it away.

"Daaaaad, Jamie took my pwincess camwaaa."

"Jame, give her back her camera."

"Daaaaad, Jamie's not giving me back my pwincess camwaaa."

"Come on, Jamie, give it back. Damn it! There's the street." There goes the street. There goes the last of his hope. Our heads all whip as my dad jerks the car down the next block, which I'm sure will just lead to more circles. I throw the princess camera at Frizzy and then give her a shot in the arm.

"Daaaaad, Jamie hit me." But he's not listening. So she takes her revenge by firing off senseless pictures of the sullen gray world outside the window. The camera, when the shutter clicks, sounds like *whaaaaa-ta-ta-ta-ta-ta-ta-ta-ta-ta…shiiiiiiittta*. The first part reminds me of the sound of a horsefly caught in a window blind. The second part is how a curse might sound coming from a native of Calcutta. I know this because the woman name Gita who works in our lunchroom at school said it once when she dropped a tray of spaghetti all over the floor. *Shiiiiiiittta*. I had pizza instead.

"What are you taking pictures of, you turd?" I ask my sister quite pleasantly.

Whaaaaa-ta-ta-ta-ta-ta-ta-ta-ta-ta...shiiiiiiittta.

"Oh, great, this street's one-way," my dad moans. "I can't figure out how to get back to the right street we passed back there."

"What. You should just stop and ask," The Snatcher insists. "That man on the corner looks nice."

Whaaaaa-ta-ta-ta-ta-ta-ta-ta-ta-ta...shiiiiiiittta.

The rain picks up. Steadier. Gloomier. My stomach turns sicklier.

Whaaaaa-ta-ta-ta-ta-ta-ta-ta-ta-ta...shiiiiiiittta.

"Oh! I think I see my earring down there...if I can just wedge my hand down in..."

Whaaaaa-ta-ta-ta-ta-ta-ta-ta-ta-ta...shiiiiiiittta.

"Turn right in point-two...miles."

"I just can't seem to reach down there."

"Damn, that's the street, right there, but I can't get over there with this being one-way."

"Shit, I think I just wedged it in there further."

"Hey, watch your language around the kids!"

Whaaaaa-ta-ta-ta-ta-ta-ta-ta-ta-ta...shiiiiiiittta.

"There! There it is!" My dad swerves and cuts off a gray Nissan. He receives a thank you in the form of the middle finger, but doesn't notice. Or care. We park and everyone hustles to the front door, as if they are all eager to see the game. And not just get out of the rain. As we step into the arena, the frigid air cuts through our damp clothes, making me shiver slightly.

"Why is it so cold in here?" The Snatcher asks. Would it be too mean to call her moron to her face? Perhaps I would if I weren't so determined to get to the game. Like, before it ends.

There are two ice rinks. Naturally we go to the wrong one first. When we find the right one, we see that Zach's team is actually still warming up. We're told by a woman with an Eagles blanket wrapped around her that the game before stretched long into overtime. The smell of pretzels and popcorn from the concession area floats out and collides with the thick stale odor of sweat as well as a dose of ammonia from the restrooms. The lights are yellowish and dim, like gigantic headlights cutting through a fog. They hang from a low moldy ceiling that makes you feel like you can reach up and touch it, just like the ceilings in the classrooms at school with their cracks and water stains. Several of the lights over the ice are protected by dented black grates, but some are exposed and open season for flying pucks.

Zach skates by the boards, smoothly and effortlessly, the curls of his sandy hair flopping out the back of his helmet. He gives me a head nod, and I return the favor through the scratched, smoky plexiglass. It doesn't take an expert to notice that Zach is the best player on the ice, evident in the fluid motion of his shot and the seamless transitions in his skating maneuvers: backward, forward, crossing over, stopping on a dime. Or a nickel. I am mesmerized watching him as usual, trying to stifle my envy, which is never good for friendships, is it? We've been friends since kindergarten, and I can't imagine anything getting in the way of our bond, except maybe my dad's plans to send me off somewhere to boarding school. Or Zach's dad's desires to send him up to Canada to play hockey. It just doesn't seem right, the idea of being torn apart like that.

He skates by again, this time not looking my way, just nonchalantly gnawing at the mangled mouthpiece half wedged between his teeth. The thud of pucks against the boards punctuates a dull murmur of indistinguishable voices in the stands and chatter by the players on the ice. I realize I am alone, my dad having taken the others to buy under-cooked hotdogs at the concession stand. That's when I hear the voice, a booming sound like it's coming through a bullhorn, but it's not: "Skate! Come on, skate! You can't loaf it in warm-ups!"

I turn and look up into the stands, which consists of about five rows of metal benches plunged into concrete steps. The echo of the man's voice continues to reverberate off the corrugated metal roof. I know that voice. I've heard it many times before. Not just in hockey rinks. In the backyard, rumbling out the kitchen window—the kitchen window to Zach's house. It's his dad. "Move it!" he screams again in the direction of his son, who continues to glide innocently across the ice in dexterous contempt for the voice that is ruining his fun.

The horn sounds to signal the start of the game. My dad returns with Frizzy.

"Where's what's her name?" I ask.

"She's gone outside," my dad says. "Too cold in here for her. She says she wants to look for her earring."

Within minutes, Zach's team goes up by a goal as he zips around two defenders, his jersey making him look like red silk as he flips the puck over the goalie's shoulder with the fluidity of a virtuoso. This doesn't stop his dad from continuing to bellow things like: "Skate faster!" and "Shoot the puck!" and "Hit that kid harder! Knock his head off…kill him!" Very nice. Fortunately, Zach doesn't kill anyone. But several minutes later he does score another goal that makes the game seem like it might turn lopsided. Just as quickly, however, the other team fights back to tie. The second period is tight, and I'm just glad my dad has decided to take Frizzy to the game room so I can watch in peace without listening to her camera cuss every ten seconds.

Both teams are checking hard and several penalties are called. That's when things start stirring a bit in the stands—grumbling from the parents about the penalty calls, or lack of calls, depending on whose side you're on. Not surprising to me, the tirade is led by Zach's dad, who has taken a break from exhorting his son to greatness so he can direct his drivel at the offending ref: "Come on, you idiot, what kind of pathetic call is that? Get in the game!" I can hear him clear as a bell from the other end of the bleachers to where I've gradually retreated so he can't spot me. No one wants to be in that kind of company. He's so loud, I'm fairly certain they can hear him all the way back on Long Island. It seems like most of the calls are going against Zach's team, which perhaps only serves to inflame his dad toward the end of the period, when a violent collision into the boards, which leaves Zach flat on his back, is followed by no call at all.

Zach's dad goes ballistic, rocketing from his seat and nearly catapulting over the green metal rail that separates the concrete steps from the rink. "What are you, blind, ref! How about a boarding penalty, you imbecile! I'm going to come out there and tear your eyes out!" Quaint. This is enough to make the ref glance up toward Zach's dad, as it now appears every person in the arena has their eyes on him. To fulfill the role of a moron requires a suitable audience, which Zach's dad easily detects, then flashes savage eyes as if he's in all his glory. Now he *is* catapulting over the rail and has stepped onto the little ledge along the boards that holds in the plexiglass. He has his arms extended and is hoisting himself high up on the glass. By now, nervous giggling from the crowd at the monkey climbing the boards nearly overshadows the applause that follows when Zach rises unsteadily to his feet and skates off the ice, trying to ignore the ignoramus who is still shouting at the ref through the glass. "I'm going to come out there and smash you into the boards and see how you like it. I'll mash you like a bug, you idiot!"

The ref now skates to the far side of the rink and is talking into that little hole in the glass where the penalty box is. The coaches are leaning over talking to a few men in the box, and they all periodically glance toward Zach's dad like he's a time bomb. The coach on the opposing team shakes his head vigorously at one point. There seems to be a lull that lasts several minutes, but it's hard to tell. Zach's dad is still yelling garbage that no one really seems to be able to understand. It's then a burly man with a red beard dressed in gray hockey sweatpants begins walking toward Zach's dad, jogging actually, keys jangling in his pocket. Who he is I am not sure; an excuse for security, I suppose. He yells something up at Zach's dad, which I can't hear, partly because they're toward the other end of the rink, but more because a palpable titter has spread through the crowd, muffling all other sound.

Since Zach's dad is never hard to hear, the sound of him yelling back at the man sounds exactly like: "Go to hell!" The man reaches for one of Zach's dad's legs, but he avoids it and reaches up for the netting that tops the plexiglass and encircles the entire rink to prevent pucks from shooting off the ice during games and dinking the heads of moms who aren't paying attention. Zach's dad now has two hands up on the netting and is climbing up like Spider Man out of reach of the security guy.

Technically, the second period of the game has ended and the players should be taking the ice for the third, but they all just sit on the bench or stand on the ice, dumbfounded at the freak scaling the net. I notice Zach at the end of the bench, hanging his head with one of his coaches talking in his ear. I can only imagine him saying, "Are you all right?" and not referring in the least to the injury Zach sustained on the ice.

"Is that Zach's dad?" The voice is my dad's, as I realize he and Frizzy have rejoined me.

"Yep."

"Jeez."

"Yeah. Jeez."

"Hey, he looks like Spider Man!" Frizzy yelps, waving her hand and clutching something that looks like a small plastic Spider Man doll.

"Hey, where'd you get that Spider Man?" my dad asks.

"Found it."

"Where?"

But before Frizzy can answer, a woman next to us blurts out, "Oh my!" in a half-chuckle, half-gasp of disbelief as if someone just mooned her. That probably would have been more conventional compared to what we see next. Spider Man—not the doll—climbs higher on the net and is kicking at the outstretched grasp of the security guy. Two others have joined the fray. One looks like a high school kid with pimples on his face and wet hair that looks like it's been zapped by an electric current. He climbs the wall and reaches up to grab a flailing foot. Zach's dad tries to jerk away, but the kid's got a good hold and a tug-of-war ensues. It reminds me of field day at my school, and I'm just waiting for one side to give in and do a face-plant. The odds are becoming stacked against Zach's dad, as the other two have now joined in the tugging, and it's a three-on-one match.

Zach's dad seems destined to be pulled down from the netting. It appears he's given up and has released his hands, but he doesn't seem to be coming down. There's more tugging from below, and I hear someone call someone a "shit-for-brains."

"Jeez, I hope the cops don't show up like that last time," my dad says. He's correct that one time the cops did show up when Zach's dad caused a ruckus at a game, that time threatening the opposing coach. He was arrested for disturbing the peace and was required to do community service, which he fulfilled by volunteering at the Boys and Girls Club. That didn't work out so well for him because he screamed at a kid during a pickup hoops game, and the kid coldcocked him. Laid Zach's dad flat out, which is not an easy thing, because Zach's dad is large and muscular. He played linebacker at Brown and is fond of saying, "I coulda played at USC." But he didn't. He did graduate college cum laude, though. I know what that means now, but the first time I'd heard it I didn't, and I recall my dad saying it means Zach's dad's not really as stupid as he acts. In fact, he makes a lot of money at an investment bank in New York City. Which my dad doesn't take kindly to. Zach's family lives in a big house the next town over, and we probably wouldn't even know each other if I had lived just one block farther away and went to a different Catholic school.

"Why is that man hanging from that net?" Oh great, The Snatcher's returned.

"Did yawl find the earwing?" Fizzy asks, which I find a little too ingratiating and can only imagine it's a tactic to deflect attention from the Spider Man doll she's stolen.

"Nope, no luck," The Snatcher says, flashing a smarmy smile at my little sister.

"Stop pulling! Stop pulling…I'm caught!" It's Zach's dad, and if he means he's caught by the three stooges below, he's on the mark. But that's not what he means, as it becomes evident to the crowd now all nervously laughing. Zach's dad is hanging by the gold chain around his neck, the pendant having caught, it appears, in the netting. This is no ordinary chain, you should know, as I've seen it up close many times. A more feeble chain would surely have snapped by now under Zach's dad's weight. But this chain is thick enough to dock a cruise ship. The pendant is a gold cross with diamonds in it. Blessed by the pope, Zach's dad likes to brag. All I can think of as I stare at it tangled in the netting of a hockey rink, stringing up Zach's dad like Nathan Hale, is my grandmother. She's likely rolling over in her grave, reciting a litany of prayers at such a desecration of the cross. She died last year, but not before she convinced me she was the holiest person on the face of the earth, the way she had a knack for conversing in prayer. Like whenever I was over at her house, she'd never say: "Jamie, dinner is being served, please wash up." She'd say: "Jamie, the dinner is being served, Holy Mary Mother of God, please wash your hands." As if that weren't enough, she'd usually throw in a "Blessed Lord Jesus," at the end of most sentences in the most sanctified cadence utterable. My dad says she was just loopy, but I can't help wishing my own loopy mother had just one bone of that kind of spirituality in her, or she might not have run off with that gay weasel.

"Stop pulling! You're going to choke me to death!" Zach's dad's insistence doesn't seem to carry much merit with the three thugs below. They keep pulling, and Zach's dad keeps screaming. At first he was just mad that he'd gotten caught, but now his screams are ones of sheer pain. The chain appears to be digging a red gash in his neck, and a couple ladies in the stands shriek in horror.

"What is the story with that guy up there?" The Snatcher asks.

"That's Jamie's friend's dad," my dad explains.

"You *know* that guy?" she asks. I don't like the tone of her voice, and rather than finding myself having to defend a freak hanging twenty feet in the air from a net, I drift away to the far side of the stands. By now, the process of apprehending Zach's dad has transitioned to extricating him from the gallows. Another man, not one of the three guys who had been doing the apprehending, begins climbing the net with a large pair of clippers, like he's out to trim the rhododendrons or something. I'm not sure if he's going to cut the net or the chain around Zach's dad's neck. He has a malicious look in his eye like he's going for the chain, but slowly clips away at the netting, and Zach's dad eventually falls free back into the outstretched arms of about five men below, who shove him violently towards the door.

At some point the game ends. Zach's team loses. He never went back in to play, which I can't help attribute more to the humiliation over his father's behavior than the actual injury he sustained on the ice. I'll never know because we don't talk about it when we see each other after he finishes changing. It's what helps cement friendships: knowing by telepathy when not to discuss an awkward topic, like problems in school or the dysfunction of one's family.

"What's with the lady with one earring?" Zach asks as we sit outside in the damp darkness gnawing on jumbo pretzels long on sogginess and short on salt.

"Huh?" I ask.

"The lady in there with your dad, the one with one earring." He nods over his shoulder back inside the rink, where my family waits, while Zach's dad continues to plead his case with rink management to let him in the next morning for Zach's last game of the tournament. If history is any indicator, he'll smooth-talk his way in.

"She lost her earring in the Front-Seat Graveyard," I say in answer to Zach's question.

"She'll never get it back," he says. "It's gone forever with all the M&Ms and gummy bears."

"No, my dad isn't allowing any candy in his new car."

"Oh, bummer," Zach says. "Anyway, like, I wasn't really asking about her earring. I was just asking who she is."

"Oh. A friend of my dad's."

"Like a girlfriend?"

"Don't know. I guess."

"No offense, dude, but your dad's way too much of a dork to have a girlfriend."

"Yeah, I suppose you're right." We gaze off down the cheerless street, with the kerosene pallor of its streetlights rippling in the damp air, and are content with silence for several minutes. I can tell Zach's willing to drop the subject of the One-Earring Lady. But I can't let it go.

"She's like an academic coach or something."

"Who?" Zach asks.

"The lady with one earring."

"An academic coach?"

"Yeah, my dad hired her to come along on this trip. She's supposed to be coaching me to get into Harvard or something like that."

"Dude, you're like twelve."

"And a half," I clarify. There's more silence as we both stare at our uneaten pretzels.

"I hope she doesn't wind up like my skating coach," Zach says.

"How's that?" I ask.

"My dad hired this guy to help me with my skating. The dude claimed he'd coached Mark Messier. Two months later he was arrested. Something to do with hanging around girls who were too young for him...or something like that."

"That stinks."

"Yeah." Silence hangs over us for several more seconds. An ambulance roars by with its piercing siren. A mother walks along dragging a little girl decked out in a figure skating outfit and wiping tears from her eyes. One of them calls the other "a bitch," but I'm not sure which.

"You know what I hate?" Zach finally says. He doesn't wait for me to answer. "I really hate how much I hate hockey." I just grunt in support.

"Hey, Jame, have you seen Ashley?" My dad has poked his head out the door. "We need to get rolling, make up some time on the road."

"Haven't seen her," I mumble, smiling at Zach.

"She said she was cold and was coming out to warm up. Damn it. I can't find her." He reaches back to hold the door open for a woman and a small boy wearing a Flyers jersey hanging down to his ankles. They walk out into the dampness. The boy stops with a startled look on his face. He turns, points at my sister, and shouts: "Hey, that's my Spider Man doll!"

My sister tucks it under her shirt and sticks her tongue out at the boy. I chuckle as I watch his face flash deep red and his lips quiver with anger. He takes a step forward. That's not good. If I were you, kid, I'd just beat it to the hills, pronto. Cuz you'd be messing with the wrong chick. Blessed Lord Jesus.

4

❦ ❦ ❦

Up in Arms

Another late night and another late morning. Four and a half weeks was more than enough time to make the trip across the country, even with all the stops he'd planned. But Doug was already feeling a little fretful, a little delayed. Why, he asked himself, did he feel like his whole life was always running behind? In reaction to this self-rebuke, he gunned the Expedition and zoomed past a slowpoke on I-95 as they neared Baltimore. Maybe his acceleration was also a reaction to the displeasure he still felt about last night. It took over an hour for them to track Ashley down after the hockey game. They finally found her wolfing a triple-scoop at an ice cream shop down the street. Frizzy had spotted her through the window sitting in a chair, eyes closed, licking the drips off a chocolate-coated waffle cone, with a dab of Chunky Monkey sliding down her chin. When Doug confronted her, Ashley said, "what," then clucked about how the arctic air in the hockey rink aroused in her an urgent fancy for ice cream. They all had to sit and watch her finish. Slowly. Surely they would have hit the road sooner this morning without that extra delay, Doug rationalized to himself. Oh well. He'd make up some time. Traffic was light for a change. They had lots to see in DC.

"I'm tired," Frizzy said from the backseat. Of course, *tired* sounded more like *tarred,* and Doug wondered how her fake southern accent might hold up now that they were crossing the Bacon-Nixon Line. Or whatever they call it.

"Take a nap," he ordered, glancing toward the backseat. Jamie had his head phones on and was reading a book.

"Can't. Don't have my blankie," Frizzy griped. Doug had forgotten to pack the blankie.

"Here, I'll give you my jacket," he said. "Use that as a blankie." She just harrumphed like you might hear any female do in reaction to the stupidity of men.

Several seconds elapsed in silence, and Doug was about to turn up the music. His favorite Bruce song was due up. But Frizzy interrupted, "I'm tarred."

"Come on, Frizzy, just take a nap, for Pete's sake," he growled.

"But what if I snore loud like that lady up there." Ashley whipped around, and Frizzy stuck her tongue out at her, more viciously than she did at the Spider-Man kid. Ashley stuck hers out in return. Doug missed the whole episode, as he was eyeing his rearview mirror at the guy tailgating him. Chalk up another pet peeve. "I'm going seventy-five, you idiot, what's your hurry!" Doug snarled, less with anger and more with pride that he was driving seventy-five. He slowed down just to piss the other driver off and boxed him in so the guy couldn't pass. This went on for several minutes— a cat-and-mouse game—until Doug glanced back again and saw the guy waving something shiny out his window. "Is that a gun?" Doug asked, thinking he murmured it quietly to himself, but apparently not. Everyone in the car jerked their heads, including Jamie, who returned from his inner world at this eruption of excitement.

The man in the other car brandished the gun menacingly. Doug pulled into the right lane, his heart beating wildly. The guy zoomed past and sped away, but not before first giving them the finger with the hand not holding the gun. The car was a beat-up, white El Dorado with a Union Jack bumper sticker and a Florida license plate.

"Great," Doug mumbled, "maybe we shouldn't go to Florida."

"Florida?" Ashley yelped. "You didn't tell me we're going to Florida. That's not exactly on the way to California, is it? What are we going to Florida for?"

"To see The Kid's grandfather," Doug said, noticeably piqued. He rubbed his hand across the prickly two-days' growth of reddish hair on his chin. "Look," he continued, "you just leave the navigation to me. We've been on the road now two days and you haven't done much training yet."

"Didn't know you wanted me to," she said. "Besides, it's not like there's been much time between traffic jams, and dry cleaners, and getting lost... and all that quizzing stuff you do. What's with that anyway?"

Doug glanced back in the rearview mirror to make sure Jamie had his head phones on. "It keeps him sharp," he whispered. "The Kid's a genius, like I already told you. He's going to be the next Bill Gates one day. I might just have him skip prep school altogether and just have him go right on to college. Hell, he's already aced the SAT."

"He's taken the SAT?" she asked.

"Twice."

"Why? He's he seventh grade!"

He started to answer, but then stopped, not knowing if he had the right answer. A moment passed and Ashley chuckled, like she was watching a funny movie.

"What's so funny?" Doug asked.

"Nothing," she said.

He waited for her to say more, but she didn't. "Anyway, shouldn't *you* be doing some of this quiz work with him?" he finally asked.

"That's not what we do at Elite Schools R Us," she said. "Besides, I'm not big on history. And I don't read much."

"Well, then, how the hell'd you get into Yale?"

"Connections. And I was pretty good at math."

"Were you a math major?"

"No, philosophy." This all seemed to confuse Doug, and he reverted to silence a while. He was desperate to turn up the music, but peeved enough to refrain until he was satisfied with this discussion. Big bucks he was shelling out for her.

"So...have you worked with many other kids who've gone to ELEGY?" he asked.

"Gone *where*?"

"ELEGY."

"What's that?"

He gritted his teeth and forced through a groan that sounded like he had a bad case of indigestion. "It's the elite academic program that Jamie got admitted to. The one in San Francisco, you know. The one we're driving to all the way across the damn country. For Pete's sake."

"Through Florida."

"Yes, through Florida."

"Speaking of driving," she said, "what is it with yours? You act like the entire world's out to get you."

"Oh, *it* is," he snarled. "Trust me."

She turned her head and laughed toward her window, then forced a straight face as she turned back toward Doug and said, "I guess I didn't realize that was the name of the program." As she finished, she cracked her window and breathed in a gulp of air like she was trying to get stoned. "Isn't that like the speech you give at a funeral?"

"What?"

"An elegy."

"Oh, I don't know. I hate funerals."

"No wait, I think that's a eulogy." There was more silence, punctuated by a fart from Frizzy. Doug glanced back. She was sleeping. Not snoring, but wheezing palpably.

"So, none of your other clients have been to this program?" he asked again.

"Nope." More silence. Another gulp of air. He cranked up the music even though he still wasn't satisfied with the discussion. Screw it. Jeez.

"So why are we driving there?" she shouted after several moments.

"What?"

"Why are we driving there?" she shouted louder while putting up her window. He turned down the music, now even more rankled.

"The Kid needs to broaden his horizons before he gets out there with all those kids from rich families who jet off to Europe like they're just going to…Coney Island, or something. Endless opportunity. That's what they have. But I won't let them outshine The Kid. Traveling the country will give him something to brag about. Up to now he's barely been off Long Island."

"Not much to see on interstates," she mumbled with her face pressed against her window.

"Yeah, well, we're going to see some good stuff. We've just gotten a little behind, you know." He emphasized *you know* so she might get the hint about the delays she'd caused. But there was no reaction, so he glanced her way beady-eyed, although he was never much good at the maneuver with his deep-set sockets. She wasn't looking anyway. His pique melted a bit as he noticed she had a nice neck. The little muscles, or tendons or whatever they were, wrapped in her olive skin looked silky and sensuous. He made sure to lighten his tone when he next said, "Mr. Hildenberger said this program's going to make The Kid a shoo-in for a scholarship to prep school." She laughed again like she was watching a funny movie.

"Maybe this afternoon you can get some time alone with him to start doing your thing…like when we get to DC, maybe." He liked the way he said *DC*. Like it was familiar turf.

"Sure, that'd be fine," she said. Doug was feeling good now. His heart had settled after the incident with the gun, so he stepped on it again to make up some time and get to DC quicker.

That's when he saw the flashing lights. He immediately tried the "my daughter-has-got-to-go-to-the-bathroom-real-badly" trick with the state trooper, but it was to no avail when the trooper looked through the window and saw Frizzy out cold. *This* despite Jamie kicking her fiercely under Doug's orders as they were pulling off the highway.

Five hundred bucks for the speeding ticket. "What!" Doug gasped when he saw it. "Five hundred bucks? That's insane!"

"Fines are doubled in a construction zone," explained the trooper, a skinny, bespectacled black man who looked more like a college professor. He had gigantic pit stains under the arms of his tan uniform. This definitely reminded Doug of his community college days, not of one of his professors, but of his girlfriend who had perspiration issues, particularly around the seat of her pants.

Doug looked out the window at the serried ranks of orange and white barricades with their little blinking lights on top. He had noticed them along the highway for the past several miles. But he'd seen no sign of workers. "I don't see much construction going on," he said.

The cop nodded toward a guy stepping out of a portable toilet, still zipping his fly. "One guy?" Doug asked. "He's not even working, he's taking a leak."

"One guy's got to stay on the job to keep the project alive until the stimulus gets here."

"Stimulus?" Doug asked.

"From the gov-ment down in Washington." The cop nodded his head in the direction opposite Washington, and Doug suddenly worried if maybe he'd been driving the wrong way.

"How long's it take?"

"What's that?"

"The money to come from Washington. It's not like it's not right down the road." Doug pointed off demonstratively in the direction he believed Washington to be, just to be sure of himself. But the cop ignored the gesture.

"Oh, you know those politicians," he said. "It could be years until we see a dime. In the meantime, this is still a construction zone."

Doug thought the longer he talked to the cop, the better chance he might have of getting let off. He told the cop he was a nice guy, that he should be a teacher. The guy said he *was* a teacher once, but it didn't work out so now he's a cop. Doug tried rationalizing that he didn't deserve a speeding ticket when there were monsters on the road driving around waving guns. This just made the cop look nervous. His nostrils flared and the sweat stains seemed to grow on the spot, like Pinocchio's nose. Doug couldn't shake the mental image of his old girlfriend, especially the time she came over and left a stain on the love seat where she'd sat. "Oh, Jesus, Mary and Joseph, look at that," his mother whispered to herself when she saw the stain later, kissing the ubiquitous rosary she held in her hands.

"Five hundred goddamn bucks," Doug muttered to himself as he pulled back on the highway.

"I'm hungwy." Oh great, now Frizzy wakes up.

"Jamie, give Frizzy some Fritos," Doug said. "We don't have time to stop for food now, we'll never get to Washington."

"I'm a little hungry myself," Ashley chimed in. "It'll be a long stretch if we don't stop."

"Have some Fritos," Doug barked.

"Like, lame," she said, scrunching up her face so her nose stuck out longer than normal. "How 'bout a real meal."

"OK, fine," Doug said. "We'll get off and get some lunch, but you need to start working with The Kid. You two can have a separate table."

Doug barely ate a crumb at lunch. His stomach was still churned up from being pulled over. Plus, Frizzy told him she saw their waitress at the pizzeria picking her nose. He couldn't get Frizzy to admit she was lying, and past experience told him she was, but he still couldn't shake the image of the woman's boogies, exacerbated by the fact that she was furry and pushing three hundred pounds. Most of all, Doug was just plain distracted, trying to keep tabs on the table across the way where Ashley and Jamie sat. Or maybe just tabs on her. Her legs sure looked slender and appealing in those skimpy linen shorts she wore, sliding up high and tight to her thighs as she sat on the red seat in the booth. Still, he also couldn't square his lust with his frustration at the appearance of she and Jamie actively disengaged.

"How's it going over there?" he bellowed across when his patience expired. Neither looked.

"Did you even talk to The Kid?" Doug asked once they'd gotten back in the car and Jamie was engrossed in his headphones and a book, with Frizzy chuckling away at a movie.

"He doesn't have much to say," she answered

"Well, isn't it your job to get him to say something?" he asked. She just shrugged.

"I asked him what he likes to do," she finally offered.

"Sounds like you two were on a date." Doug laughed at his own joke, then asked, "What'd he say?"

"About what?"

"About what he likes to do?"

"Shouldn't you know that? You're his father?"

"Don't be a smart-ass. I'm paying you a lot of money."

"Not me, my boss."

"Well, whatever, I trust you're getting a fair share, and you've been hired to train The Kid to get a scholarship to prep school so he can be a slam dunk to get into the Ivy Leagues."

"It's league. There's only one. Ivy League."

"Yeah, well, I don't care how many there are. That's where he's going."

"You *do* realize," she said, after a momentary pause, "that he doesn't have to go to some fancy prep school, you know...like to go to a good college."

Doug flinched in surprise and then said, "That doesn't exactly sound like the type of advice I'm paying you to give...or your boss is paying you to give." He rubbed the sides of his mouth nervously with one hand like he was trying to clear away some dried spit, then added, "And like I said, he's good enough to skip high school anyway."

"Maybe so," she said. "But he's got to do more."

"What do you mean?" Doug said irascibly.

"He told me he likes to read and hang out with his friends. His competition out there is pretty tough, you know. Kids starting businesses, writing novels, working on cures for AIDS. One of the things we coach kids on at Elite Schools R Us is that they need to diversify."

"Jeez," Doug said. "AIDS? I thought that *was* cured."

She snickered, then said, "At the least he should be involved in the arts, athletics…other extracurriculars."

"He played piano a while, but his teacher was like this Korean Nazi woman. He hated her, and she was costing me a lot of money." Ashley didn't respond, and when he glanced over, he noticed her flipping through a J. Crew catalog.

"Unfortunately, there's not been too much of an athletic streak in the family," he continued. "I mean, I'm a runner and all and anything he gets, he gets from me. His mother's a klutz. Don't get me wrong. He loves sports. He watches football on TV and calls the exact plays before they even run them. And he's tried to play a whole bunch of sports…soccer, hockey, basketball, lacrosse. He just hasn't had the knack. It's his mother's fault."

"Maybe he should trying fencing or something like that?"

"Fencing! What the hell is that?

"It's this thing they do with swords."

"What the hell? Like stabbing?

"No, they don't really stab. The swords have little balls on the ends, and the people wear armor."

"That's a sport?"

"Big time, in the Ivy League."

"Jeez," he said. "I don't know. When you mentioned athletics, I was thinking football or something. Isn't that big time in the Ivy Leagues?" She turned over her shoulder and looked at Jamie, then looked at Doug and winced.

Fencing. He thought about it for the next hour, until they'd made it into downtown DC. Screw it, this time he stopped and asked someone how to get where he wanted to go: The Jefferson Memorial. But he still got lost, and he had to ask five more people, not including the one guy speaking some African language he couldn't understand. When it was finally in view, his heart leapt. "There it is, kiddos! The Jefferson Memorial." He pointed out the window toward the back of the renowned white dome, half-shadowed by the late afternoon sun and sitting so ponderously that the supporting columns seemed to be oozing sweat. The air *was* thick. He could feel it draining into the car like motor oil. He zipped up the window and cranked the AC higher. He was feeling victorious. "This is perfect timing for the book you're reading, Jame," he chirped while peering in back through the mirror. "You almost done with that Jefferson biography?"

"Ahhh, yeah, right, Dad," Jamie said.

"You are reading the Jefferson biography, right?"

"Ahhh…yeah…yeah," Jamie stammered, as he stuffed the book he was reading into his backpack. He looked out the window again at the Jefferson Memorial. He could see the silhouetted statue through the reverent ivory columns and shards of sunlight enameling the surface of the tidal basin beyond. Soon, they would get a closer look. After Doug parked the car, as he was now doing. Despite a sign that said *No Parking*. Hung on some high metal fencing.

5

❖ ❖ ❖

ALL THAT BUGS ME

I'm exhausted. And nauseous. I can barely read the numbers on the elevator panel. I punch *L* with my finger, too tired to abide by my dad's rule to always use the point of the elbow. Germs are the least of my worries. Two hours. That is about the amount of sleep I figure I got last night. When I first woke up, I couldn't even remember where we were. But it all quickly came back to me when I thought of the hobo. He kept us from getting a parking ticket yesterday afternoon and—in an indirect way—from seeing the Jefferson Memorial up close and personal. He looked like Grizzly Adams, the hobo did, which I gather is a fashion admired by the hobo crowd in general. Steve was his name. He introduced himself with the most impeccably genteel manners, devoid of the slightest slurred speech you'd expect from a homeless person swigging from a giant bottle of beer. I was positive he was homeless, because he told us so. He pointed to a culvert where he said he sleeps—day and night—often waking to the sound of a tow truck hauling away illegally parked cars. He suggested we try the parking lot across the street, but since we couldn't see the parking lot, or the street, I suspected my dad was just slightly distressed about the idea of loading up the car and getting lost again. So he started to walk away from Steve's advice. We might have made it all the way to the monument if we didn't realize The Snatcher wasn't with us. When we turned to look for her, we saw her back with Steve, dividing up a pack of Twizzlers. My dad whistled peevishly, and when The Snatcher caught up, she informed my dad that Steve said it would be several hundred bucks to get his car back after it was towed. This was enough to change his mind and head for the parking lot. Unbelievably, we found it. Believably, it was full. So my dad insisted we try the Lincoln Memorial, making some comment about how Abe was more his type anyway. But we couldn't find Abe. We did, of course, find the Washington Monument. I use the word *find* liberally in support of my dad, because really any moron can see the gleaming obelisk jutting up into the sky from just about any vantage point in the city, right? The fact that we never really got close to it, I will opt not to dwell upon, lest I impugn my dad's contentment with his version of "delivering the goods."

He was feeling so resuscitated, in fact, that he pledged he would take us to see the Capitol and the White House the next day. That would be today. The day after last night. He had booked us in a Holiday Inn he claimed was right near all the sights, but when we struggled to find it for an hour, he finally gave up and checked us in somewhere else. It was clearly *not* near all the sights.

My dad had looked petrified when we first turned into the hotel parking lot, forcing a sizable suspicious- looking crowd to disperse as we did so, each one of them eying us, I assume, for our extreme whiteness. I can't remember the name of the hotel—not one I recognized, and it didn't help that the sign out front just said *Hotel*, although a few lights were burned out, so it really just read *Hot*.

My dad executed the check-in process like a zombie, as if his thoughts were spinning in his head like those balls you see in the lottery machine on TV. I couldn't believe we actually made it all the way into the rooms; I chalked it up to my dad's fatigue. We didn't stay long, however. Not after we saw the wet towels with brown stains in the tub and the iridescent streaks of green down the walls of the bathroom. It smelled like someone had died in there, which I suppose, given the neighborhood we were in, was not an outlandish possibility. We turned and left without even saying good-bye to the nice woman at the front desk with a coiled snake tattooed on her face.

We hauled ass out of DC in the dead of night, not looking back. It was as if someone were chasing us out of town. When I commented to this effect, my dad said, "Yeah, well, that's Washington. It's kinda what they do to a president right after they elect him." I suspected the manner in which we were escaping pretty much squelched any hope of seeing the White House and the Capitol, but I shrugged this off with the presumption that it might be better for my dad's mental health that way anyhow. By the time we checked into a Days Inn somewhere in Northern Virginia, there was still enough time to log a decent night's sleep. But this was clearly going to become everything but a decent night. As soon as we got to our room, we smelled cigarette smoke. My dad cursed about how it was supposed to be a non-smoking hotel. He called down to the front desk, but the man said there were no more rooms. A few moments later, he called down again to find out what room The Snatcher was in so he could ask her to switch, but the man said my dad had to come down to the lobby to make that request. My dad said he was too exhausted to go down to the front desk, so we settled in for all of about thirty minutes before Frizzy started wheezing. My dad gave her a few puffs on her inhaler, but the wheezing continued until it evolved into a frightful hacking like an old man with emphysema.

My dad told me to watch Frizzy while he marched down to the front desk to find The Snatcher's room. "What took you so long?" I asked when he finally returned. My heart was beating wildly the whole time he was gone, as I was afraid Frizzy might expire on my watch.

"The man at the front desk wouldn't give me her room number. He accused me of being a rapist."

"What's a waypist?" Frizzy asked in between coughs.

"Never mind," my dad said. "I had to explain the whole damn thing about our trip to San Francisco and Elite Schools R Us, and all that. The guy was a real bastard," my dad mumbled, as he searched under the bed for Frizzy's shoes.

"Bastard," Frizzy repeated, as if I might have missed it the first time.

Finally they headed out, my dad informing me that he and Frizzy would take The Snatcher's room and he'd send her up here to sleep. "Great," I muttered despondently. I lay in bed waiting for what seemed like forever. At least I didn't have to worry about Frizzy croaking on me, but the cigarette smell was making me ill. My chances of dozing off grew worse when a banging noise began in the room next to me, mixed in with some weird moaning. *Thump, thump, thump...ahhh, ahhh, ahhh*, it went. *Thump, thump, thump...ahhh, ahhh, ahhh.* I put a pillow over my head, but it didn't work. In fact, it got worse when I tried to deflect my thoughts with peaceful images of mountains and oceans. Because every time I was about to conjure an image, it was strangled by recalcitrant visions of Frizzy taking pictures to the equally annoying sound of *whaaaaa-ta-ta-ta-ta-ta-ta-ta-ta-ta...shiiiiiiittta.*

The Snatcher suddenly stormed in the door, which nearly made me jump out of my skin. "Man, your father can be a crank," she groused.

"What took so long?" I asked.

"I don't know. He said he was banging on the door for fifteen minutes, and I was like, sorry, you know, I sleep with earplugs in." It was then I noticed she had on Winnie the Pooh pajamas and red slippers in the shape of lobsters. She climbed promptly into bed, inserting her earplugs and then pulling a black mask over her eyes. I turned off the lamp and within moments heard her expelling the heavy breath of deep sleep. I stared her way disbelievingly through the amber glow seeping in the window from the street. The light threw an oversized shadow of her face onto the wall next to the bed, and as it refracted from the shifting tree limbs outside, it made the shadow of her long nose hook like the Wicked Witch of the West's. Great, this was all I needed in my renewed efforts to conjure peaceful images. I threw one of my pillows at her to get her to roll over, but it was to no avail. I then contemplated reaching over and snapping the mask back into her face but couldn't summon enough malice. So I meekly rolled over and stared at the chair in the corner. Surprisingly, the room grew quiet. For several seconds. And then: *Thump, thump, thump...ahhh, ahhh, ahhh...*

The elevator crashes to the lobby with such a jerk that I feel like I might vomit right on the boots of the biker dude staring at me from the hallway when the door opens. He scratches his beard and burps as I walk by him to get off. I catch a whiff of his horrendous case of halitosis. In addition to making my stomach more ill, it reminds me of Jessica. She calls our social studies teacher, Harold Meaks, "Halitosis Harry." I am backed up on returning her e-mail, and I'm sure she's getting pissed. The ding from the elevator is still ringing in my ears, and it takes me several moments of mindless wandering to find the dinette area where I am supposed to meet my dad and Frizzy for breakfast.

"Where's Ashley?" my dad asks when I walk in. I shrug my shoulders to indicate I don't know, because I really don't know. Or care.

"She went somewhere, I guess," I mutter.

"What do you mean 'went somewhere'?" my dad asks.

I just shrug my shoulders again disdainfully, then add: "All I know is she stunk up the bathroom before she left." My stomach turns as I speak the words, and my infirmity is not aided by the smell of the biker dude's breath stuck in my nose and now mixed with the nasty odor of hard-boiled eggs. I hate eggs.

I grab a stale bagel from the luxuriant breakfast buffet and pick at it while the rest of my family remains silent...for about thirteen seconds.

"I had a waffle," Frizzy says. "That bwack lady made it for me." She points across the room, all ten feet of it, to a bony woman humming as she wipes down the other table.

My dad leans over to Frizzy and whispers, "Frizzy, we never identify people by the color of their skin."

"That's what you do," she says.

"Do not."

"Do too."

He moans and shakes his head in quick surrender. "You know, Jame," he says, turning his attention to me with surprising alacrity. "We should do a little work while we're sitting here waiting for Ashley." I find this last phrase overly optimistic, perhaps delusional, as if anyone could possibly expect her to appear promptly. "You want to work on some Jefferson," he asks, "now that you've finished that biography?"

"Ah, I'm not quite through it yet," I stammer. In fact, I haven't even started it. "Maybe we should do some more Civil War stuff." But I see him glance down at his binder and know he's only prepared to talk about Jefferson.

"When was he elected governor of Virginia?" he asks.

"In 1814."

"Come on, Jame, don't screw around." OK, he's not that clueless. We spend the next several moments talking about Cornwallis and Tarleton. But gradually, I notice my dad's attention wane as his impatience deluges him like a tidal wave. He's checking his watch, and his face begins to redden to match the puffs of flaming sideburn poking out of the grungy Mets cap he's poached from me, despite his opposing allegiance to those other guys who seem to have much more success buying their way to the top.

"You done with that bagel?" he asks me, a question I find completely incongruent to the proceeding one about Alexander Hamilton. Before I have a chance to answer, he's risen and Frizzy and I are trailing in his wake.

"Where the hell is she?" my dad says as we step outside. Frankly, I'm rooting for The Snatcher not to return so I can ride shotgun from here on out to California. The humidity feels suffocating, and I stare out at the haze that appears to perch perfectly atop a lush ridge off in the distance. We take refuge from the heat under the shade of a huge oak tree, its leaves stippling the sidewalk with shadows, and its roots shouldering up through the grassy rectangle that exudes the sweet smell of being freshly mowed.

"That's the wench there!" Frizzy finally says after several moments, pointing up the hill leading out to the main road.

"Frizzy! Watch your language!" my dad reproaches lamely.

"It's the movies, Dad," I explain. "You've got to cut her off." We all stare up the hill like we're waiting for Godot; indeed my dad does seem to have a bit of a suicidal glint in his eyes. "Yeah, that's her," I confirm. We expect her to turn down the driveway toward the hotel, but she doesn't. She keeps going straight. My dad lets out a shrill whistle. One of those ones produced by putting your fingers in your mouth, but he can do it without the fingers. It pierces my eardrums, but is not heard by The Jogging Snatcher. Maybe she still has those ridiculous earplugs in from last night. I wouldn't be surprised if she has the mask on too, and is jogging in the lobster slippers.

We watch helplessly as she disappears over the crest of the hill. I glance down and notice Frizzy poking her finger into a gnarly piece of chewed gum stuck to the sidewalk. It could have been cinnamon gum, or spearmint. Who knows. It's black now. I wait for my dad to see her and bark for her to stop, but he's still staring after The Jogging Snatcher, with a look of sheer befuddlement.

He turns toward me instead of Frizzy and says, "She's really pissing me off." As if this rattles an unsavory memory in his head, he then says, "You really need to call your mother back. She keeps hounding me about why you won't return her messages." It's true. There have been seven of them left on my voice mail since our lovely chat on Long Island. I'm not exactly ecstatic about devoting much thought to when I'll call her back; luckily my thoughts are saved by the reappearance of The Jogging Snatcher.

She is now heading down the hill toward us. It's then I notice something unusual in her jogging style. She is somehow running without bending her knees, as if her heels are scraping the ground with every stride. But that's not the queerest thing. It's her arms too that are straight down at her sides, as if they are in casts. They hold this position for a few seconds until one of them twitches upward over her head, at which point she scoops out with her hand. The first time she does it, I think maybe she is merely trying to catch a bug, for what purpose I can't immediately fathom. Hungry, maybe? But when she does it several more times in the span of about fifty yards, I realize the bug-catching thing is part of her exercise routine. Or perhaps just part of a jogging style she is entirely too self-possessed to alter.

"Oh, my, will you look at that?" my dad says with the stupefied voice one might use as he watches a building go up in flames. The absurdness even snags Frizzy's attention away from the germ-infested gum.

As The Bug Catcher draws near, my dad's befuddlement quickly evaporates and his ire returns. He silently but emphatically raises his arms like he is signaling a game-winning fifty-yard field goal.

The Bug Catcher closes in and slows to a stop. I have to say I'm a little sick of words like *snatcher* and *catcher* and stuff like that. So I'll just go with Bugsy. She bends down with her legs together and touches her toes and then raises up and says, "Whewwww, that was nice!" It's really loud because she does indeed have her ears stuffed. Not with the earplugs from last night, but with headphones to an iPod.

My dad does the field goal thing again, but this time adds, "Where the hell have you been?" Bugsy flinches and peeks back over her shoulder as if she's confused about who he's yelling at. "I can't believe you went jogging," my dad adds.

"What," Bugsy says, reverting to her use of that nervous antecedent. "I haven't had a chance to jog since we left." She bends over, touches her toes, and then rises and says again, "Whewwww, that was nice!"

"You realize you've held us up about an hour?" my dad snarls.

"What. Where are we going?"

"Where are we going?" my dad says...screams, actually. It seems to fall ineffectually on her ears, as she has now done yet another forward bend. This time she's spread her legs really wide and her butt sticks way, way up toward the sky. It's awfully silent for a while as my dad stares long and hard. A dump truck rumbles by up on the main road, and Bugsy rises.

"You should go for a run yourself," she says to my dad. "You said you were a runner. Looks like you could use a little exercise." She nods in the general direction of my dad's midsection, which swells out slightly under his gray Giants T-shirt as if he has a pool noodle under there.

He turns and I hear him mumble under his breath, "Un-fricken-believable" as he walks back inside the hotel. The rest of us remain on the sidewalk. Frizzy's picking at the gum again.

Once we're back on the road, I glance through my e-mail and notice a message from Jessica she sent the night before. *hey. why did the whale cross the ocean?*

dont no, y? I say in my very delayed response.

o, so now r u done ignoring me? she answers promptly.

havent been ignoring u. just busy n distracted. After typing, I glance toward my dad in the front seat and think I still see smoke coming from his ears. He's also sniffing out the side of his nose like a dog toward Bugsy. She does smell awfully floral, and I think he wonders if she snuck on some perfume at some point during the hour and a half it took her to get ready after her jog. I look back at my phone. No response from Jessica. She's miffed.

so? I type.

so, what? she types back after a delay sufficient enough to express her displeasure, but intuitively not long enough to let me go.

so, y did the whale cross the ocean?

2 get to the other tide, tupid!

thats funny. im laughing. haha

yeah right, u DORK :)

The car is meandering up and down hills like a little kids' roller coaster. I try to keep my gaze out the window so it, the meandering, won't turn my stomach too much. We cross over a bridge with a sign indicating the Shenandoah River below. We then ascend a hill and pass an auburn field where a dead apple tree stands lone vigil over the ruins of a deserted house. Only the chimney remains, stretching upward and seeming to call in silence to the kids long ago who must have played hide-and-seek in its shadow. From there we soon pass rows of tired-looking homes in multi-hue, followed by an Arby's, a McDonald's, and a Pizza Hut, all encircling a rickety-looking hotel.

hey. thanks for the compliment, I finally type back to Jessica.

any time! where r u?

virginia. my dads trying 2 find the shenandoah national park.

ok. got another. wat do elves learn in school?

?

the elf-abet! good one, dontcha think, Bilbo Baggins?

sure, haha. im really hysterical

thats good. i am imagining u laugh cuz maybe it will help me stop crying today :(

????????!!!!!!!!!!!!!!!??????????

my moms dying

dont say that!!!!!!!!!

gotta go. dads calling

jess???? write back soon! I can feel my own eyes tear up. I told you she makes me cry, although I've never been one to hold back tears too easily. I never cried when I went to school the first time—or when my parents made me play soccer—like a lot of kids do. But I cry easily when I think of something sad. Sometimes tears don't actually come out, but I know I'm crying anyway.

I think my dad's probably about to cry too. We're lost again. He didn't want to make this diversion to begin with. Sure, he raved about it before the trip started. But after the incident this morning with Bugsy, he wanted to make a beeline to our cousins' house, as if he knew just how to make a beeline there.

We all fought for the side trip to the national park; Frizzy's and Bugsy's voices carried no weight, of course, but mine did as soon as I reminded him that the experience would enrich me for my encounter with all those pampered kids I'd meet at the program in San Francisco. "Just think how many of them have done Outward Bound in Alaska, and…"

"All right, all right!" he had snapped back.

I'm beginning to wonder if he's getting lost this time on purpose. We pass a restaurant called the Stonewall Jackson Tavern for the third time. They're advertising "steak, seafood, pasta, and chicken," on their sign, and I wonder what else is there.

"Stonewall Jackson, Jame!" my dad shrieks for the third time. I'm hoping we don't pass the tavern again. He—my dad, not Stonewall—is maintaining the appearance of buoyancy, but I can tell he's sinking fast. Who knew finding a 200,000-acre national park stretching for more than a hundred miles would be as difficult as finding a one-hour dry cleaners in New Jersey.

"That's your reason right there," my dad says, as he points to a minuscule sign for Skyline Drive, which is the name of the road that goes through the park. We turn up the hill, and a smile spreads across my dad's face.

"Wook y'all! There's Bambi!" Frizzy shouts in her grotesque accent, while pointing out her open window to a deer standing like a statue on the side of the road.

"And over there!" Bugsy shouts. "There's three more...look, Frizzy?" It was the first time I'd heard Bugsy acknowledge my sister, other than the tongue-sticking-out incident. Now's she's calling her Frizzy like they're best buds. Then she turns and smiles at my sister. What's going on here?

We whip around a turn entirely too fast, and my heart sinks as I peer out my window, realizing my dad was within inches of sending us cascading down a hundred-foot cliff. We pass another deer and this causes another swerve, this time on a straightaway. Another sharp curve gets in our way again a few moments later. My dad slows slightly, and by about the fourth or fifth bend, he's got the hang of it, but I'm definitely feeling ill.

"Stop!" Bugsy orders. My dad screeches on the brakes, and I'm wondering if the lady was trying to save the squirrel scurrying across the road. But I realize she's not even looking at it. She's got her eyes on the side of the road where a sign points to a scenic overlook. "Pull in here," she directs my dad. He obeys.

We all step out of the car, and the rush of fresh air into my lungs immediately appeases my churning stomach. The view out over the trees is stunning. We all stare amazed. Rolling hills of green appear to stretch out below us for hundreds of miles, and I notice a hawk circling above, hovering as if it were floating by strings tied to heaven. No one speaks, and we can hear the gentle breeze whistling through the pines. A chipmunk scurries through some dried leaves, and Frizzy is ecstatic.

"Look, bears!" My dad flinches and the rest of us turn calmly toward Bugsy's voice. She's drifted away and is looking at a sign describing most of the significant wildlife in the park. "There are bears up here...cool."

Reading the sign means standing still, which is enough to remind my dad that his time is short. He jams us back in the Expedition and heads off for the next curve. Just past it is another overlook. "Pull over! Pull over!" Bugsy screams.

But my dad zips by it. "Pull over! Pull over!" she shrieks again.

"Sorry, we've got to get moving along," my dad says authoritatively.

"Pull over, Daddy!" Frizzy wails.

"Yeah, come on, Dad, pull over," I add just to stir the pot. But he ignores me (a rarity) and keeps going. Frizzy begins bawling. Shrieking. Emitting a piercing wail.

"All right!" my dad yells above the din, while slowing the car. He pulls off to the side of the road, except there is no side.

"Yikes," Bugsy says sarcastically, as she peers out her passenger window directly down a steep bank. My dad begins to maneuver a U-turn. He pulls across the road. Backs up. Pulls across the road. Backs up. Pulls across the road. Backs up. There's just no room. The other side of the road is a face of granite boulders. He inches the nose of his car up to the boulders one more time, then turns the steering wheel with so much force, it looks like he's trying to pilot a battleship. Then he backs up again, inching the rear of the Expedition toward the slope behind us. I close my eyes and pray we don't flip off backwards like a platform diver. My dad's sweating. "Shit," he mumbles under his breath.

"Shit," Frizzy repeats.

I look out the window and spot two cars up the road, stopped and waiting for us. I glance the other way. Three cars stopped and waiting for us that way. At least we're not in New York or they'd be honking like idiots. Frizzy finds it all amusing and begins snapping pictures. *Whaaaaa-ta-ta-ta-ta-ta-ta-ta-ta-ta...shiiiiiiittta.*

Finally, my dad completes the U-turn and we pull into the overlook. The view here is more awesome than the first. But it's soon ruined by the sound of: *Whaaaaa-ta-ta-ta-ta-ta-ta-ta-ta-ta...*shiiiiiiittta. She even lets Bugsy try it. *Whaaaaa-ta-ta-ta-ta-ta-ta-ta-ta-ta...shiiiiiiittta.* This reminds me of *Thump, thump, thump…ahhh, ahhh, ahhh*. For the next hour, this scene repeats itself endlessly while Bugsy screams to stop at every single overlook, and Frizzy echoes the demand with a shrill of delight. It soon becomes clear we're going to miss not one. "Here's another!" Bugsy buzzes. Then she turns and glances at my sister and they giggle.

"Look, a bear!" Frizzy shouts. We all turn and look to where she's pointing across the road, into the dark woods.

"There's no bear, you liar," I say.

"Yes, I saw it," she repeats.

"I saw it too," Bugsy says. She and Frizzy smile at one another, and I'm feeling game to smack them both.

I do my best to allay my dad's anxiety over all the frequent stops by spouting off a few Civil War facts along the way. "Look at this, Dad," I say gleefully when we come upon a sign at one of the overlooks. The sign explains how it is the site of Stonewall Jackson's last mountain crossing before his death at Chancellorsville in 1863. I even throw in a few bonus facts about Jackson to cheer up my dad, like how it was General Bee from South Carolina who helped Jackson earn the nickname, Stonewall. My dad seems to lighten up, but he's clearly not eager to indulge the views. He starts to head for the car when a scream pierces the still air, echoing through the valley below and perhaps felling a few birds from the sky.

"My caaaamwaaa! She dropped my caammmwaaa!" Frizzy's in tears. Bugsy's peering off the edge of a huge granite boulder like it's the top of the Empire State Building. She's too far away for me to tell if she's saying anything, but I can hear the words in my head anyway: *"What. It slipped."*

Shortly, all four of us are peering over the boulder, with one foot forward, barely close enough to really see since we're all afraid of falling off.

"Can't see it," I say. My dad gets on all fours. Like a scared dog, he edges forward to get a better look over the precipice.

"There it is."

"Get it, Daddy, pweeease get it."

My dad walks about fifty yards up the road to find a suitable place to descend the hill without the risk of falling about a two hundred feet. As he moves below us, we can't see him. But we can hear sticks cracking, the word *shit* several times, and I do believe *bimbo* once or twice. We give up gazing down to try to watch him and all sit on the curb as if we're waiting to be picked up after soccer practice. A car pulls up, and a man with silver hair and a *real* camera in his hand gets out. He looks at us suspiciously and then asks if everything's OK.

I say, "Yes, my dad's just down there going to the bathroom. He's got the runs." The man winces like he just swallowed a raw squid, like this kid at my school did when we were dissecting one in science class. Frizzy is pouting, her lower lip protruding farther than normal, and I can see her glaring at Bugsy. I'm relishing this, because I'm assuming it will sever whatever seminal relationship it is they've been conspiring together. Then Bugsy leans over and whispers in Frizzy's ear, and Frizzy's face breaks out in a huge grin. I haven't felt ill since those first hairpin turns, but this episode is making my stomach turn again, so I get up and walk away.

Finally, my dad returns. His shirt is ripped at the shoulder and I notice a nasty scrape on his neck. The curly russet hair on his head is mussed like he just woke up, and a large twig is nestled in the side as if a bird had begun to build a nest and quickly discovered the error of its ways. My dad appears not to notice the twig, or not care. He hands the camera to Frizzy and glowers at Bugsy. The camera clearly has a piece broken off the front, and I'm excited that it will no longer work. Frizzy raises it to her eye and clicks away. That familiar irritating sound is gone. But unfortunately it's replaced by another: *Whop...whop...whop...whop... fllllizzzzzzzzzzzz.* Frizzy seems pleasantly surprised. Why didn't I think of dropping the damn thing off the cliff, I say to myself. Heaving it would have been better.

Once back on the road, there's great anticipation as we near the next overlook. "Look..." Bugsy begins to shout.

"Enough!" my dad roars. Silence stuns the car for several moments until Bugsy says to her reflection in the side window, *"Someone's* a little testy." We drive on, and several twisting turns in a row begin to make me sick again. Without the sightseeing distractions my mind drifts back to Jessica. Her mom has been fighting cancer for several years, and they said she probably won't make it through the summer. I wonder if the end is near. Tears begin to swell in my eyes.

As if that's not bad enough, I hear: *Whop...whop...whop...whop...fllll-lizzzzzzzzzzzz.* But it's only one time, as Frizzy puts down the camera to sneeze. She sneezes again. Then again. My dad glances at her nervously in the rearview mirror. I glance nervously at my cell phone, wondering if Jessica's been in touch. Bad news: no service. Oh well, at least my mother can't call.

6

❖ ❖ ❖

HEW AND CRY

Doug slid open his window and let the cool air rush in as he sped down a steep incline on the highway. His spirits lifted a bit now that they'd finally left the national park, but he still felt irked. More than five hours it took them to go a hundred miles, what with all the stops and twists and turns. *Unbelievable*, he thought. Something felt like it was scratching his head on the right side, so he reached up and pulled out what he now saw was a sizable twig. "Thanks for telling me," he said to Ashley when he noticed her observing him. His effort fell short of the contemptuous tone he was intending, and she just chuckled in response.

Doug held his phone in one hand and reached into his jeans pocket with the other, steering with his knees as the car careered down the hill. After having no luck in that pocket, he switched up hands and began reaching in the other pocket, his butt lifted high off the seat to straighten his torso and make the plunge into the tight-fitting pants a little easier. "Damn, what'd I do with that paper," he muttered to himself.

He slowed the Expedition and pulled it off onto the shoulder. As he flung open the door, a tractor trailer roared by within centimeters of ripping the door off. Doug cursed loud, but it was drowned out by the whoosh of the truck and its deafening horn, which still echoed even as the truck disappeared around a curve.

"Holwy shit," Frizzy said casually after the truck was gone.

"Frizzy!" Doug objected. "You've got to stop..." But his voice faded outside the car as he pushed open the door. He stood and reached deep into his jeans pockets on both sides, still to no avail.

"What are you looking for, Dad?" Jamie asked out his open window.

"A little piece of paper with a telephone number on it. I need to call your cousins' house and tell them we're running a little late."

"Is this it?" Jamie asked, reaching down to the floor. He picked up the paper and brushed some M&Ms under the seat quickly so his dad wouldn't see them.

"Ah, yeah, great," Doug said, reaching for the paper through the open window. He slunk back in the car and pulled onto the road without looking. Another eighteen wheeler zipped by in the left lane, this one not blasting its horn but rattling the Expedition with its violent draft.

Doug dialed the number and waited several seconds. "Hello? Hello?" he said. And then finally, "Oh, hi. Is this Bertha? I mean Bethany! Hi, Bethany, this is Doug...Doug Shoop...Corrine's husband...I mean ex-husband...I just wanted to let you know we're running a little late...very late, actually." He paused for several seconds and listened intently, then said, "To come to your house...When? Today, like we'd planned...Oh, I see... No, no, that's OK. We'll find a place for tonight, then we'll come by in the morning. Not morning? OK, how's noon?" He looked out the window and rolled his eyes. "One o'clock...fine. We'll be there."

"They're eager to see us, huh?" Ashley quipped when Doug disconnected the call. He ignored her and several minutes passed in silence, except for the rush of crisp air blowing in the windows. Doug glanced at Frizzy, now crashed in the back from her double dose of antihistamine. Ragweed, Doug had figured. That's what had set off her sneezing. He sometimes feared that by upping her dosage, it might one day knock her out for good. But he had to admit, the risk was sometimes better than listening to her sneeze like a freak. Or talk in that stupid accent. There was peace and quiet in the car. Briefly.

"These people are your wife's family?" Ashley asked. Doug had no desire to engage her, so he barely mumbled, "Yeah." The air continued to rush in, but it was quieter now since they had slowed while ascending a steep hill.

"I take it these people don't know you too well?" Ashley pressed on.

"Never met 'em."

"And it's your kids' cousins?"

"Not first cousins, actually."

"Hmmm..."

Doug was desperate to end the conversation and tried to squelch his irritation by admiring the sprawling estates along the side of the road, with their gleaming white four-post fences stretching on for what seemed like miles. But that didn't help to calm his nerves, because it just made him feel envious.

A moment passed, and then Ashley plowed on with her questioning. "Does your ex-wife know you're visiting her family?" she said. "And is there a particular reason why you're visiting *her* family...I mean, I take it you two are not involved in one of those nicey-nice divorces, if you know what I mean..."

"Look..." Doug growled, "why don't you worry about just doing the job you were brought along to do, and keep your nose out of our family business."

She looked unfazed and flipped down the vanity mirror to primp her hair. "It's not exactly easy staying out of your business, you know..." she continued, "when I'm stuck in this car with you all summer. And you don't exactly do a great job of keeping things hidden too well."

Doug could feel his skin begin to tingle as he fumbled in his brain for a clever response. But nothing came out.

"And to get your son into a top college," she added, "I need to know as much about his family as possible, the warts and all."

"What do you mean, 'warts'?" he howled. She just shrugged.

"Going to see these people is not a wart," he continued sorely. "This happens to be a very prestigious family. They're descendants of Thomas Jefferson, and a few of the ancestors were top officers in the Civil War."

"Which side?"

"What do you mean, 'which side'?"

"Which side in the war, the North or South?"

"Oh, the South...I guess," he said hesitantly. "The point is, it's important for Jamie to meet these people who are part of his esteemed heritage. Something to brag about out in San Francisco, you know?"

"Oh, yeah, absolutely," she said.

Doug just shook his head. *Enough with this worthless discussion*, he thought. He was feeling too anxious that Bertha, or Bethany—whatever her name was—seemed to have no clue on the phone about their visit. But he quickly boosted his spirits when an idea popped into his head. "Hey,

Jame?" he said, glancing back in the rearview mirror. No response. "Hey, Jame?" this time a little louder. No response. "Jamie!" The Kid jumped, almost hitting the ceiling, and pulled the headphones out of his ears. Satisfied, Doug continued in a calmer voice: "Your cousins can't see us until tomorrow afternoon, so I thought we'd go see the Jefferson home today, and then the Virginia University tomorrow morning."

"University of Virginia," Ashley corrected him.

"Yeah, whatever, same thing." He glanced back at Jamie again. "Shouldn't you be finishing up that Jefferson biography by now?"

"Oh, yeah, Dad, it's done," Jamie said. Doug smiled proudly and resolved to make the rest of the trip perfect.

It would start at Monticello, the historic home of Jefferson, which Doug repeated called Monte Cristo. But he didn't care about being corrected. The azure sky framed by towering green oak trees and the gleaming white columns and dome of the historic home sparked a visceral feeling he'd never had before. They strolled through a sprawling vegetable garden lush with tomatoes, beans, squash, figs, peas, and too many other varieties of plants they couldn't identify, especially the one Frizzy stepped on and mashed flat. They wandered down to the family graveyard, and Doug squinted through a black wrought-iron gate to read the words aloud on Jefferson's obelisk headstone. "That's quite an epithet," Ashley said when he was done.

"I agree," Doug said cheerily.

Next, they headed toward the house. Doug and Jamie went inside for a tour, shuffling along with a group of old people, mostly, and listening to the guide explain about a clock driven by weights nearly the size of bowling balls, a revolving bookstand in a reading room and a wine dumbwaiter that fetched bottles Jefferson imported from France. Doug was a little nervous that he'd left Frizzy outside with Ashley, but he felt it necessary due to the dust and mold he worried might exist in the old home. At one point he spied them through a window. Frizzy sat in the grass picking at the dirt with one hand and picking her nose with the other. All seemed well. Ashley lay next to her in the grass sunning herself, like she was at Jones Beach. Doug chuckled, feeling carefree.

Things got even better when they went to the university the next morning. They took a tour, which Ashley begged out of so she could do some shopping. Doug flashed his irritation, but she claimed to have seen enough universities in her experience, an impressive answer which made Doug feel palpably more at ease. What absolutely intoxicated him a few hours hour later was her prompt return and her request to spend time with Jamie "doing some work."

Wow, Doug thought, *this is really turning out OK.* They found their way to this long rectangular courtyard they call the Lawn and spread out a picnic with some sandwiches they'd bought. Jamie and Ashley set up their own location across the way so they wouldn't be interrupted. Doug gazed across with grand visions of his son walking along the grounds of such a prestigious university one day. Just like some of the young men strutting by on their way to summer classes. Doug detested them with every scrap of envy deep inside, but that didn't stop him from wishing his son might one day be one of them. He tried to deflect this raw combat of emotion by ogling the younger women slithering by with their long tanned legs and tight shorts. But in the end he stopped doing that too, in surrender to the repugnant sense of inferiority it stirred in him. They were way out of his league, even if he weren't fifteen years too old. By the time they left the Grounds, his euphoria had given way to manic gyrations in his head. To add to the angst, he craved a chance to ask Ashley how the session went with Jamie. But The Kid decided not to tune out in the car for a change, despite Doug's several suggestions that he do so. "No, I just want to enjoy this experience," Jamie said. *Great*, Doug thought. "Hey, Dad," Jamie continued, "did you know Jefferson..." But by the time Jamie finished his sentence, Doug had tuned out himself.

It was this numbness he attributed to getting lost again. *I just need to think straight*, he admonished himself, as he pulled off into a used car dealership so he could call Bertha to get better directions. Frizzy was sneezing again like mad, and every time she did, it sent a tremor through his entire body.

"They're not home," he said after disconnecting the call and looking at his watch. "It's just after one."

"Maybe they left when we didn't show up at the time they'd booked us on their calendar," Ashley joked.

"You're a big help," he muttered. He drove until they finally found the house, but he wasn't quite sure he felt good about it. They turned off the road into a driveway whose entrance was flanked by two stone pillars about as high as football goalposts. On one of the pillars a sturdy square gilded sign read *Hewed Meadows*. Once past the pillars, they arrived at the crest of a hill and stared down at a tiny white house. Actually, it was an immense white house, he knew, but it looked tiny since it was so damn far away. "Holy shit," he mumbled.

"Holwy shit," Frizzy echoed.

"This is their *house?*" Ashley asked. "Holy shit."

"All right, that's enough," Jamie reprimanded.

By the time they completed the winding drive to the house, which grew in opulence with each view over hill and dale, Doug's heart had sunk into his stomach. *Maybe this wasn't such a good idea,* he thought.

"This is cool," Ashley said, as she stepped out onto the flagstone drive under a gaping portico. "This is, like, totally cool," she said again.

"Shut up," Doug said wrathfully.

A woman opened the door and gazed out at them. *Bertha?* he thought. She was plump and hirsute, this he could tell even from several paces away. She wore a gray frock that hung down below her knees where two stubby calves plunged into white tennis shoes without the aesthetic benefit of ankles in between. As Doug appraised the woman, he felt a sense of dignity return inside himself, a sense of superiority he desperately needed.

"Bertha?" he said.

"No," the woman answered.

"I mean, Bethany," he quickly corrected. "I'm so sorry."

"Noooo," the woman said again more forcefully. "Ms. Bethany not home. I am...deee, deee, house keepa," she said with an accent Doug couldn't figure out, but then again, he hadn't much experience with house-keepers. He felt his sense of superiority quickly vanish as he explained to the woman that they were family visiting for a few days.

"Ooooh, yessss," the woman said. "Shoot!"

"What's wrong?" he asked the woman.

"Shoot!" she repeated. As she did so, her frothy eyebrows scrunched together and formed one long arc across her head.

Doug turned and looked quizzically at Jamie, who just shrugged his shoulders. Ashley and Frizzy had already drifted off down a path leading to the far side of the house.

"Ummm..." Doug muttered, not knowing what else to say.

"You shoot, no?" the woman said, becoming visibly impatient. It was then Doug noticed the barking dogs inside the house, behind the massive dark wooden front door that the woman had pulled shut behind her. The barks were yippy and piercing. Doug felt a sharp pain rattle between his ears.

"You mean...Shoop?" he said, as the light slowly clicked on in his brain. "We're the Shoop family."

"Yes, yes, Shoop family," the woman echoed, but he wasn't certain she still wasn't saying *shoot*. They were informed Ms. Bethany would be back with Amanda in an hour.

"Amanda? Their daughter?" he asked.

"No, Amanda dog," the woman said, holding her hand level to estimate the size of the animal, which if she was accurate would mean Amanda was the size of a mule. "Chelsea daughter."

"Right, OK," Doug said, figuring it best to leave the conversation there. He and Jamie wandered around back to find the girls.

"Daddy, y'all wouldn't believe what we just sarrrw!" Frizzy said. Doug winced at the accent that sounded like an indigestible blend of redneck Brooklynese. It was the last thing he needed. Other than an annoying lie from his daughter. She didn't wait for an answer.

"Buffalo!"

"Yeahhhhh, right," Jamie said.

"No, really we did," Ashley said. "They just disappeared over the hill right down there."

Doug completely ignored the fabrication and stared off at some horses grazing along a fence. As Doug did so, he felt a vexing pang grow in his stomach. It wasn't the novelty of seeing horses in a backyard. He'd seen it before on Long Island. No, it was the thought of *where* he'd seen it that was gnawing at him. Rex McGinley's house. *Damn him,* Doug thought. Maybe this whole trip wasn't going to be perfect, and if it wasn't, it was going to be McGinley's fault.

Ugghh, he said to himself. *I just need to shake this off.* "Hey, Jame," he said, as he turned to his son. "Pretty neat here, huh? This house may look new, but I bet they've had this property in the family for hundreds of years. Just imagine Jefferson riding up over that hill on his horse to visit with the family."

Jamie didn't appear to hear the words as he stared off like he was trying to scope out the buffalo. Down the hill Ashley gnawed on a piece of Twizzlers and propped the jumbo bag open so Frizzy could reach in for her share.

"And just imagine, Jame," Doug droned on. "One day, you'll be successful enough to own a spread like this, I know it."

Jamie seemed to squirm a bit and began to speak, but he was cut off by a voice. It was a deep voice, and he and his dad turned and looked toward the house. Standing on a deck surrounding the huge pool, with his foot propped up on a stone wall, was a man. He was dressed in a pink polo shirt tucked neatly into khakis. The man was very tall, sophisticated looking, even from a view of about fifty yards away. His hair was salt and pepper, and his chin long and chiseled.

Doug stared and his jaw dropped. "What the hell..." he said, dazed, as if someone had just slapped him in the face.

"What's wrong, Dad?" Jamie asked.

"Oh, nothing," he said. "That guy up there just looks like someone I know."

7

❖ ❖ ❖

MENAGERIE

"So *who* are you?" the girl asks.

I'm panicking over being marooned with her in the kitchen alone. I'm not sure if it's her beauty or the fact that the kitchen is the size of a gymnasium but somehow makes me feel claustrophobic. Like I'm locked in a janitor's closet at school. Which actually happened to me once in fourth grade, when Mrs. O'Hara sent me to get that powder stuff that soaks up barf. Billy Schneider's it was, the morning before our Christmas party, which was ruined because the barf smell lingered the rest of the day. At least that's what everyone in my class claimed, although I couldn't smell it because I had ammonia residue lodged in my nose all day from being stuck in the closet until the real janitor showed up with the keys. Twenty whole minutes I was in there. Which is about the length of time I feel like I have been standing mute in this kitchen like a numbnuts. I can't keep my eyes from drifting around the ceiling, but they invariably fall back on her. She's striking. Tall with long, silky blonde hair that is meticulously brushed down the length of her back despite the fact that she's just returned from a very strenuous horseback riding practice. This is obvious because she still has on those tight tan pants they use for riding. Jodhpurs they're called, which I know from reading this book once about a girl who was a horseback rider. It was definitely a girly book, but I enjoyed it, although I did make sure it was hidden away when my friends came over. Anyway, I know this girl exerted herself—despite the manifestations of her grooming—because her skin has the shiny glow of dried perspiration, and it's catching the late afternoon rays beaming through a Palladian window tall enough to adorn a cathedral.

She is older than I am, although I haven't confirmed her age. She looks
like some of the girls at my school who were in eighth grade last year, so
I'm guessing she's going into ninth. She's very slender and doesn't have the
round, plump caboose that her mother has. Not that I'd notice; I'm just
mentally repeating what my dad has assured me. Ever since the girl arrived
home with her mother, my dad has leveraged every opportunity to whisper
that the mom's a little plump. I didn't quite see it that way; indeed she
looked as attractive as her daughter, but I guess I'll have to go with plump
since I'm not one to judge these matters, and I trust my dad has much more
perspective. Indeed, he said her butt looks like a couple of watermelons. He
didn't precisely say this to me, but he whispered it like in a sleepwalking
soliloquy. This was right before I mistakenly admitted I was thirsty and
was summarily dispatched to this kitchen with this girl to get a drink.
Which I now hold unsteadily in my hand.

"I guess..." I stammer. "I'm your cousin, or distant cousin, or something like that...sort of."

"Really," she says with a tone that suggests she thinks I might be delusional, which is not a good trait to have unless you want to grow up to be
a serial murderer. I'm not exactly sure how to continue the conversation,
what with my knees knocking together and my mouth so parched from
having placed the water on the counter without having taken one mere sip.
It's a granite-top counter, and the clink from the glass reverberates high up
to the ceiling. This makes me flinch and hastens my exit, which is embar-
rassingly haste enough as it is. I dread running into this girl again, Chelsea,
my distant cousin, whoever she is. I flee out the back door looking for
Frizzy and Bugsy. Frizzy's been relegated to the outdoors, where it has been
decided she is at lesser risk from the ragweed than she is from the four dogs
inside, the three little yippy white ones and the big one named Amanda,
which is one of those massive Great Pyrenees with so much fur, you could
lose a small child in it. I have no luck finding the girls, which is just fine
anyway, because I'm still befuddled and annoyed by the conversation I had
with Bugsy on the Lawn at the University of Virginia earlier today.

In fact, I now can't help but call her Dog-Doo Breath. It's like this:
When we were sitting in the grass, several long, awkward moments passed
without our saying peep to one another. She had her eyes closed and her
face flashed up at the sun, with a smug grimace that made me think she

might have had visions of sugarplums dancing in her head if it weren't July. I considered asking her if she knew what a sugarplum is; then I toyed with a snide remark to the effect that I wondered when she was going to start consulting me. My strongest impulse was just to get up and walk away, but I glimpsed across the courtyard at my dad, and he looked so peppy, I just couldn't ruin his day. "So, how was Yale?" I finally asked. She responded with such a startled look, you'd think I asked her how was jail.

"Oh, Yale was stupendous," she finally said after collecting herself. She proceeded to tell me how much fun she had, particularly all the times she went to this place called Mory's with her boyfriend. At this place, apparently students sit at a large table and pass around a gigantic silver cup filled with a harsh concoction that makes the participants really drunk and want to sing stupid songs. The person taking the last sip has to put the cup on their head and spin it around. Bugsy, heretofore Dog-Doo Breath, said she loved to lose. When she told me this, I winced, thinking of her Brillo Pad hair scratching against the inside of the silver cup. "So, how big was this cup?" I asked. "Real big," she said, measuring with her hands. This made me think of my friend Zach and the Stanley Cup. Zach's always talking about the Stanley Cup. Sometimes he does so derisively, like when he mocks his dad for his frequent claims that Zach will one day win it. Zach says he has about as much of a chance of winning the Stanley Cup as the New York Islanders. This is a defeatist trait in Zach that sometimes annoys me. But I guess he's right, about the Islanders. I'm no expert; I can only judge by what Zach tells me, and he tells me the Eighties Dynasty will never be back. I'm like, wow, that's way before we were born, but Zach knows everything about the team, and what he tells me, of course, I facilely commit to everlasting memory. There's Nystrom, and Gillies, Bossy, Potvin and of course Trots. "Trots?" I had asked him the first time he ever mentioned the name, which immediately made me think of Trot Copperfield. "Yes, Trots," Zach had continued. "Bryan Trottier. Amazing center." I erupted into laughter. "That's fine and all," I said, forgetting about Dickens and trying to be cool. "But I wouldn't want the nickname *Trots*." "Why not?" Zach had asked. "Because," I'd said, "that's like what they call it when you have the runs, like diarrhea, you know?"

I laugh again as I think of this while standing out in the back field of my cousin's house, or whoever's house it is. "Trots," I whisper, having a jolly good time with myself, mind you. I would have called Bugsy *Trots*, but Zach would be pissed if he ever found out, so I'm going with Dog-Doo Breath. I know it's all a bit of a stretch—just slightly more convoluted than the Shotgun Snatcher. But it's stuck in my mind. What can I say? It won't come out. Like stains in underwear. And truth be told, there's more to the story. When we were sitting on the Lawn, after she finished telling me how drunk she always got at Yale, she proceeded to tell me I had a lot of work to do to get in. I figured this was where her consulting began, and I'm thinking, first of all, lady, I haven't even started seventh grade yet. I thought of a few choice words to call her—borrowed from my dad, of course—but instead opted for the meek approach. "I know," I said, "my dad's already informed me that I need to start thinking about starting an Internet business, or writing a novel...or trying out for the football team."

"Football?" she said wincing. "What about fencing?"

"What?" I asked with mock fascination. "Fencing? Hmm. I guess I might find it fun to be like the goddamn manager, or something...if you want to know the truth."

"Wow," she said, "that's some fresh mouth you have for a kid."

"I'm not a kid. And it's nothing like Holden Caulfield's."

"Who's he? One of your friends from school?"

"Um, no," I said. "No. Never mind."

"OK. Never mind." She blew the furry stuff off a dandelion and then said, "Listen, forget about that crap for now. What's more important is how well you know how to kiss you-know-what."

"Huh?" I said.

"Kiss ass," she said, whispering the cuss word through cupped hands and with feigned force as if she were trying to spit it across the Grand Canyon. That's when I caught the full fury of her nasty breath, which smelled like the most rancid diarrhea. This made me think about her comment moments earlier about how scrumptious (her word) her lunch was. She said she had a falafel. Two, actually. I don't know what a falafel is, such ignorance doing nothing to help me not refute the idea that it makes one's breath smell like diarrhea. Or worse: dog doo. I looked dazed, although she mistook my olfactory repulsion for cerebral inertia, so she continued, "You know, like sucking up."

"Yeah, I know what it means."

"Well, how good are you at sucking up to like teachers and coaches, and just adults in general?"

"Oh, to all those?" I said caustically. "Um, I guess I need some work there."

Truth be told, I'm no good at sucking up at all. No way. Not at all. And if that means I don't get into Yale, well then, I don't give two shits... to borrow a phrase from my dad. He's never said it in front of me purposely; I've just overheard him say it a few times on the phone when he's talking to my mother. What does it mean, anyway, not to give two shits? Maybe, I now contemplate, it has something to do with horses, as I watch one of the shiny brown ones in the field before me unleash a bowel about the size of a bowling ball, or those balls on the clock at Monte Cristo.

I am still staring in disbelief when I am called for dinner. Great, I think, now I need to see Chelsea again. But, oh thank God, she's not there. Upstairs packing, we're told by her father. That's the man whom my dad seems to eye suspiciously as if the guy might shoot him in the back at any moment. Chelsea's two older brothers, twins going into twelfth grade, are gone too. They've not been here at all since we arrived. In fact, we've learned they've been gone for several weeks. They're in the Himalayas on some leadership excursion where they are practicing survival skills in the shadow of K2. We learn this just as we're getting ready to sit down, and Dog-Doo Breath shrugs her shoulders at my dad as if to say, "Told you so." We also learn that the twins attend Choate, which is where Chelsea will also be going to school in the fall.

That's when Dog-Doo Breath pipes up and says she has lots of clients who go to Choate.

The man, my distant uncle or whatever, whose name is apparently Thomas, but whom my dad has twice mistakenly called Rex, responds to Dog-Doo Breath's comment by saying, "Oh, really, what do you do?"

She explains truthfully what her job is, which somehow does not seem to register as a subtle negation of the lie my dad earlier told Uncle Thomas that Dog-Doo Breath is a neighbor hitching a ride to Florida so she can visit some family for the summer.

We sit down at the table outside, which is where my dad requested we eat so that Frizzy would not be exposed to the dogs. It then becomes apparent someone else is missing, so my dad says, "Where's Bertha? I mean Bethany?"

"Oh, she'll be here in a moment," Thomas says. "She had to pack too." The moment promptly arrives, and Bethany swoops out the door as if she's running from a house fire. She's panting and out of breath, as I'm still trying to reconcile the image of her watermelon butt. I just don't see it. She's dressed in very tight white pants into which you could never fit two watermelons. Or one. Her hair is very curly and blonde and her nose quite bulbous and overly caked with makeup. I would like to think she's been exercising by the way she's panting, but she's not sweating, and I'm just eager for her to sit down because her kinetic behavior is making me a little agitated. The salads have been served by a large woman wearing an apron. This is not the same hairy, ethnic woman who greeted us earlier at the door. This woman is black, and I'm tempted to comment on how I thought slavery was banned after the Civil War. I wonder if her name's Eliza, just like the redoubtable character in Harriet Beecher Stowe's story.

Aunt Bethany picks a plum tomato from her salad and pops it in her mouth, which seems rude in and of itself, but is more acutely rude due to the fact that she's still standing. And still making me agitated.

"Listen, y'all," she says, with an accent I find disturbingly contrived. Hell, even Frizzy's is more authentic. "I'm so sorry that I can't sit and stay for dinner. Chelsea and I need to be off."

"That's too bad," my dad says. "Where to?"

"Field hockey tournament." As she says *tournament*, a glob of red juice dribbles onto her chin from the second plum tomato she's snarfed. She dabs the dribble daintily with the point of a folded cloth napkin like she's Queen Elizabeth.

"Oh, that sounds fun, we should all go," Dog-Doo Breath chimes in. My distant aunt chuckles haughtily.

"No, no, sweetie," she says. "The tournament's in Maryland."

"Beth has been running Chelsea around to tournaments all summer, ya know," Thomas adds proudly. "I barely recognize them these days." He punctuates the sentence with a forced laugh that begins with such a violent inward draft of air, I'm worried the dude might asphyxiate right on the spot. It makes his chin grow to the size of that Leno guy's on TV. "But she's already getting looks from UPenn," Thomas continues, "and she hasn't even started high school." He finishes with another laugh, and I can't help but stare at the chin, upon which I now notice sits a tiny tomato seed, which I'm certain must have been fired from the mouth of his wife.

"Well, gotta run, y'all," Bethany says. "First game's at 5 a.m. tomorrow morning. Sorry I couldn't spend more time with such dear family. Do stop by again next time you're in Virginia." She nods at Dog-Doo Breath, almost ignoring the rest of us, and Dog-Doo Breath smiles back inanely. Into Bethany's mouth goes another tomato, and I notice it's her last one, so I instinctively shield my salad plate with my hands to protect my own supply. "See you Saturday, honey," she says to Prince Thomas, then bends to peck him on the cheek but misses and catches his chin, where I think she may have hoovered that tomato seed. "Don't forget to get the Mercedes out of the shop," she continues to say to her husband over her shoulder as she's walking away. "The boys will need it when they get back from their trip."

I'm certain my dad's apoplectic by now. As I glance across the table, I realize that he's inhaled his entire salad already, as well as two dinner rolls. He does that—eats fast—when he's anxious. It gives him reflux, which usually starts with the hiccups and then grows so violent, he has to barf so he can clear his airways. Usually he makes it to the bathroom, which is a good thing, because I can't stand the sight of other people's puke. It's the Billy Schneider effect; it'll plague me the rest of my life. There it is, the hiccups. He quickly gets up to excuse himself, and that's when the first rumble of thunder can be heard rolling over the hills like a freight train.

Not five minutes later the skies darken to the color of coal, and blowing rain pelts the deck around us. We're under cover, and the thunder still seems distant, so no one makes a move. I'm thinking that's a bit careless, but then I look at Frizzy and I can tell she's itchy and wheezy and I think, OK, let's wait it out. The pelting rain quickly grows louder and that's when the slave saunters over and begins pulling some of the outdoor furniture in from the edges of the covered deck. "Thanks, Eliza," Thomas says, as I just shake my head dumbfounded at the sound of her actual name. The iron furniture scrapes stridently on the stone floor, so I cover my ears and look away, at which point I spot my dad returning from the bathroom and grimacing the way he does after he's just cured his reflux.

Uncle Tom's a trooper. He's completely unflustered by the storm, as if he were sitting out here alone reading a novel on a wispy, clear day. "So, how is it we're ahhh..." he stammers and does this twirling thing toward my dad with his pointer finger... "related?" I hear him barely, even thought he's sitting right next to me, because the rain is pounding.

"What's that?" my dad shouts.

"How is it we're related?" Uncle Tom repeats, louder than my dad. The ensuing conversation takes place as if they were conducting it at the door of an open airplane at twenty thousand feet, like you see those skydivers do on TV before they jump.

"Oh," my dad says. "My wife... I mean my ex-wife, is a Hanneford. Her great-great-great-grandfather (he counts the *greats* on his fingers) was a Randolph, from Virginia, and I understand his brother's family settled right in this area and has never left. It's your family, I'm told."

Uncle Tom just nods his head pleasantly. Then he screams, "We're from New York!" before stuffing his mouth with a forkful of lamb. Which I by the way find detestable. Frizzy has chicken fingers and French fries, just like off the kids' menu at a restaurant. I try to poach some of it, but she's too far away. Next to her, Dog-Doo Breath snags another large spoonful of mashed potatoes, her third helping. Each of the previous two have disappeared into her mouth quickly, but not as quickly as the three glasses of red wine.

"What's that?" my dad shouts.

"We're from New York!" Uncle Tom screams again. "Just moved here four months ago. I made a killing on the Street..." he hesitates and opens his mouth to let out one of his annoying laughs, but the sound is consumed by the roar of the rain and a rumble of thunder that seems to be closer than the last. "I figured, why not enjoy life, you know, so I decided to buy this spread down here. Still got the pad in New York, though. Scarsdale."

"Scarsdale!" Dog-Doo Breath shrieks with a violent slur of her speech. "How wonderful! It's just soooo phoophie there!"

Did she just say *phoophie*? I glance at my dad and Uncle Tom for a reaction, but both have ignored her.

"I feel just like a real Southerner already," Uncle Tom says, his laugher registering above the storm this time, as I now notice the rain has shut off like a faucet. My dad picks at his lamb, and it's so quiet you could hear a pin drop.

"So…your family is *not* from Virginia?" my dad finally asks, loudly, as if his voice level is stuck in yell-mode.

"Well, let's see…" Uncle Tom shouts back. "My grandmother was a Hanneford, indeed, yes. But her family was New York through and through. Her granddaddy…you like how I say that just like the Southerners?—ha-ha-ha-ha—worked in Teddy Roosevelt's administration when he was governor. One of her ancestors gained acclaim for helping get the guns of Ticonderoga to Boston."

I stare at my dad, knowing full well he has no clue what this means, but he tries to look impressed regardless.

"I know all this," Uncle Tom says, "because Chelsea had to do a genealogy project in school last year. She aced it, of course!" He accompanies this fawning exclamation with a dumb smirk. Dog-Doo Breath reaches across to snag a fry from Frizzy's plate and knocks a glass of water over. "Ooops," she says mildly. Nobody else reacts, but Eliza is on the spot and begins sopping it up.

"Now, I do recall," Uncle Tom continues, "that there is a Randolph branch of the family here in Virginia…" Why he's still shouting, I can't fathom. My dad stabs at a pea like he's trying to draw blood. He misses and then watches it shoot across the table and land on the ground, where it rolls for several yards before stalling in a small puddle.

Uncle Tom glances amusingly at the pea, then repeats, finally in a quieter voice, "Yes, I believe there are some Randolphs around here. Chelsea may have mentioned that, but you'd have to ask her." I'm wondering if this is an invitation for us to stay four more days until Chelsea returns home with the field hockey Stanley Cup spinning on her head and her mother drunk with rapture.

But staying another day is clearly out of the question when the next morning arrives and my dad appears in the kitchen looking like he'd just been through a war. He and Frizzy had been relegated to the "far wing" (Uncle Tom's term), where they'd been assured the dogs never enter. But clearly my dad and Frizzy had a sleepless night from her wheezing and coughing, and he's in no humor. Especially when Dog-Doo Breath appears perkily and announces she's heading out for a run. She looks no worse for the wear despite tripping on one of the chaise lounge chairs after dinner last night and bumping her head on a marble statue of Adonis, which didn't budge.

"Ohhhhhh, no, you don't!" my dad bellows. He reprises this order several moments later when Eliza asks if we want eggs Benedict for breakfast.

"That'd be swell!" Dog-Doo Breath shrieks. But her response still seems to be hanging in the air as we peel out of the driveway a short time later without any breakfast at all. Uncle Tom's not even there to say good-bye. Early tennis match, we were told by the housekeeper, the same one who had greeted us the day before.

I can hear the dogs barking at us over the roar of the Expedition as we charge up the first hill of their long and winding driveway. By the third hill my dad has slowed slightly, and the steam from his ears seems to be subsiding. That's when Frizzy shouts: "The buffalo!" We doubt this time she's lying because Uncle Tom had indeed confirmed that there were buffalo on the property. Although he insisted on calling them bison. He just laughed when my dad asked him about it and merely said, "It's *the thing* to do, you know."

So there's no hesitation in my dad slamming on the brakes. We all hop out and head up a steep, slick hill in the direction of the buffalo...the bison. My dad gets out but lingers behind as his excitement clearly lacks punch. The ground is still very wet from the night before, and I notice Frizzy trip a few times, then wipe her hands on her white shirt, which is quickly turning the color of terra cotta. We search for several minutes, but there is no sign of bison. Or any large mammal, for that matter. Just a few birds and a chipmunk.

I shoo us all back to the car, knowing full well my dad's patience is likely exhausted. He starts the car and glances toward the passenger seat and then lets out a howl you might associate with your scariest nightmare. "What the hell is all that red mud in my car!" he screams at Dog-Doo Breath.

This might be a perfect time for her to nervously say "What," with her characteristic charm, but I've noticed within the last day she's begun to forsake that word. Indeed, she seems startlingly comfortable, like a new shoe that's suddenly old. When she gives my dad a blank look, he screams again, "What the hell's with that red mud!" to which she casually looks down and shrugs dismissively. So he flings his head back toward me and Frizzy, and

I try to shield his view from the pancakes of red clay ground into his gray floor mats. But it's too late. Hey, I consider saying, at least it matches the exterior color of your car. Sort of. In fact, I can't think of anything to say that might appease the deep moans coming from his throat and making me wonder if his appendix might burst like Madeline's.

The moaning subsides gradually and silence reigns when we get to the main road. That's when Dog-Doo Breath says, "I sure can't wait to meet the *real* Virginia cousins." She spews this with the authentic excitement of a child on Christmas morning. News that some *real* Virginia cousins might actually exist was met mutely by my dad the night before. Uncle Tom had called Chelsea in Maryland and when he hung up, he said, "Well, she believes, based on her research, there's a Randolph family related to us up in Fauquier County." When he said this like *Fuck-queer*, I thought he was using a "fresh mouth" as a way to pull a joke over on us. But Uncle Tom was way too stiff for such chicanery, despite what his incessantly stupid laugh might otherwise attempt to betray about his personality.

My dad answers Dog-Doo Breath's comment with a steel wall of silence. Any doubt as to whether he's considering a detour north to find the *real* Virginia cousins is refuted by the compass indicator in his car that reads bright green with an unfaltering *S*. I think I hear a sardonic snort from Dog-Doo Breath, which I'm really relishing because I've been catching some good vibes lately that my dad's so irritated by her, he's considering switching our places in the car. The only obstacle to this welcome change is Frizzy. I don't think my dad trusts Dog-Doo Breath with her back here. I glance at Frizzy to give her a random leer, which she unfortunately returns with much more stylistic flare. Defeated, I begin to pull my eyes off her, but not before noticing something in her lap. She's clutching it, and the best I can tell, it looks like a porcelain elephant figurine, small enough to fit comfortably in her hand.

"Where'd you get that?" I ask.

"Nowhere," she says evilly.

I consider yelling up to my dad that Frizzy has stolen something from those people we just left. But my dad's now whistling away, like he hasn't a care in the world. And I begin to wonder if he already knows.

8

SUMTER NICE

"Dad, you need to pull over! Now!"

Doug swerved off the road, and the moment the Expedition rolled to a stop, Jamie flung the door open and vomited. Even in his delirium he was alert enough to climb over to Frizzy's side so he wouldn't have to open his door into the face of barreling trucks on I-95.

"Eeeewwww!" Frizzy shrieked as Jamie hurled a second time.

"You getting it all outside there, kiddo?" Doug asked delicately. "None on the car, right?" None on the car, but Jamie had drowned the porcelain elephant...or what remained of it. When he'd opened the door, he had kicked it out by accident, or perhaps subconsciously on purpose. It shattered into a dozen pieces, the sound muffled by the ambient noise from the highway so that no one else in the car noticed.

Finally, after Jamie gave his dad the *OK* sign, Doug pulled back onto the highway, but exited another few miles down the road at a rest stop. They all insisted on it. *Fine*, Doug silently conceded, Frizzy needed another puff on her inhaler anyway. She was the first to react adversely to the upholstery cleaner. Jamie was next with the vomiting. Doug knew it was a risk buying the stuff, but he couldn't stand the sight of the clay stains on his floor mats. He'd pulled into a Home Depot and bought the cheapest cleaner on the shelf.

"The stuff really does stink," Ashley groused, as they leaned against the car and watched Jamie stagger around the parking lot guzzling big breaths of air like a blowfish, trailed by Frizzy snapping pictures, the sound silenced by the roar of the wind and traffic on the highway. "It's making *me* nauseous too, you know."

"Are you sure it wasn't all those dirty water dogs you had back at Home Depot?" he asked.

"Dirty what?"

"Dirty water dogs."

"What the heck are you talking about?"

"The hot dog guy, out front…he cooks his dogs in water he scoops from the gutter."

"How the heck do you know?" she asked.

"I've seen them do it countless times in New York."

"Yeah, well, not every place is like New York."

"Don't bank on it," he said. He glanced at his watch and then whistled for Jamie and Frizzy to return. "How many of those things did you have anyway?" he asked Ashley. "I mean, jeez, it's barely ten o'clock."

"I don't know, three…four," she said, unembarrassed.

The thought of four of those germy hotdogs turned his stomach. But not as badly as the vision of that hairy housekeeper's two flabby gazongas as she straddled a man naked in bed. Doug stumbled upon them in the faint light earlier that morning as he groped around for the bathroom. When he opened the door, all he heard was her low moaning, like some wild animal in heat. She was squeezing her breasts savagely, and they were squirting around in her hands like under-filled water balloons. She didn't flinch at the sound of Doug's entry, but the man under her did. It was Thomas. He turned his head toward Doug and just winked casually, then glanced at his watch as if he suddenly wondered if he was cutting it close to the start of his tennis game.

It was this smugness that irritated Doug all the way to Virginia's southern border. But a different state offered new hope, so by the time they crossed into the Carolinas, he felt a renewed peacefulness settle in. The day was brilliant, a deep blue cloudless sky unfurling in a thin strip above the towering oaks and pines that flanked the highway. He cranked up Gerry Rafferty. Frizzy made a comment about how it was his favorite song to sing when he was sitting on the toilet. This made him blush as Ashley snickered, so he advanced to the next song and opened his window to let the fresh air wash away his embarrassment. Finally, Ashley fell asleep and the Victoria Secret catalogue she had on her lap slid to the floor. Doug eyed it covetously and considered reaching down to swipe it, but knew it was a risky move. Frizzy was now glued to the TV screen, and The Kid had his nose in a book with his headphones on. Doug felt euphoria fill his veins and make him tingle, and he began to embrace an elusive certainty about the trip's success. He believed it could be a milestone in his son's life. The adventure. The ELEGY conference. The family bonding. And (he still held out hope) some helpful direction from the consultant as to where to focus The Kid's future so he could get into a top prep school and then into Yale. He gazed over at the consultant. She'd blown up one of those inflatable neck pillows. The one time he'd flown anywhere—to Jamaica for his honeymoon, his father-in-law paying for the trip—his wife had insisted on using one of those pillows. She used earplugs too, and a mask. Hindsight being twenty-twenty, of course, Doug could never quite reject it as it not being a bad omen for their future together. On the return flight, when she was sound asleep, his stoicism collapsed abruptly, and he reached over and punctured the thing madly with his ball-point pen.

Maybe all women use those pillows. As his mind drifted, so did his car. He heard honking as he swerved into the right lane, which is where he remained, content to sail along at the speed limit while cars and trucks zipped by on his left. Where had things gone wrong with his wife anyway? It wasn't the pillow, was it? Maybe that just summed things up in a mind that was truculent toward the ambitions of deep thought. It was just more than a year ago that he'd learned about her affair. His friend Rex had called him and told him he'd seen Corrine out at a restaurant with the weasel. Rex knew the weasel from business school, or *B-school* as he liked to call it, to Doug's vexation. The fact that anyone would tattle, or that it was actually Rex who'd tattled, seemed at first to weigh more thornily on Doug than the actual affair itself. But deep down inside, the collapsed marriage was just another failure that he dragged around like a sack of potatoes.

Now let's see, Ashley would have been a good option for an affair, Doug thought, as he cruised along oblivious to the passage of miles. He ignored the fact that he never considered having an affair when he was married and never would have. But it was fun to imagine. He had to figure she was in her late twenties, considering the work experience Mr. Hildenberger had listed in the e-mail he sent Doug about her. Even though she ate like a cow, she looked like the kind of woman who could remain rock solid well into her fifties, like some of those Hollywood women. Not like Corrine, who began to droop the first day of their marriage. So what if Ashley jogged funny, the results were just fine, and he admired physically fit women. From the neck up he could do without, especially the stuff that came out of her mouth. Unbelievable. Sometimes he thought she acted more like Jamie's age. Then there was the stuff that didn't come out of her mouth. He'd made up his mind to call Hildenberger as soon as he could get some time alone. He'd let her boss deal with her incompetence. Then again, Doug worried that any reprimand from her boss might make him looked like a backhanded nitwit and make her a little less inclined to see him in a positive light. *Eh, what the hell,* he thought, he'd see what happens.

His mind re-engaged on the road. He glanced at his watch and figured they must be halfway through Georgia by now. He'd turned off his GPS when they left Virginia, swearing that it caused him to get lost more often than not. He knew he wasn't lost now. It was a straight shot to Florida. Easy. That's why the next sign he read made his placid demeanor shatter like crystal: sixty miles to Savannah!

"Holy jeeeeez!" he shouted. All three passengers in the car snapped to attention with looks of sheer fright, as if they were all about to face the fleeting moments before a wild crash that sends them into violent unconsciousness and a dreamy netherworld hitched to the gossamer wings of angels with the bodies of little girls and the heads of old men with Rasputin beards. But instead of St. Peter's voice at the gates of heaven, it was Doug's that came through again.

"What's with this state! You go thinking some place is totally puny, and it takes forever to drive through. It's bad enough they have two of 'em."

"Two of what, Dad?" Jamie asked.

"Carolinas."

"Oh," Jamie said, "I thought we were going to stop at Fort Sumter."

"Whoops, is that in North or South?"

"South, Dad. I think we might have passed the exit a little ways back." As his son's voice trailed off, Doug scratched his head nervously and slowed the car down to the minimum speed limit as his indecision reigned. Another car was right on his tail, so he gave the guy a hand gesture, like flipping him the bird, without the bird going up.

"I don't know, kiddo…we're quite a ways off from Florida," he said. "We're not as far along as I thought we might be by now. Maybe we can visit some Civil War sites in Florida when we're visiting Gramps."

"Civil War sites…in Florida?" Jamie said. "That'd be like hoping to buy a Picasso original in Walmart."

Ashley yawned and rubbed her eyes, then said, "I hate Walmart. Target's sooooo much better."

Doug picked up his speed again and tried to stifle the guilt that was making his skin prickly. For the next several miles, he quietly debated the merits of turning around. He'd pulled out his road atlas, which he generally refused to consult, and saw that they weren't too far past the exit for Fort Sumter. But with one eye on the road and the other on the map, he thought it sure looked like a haul to get there from the interstate. It could cost them an extra day, and they were already behind. Plus, Dale was expecting them tomorrow morning.

It was almost as if Ashley was reading his thoughts. "Where in Florida does your dad live?" she asked.

"My dad doesn't live in Florida," he said. "He's dead."

"Well, what the heck, you told me we were going to visit your dad in Florida."

"No, I said we were going to visit the kids' grandfather in Florida. Dale is his name. It's Corrine's father… my ex-wife."

"Wow," she said with stunned reserve. "This is really getting weird. Is it *really* her father? I mean, are you sure this time?"

"Very funny. Yes, I'm sure it's her father." Indignant, he glanced in the rearview mirror and saw that Jamie had resumed his reading with his headphones on, having given up on Fort Sumter. Frizzy was giggling away at the TV, chewing on a Twizzlers.

"Where'd Frizzy get the Twizzlers?" Doug asked petulantly.

"I gave them to her," Ashley said.

"I'd appreciate it if you wouldn't do that," he said.

"Ha! It wouldn't hurt for her to get a little attention once in a while."

"What's that supposed to mean?"

"Well, it seems you're all about The Kid. The Kid this. And The Kid that. It's a little much, you know."

"Listen, the day you become a parent, you can give me advice. That's the thing about you people without kids. You think you know everything. It all seems so easy and straightforward, doesn't it? 'Oh, I can't believe you let them watch so much TV,'" he ranted in a contrived, high-pitched voice. "'I can't believe you let them get away with talking back. I can't believe…'" he grasped for something else but failed and merely said, "It's not so easy, once you have to do it. So, until then, back off."

"I'll be sure to call you."

"Huh?"

"When I become a parent. I'll be sure to call you. Maybe by that time The Kid will be famous."

"Yeah, well," Doug said. "I'm sure he will."

"Not if you don't ease up on him a bit," she said.

"What does *that* mean?" he asked.

"I don't know…" she said. "It just seems to me, a stupid non-parent, that you're putting a lot of pressure on him. Kids like that sometimes wind up famous for the wrong reasons, ya know."

"I don't see where you get off lecturing me about pressure," he said, the exasperation in his voice building. "It's people like you…all you high-priced consultants…who are putting the pressure on everyone to keep up."

"You hired me," she said.

"Yeah, well…" he said. But by the time he could scrape together the rest of his retort, she'd lowered her window and turned her face into the rushing air. He shook his head, reached down and cranked up the music. He was eager to get Florida. Unfortunately he was running low on gas, so he pulled off somewhere in Georgia. Ashley took the kids into the mini-mart, and Doug flipped through some things in his binder while he gassed up. He'd really slacked off the last few days with Jamie, and he worried he wasn't keeping his brain sharp. *Screw what the broad said,* Doug thought. *She really doesn't know what the heck she's talking about.* He opened his binder and the first page he saw were some facts on the beginning of the Civil War, the Battle of Fort Sumter. His skin immediately tingled again with guilt, so he slammed the binder closed and tossed it on the front seat. Some thunderheads were building in the sky. That's when it occurred to Doug they'd not had any rain so far on the trip, except for that brief shower in Philly.

But who counts Philly? How lucky they were. The Expedition was purring along like a kitten. No accidents. No flats or exploding Firestones. Things weren't so bad, were they? He began to whistle and carried the tune into the mini-mart, where he picked up a tall bottle of iced coffee.

"That's sumter nice family you got," said the man behind the counter, as he nodded his head toward the parking lot like a mechanical doll.

"Huh?" Doug said. Did he just say *sumter*? And then quickly he added, "Oh, thanks," nervously so as not to appear rude and invite the barrel of a shotgun to his forehead. He reached for his change. The quarters looked like tiny buttons in the man's puffy palm. Doug couldn't help but trace his eyes along the tattooed forearms, with all sorts of dragons and snakes shooting fire out of their mouths. The man's biceps were as large as Doug's thighs, he thought, although they lacked any hint of muscle under the flab. Still, Doug wondered if the guy couldn't tip a school bus. His Expedition, definitely. He didn't, however, have such malice in his eyes. They peered out smiling at Doug, deep blue they were, in a sea of hair, lots of it wiry and dark, hanging over his brow and down the sides, where it impregnated a riotous beard.

"Y'all have a good day now," the man said, with a tone that you sometimes hear from people when you suspect they're inside your head. Doug nodded and hesitated, spying his "family" through the plate glass window. Ashley was bent over in front of the car, with her rear end facing alluringly toward him. She was helping Frizzy clean dead bugs off the front grill with the squeegee. Doug resisted the urge to run out and lecture them about how germ-infested the squeegee was. So he just stood and stared instead. He could see the silhouette of Jamie's head and shoulders through the tinted windows of the car. Doug instinctively glanced back at the gentle giant behind the counter and felt relieved to see the man engaged with another customer. Then Doug chuckled, as the thought occurred to him— as they rarely do—that messages sometimes come from the most mysterious places. He gazed at his family one more time, and whispered comfortingly to himself, "Thanks Corrine, for not wanting them."

"So why are we going to see...Dale, is it?" Ashley asked after they'd been back on the road a few minutes. "You never quite got around to explaining that to me."

"I didn't think that was required."

"Whatever." She pulled out another catalogue and began flipping through while chewing on a piece of Twizzlers like it was rawhide. After several miles of quiet, she finally garbled through a mouthful: "It's about..." she paused and nodded her head toward the back of the car... "The Kid."

"What?" Doug said.

"The Kid...Jamie," she whispered. "It's about him, isn't it?" When she saw the puzzled look cross his face, she continued, "Going to Florida to see this Dale guy has something to do with The Kid."

He steeled his gaze straight ahead and completely ignored her for several long, quiet minutes, his blood curdling at the intuition of women, as well as her incessant gnawing on the candy...in his new car, no less. How do they do it? he wondered. Women are always one step ahead. It used to drive him crazy with Corrine...she always reading his thoughts and intentions with pinpoint accuracy. He was proud of himself for eventually accepting it as a fact of life, and usually stuck to honesty as a result, to avoid conflict. A few of his friends, on the other hand, seemed to masochistically fight against the tide, telling lie after lie and deluding themselves into thinking they were getting the upper hand in their marriages. *Funny how most of those guys are still married,* Doug thought, *and I'm not.*

"Dale's brilliant," he finally mumbled, barely audible above the air conditioning, which he was now blasting against the outside heat that seemed to be rapidly penetrating the car.

"Brilliant as in 'it's a brilliant day'? or brilliant as in he's really frickin' smart."

"He's smart. Really smart. He was like a chemical engineer or something like that. Whatever that is. All I know is he made a pretty damn good living at it. And yes, I thought it would be good for the kid to be exposed to him some more. He doesn't exactly get his brains from me, you know."

"Don't sell yourself so short."

"Thanks," he mumbled self-consciously. They drove on for several more minutes. "He's not a bad guy, you know," he finally continued.

"Well, that's good. So you think you'll be a little less uptight than you were at that other place back there in Virginia?"

Doug ignored her comment and said, "He is a little quirky though. You'd think he was living on food stamps when you see how frugal he is.

And he takes forever to make decisions. He'll spend thirty minutes buying a pack of gum, comparing the cost of each and every pack on the shelf, measuring their net weights, their cost per net weight, cost per stick of gum. It's maddening."

"Old people get that way."

"Noooo, he's always been that way. He paid for our wedding and our honeymoon, which was nice. But I had to sit down with him and plan the trip, and you'd think we were preparing for a yearlong stay at the space station. He had stacks and stacks of brochures all spread out on the dining room table, with all sorts of charts comparing costs at the different hotels. He even researched the thread count on the bedding at all the hotels we were considering."

"Wow, sounds like it will be a fun visit."

"Yeah, well, I'm not sure fun is really the motivating factor. Like I said, I just think it will be good for Jamie to be exposed to him a bit more." He paused for several seconds. "And for the kids to see their grandfather."

"Ahhh, now you're talking more like a normal person," she joshed.

"I can handle the history stuff and some of the literature," he pressed on. "But when it comes to math and science, forget it. The Kid needs some work there. Math and science are critical to getting ahead these days. You should know that."

"Yes, of course, absolutely," she said, not camouflaging her sarcastic tone.

"Maybe you can help when we get there."

"Help with what?"

"You know, working with The Kid on some science and math, along with Dale."

"Oh, we're back to that again."

"Back to what?"

"Never mind."

"You said you were good at math."

"I did, didn't I? But I hated it. Took one course in college and that was it. Went with philosophy instead. Don't know much math."

"Well, whatever," he said. "Maybe you could test The Kid on something you *do* know."

"I told you that's not what we do at Elite Schools R Us. That's for teachers."

Well, what the hell do you do? Doug said to himself. He sighed deeply and rubbed his eyes. He was getting tired and thought he needed a rest. He was about to pull off, when a giant sign along the side of the road made his spirits soar. Welcome to Florida.

"The sunshine state, kiddos," Doug chirped. But no one responded. He turned up his tunes and fixed his eyes on the road ahead. A few miles up, the hazy, blanched sky suddenly flickered dark, like a great big black veil had been draped over the highway. He'd never witnessed anything like it. It seemed like the end of the world. The Apocalypse. He half expected to see a white horse come down from the heavens. With a rider named Faithful and True. Words *some* people don't quite get, do they?

9

❖ ❖ ❖

MY SISTER'S COKE

I lean over the front seat and confirm what I believe. The speedometer reads forty-two. "Um, Dad," I say delicately, "Do you know you are only going forty-two on the interstate?"

"Well, who can see in this ridiculous monsoon?" he shoots back irritably. He's right, you can't see much outside through the wall of water. That isn't stopping Frizzy from taking pictures. Thank God I can't hear the sound. I can't hear much, really, above the roar outside. Remember the rainstorm in Virginia? This is like a hundred times worse. It sounds like we're all stuffed in a metal garbage can and someone's banging on the outside violently with a hammer. My dad's knuckles are white as he grips the steering wheel, and I can't resist feeling comforted to know he's being extra careful. Why lots of other people on the road aren't is definitely a source of curiosity to me. And concern. Although I can't see my dad's face, I know it's tremulous with anger, and I can visualize the puffy skin right under his eyes red with rage and jiggling a bit like Jell-O, as it usually does when his dander's up. And it's definitely up. His grits his teeth harder as each car zooms by on his left...red, blue, and black phantoms cloaked in shrouds of meteoric raindrops that seem as big as lemons. I begin to wonder if Florida might not be the best fit for his unlicensed petulance behind the wheel.

I can't help but notice that many of the cars passing us are not cars at all. They're trucks. Pick-up trucks. The last one that eases by more slowly than most has the words *Boss Man* painted in bold letters on the cab's back window and something hanging from its trailer hitch that looks like gigantic testicles. I think I've seen more—pick-ups, that is, not testicles—in twenty minutes than I've seen in my entire life on Long Island. This reminds me of a joke Jessica told me once about rednecks and pick-up trucks, but I can't remember the punch line. I consider e-mailing her, because I know she'd remember it. I spent most of my time driving through the Carolina's e-mailing her back and forth. I was glad to hear her mother is back on the upswing. I told her all about the experience in Virginia. Dog-Doo Breath getting drunk. My dad barfing in the bathroom. Frizzy stealing the figurine. Despite learning of all those riveting tales, she simply wrote back: *sounds like u have the hots for your cuz. Is that legal?*

thats a joke. HAHA, she'd written back later when I never responded. I still haven't written back, so you could say I'm stonewalling. I've been waiting for the chance to try that sometime. Besides, I can't find my phone, and I'm about to rummage through Frizzy's backpack when I glance up front and notice that Dog-Doo Breath has my phone. At first I thought it was hers, as they look alike, but it's definitely mine.

"Ah, excuse me, can I please have my phone back," I say forcefully. OK, check that, maybe it was a bit more wimpish than I intended. Besides, she can't hear above the din, because the rain is still pounding. I feel like we're driving through a herd of elephants. So I repeat my request, much louder.

She hears me this time and yells back, "Wait, wait, wait," as her fingers move frantically over the keys on the phone. She tilts the phone sharply one way and then back the other. "I'm almost done with this game, and I have a high score going," she says. "Your phone has like way better games than mine."

It's another hour until I get it back, which is when we finally stop for the night. Thank God, as I have no idea how far my grandfather's house is, but I figure at the speed we are driving, it might take us three days. Hopefully tomorrow will be a new day. We check into the hotel and are soaking wet, so we have to change for dinner, which entails eating in a dark, dingy room they call a restaurant, because my dad has no desire to go outside again and battle the rain that is still falling in tropical torrents. The food is as soggy as the weather, and even Dog-Doo Breath seems repulsed. I've ordered a hamburger that tastes like a hockey puck wrapped in a wet napkin. Fries come on the side, and I have to peel them off the plate, hanging several of them limply and inspecting them before deciding they're not worth risking death. I finally give up and resolve to snack on some Fritos in the room. Unfortunately, things up there fail to improve through the evening. The rain pours down harder, which I didn't think was possible. The thunder cracks about every minute for what seems like hours on end. It keeps me wide awake, and I can hear my dad tossing and turning in the other bed, although I can't tell if he too is bothered by the thunder or by Frizzy kicking him. Or both. Frizzy sleeps with him now after the second night of the trip when I protested that she kicked me in the nuts during the night, and that I would not be able to focus on his quiz work if I didn't get sufficient sleep. So now he's got her. And she's sleeping like a log, despite the cacophony blaring through the window until the wee hours of the morning.

I'm relieved to see hope shining through the thin filthy curtain when I awake after my brief slumber. It's sunlight. Hurray! After dressing, I'm sitting on the bed with Frizzy watching Disney Channel while my dad uses the bathroom—for a long time—when I hear a thumping in the hallway. I assume it's just someone walking to or from their room. Then it happens again and it begins to sound like quite a commotion. Curious, I walk to the door and peer through the peephole, where I see a bluish blur drift by, accompanied by a sound that resembles humming. I stand near the door and wait for a moment, wondering if it will come back. It does. So I open the door a crack and peer out. My eyes follow a person who is moving away from me down the hallway. It's a woman, and I know immediately who it is. She disappears out the exit door, so I stand there with my room door slightly ajar and lurk. Like an axe murderer. Sure enough, she appears momentarily at the exit door on the opposite end of the hallway, now running right toward me. Of course she's trying to catch bugs, and I doubt there are any in the hallway, although I do spot scurrying along the far wall a cockroach that's as big as a small dog. Bugs or not, I hereby revert to her former nickname, because frankly I'm just sick of thinking about dog crap. My stomach problems are bad enough.

She sees me and stops. "Hi there, kiddo!" she shouts above the blare of her iPod music, trying to imitate my dad's cadence, much to my chagrin.

I return the greeting with a dark frown and say, "What in the world are you doing?"

"Why, jogging, of course," she yells, not inaccurately because she *is* still running—in place, a feat I can't quite reconcile when you consider that she is not bending her knees one degree.

"Ummm…" I say, "like in the hallway?"

"Well, the stairs, too. I go up a flight, and then down, up a flight, then down…" I'm now really curious how in the world she runs up the stairs stiff-legged, but more curious as to why she is running inside and not out, so I ask her, not necessarily eager to see a repeat of her last disappearing act in Virginia.

"Have you been outside," she says back, more as a statement than a question, before quickly adding, "Gotta go" and running off like a drunken beefeater being chased by crazy rats.

Soon I know what she means. About outside. When the sliding glass door to the hotel lobby whooshes open, it hits us. Literally, like a punch in the gut. The air, I'm talking about. It's so thick and heavy with heat and humidity, I actually feel myself stagger. It reminds me of the time Zach took me to his dad's golf club and we tried the sauna, thinking it would be fun to see how long we could stay in it. It was definitely a long time, and we only left when some old dude walked in buck naked and chased us out. I fainted immediately after and could never quite tell if it was from the heat, or from the sight of that man's penis hanging under the dark shadow cast by a roll of stomach blubber. I don't think the penis was circumcised, and if not, it was the first time I'd ever seen one like that. OK, it was also the first time I'd seen an old man's. So I didn't have much perspective to judge by. All I know is it was scary looking. It was long and hooked. To the left. His left, not mine. It was withered and wrinkled, yet puffy like it might have been afflicted with poison ivy. Again, I'd never seen one afflicted with poison ivy, but I'd done a lot of thinking on the matter earlier that summer. That was when I picked up a bad case of poison ivy God knows where, as my mother would say. It was all over my hands, and my dad ordered me not to touch my privates or I'd be in for a nightmare. He made me pee sitting down like a girl until things cleared up. That took about three weeks.

There is no nightmare-withered-hooked-poison-ivy penis dangling in my face right now, thank God, so I definitely know it's the heat making me feel faint. I'm not alone either. The other three also appear to be staggering across the parking lot toward the Expedition. Bugsy says, "I can't believe people live in this place," and then my dad mutters something incoherent that sounds a little bit like he is speaking in tongues.

The situation isn't improved by the fact that we've skipped breakfast at the five-star restaurant in the hotel. We search out a Starbucks, which gratefully is not difficult, as there appears to be one in every strip mall, there being an unbroken string of strip malls along the road back out to the interstate. In fact, we'd have multiple opportunities to visit just about every chain store and restaurant if we wanted to. There goes the fourth McDonald's I've seen in the last five minutes, another Denny's and another place called Publix, which appears to be a supermarket. Why they need one every mile makes me wonder if all people do in Florida is buy groceries.

My dad's got his road atlas spread out on the table at Starbucks and this is beginning to make me nervous. Only when we're back on the road does it become apparent that he's determined to make amends for missing Fort Sumter. He declares that we are going to St. Augustine, which he proudly reveals is the oldest city in the country, and I realize that what took him so long in the bathroom this morning was not an upset stomach from our nasty dinner last night, but frantic Internet research on his dumb smartphone. He seems to know all the facts about St. Augustine, and admittedly I'm a little bit in the dark on the place myself to be able to quibble with him.

The place isn't so bad at all. It sure seems different than the homogeneous stretch of interstate and strip malls we've seen in Florida so far, and my dad is noticeably intoxicated with his decision. We visit a huge stone fort called Castillo de San Marcos, which was built by the Spanish explorers in the seventeenth century. It has a majestic view out over water, which appears to be some sort of inlet leading to the ocean. Up on the gun decks there are dozens of old-fashioned cannons, which I think are really cool, until I look over and see Bugsy riding one like a pony. Talk about spoiling a kid's fun.

My dad, on the other hand, continues to be beside himself. "This sure is better than Fort Sumter, isn't it, kiddo?" he asks me.

"I don't know," I say. "I've never been there." I'm not trying to be a wise-ass, just honest, but either way it doesn't register with my dad. He asks me two more times, and each time I give him the same answer. The fourth time he asks, though, I notice his enthusiasm has waned. I am certain it has nothing to do with my pending response. In fact, I don't respond at all but just stare at him sympathetically as I notice his gray Knicks T-shirt soaked with sweat and clinging to his back like Velcro.

"Jesus, Mary, and Joseph, it's fickin' hot," he swears as he staggers slightly, and somehow I think my dead grandmother up in heaven must be roiling at the improper usage of her favorite supplication. The remainder of our visit to the fort becomes a blur, and I hear my dad curse some more under his breath when Bugsy protests that we didn't even get to see the chapel. She says this as she's staring down at her huge unfolded map of the fort, which is just seconds before she walks into a wall, knocking those gigantic sunglasses off her face. Surprisingly, and disappointingly, they don't break when they hit the cement walkway, but they shortly succumb to the unwitting foot of some crusty old guy dressed in a blue and red Spanish soldier uniform with a musket flung over his shoulder. The guy marches on steadfastly like he's off to battle, and I just stare laughing while Bugsy sinks to her hands and knees to collect the pieces.

The fact that she has taped the pieces together with the duct tape my dad has in the back of the car and is now wearing them crookedly on her falcon beak is even better entertainment. At least for a little while, but I soon tire of it and retreat into my own little world as we drive down the interstate. My dad has announced that it will be about three hours to Dale's house, which I extrapolate to mean about five hours...after we get lost. I'm particularly pessimistic that he'll find his way this time, not just from past experience, but because I'm certain it's going to be very hard to find a place called, Sara's-Soda. Back before we left New York, when my dad was taking directions from Dale over the phone, he wrote down, *take I-75 south to the third exit for Sara's-Soda.* I'm hoping he did this in a joking manner, but I can't help but have my doubts.

hey. are u near My Sister's Coke yet? Jessica writes as we're passing through Orlando. Before we left I had told her about Sara's-Soda and how I'd evolved it so creatively to mean that my grandfather lives in a place called My Sister's Coke.

I respond: *not yet*, because I'm no longer stonewalling.

thanx for all the detail, she writes back, which is the kind of sarcasm that makes me revert to some more stonewalling.

Shockingly, a little over an hour later, my dad finds the third exit for My Sister's Coke. The fact that he almost flies by it and gives us all whiplash when he veers for the exit is beside the point. We're on another road that looks just like the one from this morning, and I'm beginning to worry that maybe we *have* gotten lost and arrived where we started. Like the line from that T.S. Eliot poem. The strip malls all look eerily similar, and I think I see the Starbucks where we ate breakfast. My dad, however, seems surprisingly confident, and when we pass a Hooters, I feel much better, because I don't recall seeing a Hooters this morning. It'd be a good place for lunch, I think. But no dice, because my dad is on a roll.

We pull up to a red light and he's humming away, bebopping to his music and clearly high on life. For the moment. "The Sunshine State," he chirps, apropos of nothing. I look out and all I see are dark clouds building as high as the stratosphere and obscuring the sun completely. The traffic light turns green, but the car in front of us doesn't move. I see my dad's hand hovering above the horn, as he exerts every last tentacle of patience to not lean on it like they do in New York. Finally, he just gives up and mutters under his breath as he pulls around the car. He stares at the car closer, then shouts: "Look at that! Unbelievable. She's talking on her cell phone *and* putting on makeup." He continues to stare at the woman in the car, as he then barks through his closed window, "The light's green, lady!"

No, it's not. Not anymore. The fact that we're not slammed broadside in the intersection by a speeding UPS truck is a great relief to me, but what comes next surely is not a great relief to my dad. I think I'm the only one to hear the siren. Frizzy's asleep because my dad gave her a dose of Benadryl somewhere along the drive. He said he was concerned about the mold in the hotel room last night, but I personally hadn't seen much of a reaction from the poor child, and I sometimes wonder if my dad just likes to knock her out as much as he can. Anyway, like I said, no one else seems to hear the siren. I can't say that with certainty, because frankly I don't give a crap what Bugsy hears, and my dad could very well be ignoring it, hoping the cop is off to catch a murderer or a few freshly baked donuts.

No such luck. It's clear who the cop's after. He steps out of his cruiser in a neatly pressed tan uniform so tight that's he's making me sweat just looking at him. This seems like a repeat of the situation in Maryland, but I quickly notice this guy's as cool as a cucumber, whatever the heck that means. He walks stiffly to the car, not a drop of perspiration on him. My dad lowers the window, and I can tell he's scrubbing his brain for a good excuse. He glances back feebly at Frizzy and mutters when he sees her out cold. I don't even get an order to kick her awake this time.

He's already handing the cop his license and registration before even being asked. The cop takes them and says, "Do you know you could get killed running a red light like that? It's one thing when all the old people do it…"

He doesn't have time to finish as my dad says, "Sorry, officer, but my wife's pregnant and she's about to barf. She has morning sickness."

The cop glances at his watch and says, "But it's after noon."

"Yeah, well," my dad stammers, "I think that's one of those misleading terms. Like the swine flu. You don't get it from eating pork, ya know?"

"Ah-ha," the cop says with genuine wonderment. I'm glad he's standing up straight and can't see my pregnant mother in the passenger seat about to barf, despite the fact that she's flipping cheerily through a clothing catalogue. Which she stops doing abruptly when she hears she's pregnant.

"Well, there's a Burger King up there you can use," the cop says. "I used it last week after my brother's bachelor party. It was good."

"The bachelor party?" my dad asks.

"No, the Burger King. The bathroom there, it's good and new and clean. The bachelor party stunk. The bride showed up halfway through and we had bad shrimp. Hence, the Burger King." Hence?

"Huh," my dad says pensively. "How about that. That's too bad." There's silence for several minutes as both men seem to be looking down the road wistfully at the Burger King. "I never had a bachelor party myself," my dad finally says.

"Don't sweat it," the cop assures him. "They're not all they're cracked up to be. I'd tell you about mine…" Here he pauses and finally leans over to look into the car. "But I wouldn't want to offend your nice family…And the missus there isn't looking too good." My dad nods in agreement.

"I'll let you go this time," the cop continues. "But you drive careful now. And move along before you get your nice new interior all soiled up." He laughs in a way that literally sounds like, *hee-hee-hee*. Hence, quite ridiculous.

As my dad pulls away, Bugsy turns around and flips the cop the bird, finger and all, while mouthing the curse words that go with it.

"Hey!" my dad protests. "What's that all about? That cop was a nice guy."

"Nice guy, my ass," she says. "I should have gotten out and kicked him wear it counts. Then we'd see who's not looking too good."

This outburst is enough to make Frizzy wake up and immediately laugh for no good apparent reason. I, on the other hand, laugh along with her for more reasons than I can admit.

Soon enough, we turn into a place called Palmetto Swamp Preserve. At least that's what it says in swooping forest green lettering on the coral-color wall, fronted with an array of blooming plants pink and purple and blood red. My dad slows to a big iron gate that's closed. He opens his window and leans out to punch some numbers into a metal box. Nothing happens, and I hear a dial tone like on a real phone. My dad says "dammit" and then punches in some numbers again.

"Hello," a tinny voice finally says through the speaker.

"Dale?" my dad asks.

"Yes?" says the voice. My dad smugly looks at Bugsy, then turns back to the phone and says, "It's Doug...and the kids."

There is a pause which seems to hang in the air for eternity. All I hear is the sound of a lawn mower in the distance. My mind is churning as I'm certain is the mind of everyone else in the car (OK, maybe not Frizzy's), and I am wondering after this long, excruciating pause whether we are to be summarily turned away.

"Haaaaaaay..." the tinny voice comes through again, as if it's fluttering through a kazoo. "All riiiiiight!" And within a split second the iron gates in front of us begin to part like the Red Sea and my heart lifts in relief. My dad sighs deeply and then begins to roll slowly through the neighborhood. The houses are big. Bigger than ours at home, but not as big as Zach's house on Long Island. They all pretty much look the same, two stories, sort of boxy, guarded at the front door by a tall palm tree on each side, and barely no yard space. The only thing that really distinguishes each house is its color, and I begin to assign flavors, like ice cream or something, as we putter along. Lemon. Strawberry-Vanilla. Mocha. Peppermint. My grandfather's is peach, I decide, as we turn into the driveway.

Instead of pulling in all the way, however, my dad stops the car halfway, and says, "Look at that ugly thing." He points out the front window, and we all crane our necks to see a humungous black snake sunning itself on the driveway. It's alive, for sure, as we can see its tongue occasionally slither out of its mouth like Lord Voldemort's. We all stare for several moments when Bugsy says, "Honk at it."

"Snakes can't hear…can they?" my dad says.

"Then just run over it."

"God, no," my dad says, "it'll make my tires a mess."

"Then get out and scare it away," she orders.

"You get out and scare it away."

This results in a quick stalemate, so we sit quietly and watch the snake taunt us. Then Frizzy cuts one and it smells like rotten eggs. "Oh jeezzzz," my dad says, as he cranks down every window in the car. I'm not sure that's an improvement, as all that we feel is the stale, stagnant humid air roll in like sludge from outside. It's what we *see* next that convinces me it was *really* a mistake. Mosquitoes. Hundreds of them.

"Put up the windows!" Bugsy shouts, and I wonder if she might have the courtesy to save us by putting her unique skills to work.

"No, we need to keep them down and get the bugs out of here!" my dad shouts back as he begins flailing his hands and trying to swat the bugs toward the open windows. We all follow suit, and now there are eight flailing hands and lots of cursing from the front seat and an increasing number of loud slaps as we all redirect our flailing toward defense of our own hides, where the bites are multiplying rapidly.

"We're losing, we're losing!" Bugsy shouts. "Put up the damn windows!" My dad obeys this time, which ends our efforts at eviction and begins our efforts at complete extermination of each and every bug trapped in the car. Slap, bang. Slap, bang. Slap, bang. It's beginning to sound like a symphony, the alternating percussion of hands hitting windows, then skin, the dashboard, then skin, the seats, then skin.

"Look at the blood you got on the seat!" my dad yells at Bugsy, who by the way I think has lost all right to her nickname.

"What," she shouts back. Uh-oh, there's that word again. "What the hell do you expect?"

"Dammit!" he shouts again, this time not at her, but at the bug that's lodged on his neck and has dug into his skin for a meal. He slaps at it, and now there is a splotch of blood the size of a penny.

I wonder how long we're at this game, until it finally settles down and we're all panting like we just ran a 5K. I glance out the window and notice the snake is gone. Probably got scared when it realized there were a bunch of lunatics in the car.

We ring the bell, which sounds like wind chimes, and the door immediately swings open. I wonder if our cartoonish assault on the mosquitoes has been observed through the long slender window next to the door. "May I help you?" the woman asks. She is clad—or unclad—in a skimpy bikini, two white triangles barely covering her chest, which is the size of two, well…watermelons. Her belly button is pierced with something that looks like a dragonfly. Hell, why not, since we seem to be stuck on the bug theme. But not entirely, since the tattoo on her left hip is a hammerhead shark. As I stare incredulously as this woman, I'm thinking she's quite a catch for my grandfather. We just call him Dale, by the way.

"Umm…" my dad says profoundly. "Is Dale home?"

"Dale?" the woman says. I notice a smear of white stuff under her eye, which I guess to be sunscreen, as her entire body of exposed skin (lots of it!) is silky and shiny from the stuff. Her hair is blonde—or more like lemon—and pulled up behind her head. "There ain't no Dale here," she says with such an easy rebuff to refinement. No Dale? Uhhhh-ohhhh.

"Oh, Daaaaale…" she continues as if a little mouse, or maybe a big cockroach, has whispered in her ear. "He lives next door." She says *door* like *dar-wer*, and we all exhale. Bigly.

Thankfully, the snake has decided not to take up residence in Dale's *real* driveway. My grandfather gives us all gigantic hugs, even Bugsy, and I'm wondering if he even knows who the heck she is. Anyway, my hug results in my nose plunging smack into his belly button. I'm no shorty; it's just that Dale is a beanstalk. I'd forgotten this, or at least hoped I'd caught up a bit more, as it has been two years since we'd last seen him in New York at Grandma Chip's funeral service. That's not really her name. It was Clara. But we all called her Chip because we thought it was funny: Chip 'n Dale, get it? Dale always thought it was funny too, and his easy laugh now swells as he digests the reality of our visit. After digging my nose out of his stomach, I glance up and see *his* nose. Sort of. It is covered with a copious bandage that stretches from the bridge down to the tip, even shooting off the end to cover his upper lip. The whole thing looks like an Olympic ski jump, which briefly reminds me of Ingrid. Remember her, from the traffic jam on Long Island? That seems like years ago and makes me shudder a bit until I succeed in smiting the recollection from my brain and refocusing back on Dale. The bandage on his nose is long, because so is Dale's nose, like every part of him. His nose without the bandage always reminded me of an icicle, one with a constant drip as a result of the warm sparkle emanating from his wide blue eyes shining down benevolently.

"What's with your nose?" my dad asks, a bit too harshly, in my opinion.

"Oh…I banged into that column going into the kitchen." He gestures over his shoulder, and it's now I notice the effect of the gigundo bandage on his enunciation. Words sound randomly muffled, slurred, truncated—in fact, strikingly Bavarian—so that the word *kitchen* comes out something like *hishun*. "It's not a well-designed feeshure at all," he adds in his funky twang. "I'm always bumpin indo it, but I caught it good dis dime."

By now we're all cautiously moving past the column as Dale guides us toward the rooms where we'll be staying. That's when Frizzy shrieks at the sight of the pool in the back. My dad is more excited about the huge library we pass as we walk down the hallway. The walls are lined on three sides and filled to overflow with books. I skip nervously past but am quickly pleased to see I will have my own bedroom. It's spacious. The walls are painted the flavor of coffee, and the bedspread is striped black and orange like a tiger pelt. Quickly, I change into my bathing suit and emerge with a rapid gait toward the pool, first dodging the lethal column before flying through the kitchen. I mean *hishun*. Just as I am about to get to the door, I stop in my tracks and watch in dismay as Bugsy flops into the pool like a drunken duck and splashes water all over the deck. Damn her, I mutter and turn around to the smell of salad. In the hishun Dale is rubbing vinegar all over Frizzy's mosquito bites, which have swelled to the size of ping-pong balls and have spared no part of her body. As we wait for her to dry into the hue of a glazed Easter egg, Dale hands me a ginger ale with an all-knowing look of sympathy as he gazes over my shoulder at the drunken duck in his pool. I'm still not sure he knows who the heck she is.

"You and I will play some golth tomorrow, Jame, 'kay?" he says. I assume he means golf, and if so, I suppose it's 'kay with me. I enjoy golth, having played a few times with Zach at his father's club. I assume it's been my dad's machination to encourage Dale to take me off somewhere by myself.

Fine. I'm just glad I won't be stuck at home watching The Drunken Duck swim all day. But then it hits me: re-emerging visions of that old man's shriveled-withered-poison-ivy penis. Because it was the last time I played golth with Zach that we did the sauna thing and that penis frightened the bejesus out of me.

I still can't seem to shake the vision the next morning as we drive to the course. At least that's what I thought we were doing until we turn into a church parking lot. St. Ignatius. I wonder if we're going to Mass. I know it's not Sunday, but I also know a lot of old people do go to Mass on week-day mornings. And that's just what I see. Not a lot. But several hunched-over ladies with blue hair. Some latch onto portly bald guys, and a few are pushing walkers through the parking lot like it's the Indy 500, dodging the big cars that mostly look like Cadillacs. We're driving behind one of them now, but this one says Grand Marquis on the back, which I have no problem reading because Dale is following dangerously close, and I'm just thankful it's not my dad in front of us.

"So…" I finally say haltingly. "We're going to church first?"

"God, no," Dale says. "Weekday Mass is for all da old farts. We're pay-ing some golth, 'member?"

Sure I 'member, but that doesn't help me understand why we've pulled into church. Dale parks the car in the far corner of the lot. Some massive thick trees heavy with dew and looking more like bushes on steroids bor-rowed from Alex Rodriquez droop over the front of his car as he pulls to a stop. Dale hops out and skips to his trunk, and by the time I join him, he's rubbing sunscreen into his cheeks—which reminds me of his buxom neighbor—and then dabs a little on his nose bandage.

"You'll need lots of dis shtuff," he says, handing me the blue tube. I immediately set it on the back bumper. I then watch him glaze his arms and neck with bug spray, and when he hands this to me, I eagerly apply it all over my body like a madman. Dale eyes me with amusement as he digs the clubs out of the back. He's already reassured me I won't have to use his jumbo-sized clubs. I'll be using Grandma Chip's.

"You'll be alright witout the non arn?" he says. I just shrug my shoul-ders, knowing he means nine iron. The few times I've played with Zach, I've proven myself to be not so bad at golth, but I still don't know what's really the difference between a nine iron and a six iron. Even if I were like one of those rich country club brats who knew the difference, I'm certain I wouldn't make a big deal of it with Dale, except now that I think about it, if I were a rich country club brat, I'd probably be protesting to Dale that I couldn't possibly be expected to play golth without a non arn. In which case he'd just have to explain one more time that the alligator ate it. Just like he explained last night when we were in his garage, and he was showing me the clubs and reminiscing teary-eyed about the day the gator wolfed the non arn. That would be right before it ate my Grandma Chip. Dale joked that if Chip actually liked golth she would have known to use a three iron instead of a nine iron because a three iron is much longer. Maybe it wouldn't have made a difference, he'd said, but it sure would have given her a little more cushion from the maw of that ten-foot long gator. I'd known Grandma Chip met an eerie death, but I'd always been shortchanged on the details. Until last night in the garage. Two years ago, along a lake near their house, Dale explained, Chip saw the massive reptile feeding on the haunches of their little Pomeranian named Beaver. She went to the garage, and the nine iron was the first thing she grabbed. Dale said he was quite confounded when the police reached him on his cell phone while he was shopping at Publix. It was the fact that they told him *first* about how a gator ate their Pomeranian. He said he couldn't help but rejoice at the news because he always hated the mutt, but his joy quickly faded when they obligingly decided to include the news that his wife was killed too. They only detected the involvement of the nine iron later when they discovered the handle—or the grip, they call it—nearby, and traced it back to her set of clubs in the garage.

"Ooops, here it is," Dale now says matter-of-factly, as he pulls the severed grip out of a side pocket in the golth bag while he's reaching in to get me some balls and tees. "I forgot it was still in here." I stare at the grip. Sticking out below the black rubber is an inch of metal shaft that's sliced off like it'd been cut with a hacksaw. Visions of my grandmother being mauled by some prehistoric-looking creature sends a bolt of I-don't-know-what shooting up my spine into my brain, and I feel myself overcome by nausea, a feeling I know all too well.

"You all right?" Dale asks. I just sit on the car bumper and try to collect myself, but I'm sweating like crazy. Dale notices and says, "It is grosshly hot out here. Dat's why we've got to get going early." He's right, it is gross.

The humid air feels like a hot iron pressing down on the back of my neck. I hear the buzz of what must be locusts, or cicadas, or something. And that's it. Except now for the church bell, which reminds me where we are and seems to be the signal to Dale that it's time to take off.

I follow him through the A-Rod bushes that scratch against my damp skin. It's then I notice several mosquitoes landing on my arms, despite the spray I'd liberally applied, and I hear Dale order, "Hurry! Hurry!" We duck through a hole in a fence, not nearly large enough for me to believe Dale will fit through, but I can quickly tell he's experienced at it.

We emerge into an open space full of sunlight and thankfully free of bugs. "The most eslusive golth course in all Forida," he says. I know he means exclusive, because I've really gotten the knack for interpreting his accent by now, having had quite a bit of experience with the wacky world of wrongful elocution from my little sister. "How do ya know if a golth course is eslusive?" he asks in answer to my question, as if I'd actually asked it. "You can play for five hours and not see another soul." Uh-oh. We're going to be out here for five hours?

I gaze around suspiciously. We ascend a small hill that leads to the flat area where you tee off. At Zach's club the grass in this area is usually finely mowed to a texture you might be inclined to eat your breakfast off of. Usually there are those markers too, which show you where to put your ball when you tee it up. None of this looks familiar as the grass is not short and luscious, but...well, actually I'm not sure there's any grass at all. It's just dirt and weeds. And the only thing I see sticking out of the ground that might look like one of those markers is a dark mound about the size of the horse dung I saw back at my cousin's house in Virginia. 'Member that place? I start to sidle a little closer for inspection when I notice it moving. Like it has a mind of its own. "Watch dat!" Dale suddenly shrieks, and I jump back like it's a bomb. "Dat's a red ant pile," he declares. Well, the pile looks brown to me, but I trust his judgment on all matters to do with this bizarro world we've just entered. "Those things bite ya, dey make ya itch like a dickens," he says. Like poison ivy?

I move to the front of the flat area and gaze out toward the hole. It's one of those ones where you are supposed to be able to hit it on the green with your tee shot. A par three, I believe. I can see the green right down a slope beyond a sandy area that's overgrown with tall grass. In the middle is a huge lake that I don't believe is intended to be there, and it's become a playground for a bunch of white birds with long necks poking in the muck for who knows what. My eyes shift back to the green. I know there is supposed to be a flag sticking up somewhere, but I don't see one. "Ya just aim for da steeple on dis hole," I hear Dale say, as if he were reading my confused thoughts. My eyes shift upward to the church steeple above the low tree line. It doesn't jibe with my internal compass at all. I thought the church was behind us. I spin around, which makes me dizzy, and when I refocus back on the steeple, I see two of them. Back down to the green my eyes drift; the area looks shaggy like it's in bad need of a haircut. Nothing is around. This place is desolate as far as the eye can see, except for the steeple, and I'm wondering if maybe when we passed through the A-Rod bushes, we stepped into the Twilight Zone.

My trance is suddenly broken by a rustling noise in the dark woods behind the tee area. I turn and see a man stepping out, pulling up his fly with a force that makes his heels lift off the ground several times before they finally settle to earth with mission complete.

"Dere you are, Dawkins," Dale says casually, and more rustling noise in the opposite direction makes me quickly turn in fear of seeing another zippering zombie coming my way. But it's only a bird taking flight out of a huge lake in the distance, whose surface is green with ooze.

Dale looks oddly at my flinching and then says, "Jamie, dis is my good friend Dawkins. 'Member, I told ya he'd be playing wit us." No, you didn't but that's 'kay. I shake the hand of Dawkins, wondering it that's his first name or last. He peers straight into my eyes, as we are equal height, which renders him about half the height of Dale. He's wearing a straw farmer's hat, and his grip encases my hand with a force that I fear might crush it as he hangs on long past common etiquette. He then nods disarmingly and says, "Hey, Sport," before unyoking a sidewinder smile that makes his left cheek puff out up like Popeye's.

"I was just telling Jamie here how we belong ta da most eslusive gloth course in all Forida."

"When the hell are you going to get that bandage off, Speed?" Dawkins asks. Did he just call him *Speed*?

"When yooooo stop peeing every five minutes," Dale answers. Uh-oh, I think again. Five hours out here?

Dawkins ignores this last comment and bends over to tee up his ball. He quickly stands up without practicing and says:

"You spotted snakes with double tongue,

"Thorny hedgehogs, be not seen;

"Newts, and blind-worms, do no wrong..." He swings the club back, then bellows, "This goddamn ball go on the green," swinging with a grunt on his follow-through and nearly tumbling over backwards. The ball rockets off the tee on a line drive, catching the tall weedy grass in the sandy area with the big puddle. The white birds scatter, fortunately none of them headless.

"Shit," Dawkins says. "If those weeds were mown, that ball would have made the green."

"Hey, Shakespeare, I warned ya about your language wiff my grandson around," Dale says with minimal censure in his voice. "And if doze weeds were mown, we sure as hell wouldn't be playing *here*, would we?"

After we all hit our balls, we're walking down a path that's heaved with huge tree roots and littered with rocks and stones, and even a discarded tire, just like on the Long Island Expressway, although this one looks like it's small enough to fit a golth cart. Dale then says to me: "Dawkins was a literature professor in college. He likes to spout off all the poetry he knows..."

I stop in my tracks, but Dale doesn't notice and keeps walking. I see what's going on here. Literature professor? If I could, I think I might run for it, but I'm too scared of who might be peeing in the bushes. So I walk on tentatively until I hear Dale shout, "Yep, just like I thought, you're right up dere on da green, Jame!" But not near the hole. Because dere isn't one. Just a lot more weeds and rocks and a few of those ant piles that Dale thinks are red.

"Ahhhh...what do I do now?" I ask Dale.

"Oh, I'll show ya in a sec," he says. "Let's wait for Dawkins." Who's in the bushes again. Sure enough, he comes out zippering. He chips his ball up to the green and it ricochets off a stone and shoots back down the far side.

"Shit, this place has my number today," Dawkins says. Once his ball finally makes it up to the green, Dale marks off a central spot from all three balls and puts a tee into the ground. That's what we putt to. Dawkins whacks his first, curses a few more times, and then storms off over a mound toward the blinding sun. Dale meanwhile takes so much time to line up his putt, I am wondering if I might keel over and croak from heat exposure.

His pace only grows more methodical on the next hole. And the weeds grow taller. The sun hotter. "You going to pee *again?*" Dale says to Dawkins as we approach the next green.

"You can be thankful I pee so much, otherwise I wouldn't be playing with you," Dawkins says. "You take so goddamn long on every shot, I feel like I'm having a dream within a dream."

"A little Poe dere," Dale explains to me courteously. Then to Dawkins, "Well, ya'd just be back at dat other club of yours, paying greens fees and playing wit doze old farts."

"Good point, Speed, my friend. You can't beat Disgusta National, can you?"

"Noooo, sireeee."

We approach another hole and I have the feeling we've played about eight of them already. But as I quickly count backwards, I realize it's been only three. And this is where it dawns on me why Dawkins calls Dale *Speed*. I watch him bend over to place his tee in the ground and adjust it several times before grunting and crouching down on his hands and knees, then scrunching his lanky body lower like a panther on the prowl, so his eyes are level with the top of the tee. He closes his left eye and squints hard with the right, then adjusts the tee slightly to the left. Satisfied, he stands up and selects a club, stares at the sky, puts the club back, then selects another. Dawkins is gone. In the bushes. Dale now has three clubs in his hand, licks his finger and holds it into the breeze. As if there is one. My eyes begin to cross and my throat stings from dryness. My mind drifts to last winter and that huge snowstorm, which makes me shiver in relief, until I'm reminded that it was the day I received my acceptance to the program in San Francisco. Actually, it was the day after because the mail was canceled the day of the storm. It was a weird day, one I will never forget. Not because I got accepted to the program. That wasn't a big deal as far as I was concerned. But at some point during the evening after I think my dad thought I was asleep, I overheard him crying. I'm sure that's what it was, but I don't know why. I guess I'll never know, but I'll never forget. Hearing your dad cry and not knowing the reason is something you never forget, is it?

It's in this trance that I walk behind Dale, neither one of us seeming to care that I've forgotten to hit my ball. My head throbs from the sun. My clothes are drenched with sweat. Bug bites seem to be multiplying on my arms like I've got the plague. "Look, dere's a gator!" Dale shouts, pointing off to the bank of a lake where a massive alligator is sunning itself. It's the first one I've ever seen, and immediately I think of *both* my dead grandmothers: Where Dale's wife failed with a nine iron, I wonder if my dad's mom would have fared better by invoking St. Francis of Assisi against the surly reptile.

Before I know it, we've arrived at a different hole, and as I look out from the tee area, for the first time I see houses.

"Jamie," Dale says authoritatively. "Now it's time for your first leshon of da day." He means lesson. And I just knew it was inevitable. It had crossed my mind several times that Dale and Dawkins had been awfully quiet since we started. Quiet about cerebral stuff, if not necessarily about sheer buffoonery. I take a deep breath and ready myself for a grilling on the sum of the angles in tessellated hexagons, or the correct sequence of the reverse Krebs cycle, or the mindless ambiguities in *Troilus and Cressida*.

"You've heard of da Masters?" Dale continues. I stare at him blankly, while thinking: masters of what?

He reads my expression and says, "Da Masters golth tournament. Da one the pros play every year in April."

I shrug my shoulders the way I'm supposed to at my age when I'm trying not to appear too clueless.

"They play at a course called Augusta National," Dale says. "One of da most beautiful courses in all da world. Dere's a part of da course on the back non called Amen Corner. It's da toughest stretch and it's sink or swim for da pros when they play doze holes. A little prayer comes in handy first, I suppose." He stops and stares up as a large prehistoric-looking bird swoops overhead. "But dat's just a game, ya know, and even doze who lose can go home proud for just having made it dere. But here, my young friend..." he pauses and sweeps his hand out toward the desolate-looking houses lining the hole in front of us. "Here, dere is no pride. Dere are no prayers left to save dese souls. Dis course of mine and Dawkins is Disgusta National, home of da greedy and depraved. At one time not too long ago, it cost hundreds of thousands of dollars just ta belong here. Just ta piss in da granite urinals. Yes, indeed, eslusive it was. So eslusive they shut out all da meek from this nice little kingdom, and now it's left ta me and Dawkins to inherit dis earth. Ah, yes, Forida, da land of da lowly. It's why we love hating dis debauched place so much, right, Dawkins?"

No answer from Dawkins.

"Dawkins?" Dale says, a little louder.

"Over here!" Dawkins shouts from behind a tree.

Dale continues, "Dis hole here, Jamie, begins Hell's Alley. Because every single one of dese people is doomed ta perdition. Forida attracts dem all. Dat house dere..." he points off to a monstrous home with towering columns inviting spiraling weeds up the sides. The windows are sheathed with metal covers. The large pool is cracked along the sides and unfilled. "...Da owner is in jail for shtealing money from his company's investors. Dat house..." he points to another. "...Da owner is dead. Took his life after shquandering millions of his company's money out in Lash Vegas..." The denunciation continues as if it were draining from the mouth of the Ghost of Christmas Past. "Dat guy," he says "...sent ta jail in a Ponzi scheme. Ahhh...Ponzi, one of Forida's original thieves..."

I can hear Dale's voice like a hum, but I've now shut off my ability to distinguish the words. Especially the mispronounced ones. Maybe it's the explanation of a Ponzi scheme that loses me. Or the mention of someone killing himself. The heat is throttling. The bugs incorrigible. Distorted visions flit across my brow: the flabby old-man penis, the drunken duck in the pool, the watermelon boobs, the evil snake in the driveway. He's actually talking to me, the snake. I sit on the end of Chip's golf bag. The broken non arn curses me from the side pocket. I feel nauseous. My ears tune back in momentarily enough to hear the words "...and dat's da leshon," as I stare blankly into the blanched sky.

"You OK?" Dale finally asks.

"It's getting pretty hot out here," Dawkins argues on my behalf. "I've had enough of this Xanadu myself."

"Here, Jamie, have a sip of dis." Dale has reached for the large water bottle tied to the side of his bag. I stare at it for several moments. The white bottle blurs in front of me. I rub my eyes with the knuckles of my pointer fingers. The bottle sways in my vision. I begin to reach, but I feel myself grabbing at air. It's den I realize, maybe I'd be better off wit a Coke. 'Kay?

10

❖ ❖ ❖

CHICKEN-MAD COW

Finally! Someone let Jamie ride shotgun. Dawkins had insisted. Like a sport. "You still don't look too good," he'd said as they were getting in the car. After they quit golthing, Jamie thought Dawkins might vaporize into the woods whence he'd come, but he followed them through the A-Rod bushes instead and plunked his clubs into Dale's trunk. Then he squeezed into the back of Dale's silver-blue Nissan, leaving his hat on, which still left his head far short of the roof. Dale's, on the other hand, rubbed it vigorously as he drove, despite his efforts to suck his neck down into his shoulders. Just like one of those white birds on the golth course. Or whatever it was.

"Could you turn up the AC a little more there, Speed," Dawkins said rancorously, as they backed up and something crunched under the tires. It was the tube of sunscreen Jamie had left on the bumper earlier that morning.

"I usually just leave it on four," Dale said. "If I turn it up ta five, I find I lose about two-tenths of a mile per gallon of gash."

"Cheapskate."

"Wussie."

"I can't wait to get my own car back."

"Yeah, when do ya get it back?"

"Feels like never," Dawkins groaned. Dale knew Dawkins' car had been in the shop for two weeks after he smashed it head-on into another car at a Taco Bell drive-through. He was not paying attention, he'd claimed, because he was in a rush to go to the bathroom.

Dale had been telling Dawkins lately that it was time he see a urologist about his "going" problem. But Dawkins continued to refuse, and Dale couldn't spite him. After all, it was the "going" problem that sort of led to their friendship. The first time they met was shortly after Dale had moved to Florida from New York under stern orders from Chip's doctor to relocate someplace warm or her rheumatoid arthritis would kill her. Dale wanted to go to the Southwest. Sedona, maybe. But Chip insisted on Florida for reasons he couldn't understand. It led to their biggest argument in twenty-five years of steady marriage, and he quickly realized at his age, he needed to go where the sex was or he was fooling himself.

The first month in town, he was shopping in Publix, in the ice cream section, when he stopped to rub his sore lower back. "You oughta get that checked out," a man said, strolling by pushing an empty cart. It was Dawkins.

"Ehhh," Dale said. "I hate doctors' offices. Especially down here. I find it so depressing sitting around with all the old farts." Dawkins laughed with a teary twinkle in his eye that you get when you feel you've made an instant connection with someone.

"I know just what you mean!" Dawkins said effulgently. "I've got this perfect doctor for you. He takes care of my problems, you know, down here." He pointed to his crotch.

"But what's a urologist going to do for my back?" Dale had asked.

"Oh, no. He's not a urologist. He's a pediatrician. It's my nephew. Sitting in the waiting room there is fun with all the kids running around with snot coming out of their nose and playing with those colorful abacuses with the twisting wires. Makes me feel alive. And they still make that *Highlights Magazine*, you know. Best thing is, you don't have to sit there too long. He whisks you right in ahead of all the other suckers who have to wait for the standard hour and a half."

Dale quickly found out Dawkins didn't want to be in Florida any more than he did. His wife also made him move down, from Chicago, to be near her ninety-five-year-old mother in a nursing home. As new friends, Dale and Dawkins left Publix together that day, Dawkins without any groceries because he lost the list his wife gave him and couldn't remember a thing that was on it. "Oh youth! for years so many and sweet," he sang in the parking lot, and that was when Dale discovered Dawkins had taught literature. Coleridge was one of his favorites.

"You like poetry?" Dale asked Jamie as they headed to get some lunch. Jamie twisted up his lips awkwardly and was ready to spout some Shakespeare or something, suddenly feeling under immense pressure. It was one thing when it was his dad asking him to perform, but someone else? Oh well, "Tomorrow, and tomorrow, and tomorrow..." But before Jamie could get the words out of his mouth, Dale reached over benevolently and tussled his hair, barely needing to straighten his long arm to bridge the gap between them in the car. No need for sound or fury, thank God. Dale smiled. He could see the boy had a good head on his shoulders, but he worried about the situation with his mother. He was embarrassed about it, really. Where had he gone wrong as a father to raise a daughter that would do something like that? He loved her, but he was angry. No doubt about it.

And Doug. He worried about him too. Sometimes he guiltily wished *Doug* were his child and not Corrine. Doug's heart was in the right place, but he always seemed to be struggling with himself.

"Here we are, fellas," Dale said, as he turned into the Costco parking lot. Jamie thought they were supposed to be going to lunch, but maybe Dale had some errands first. Or they could be getting pizza. Jessica's mom had brought them to Costco on Long Island once for some pizza on the way back from one of Jessica's modeling sessions that she let him attend, grudgingly.

"I want ta look at doze shmartphone dings," Dale said as they entered the store. "I'm thinkin' of getting one."

"Great, this oughta take about two hours," Dawkins quipped. They walked toward electronics; Jamie could smell the pizza. He looked around and wondered if he was the only kid in the store. The only person under the age of sixty-five, maybe. Dale bounced with a long stride, and the others lagged behind. That's when he made a sudden maniacal duck of his head, like he was avoiding a roundhouse blow from Muhammad Ali. When Jamie and Dawkins caught up, Dawkins erupted into hysterics. His loud guffaw stretched for several seconds, until he choked it off with a violent gulp, like a kid swallowing water in a pool.

"That bird crapped on your head!" Dawkins finally said, as he collected his breath and pointed to Dale. Sure enough, a long stream of blackish gray goop ran from the crown of his head down the side, leaping across the part in his silver hair, which still looked crisp even after several hours in the morning broiler.

Dale instinctively reached up and touched it with his hand. "How 'bout dat," he said calmly, staring at the goop now smeared across his palm. "Firsht it tries ta attack me, then it craps on me. I wouldn't exactly call dat good cushtomer shervice, would ya, boys?"

Before they could answer, Dale was off to clean up in the bathroom.

"What's a bird doing in here?" Jamie asked.

"You build a store as big as a football stadium, the birds are bound to get in," Dawkins answered. "Next thing you know, they'll be letting the cows wander in." He turned his head and followed a wrinkly old rotund woman as she waddled by. "Whoops, maybe they already have."

Dawkins chuckled at his own joke, then turned abruptly and headed for the TVs, with Jamie following. "Let's see if we can catch that nice-looking broad on CNBC," the old man said. But suddenly before them, the hundreds of screens exploded with a spectacular image of a massive rock jutting up into a deep blue sky with evergreens silhouetted in the foreground. "El Capitan, Yosemite National Park," the caption read on the screen.

"Priceless," Dawkins said, mesmerized. "Ever been to any national parks?"

"One."

"The parks are the best idea we ever had." Jamie nodded slightly at Dawkins' assertion, doubting his dad would think so. "Wallace Stegner said that," Dawkins continued. "Ever heard of him?"

Jamie squirmed, then said: "No." Dawkins fired a long, suspicious glance out the sides of his eyes. He wondered if the boy was lying. Dale had said the kid was sharp and read like a fiend.

When Dale returned ten minutes later, they headed toward the back of the store, passing the pizza. "I thought we were getting lunch?" Jamie finally asked as politely as he could, his curiosity overwhelming him and his stomach screaming for food.

"We are," Dale said simply.

"Golly, Speed, you could at least admit to the boy you're too much of a cheapskate to buy him lunch."

"If I'm going ta eat lunch surrounded by a bunch of half-dead people, at least I'm going ta get it free."

"You should just eat at home then," Dawkins said.

"What fun is dat! I wanted ta take my grandson out for lunch if that's 'kay wit you. Look at dis pro-shoodo," Dale slurred through his bandaged nose. "It looks deeee-lithshus." He reached down and picked up a small piece of meat sitting in ruffled white paper like you see around the bottom of cupcakes.

"It has a little piece of mozzarella inside that's been marinated in pesto," said the little old woman behind the cart, who was wearing a piece of plastic on her head that Jamie thought looked like a shower cap.

"Mmmmm," Dale said as he picked up the piece of cardboard with the nutritional information on it and read it out loud. "A little high in shodium for me, but low in sashurated fat. Have one, Jame." Jamie reached over hesitantly and picked up a sample. "You watch," Dale continued, his cheeks full from a second helping and his bandaged nose oscillating with each chew. "Dawkins here will be stuffin' his face in no time. He complains, but deep down he loves fleecing corporate 'merica. He'll take all da free shtuff he can get and not spend a penny in dis place."

"What would really tickle me," Dawkins said after grabbing his own sample and veering a bit too close to Jamie's face, so that a speck of mozzarella shot out onto the tip of Jamie's nose, "is to come in here one day and spike all this stuff with Ex-Lax. Wouldn't that be a hoot...watching all these old farts running for the bathroom at once." He erupted again into his guffaw and more mozzarella flew out, but missed Jamie this time and landed on the shoulder of a portly old man with a cane, shuffling over for his own free sample.

"Dawkins is full of pranks," Dale said to Jamie. "Like a school kid. Problem is, last time it almost got him thrown in jail when he pulled da fire alarm at da old geezer's home where his mother-in-law lives."

"During the Christmas party!" Dawkins hollered, and several heads jerked to stare at him.

"Stop, dat's enough!" Dale said, still laughing and slapping his leg. "You'll give my grandson bad ideas."

"I pulled the fire alarm at church once," Jamie declared proudly, and both old men turned abruptly with a fleeting sparkle of admiration in their eyes. It quickly faded, though, when Jamie continued in a more timid voice: "By accident...actually. It was really crowded on Palm Sunday, and we had to stand because we were late as usual. I leaned on the fire alarm and it went off. They had to clear out the whole church. Three fire trucks showed up. They never finished Mass. Or maybe they did, but we'd fled." By now all three were laughing again, food spewing all over the floor of Costco and the flock of old people jostling for the new batch of prosciutto samples. Another bird darted over their heads.

"That was the last time we went to church together," Jamie added a few moments later. "As a family, I mean. My mom left us that week, couldn't even hang around for the Easter Bunny." As he spoke, Dale's smile quickly faded to a grimace, and he felt his cheeks turn stiff and pale. "I had to lie at school that I was still going to church every Sunday," Jamie said.

"He goes to Catholic school," Dale explained to Dawkins stoically.

"Oh, that's too bad," Dawkins said.

"Dawkins claims he's agnostic," Dale explained to Jamie. "I call it apathetic. Or just plain pathetic. Let's move on and see what's in da dessert section, shall we?"

As they shuffled along through the store, Dawkins said to Jamie, "Did they find out?"

"Find out what?"

"At school. Did they find out you were skipping church on Sundays."

"Naaaa. Because I eventually decided to just start going on my own. I'd ride my bike to five o'clock Mass on Saturdays and just tell my dad I was going to my friend Zach's house."

"You lied ta your dad about going to shursh?" Dale asked, with a marvel that seemed to excite his speech impediment.

"Well, yeah, I guess."

"Dat might be a tough one ta sort out in da confessional, don't ya think?"

"No one goes to confession anymore, Dale," Jamie said.

"Guess you're right. In my opinion, folks should be going every day. But who's got da time when dere givin' out free shtuff at Costco, right?" He winked at Jamie, then said, "Why didn't ya just tell him?"

"Tell who? What?"

"Your dad. Dat you were skippin' shursh."

Jamie shrugged his shoulders, and Dale just said, "Dat's 'kay, never mind." They arrived in the bakery section, but couldn't get close enough to the cart to see what the free sample was. The wide crowd of old geezers was three rows deep. "Let's just get da hell out of here," Dale said. Jamie was still famished.

They stepped outside, where it was pouring rain. For thirty minutes they waited for it to let up, but Dawkins finally said "Screw it," and walked leisurely to the car.

After dropping Dawkins off, they arrived home at Dale's to a perfectly still house. The only sound was the rain pounding on the roof like an invading army. Dale and Jamie stepped into the living room and saw the three bodies. Doug sprawled out on the couch. Ashley in an armchair with her feet up on an ottoman. And Frizzy face down on the carpet. She was wearing a bathing suit, and her back was red as a beet. Jamie might have thought they were all dead, except he could now hear his dad snoring loud enough to be faintly heard above the din of rain. Dale clapped, a loud one, and Jamie thought the lights might come on just like in that commercial that sometimes runs on cable when he's watching Travel Channel. But they didn't come on. It was dark and dreary, even though it was still only mid-afternoon. Doug roused slowly and rose to his feet.

"Oh, you're home," he said. Ashley slowly woke up too.

"We're pooped," she said. "We went swimming all day. Even your dad!"

Doug turned his head away sheepishly, then said, "How was golf?"

"Good," Jamie said.

"What'd you talk about out there?"

"Nothing."

Doug turned to Dale. "How was it?"

"Good?"

"You kiddos get to talk about much out there?"

"Not much."

Jeez, Doug swore to himself. *I'm starting to feel like my life is one endless exercise in futility.*

"Hey what's wit my pink elephant?" Dale asked. He'd wandered over to a large sliding door looking out toward his tiny patch of grass—the prickly southern kind that he refused to call grass. The rain had suddenly stopped, but the bushes and trees in back drooped so low with moisture, it looked like they might keel over. Jamie had joined Dale and saw the elephant lying on its side. It was about the size of a large dog. Too big for Frizzy to steal, Jamie hoped.

"Oh, sorry, I was riding it and fell over," Ashley said. "Then it started to pour, so we came running in."

"Riding it?" Dale said, mildly amused. "Never thought of dat one before." He stared at the girl...young woman, he supposed. Who the heck was she anyway? "Well," he continued, "I better go out and fix it or the birds might get pissed."

"What birds?" Jamie asked.

"Dese big birds dat come ta visit. Woodstorks, they're called. They're humungous. Tall and gray with dese long necks like an ostrich. Dere's a family of three of dem. They hoot so loud, they can make a honking flock of geese sound like crickets. For some reason, God knows why, they love da pink elephant. Dey tiptoe around it and often rub right up against it. Sometimes I think dey might be trying to hump da thing." Ashley giggled, and Dale said, "Oops. Sorry, Jamie. Da birds come by several times a week, usually in da morning. Maybe we'll see dem tomorrow, but I figure we'll have ta get up early to go ta Disney World."

"Disney Woooooorld!" Frizzy miraculously awoke and jumped up from the floor.

"Disney World?" Doug echoed with chagrin. "Who said we're going to Disney World?"

"I did. If you're going ta subject your kids to dis hellhole of a state, ya could at least take dem to Disney World."

"But..." Doug protested. "We really need to get on the road to California. We don't want to be late for Jamie's program."

"When's it start?" Dale asked.

"Three weeks from tomorrow."

"Three weeks!" Dale said. "Dat's more than enough time. Even Sal Paradise made it ta San Francisco quicker dan dat."

"Who the hell's Sal Paradise?" Doug asked.

"Oh, never mind," Dale said as he winked at Jamie.

But Doug couldn't not mind. All night it bugged him, and he barely slept an hour straight. It was still on his mind the next day when they all piled in the Expedition again. He didn't care who the hell Sal Paradise was.

But Sal *was* the name of the guy who lived in the apartment next door to Corrine when she and Doug were engaged. He could never prove they were messing around, but he always had his suspicions. It was Sal Gambino, or something like that. Not Gambino, but close. Doug always worried that the guy might have Mafia connections and take him out if he ever confronted him about his fiancé. Sal...Sal...Sal...Sal Barbino!

"Dat's it!" Dale's shout interrupted Doug's focused thoughts like a rock shattering a window. "Dat *was* it. You just passed da exit to get on da highway," Dale commanded from the backseat, where he was wedged between Jamie and Frizzy. "Make a U-turn up here at dis light. You have a green arrow. Quick!"

"No, no, no," Doug said as he continued straight. "I hate when people make U-turns. It causes accidents. I've seen it. You think a car is making a left turn, but then it slows to make a U-turn, and then...Wham! You smash right into it."

Dale glanced down at Jamie and arched his left eyebrow with a look of amusement. "My dad hates the way other people drive," Jamie whispered.

"Oh, den he must be loving it down here in da Land of da Idiots," Dale said. He laughed the whole way to Disney as Doug cursed at just about every car on the road. He laughed again when Doug asked him if he was going to wait in line to buy the tickets.

"I'm paying," Dale quipped. "You're waiting." Dale handed him a wad of cash.

"That much?" Doug asked. "We're not spending a week here, are we?"

"Just one day does enough damage," Dale said. When Doug returned forty-five minutes later with the tickets, his face was flush and his shirt soaked with sweat. He doled them out. One for Dale. One for Jamie. And one for Frizzy, which he held onto with his own.

"Hey, what about me?" Ashley cried.

"You can wait out here," Doug said irritably. "I didn't hire you to waste eighty bucks at Disney World!"

"But he's paying," she said, pointing to Dale.

"But I hired you."

"Who are you anyway?" Dale interrupted.

"She's my friend," Frizzy squealed. "I'm not going in if she doesn't go in."

"You're not going to leave her out here," Jamie said to his dad with a mixture of goading and glee.

"We won't be in there long," Doug said.

"It's not like we're running in for a burger at McDonald's," Dale said.

"It'd be cheaper," Doug answered.

"Get me a ticket," Ashley pouted.

"Yeah, get her a ticket," Frizzy echoed.

"Get her a ticket," Dale said. Doug looked at Jamie. He shrugged his shoulders. When is The Kid going to stop with that idiotic shoulder shrugging? Doug groaned to himself. He stormed off without getting money from Dale. Forty-five minutes later he returned with another ticket. His treat.

"No!" He screamed. That was several sweaty, exhausting hours later when Ashley asked if they could go into the souvenir store.

"Party pooper," she said.

"Party pooper," Frizzy repeated, sticking her tongue out at Doug. He did, however, let them go on Thunder Mountain again. For the third time. Frizzy just barely made the height limit. Not bad for a five-year-old. She must have Dale's genes. It gave Doug a chance to sit on a bench and decompress. Dale wandered off to get an ice cream. Several people walked by, their arms full with stuffed animals. Goofy, Donald Duck, and some other one he didn't recognize. Nor did he recognize what they were saying. Was it in German? It seemed that so few people in the park were speaking English. He definitely couldn't tell what language a family of four was speaking as they sauntered by a short distance away, all of them—the parents and a little boy and girl—eating corn dogs. It looked to Doug like they were regular corn dog eaters. The boy was a little younger than Jamie. Probably weighed twice more than his own kid, though. And he certainly didn't look like he'd ever be anything in life. But the family looked happy, carefree. How did they do that? Doug wondered. Low aspirations? Maybe that was the key to life. No more comparing yourself to those cocky Wall Streeters and corporate bigwigs out there. Or the pompous doctors, or dickhead lawyers. Hell, The Kid even has a friend whose dad's a famous author. What a horse's ass he is. Low aspirations. That's it. Then you never set yourself up for disappointment and can just be content with being fat and eating loads of corn dogs and wandering around Disney with the rest of the schleps.

"Where's your ice cream?" he asked Dale when he returned empty-handed.

"I couldn't decide what flavor ta get. Den I realized it was too damn espensive anyway. Dat's da nice thing about lack of compulsiveness. You save money and shtay thin."

Doug stared off with a glaze over his eyes that turned the world in front of him into a kaleidoscope. "Quite a place, huh?" He heard Dale's voice, like some distant echo you hear in a dream.

"Sorry I dragged ya here," Dale continued.

Doug let the words sink in. He'd never heard his own father say he was sorry for anything. Just one time might have helped. One apology might have made up for the hundreds of times his father called him a loser. "Oh, that's OK," Doug finally said, still staring numbly in front of him. "I'm sure this will be the *first* thing Jamie will talk about when he gets to San Francisco."

"Eh…what do ya expect? He's still a kid. Dey eat dis shtuff up."

"Yeah, well, it's just that…" he let his words hang in the air, mixing with some Korean chatter from another foreign family flitting by and taking video of the flowers in the garden behind the railing.

Several moments of silence had passed between Doug and Dale, when Dale finally said: "Listen, Doug…" then hesitated. Doug was expecting a lesson on the perils of over-parenting. He knew the ropes. He mocked the crazy hockey parents and the rich Superman-parents. And he really hated the ones who made their kids' science projects for them in school, probably because he knew he'd do the same thing…if he could. Oh yes, he was just as guilty. And he knew he couldn't help it. Like it was some kind of drug he needed, or he'd end up like the corn dog people.

"I just wanted ta say…" Dale stammered, "dat I'm really sorry 'bout Corrine." Doug glanced at him surprised and noticed a tear puddling in one of Dale's eyes. Before Doug could respond, he spotted the kids skipping wildly toward them with Ashley in their wake.

Doug glanced at his watch, eager to get back on the road. Ironically, it was driving that seemed to be offering him the most solace lately. "You kiddos ready to get going?" he said.

"Oh, we haven't gone to Pirates of the Caribbean yet," Ashley said. He gave her the I-didn't-ask-you look, which became the I'm-going-to-strangle-you look when Frizzy squealed, "Yes! Pirates of the Caribbean!"

The stale damp air in the dark tunnel was no relief for Doug's pounding headache. At every turn, surly pirates squawked and Frizzy took pictures. *Whop...whop...whop...whop...flllllizzzzzzzzzzzz.* They all thought she'd lost the damn camera, but Ashley found it for her under the backseat of the car just before they'd left that morning for Disney. "Frizzy, can you stop with the pictures," Doug groaned. He glanced at his watch glowing in the dark. This was one long ride. *Whop...whop...whop...whop...flllllizzzzzzzzzzzz.* "Frizzy!" Doug yelled. "Oh, this is so much fun!" came Ashley's voice from behind him, where she sat alone. Doug thought he saw some light around the next corner and knew it had to be the end of the ride. That's when he felt the jolt. The moving boat they were in came to a sudden stop. Must be part of the experience, Doug hoped. One of the pirates was howling, "Strike up your colors, you scurvy wench, don't expose your superstructure..." Followed by: *Whop...whop...whop...whop...flllllizzzzzzzzzzzz.* They didn't move for several moments. Then several more moments. "Strike up your colors, you scurvy wench, don't expose your superstructure..." *Whop... whop...whop...whop...flllllizzzzzzzzzzzz.* "Wonder what's going on?" Dale asked. "Oh, my God, we stuck!" some lady with a Hispanic accent shrieked from the back of the boat. "Strike up your colors, you scurvy wench, don't expose your superstructure..." *Whop...whop...whop...whop...fllll-lizzzzzzzzzzzz.* "Someone get us out of here!" "Strike up your colors, you scurvy wench, don't expose your superstructure..." *Whop...whop...whop... whop...flllllizzzzzzzzzzzz.* Doug leaned his head forward on his folded arms and closed his eyes tight, wondering when their perfect summer trip was going to start.

Two hours later they were evacuated from the broken-down ride. Doug stormed toward the exit of the park. Dusk was settling in. "We should get some dinner," Ashley chirped. Right.

Their empty stomachs growled the whole way home. "We'll make it just in time for da eleven o'clock news," Dale said from the backseat. "We need ta find out about dat hurricane."

Hurricane?

"Channel Eight! Channel Eight!" Dale ordered as they all came barging in the door. The TV screen exploded from blackness to sharp color. Car commercial. Another car commercial. Then a pharmaceutical commercial.

"Dat's da one I told Dawkins he should use," Dale said.

"Who's Dawkins?" Doug asked.

"The guy we played golf with," Jamie said.

"There was someone else?" Doug asked. But no one answered him. Another commercial. This one for electric scooters. An old man riding around like he's Mario Andretti.

"Isn't it a little early for a hurricane?" Doug asked.

"No, no," Dale said. "Hurricane sheashon started back on June firsht. We've had a couple threats already. Dey say dis is supposed to be da worst sheashon ever."

"Who's they?" Jamie asked.

"Da people on dis news shation," Dale said emphatically. "It's da best. Two years ago during a big one, dey predicted ten people would die before da storm even hit. And guess what? Ten people died." They all stared at the screen, waiting through another commercial, this one bragging about the station's weather coverage. Video showed a helicopter zooming over the Gulf of Mexico. An ambulance. A family fleeing a house with terrified looks on their faces. "When lives are threatened," a deep voice bellowed from the set, "don't panic and fear...Channel 8 weather is near."

The commercial ended and dissolved to the anchors on the set. The man and the woman wore grave expressions on their faces, which were caked with makeup like clowns. "Dis one's a real fireplug," Dale said, referring to the woman anchor wearing a tight red sweater.

"Nice knockers," Frizzy chirped. The three adults, still standing around the set, stared solemnly at the screen and nodded their heads affirmatively.

Evacuate. They'd said the word about thirteen times by Doug's count. And that was only *after* he started counting.

"Do you really think it's necessary?" Doug asked the next morning. "I just flipped around to a few of the other stations, and they didn't say anything about evacuation."

"Doze other shations don't have Super Miraculous Extra Powerful Radar," Dale said seriously. "Dey just don't know what da hell dey're talking 'bout." He rubbed at his bandage as if he had an itch underneath. "Look, I can drive my own car up dere if ya want, but it really seems like a waste of gash when you're going dat way."

But I wasn't going that way, Doug thought. Dale had requested they drive him up to his brother-in-law's house in northern Mississippi. It's where Dale rode out the last storm. Doug's plan after leaving Florida had been to head north through Georgia and then cut west toward Memphis. This way he could avoid Alabama and Mississippi at all costs. Just the thought of those eerie places made him shiver. Those hicks there would spot Long Islanders from ten miles away, and who knows what kind of trouble they would stir up.

"I don't know…" he stammered. "It is quite a bit out of the way."

"No, it's not, Dad," Jamie said. "I think it'll actually be quicker. I checked it out on Google this morning on Dale's computer." Great.

At least it was a good excuse to hightail it out of Florida. They wasted no time packing. As Doug headed up the stairs to grab his suitcase, he met Dale on the landing. He had his back turned and seemed plunged in thought as he was staring out a window. He either didn't hear Doug or didn't mind his presence. "What are you looking at?" Doug asked, just as he let his own gaze drift out the window and lock in on Dale's sightline. At the next house his neighbor was high on a ladder screwing plywood to her windows. She was wearing the same white bikini she had worn the day before last when she greeted them at her door after the mosquito attack. Only this time, Doug caught the rear view: the round, shapely cheeks somewhere hiding the thong string that slid up between.

"She's a stripper, ya know," Dale said, as both men stared vigorously.

"That's fairly unsurprising."

"Works at dis place up on Highway 33…I'm told. And guess what? Her husband's an author. Writes children's books. How's dat for a combination?"

"Brings new meaning to the cat in the hat, I suppose."

"One night I saw dem out there playing naked Frisbee together."

"Really?"

"Yeah," Dale said. "I'd say he had quite a hungry caterpillar, by the looks of him." Neither of them flinched a muscle as they stood at the window listening to the whirl of the cordless drill and watching her cheeks jiggle harmoniously. "They're quite a pair," Dale asserted pensively.

"Yes, indeed," Doug said.

"I mean she and her husband. They're quite a pair. Very happy together. Not like da couple across da street. Always fighting. Da cops have had to break it up several times. Da worst was when they got their guns out. She shot at him first, apparently. He shot back. Hit her right in da buttocks. Both of them actually."

"Wow. That's something."

"Dey became infected. Her buttocks, dat is. Dey had to lance dem off, den put in some shynthetic ones. I mean, I've heard of women getting dem up here..." he paused and cupped his hands together against his chest like he was feeling himself up. "But not in da buttocks. You should see dem. Dey're huge. Like, um..."

"Watermelons?"

"Yeah, dat's it, like watermelons." He paused. "Dey still fight, but at leasht they've agreed ta take the guns out of da house. You really do get all da wackos down here."

"This seems like a decent neighborhood, though. I like your house."

"Thanks, but it was somewhat shpur-of-the-moment. Clara and I needed ta move down quickly, so we bought dis. I really wanted ta buy an empty lot somewhere else and design my own place without columns stuck in shtupid places where ya can bump inta dem. But den, well, da alligator attacked. I guess I just want ta get out of Forida altogether now dat she's gone."

"Where to?"

"I don't know. Shedona's shtill tops on my list. But I have a bunch of other places I'm evaluating."

He'll be stuck here until he dies, the way he belabors his decisions, Doug thought. Then he said, nodding his head out the window, "She's got three more to go. How long do you think that'll take?"

"Half hour."

"Hmmm...sounds tempting, but maybe we better get on the road. We've got a long trip."

Bastard. Jamie heard Dawkins whisper the word to Dale as they were scrambling to get the car packed. Dawkins had come over to say good-bye after Dale called and told him he was evacuating. "You're never coming back, are you?" Dawkins continued in a bilious whisper to Dale.

"Of course I am," Dale said in a chirpy voice. "I'll catch a flight back out of Memphish or someting." As Jamie headed back into the house to get his backpack, Dawkins blocked his way. His straw farmer's hat from golth was missing, and Jamie saw the man's round face in the full light for the first time. It wasn't fat, just perfectly round like a basketball. His nose the size of a foosball. His hair was so thin, some large freckles were noticeable on the pate that had been previously concealed by the hat. His baldness exaggerated his eyebrows that were sprouting wildly like carrot stalks. They threatened to scratch at Jamie's nose as Dawkins leaned in and said with medicinal breath: "Next time, I'll take you to *my* course."

"OK," Jamie said. Dawkins cocked his head and looked over his shoulder toward the car. "But I'm not certain they'll be a next time." He reached and grabbed Jamie's arm around the bicep, squeezing hard. "Always smile, sport," he said, "and the world will always smile back."

Dawkins let go of his arm, then tussled his hair. He turned and glanced at the darkening sky, then ambled toward his car and opened the door as a Taco Bell wrapper blew out. "God bless, Speed, God bless," Dawkins, the agnostic, said apathetically, barely glancing his friend's way before getting in and driving off.

As Doug pulled out of the gate at Palmetto Swamp Preserve, he turned left onto the main road. "Ah, Doug, you're going da wrong way," Dale said from his renewed perch in the backseat between Jamie and Frizzy.

"You said turn left."

"Yes, but you're going da wrong way, down the wrong side of the shtreet."

"What?"

"It's a divided highway. You're going da wrong way!" Two cars rounded a bend ahead, flying straight at them.

"Shit!"

"Pull over!"

"Oh, my God, we're gonna die!"

"Shush, Ashley!"

"Pull over!"

"Where?"

"Over dere!"

"They're coming!"

"Shit!"

"Oh, my God, we're gonna die!"

Whop…whop…whop…whop…flllllizzzzzzzzzzzz.

Everyone shut their eyes. Doug jerked the wheel right. The car boomed and bounced and shook and rattled. Their heads all shot up and bashed the ceiling, Dale's nearly slicing through the roof. Another bounce. Another shake. Then, level ground. They opened their eyes. Jamie glanced out the window at the meticulously landscaped median they had just crossed. "What kind of plants were those?" Jamie asked Dale.

"Bougainvillea. Dead ones now."

Doug's heart was still pounding when they pulled into Publix. Dale said he needed to pick up a pain prescription for his nose before leaving town.

Jamie was excited to finally get to go inside Publix to see what all the fuss was about, but was quickly disappointed. "How come the shelves are all empty?" he asked as they walked toward the pharmacy.

"Shtorm's coming," Dale said matter-of-factly.

"Didn't they say it was still off the coast of Venezuela?" Jamie asked. "That's pretty far."

"Close enough."

The line at the pharmacy was six deep, two of them wheelchairs. "We'll just go stock up on some water," Doug said.

"Good luck," Dale chuckled.

Moments later Doug was walking down the frozen foods aisle, pushing a cart with five bottles of root beer. It was all they had left. As he passed the waffle section, he noticed one of the freezer doors open and...oh no, not again. The second time in one morning. Pasted on a rear end sticking out of the freezer was a pair of tight jeans sliding down as the woman bent over, forcing the lace of a purple thong to slide up. Just above the thin string was a small butterfly tattoo. Doug felt a tingle in his pants and continued to push his cart as his head swiveled back toward the waffles. *That should be illegal*, he thought. It's not like he'd never seen it before, a woman flashing her thong in a public place. It was like a fad to taunt the meek. Even in church he'd seen it countless times. Sinful. *There* he always tried to turn quickly away. But sticking out of a freezer of waffles? For some reason, it seemed to make staring a bit more excusable. Dazed, he eventually passed on to the breakfast burritos and then the frozen juice. Blueberry Pomegranate was the last thing that caught his eye before he turned his head forward and saw another pair of underpants staring him square in the face. Not a thong, but princess briefs. Frizzy's. Flashed skyward as her dress parachuted over her head while she bent to scrape at something on the floor with her finger.

"Frizzy!" Doug yelled just as he plowed the cart into her behind. "Ouch!" she yelled as she shot forward like a rocket. He watched helpless as she sailed toward a display of stacked wine bottles at the end of the aisle. It wasn't a bull's-eye; her shoulder just grazed the edge of the display as she fell to the ground. But it was enough to rattle the bottles, one of them shaking loose, crashing to the ground, and splattering blood-red zinfandel all over the industrial tile.

"Oh, dere ya are. Ready ta go?" Dale said as he rounded the corner, then looked at the floor. "Uh-ooooh."

A man arrived with a mop and insisted that he needed no help cleaning up, but Doug couldn't abandon the disaster he created without the burden of guilt. So he stayed and searched along the edges of the freezer for shards of glass. And the woman with the purple thong. But she was long gone. The manager arrived and insisted they didn't have to pay for the broken bottles. A half hour later, the mess cleaned up, Doug sighed deeply and rubbed his hands through his wiry hair. "Let's go," he said to the others.

"What about the root beer?" Jamie asked, pointing to the cart.

"Forget it, we don't need it."

"Ummmm, but I need to pay for something," Ashley said, holding a blue box furtively down at her side.

"What?" Doug said irritably.

"Just something."

"What?" he said again, his voice rising.

She pulled him away from Dale and the kids and whispered, "Feminine product."

So they headed toward the express line. Ten items or less. Only one person was ahead of them: a short old woman with three chickens. She looked like Betty White, except for the permanent frown etched into her jowls.

"This is for Tysons," said the checkout person, a young black girl with magenta streaks in her hair.

"What?" said Betty White, turning one ear toward the girl.

"This coupon y'all gave me's for Tysons. Yous got Perdue chickens there."

"But I don't like Tyson."

"Thaaan, you can't use no coupon."

"Why not? It says buy two chickens, get one free."

"I know what it says, but that's for Tysons. Yous got Perdue."

"What's the difference? A chicken's a chicken."

"Accept one's a Tysons, the others a Perdue."

"What kind of policy is that?"

"It's no policy. It's just the coupon."

"Don't get snippy with me, young lady."

"I'm not getting snippy. I'm just tellin' you like it is."

"I'll call the store manger over here, if I have to."

Doug groaned and shifted his weight as he listened to this absurd debate. He harvested thoughts of the purple thong to calm his mind and thought he actually saw the woman checking out in a far lane, but then again he hadn't actually seen enough of her upper half—above the tattoo— to be sure.

"Yous go ahead and call the manager if you want to," the checkout girl continued.

"I've never been treated so poorly in my life. If this were Kroga in Indiana they'd take my coupon." the lady said.

"Not if it was Tysons."

"Oh, certainly they would."

"Then y'all should shop in Indiana."

"Well, I certainly know I'm never shopping here again."

"Fine."

"Fine."

A silent stalemate ensued. Purple thong. Purple thong. Doug was desperately beseeching a state of serenity, but thoughts in his head kept getting crowded out by the echo of a shattering wine bottle. His skin was tingling. His heart racing.

"Y'all want the chickens?" the checkout girl finally asked.

"If you say so."

"I didn't say so. I axed you if you want the chickens."

"Fine." Several more moments of silence. Shattering glass rattled in Doug's head again. Punctuated by the real sound of a flushing toilet in a nearby bathroom.

The chicken lady snatched her receipt and examined it. "Hey, you charged me for three chickens!" she hollered. "I only wanted to pay for two."

"Lady!" Doug screamed. "If you don't cut the crap and move along, I'm going to stick those chickens up your ass!"

Silence. Staring faces from every checkout lane in the store. Another flush of the toilet, followed by a deep groan from the bathroom.

Rain began to fall as they headed into the parking lot. Doug stormed toward the car, Jamie trying to keep pace. Behind him were Dale and Ashley. He could hear them both giggle, as Frizzy at their side mocked: "...stick those chickens up your ass...stick those chickens up your ass..."

It was pouring by the time they left the parking lot. Doug had a full tank of gas, and he wasn't stopping until they got out of Florida. "I gotta pee," Ashley said twenty minutes after they got on the interstate.

"Hold it."

But even he couldn't hold it ten hours. That still wasn't enough time to get them out of Florida. "They coulda made a separate state out of this panhandle, it's so goddamn long," Doug muttered to himself. "Like another Rhode Island or something." They spent the night near Pensacola, where Doug tossed and turned to the sound of the pounding rain outside and the whoosh-thump of the elevator inside, its shaft feeling like it was centimeters behind his headboard.

By early afternoon they neared Jackson, Mississippi. Sunshine blazed overhead. Doug's mood resurged. Mississippi didn't seem so bad at all, especially after they exited onto a state highway to find Dale's brother-in-law's house near Oxford. Verdant hills undulated for miles, interspersed with fields flush with rows and rows of maturing plants. Doug wondered if it was cotton. He'd seen similar-looking plants in South Carolina.

"Ah...Civil War country, huh, Jame?" He glanced into the rearview mirror and felt himself jump a bit as he surprisingly caught sight of Dale's towering frame, his head scraping the ceiling. He'd forgotten he was there.

"Hey, Jame!" Doug yelled so that everyone jumped. The Kid pulled his earphones out. "What were the big ones in Mississippi?"

"Big ones?"

"You know, the big Civil War battles."

Jamie glanced self-consciously at Dale, who seemed to be more focused on Ashley as she leaned over into the backseat to hand Frizzy some candy.

"Ummm…" Jamie stammered. "Corinth. Vicksburg."

"Vicksburg. Oh yeah!" Doug said like he'd just hit a swish shot. But that was it for the quizzing, because he had been completely unprepared to go through Mississippi.

They drove on for several more miles. The sun began to drift lower in the sky, an igneous orb throwing long shadows from the huge oak trees and white rail fences that painted oblique latticework along the rolling countryside. "Dis is the driveway," Dale said, as they slowed along a narrow lane with horses grazing on a far hillside.

Doug stopped the car in front of a wrought-iron gate, hinged to pillars of red brick with ornate cement coping. "Nice spread," he said, as he stared up at a large antebellum house, sparkling white in the late-afternoon sun. It had high columns in front surrounding a porch that sheltered three empty rocking chairs wobbling ever so slightly in the warm breeze.

Doug stopped the car and they all walked up the steps to the front door painted jet black to match the shutters on the windows. He looked for a doorbell, but didn't see one. In the meantime, Dale had reached for a knocker on the door. The knocker was brass and sculpted in the shape of an eagle. When Dale struck it down, it thudded heavily with the sound of a sledgehammer hitting a railroad spike. The echo leaked down the hillside and then faded beneath the sound of the wind blowing through a massive oak tree in the front yard.

The door swung open slowly as if it were the opening of a vault. A cherubic black woman wearing a pastel floral dress that hung neatly from her large bosom smiled a dignified salute full of gleaming teeth like piano keys. "Mr. Daayyle," she said without wonder.

"Martha," Dale responded. "Good ta see ya."

"What happened to your poor nose?"

"Oh, just a minor scrape, dat's all." He introduced his family. And then "Amber."

"Ashley," she corrected. Jamie giggled.

"Ahhh, Mr. Coulter's not here," Martha finally said after several moments of awkward silence. Doug shifted nervously, but Dale took it in stride. His brother-and-law, Lachlan, traveled quite a bit. He was a retired lawyer from Memphis and had been very successful. His wife—who was Clara's sister—had died of cancer a few years before Clara was munched by the alligator. Lachlan had been in Africa the last time Dale rode out a hurricane there. The invitation was always open. Dale had left a message on Lachlan's voice mail before they'd left Florida, and he knew at least Martha would be there.

"He's dead," Martha said, quickly putting her fingers up to her lips, as if the announcement was newly shocking to her.

"Dead?" Dale said. "But..."

"No one called you?" Martha asked.

"Well...no," Dale said. "Den again..." his voice faded as he couldn't quite articulate the fact that a tie between two brothers-in-law connected only by their dead wives is a feeble one at best.

"When did he die?"

"Month ago." Martha then leaned in and whispered, "Mad cow disease."

"Mad cow disease!"

Martha glanced around nervously as if she expected the FBI to appear. They all stood silently. The birds sung. The breeze blew. The echo of neighing horses filtered up the drive. Frizzy farted, a slight squeaky one. Then Doug realized it was Dale.

"I never even knew he was sick," Dale said.

"That's not a disease you brag about," Doug said dryly, as Martha wrenched up her mouth in concurrence.

"I'd offer you to still stay here, Mr. Daayyle," she said, "but they's closing up the house tomorrow. It's to be sold. This is my last day." As she spoke the words, she tilted her head forward, and her eyelids heavy with thick lashes dipped and rose mechanically.

"Well, now...." Doug said awkwardly, as they sat in the car in the driveway with the engine off, all their faces pale with the look of death.

"I guesh I could stay at a hotel," Dale finally said after a long pause.

"Good idea," Doug said promptly. "We'll find one in Memphis. We're heading there anyway."

It had been a planned stop, so it was no sweat off his back. They found a satisfactory hotel right on Union Avenue. In fact it was one of the best of the trip. No mold or cigarette odors in the rooms. No elevators banging in your eardrum while lying in bed. No rain pounding outside. Doug even liked the complimentary lavender shampoo. He snagged a few extra from the room service cart in the hallway and stuck them in his toiletry kit. Yes, indeed, it would be a good place for Dale to spend a few days. He liked the guy and all, but there was no doubt he made him a bit nervous. Put him on edge. It wasn't just the intimidation from Dale's intellectual prowess, but the deliberateness too. And that speech problem was really getting annoying. Doug didn't have time for any of it. And then, of course, there was the situation with Corrine. Dale never made an issue of it, but he was her father after all, and blood's thicker than water, as they say.

A few days in Florida with Dale were fine. Good for The Kid, although now that he thought about it, Dale didn't exactly work much with Jamie the way Doug expected him to. And then for two days in the car, they sat side by side, The Kid mostly listening to his music and reading and Dale staring out the window, and sometimes at Ashley. There were giggles occasionally from the backseat, but Doug always seemed on the outside listening in. Enough's enough. Yes, this would be a good spot for the old man. Time to head west. Doug spread out his road atlas on the hotel room bed and surveyed his route. They'd shoot up I-55 to St. Louis and then head west on I-70. Lots of open road. It'd be a good time to get back to quizzing The Kid. And to finally putting that consultant to work. He needed to start getting his money's worth. In fact, he'd decided it was time to send her to the backseat next to Jamie so there'd be no more time wasted in the car. They'd be in Denver in about three days. Then they'd make their detour up to Mount Rushmore. The Kid was dying to see it. And it'd be something to brag about in San Francisco. Then they'd pick up I-80. There'd be nothing to see in those other states: Wyoming, Utah, Nevada. *Painful*, he thought. He'd just zoom right through them. "Right into Frisco!" he said as he slammed the atlas closed.

The door to the bathroom opened, and Dale stepped out smelling like Clubman. "Ready for some grub," he said. The kids and Ashley bounced off the bed where they'd been watching TV. The dining area in this hotel looked "A-OK," Doug had declared the night before. That's where they'd get breakfast, although he wouldn't be joining them.

He was headed toward the church. Last night when they arrived in town, he had called his friend Brian. "We just got into town," Doug had said. "Can you still get together in the morning?"

"Sure," Brian said.

"Is there a place you can recommend for some coffee on Beale Street? I was hoping to maybe check it out and catch some of the scene down there."

"The only thing you'll catch down there that time of day, Doug, is the fetid smell of stale beer and urine fermenting in the morning heat," Brian had said.

Morning heat. That was an understatement. It was downright stifling. The sun beat viciously on his back as he stepped out into the hotel parking lot. Not a wisp of air stirred. The combustion of city noise—a transit bus pulling away from its stop, a taxi honking, and a clink-clink that sounded like a crane at a construction site—all pecked insidiously at his sense of balance. He stopped and leaned on a black Escalade and then swigged from his bottle of water.

Danny Thomas. Danny Thomas. Who the hell was he again? Doug kept asking himself the question as he drove down South Danny Thomas Boulevard for the third time looking for the side street Brian had indicated in his directions. He was on TV, Doug knew that much. But he just couldn't remember the show. Not much of a TV watcher when he was a kid. *Rockford Files* was his favorite. Watching on that old TV in the basement encased in the heavy, honey-colored cabinet and dialed up to the loudest notch on the volume control so he could hear it above the clothes dryer and the furnace blasting. He liked the way the guy peeled out of parking lots and did those three-sixty spins. He'd done one of those himself once in drivers ed. The instructor said he'd fail him next time he tried a stunt like that. But he wasn't trying. Wonder if Brian would remember? They took drivers ed together. They did most things together in high school. He, Brian, and Rex, of course.

Doug finally found the church and pulled into the parking lot past a black woman pushing a stroller and holding the hand of a little girl walking alongside with pigtails tied at the end with little colorful balls like marbles. Smaller than the lollipop she sucked, but the same rainbow of colors. The woman looked like a grandmother. She was shuffling in tiny steps to ward off the heat, letting go of the stroller every few steps to fan herself with a diaper, which was neatly folded and pressed like when they first come out of the package. The parking lot was empty. Doug stared for several moments up at the cross, towering piously and intimidatingly into the milky sky. What was the delay? Facing the heat? Wondering what it would be like to see Brian?

A dozen years it had been. Their ten-year high school reunion was the last time. Before that, they'd only seen each other a handful of times since high school graduation. Brian left that summer to work for his uncle doing something or other in Newport and then went to college at Holy Cross. Doug visited him up there once, just before Christmas that first year. How could he ever forget? It's where he met Corrine.

Boredom. That's what made him leave the campus, where Brian seemed to have his nose perpetually in the books, and go downtown to the shopping mall. Worcester. Cold and gray and dreary in early December, brown hills dotted with sooty, melting snow and circled by looping highways thick with exhaust. Why not knock off some Christmas shopping? He ran into Corrine in Filene's Basement at the galleria while he was picking out a sweater for his mother. It wasn't the first time he'd really seen Corrine. He'd recognized her from home, where she hung around with some girls he knew in high school. She was attending college in Connecticut and had gone up to visit a friend who went to another school near Worcester.

Doug promptly broke up with his then-current girlfriend over Christmas—left her sweating in an overly heated bookstore—then commuted to Connecticut regularly, fighting traffic on I-95 and incubating his disdain for other drivers. His mother never liked Corrine. She was too saintly to say so, but she left no doubt in the way she'd purse her lips and draw her chin into the folds of skin around her neck every time Corrine opened her mouth in her vicinity. By the time he and Corrine had married, Brian was off becoming a priest, a development Doug's mother cataloged to him at every conceivable opportunity with the inference that her own son had let her down. Maybe this is why he decided to lose touch with Brian, a development assisted by Brian's departure for missionary work in South America.

When Corrine left him, Brian was the first person he really wanted to call for support, but he didn't. At first he thought he was afraid of being judged, but realized that wasn't it. Fear of being judged is something that peaks in the teenage years and then gradually fades to nothing over time. It's why senior citizens fart in public without compunction or rashly spout whatever random thoughts pop into their minds. Doug was already feeling it at the age of thirty-seven. He noticed he didn't really care anymore about what people thought of him, or his actions. Fear of being judged? That definitely wasn't it.

Fear of misjudging. Now that's what gnaws at us as we get older. Sealing friendships as a kid is easy. You find a few things in common with the other person and you just do it: become friends. But adults get burned once or twice and they get a little gun-shy. They start to feel frustrated, a little stupid, perhaps, that the solid judgments they formed about someone are totally off the mark. That's what addled him about Corrine. And was probably why he'd steer away from ever getting involved with another woman. Just another person to worry about measuring incorrectly. It was similar now with Brian, he'd concluded. It was really more like Doug was starting a new friendship with him. The old friendship was gone; it offered no guidance as to the kind of person he was as a priest. That *should* make him warm and kind and compassionate and all, right? But what if Doug shared with Brian the misery about his life, expecting a soft shoulder to lean on, and it was nothing but cold and hard? He'd feel burned.

Burned like he was by Rex. Doug knew he had definitely not misjudged Rex by the sheer fact that the initial judgments had been cast long ago in high school. So those didn't count. The problem was really with Rex. The guy just changed...he got obsessed with money and power and high society, and Doug kept telling himself he didn't care about the guy anymore.

But he *did* care. He clung bitterly to every word Rex uttered. "I wonder if Brian's gay," Rex had quipped the last time Doug was at his estate in the spring and Brian's name came up. "It must be a little humiliating being a Catholic priest in Memphis with all those Southern Baptists." Doug laughed right along deceptively, but the words jarred him inside. Enough to force him into arranging a visit with Brian. A reversion to high school when allegiances shifted with the slightest act of perfidy. Good word. He'd seen it recently when he was doing some research on some history material to quiz The Kid on. He liked that his son was making him smarter.

He blew a deep breath of warm air out against the tide of air conditioning still blowing from the idling Expedition. He was enjoying the solitude,
although the vestiges of other occupants were present enough to distract
him. *She* is *a slob*, he thought, as he stared at the passenger side, the array
of catalogues scattered on the floor, among an open pack of Twizzlers, a
hairbrush, and two empty Evian bottles. Her duct-taped sunglasses sat on
the dashboard, where the black frames looked molten from the sun searing through the windshield. He clicked off the ignition. His brain quiv-
ered from thinking too much. He wasn't used to it. Preferred to just plow
through life.

"Thanks for coming," Brian said as they shook hands and let themselves melt together into a tentative hug. "Not only is the pastor laid up
from his hernia surgery, like I told you on the phone, but now it looks like
we need a new water heater in the rectory. Plumber's on his way back."

"No problem," Doug said, trying to feign a cavalier tone.

"Hey, where are the kids?" Brian asked.

"Oh, I thought about bringing them," Doug lied. He knew if he'd
decided to invite them along, somehow Ashley would wind up there too.
"But I thought it might be best for us to catch up alone. Next time you
can meet them."

They moved into the rectory kitchen, the smell of fresh coffee waft-
ing with the faint smell of construction—recently dried caulk or drywall
or something. "Nice digs," Doug said as he ran his hand along a black
Corian countertop, smoothly reflecting his face so he could look up his own
nostrils.

"Thanks," Brian said. "Recently renovated, thanks to a donation from a
parishioner, a recent convert from the Baptist Church."

"Wow, that's a stunt."

"Yeah, Memphis has been good to me. When I first arrived, I was angry
that I got stuck here. I thought that at least if I was going to be subjected
to the South, I could get New Orleans. But this is OK."

As he spoke, Doug watched Brian's crow's feet lengthen and then
retract slowly, like a drying river, as his mouth came to rest. Brian's buzz-
cut hair was completely grayed, belying a youthful twinkle in his eyes and
an adherence to fitness that might be a recent development, if the looseness
in his collar was any indication of his less recent girth. The collar sagged a

bit, the white square angling down instead of staring you strait in the eye with seraphic calculation like it usually does.

Within moments all stiffness dissolved away and they surprisingly talked like old friends who hadn't been apart for more than a few weeks and didn't need to cast new judgments. Maybe it was the coffee, which Doug thought was making him a little giddy, the nutmeg or whatever it was, dark and rich like the tabletop they set the cups on, grooved and distressed to make it look like it had been dragged right out of the woods. Really nice digs, Doug said again to himself. In a church, for Pete's sake.

"So..." Doug said, feeling loose and trying hard be witty. "I always thought it was kind of ironic and all that you became a priest..."

"Why, because I cheated off you in religion class?"

"Yeah, there was that, I suppose."

"You forget, Doug, that while your mother was training you with daily recitations of the Angelus, my mother was drinking her way to oblivion. The closest she ever got to church was that time she drove into the brick wall in front of St. Pat's on Thanksgiving morning."

"And look where it's gotten both of us."

Brian just chuckled and took a sip of his coffee.

"What I was talking about," Doug continued, "when I was joking about the irony of you becoming a priest, was...well...how you were the one always getting lai— Well, you know what I mean."

Brian ran his finger around the edge of his cup, not with discomfort but with the deliberation of one who always thinks before he speaks. "I guess I lied quite a bit back then."

"You lied about getting lai—. Sorry."

"That's OK, Doug, you can say it. Being a priest doesn't automatically make someone a prude...which I suppose might be at the heart of our little image problem these days." He stopped and chuckled sardonically, then said, "I guess I just chalk up the lying to teenage angst. Back then I thought everybody was doing it...you know, what you said."

"Getting laid."

"Yes. But now with the wisdom of age, I realize perhaps more kids were lying about it than you think."

"Jeez, I guess you're right. Poor Cheryl Pompiano. Maybe she wasn't a slut after all."

"Yeah, I tell the twelfth graders I teach over at the high school that if fewer of them would lie about it, maybe fewer of them would be pressured to actually do it. It works better than the strict abstinence sermon."

"Yeah, but do they actually listen?" Doug said. "I mean, kids aren't too good at listening."

"Oh, you'd be surprised, Doug. Kids are better at listening than we think." With that, Brian rose to refill the coffee cups from a brushed metal pot.

"So, that must have been a tough one to handle when you became a priest, huh?" Doug said, his continued attempts to be witty sounding stiff and contrived.

"What's that?"

"You know, lying about getting laid. You got two competing sins going on there."

Brian started to respond, then sucked in his breath like a faint hiccup and took a sip of his coffee. He tried to shift the subject: "I'm sorry about things with Corrine."

"Yeah, well," Doug said awkwardly. "Shit happens. God's way, right?"

"Maybe I should apologize for being such a boring friend that time you came to visit me in Worcester," Brian said, trying to sound lighthearted. "You might not have ever bumped into her."

"Well, don't sweat it," Doug said. "It's no one's fault but my own, I suppose. That's what I'm supposed to say, right?"

"Don't be so quick to sell yourself down the river."

"Well, I already have. And the only thing that keeps me from drowning is that I have my son."

"Daughter too, right?"

"Oh sure, sure. But you gotta see this boy. He's really gifted. He's going to be a star one day." Doug tried to run his finger around the rim of his cup, but it slipped and the cup wobbled, splashing a bit over the side, the liquid blending with the color of the tabletop. "Whoops, sorry about that."

"No problem." Brian sopped it up with a towel, baby blue striped, like it had jumped off the page from the Williams-Sonoma catalogue. Ashley had one in the car.

"Anyway," Doug continued. "My kid's sure going to blow the doors off Rex's kids someday."

"Ah, Rex, how is the old boy? Seen him much?"

"A little too much lately," Doug said, thinking of the haunting Rex look-alike in Virginia, the one who favored early-morning trysts with his hairy housekeeper, perhaps in rebellion against his wife's fat ass. Wish he could claim the real Rex had a wife with a fat ass. But she was perfect. Like everything that belonged to Rex. The sprawling, leafy estate up on the hill overlooking Long Island Sound. The $50,000-a-year private grade school he sends his kids to. The country club with its summer camp, where the kids dress in prim white outfits and learn to sail and write poetry and take golf lessons from tour pros.

"I hear he's retired," Brian said.

"Oh, yes, at the ripe old age of thirty-seven. Walks around like he's some sort of aristocrat or something. I'm done going out there. I can't take it anymore."

"That's too bad, we were all good friends back in the days. You and him especially."

"Yeah, well...screw him. Sorry. One day I'll show him."

"Your *son* will show him?"

"Yeah, that's right."

"And that will make you satisfied?"

"What's more satisfying than having your kid be successful?"

"I wouldn't know. Some argue that's why priests should not get married. They'd get too absorbed in their kids at the expense of their congregation."

"I thought it was the whole carnal thing?"

"Well, now, some would argue that's why priests *should* get married..." A knock cut him off. A man stood in the entryway, his blue shirt stenciled in red with the name *Dave*. Brian excused himself to sign off on the bill for the new water heater.

"So, what's your definition of success for your kids?" Brian said when he sat back down, glancing at his watch as he did so.

"Well, for Jamie, my son, I guess that would be acceptance to the Ivy Leagues...then a job as a high-powered CEO... I don't know..." Doug's voice trailed off as he turned his head up to the countertop. Indianapolis Colts canisters stood in a row. Three different sizes, for sugar, flour and... what *do* you put in the third one?

"You know, Doug...remember Tony Dannafrio?"

"What a tool. Unfortunately, I still get to see these people back home. You're lucky you don't."

"Well, maybe so. I remember the time he wanted to stick the dog crap in the mailbox of that crazy old man that lived down the street from you... what was his name?"

"Old Man Maplethorp."

"Yeah, that's it. And do you remember what happened?" Doug shrugged self-consciously. "You stuck up for the old man," Brian said. "Wouldn't allow him to be harassed, even though Dannafrio threatened to beat you to a pulp."

Doug tried the rim thing again. This time a little more successfully. "Yeah, so..."

"You tell me." But Doug didn't answer. Brian rose. "I'm going to need to excuse myself, Doug. I need to start working on my homily for Sunday. I'm way behind." He picked up both coffee cups and rinsed them quickly in the sink, the water sputtering the way it does after the main line's been shut off a while. Brian wiped some spray from his chest and then turned around and folded his arms, the black sleeves riding up and revealing muscular forearms veined from exercise. "You still go to church, Doug?" He watched his friend squirm as the question came out. "No judgment, Doug. I'm just curious."

"Not much since Corrine and I split. I haven't felt the desire. Sorry."

"No need to be sorry to me. This isn't confession right now. This is just friends. Think about it. Church, I mean." Doug stared blankly, so Brian continued, "I'll leave you with one of my favorite quotes from the esteemed John: 'Life is what happens to you while...'"

But Doug cut him off quickly with raised hands, like he was blocking a punt. "Whoa! I have to confess again, Father, I haven't been reading the Bible too much either these days. Since we were forced to in high school, I suppose."

"Oh, I wasn't talking about the Apostle John," Brian said. "I was talking about John Lennon."

John Lennon. Jeez. *I never was much of a Beatles fan*, Doug thought as he cruised Union Avenue twenty minutes later, hot and tired. The *White Album* was fine. Do-Re-Mi. Life shines on, or something like that. Where the hell was that hotel anyway? It was nearing noon, and he wanted to be on the road—rid of Dale and heading west.

"We decided he's coming with us," Jamie said, when Doug finally found the place and located Jamie, Frizzy, and Ashley frolicking in the pool.

"Who's we?" Doug asked petulantly. They all stared at him, their hair plastered to their heads, drips running down their cheeks like raindrops on windowpanes.

As they left Memphis an hour later, Doug was definitely feeling the blues. "The Mighty Mississippi, kiddos," Doug said as they crossed the bridge, but his voice sounded flat. At least he'd made one good decision: The Kid was riding shotgun.

11

Fourteeners

I just knew shotgun wouldn't last long. About five hours was it. The most exciting part, I suppose, was the beginning—driving over the Mississippi, although even that fell short of my own grand expectations. Which, by the way, I've been learning in life to temper for my own well-being. After we crossed the river, it was all downhill. Or more accurately, rather flat.

We spent an hour stuck in traffic a stone's throw from the river. The road narrowed to one lane for construction while we inched along through a thick haze of dust swirling from the back of earthmovers and acrid smoke belching from some low, ugly, rectangular buildings along the highway. The correlation between my dad's mood and the speed of the Expedition on this trip was now without question, so it was pretty grim for a while. But by the time we cruised into Missouri up near (but not above) the speed limit, he was whistling away. I had been excited to stop and see the Gateway Arch up close and personal. After all, that was part of the original itinerary to the best of my recollection. But perhaps my recollection no longer ranked up there with the best. Or perhaps, more likely, the itinerary had changed again.

"I thought we were stopping?" I said to my dad, in a low, calm voice one can use when you are in the navigator's perch and the rest of humanity is relegated to the cheap seats. By the time I'd finished my sentence, I could see the very crown of the Arch sinking below the treetops in the murky distance behind us, a shard of afternoon sun catching it in one spot and giving it the look of a woman's bracelet with a single glittering diamond.

"Uggh…I don't know, Jame," my dad murmured, as he rubbed his free hand through his hair—always a dead giveaway that his thoughts are somersaulting in nervous regret. "We've been making some good time, and I'm a little hesitant to stir the pot, if you know what I mean." As he said this, he glanced in the rearview mirror at the Three Musketeers in the back. They'd all dozed off, Dale snoring the loudest. No doubt they were recovering from a spell of irritating giddiness a short time before that, all of them laughing at jokes and comments that my dad and I couldn't hear. It agitated him enough to consider sending me to the back again when we had stopped for gas before hitting St. Louis. I could only imagine that this meant Dale going to the front seat and me being stuck back there with the...the...oh, hell, I don't know what to call her anymore. Anyway, I begged and pleaded with my dad, and the status quo reigned.

"That's all right, Dad," I said as we left St. Louis in our wake. "Maybe on the way back."

"Yes, that's it! On the way back, kiddo." He began to whistle again, and I suddenly noticed he hadn't cursed at another driver since we left Arkansas. Why stir the pot?

As we drove monotonously through the farmlands of Missouri, the sun began to set in the far west and we were heading straight toward it. This felt good. I could imagine San Francisco rising before us on the horizon, but I knew we had a long way to go. "When do you think we'll get there?" I asked my dad.

"Oh, I'm thinking about seven or eight days, kiddo, when you toss in the little side trip up there to Rushmore. That'll give us a good week to spare before your program starts. I figure we can tool around Frisco, maybe head up to the wine country or something.

You don't like wine, I considered saying. But instead I said, "Sounds great, Dad," laying the enthusiasm on like a slab of thick butter...which he *does* like. He smiled and that's when I noticed Ashley's—there, I said it!— sunglasses sitting on the dashboard, wedged up against the windshield. These were not the old ones, the ones that were trampled at St. Augustine. She bought a new pair back in Memphis, right before we went swimming in that pool in the hotel, which I regretfully admit was kind of fun. The new glasses are not quite as big as hubcaps like the old ones, but just as round and just as goofy. A sudden impulse rooted only in my desire to keep my dad as chipper as possible compelled me to pick up the glasses and slip them on. The earpieces were hot from sitting directly in the sun, so I quickly pulled them off, rubbed them cool, and then slipped them back on. The orange-tinted orbs covered my entire face. "Look, Dad," I said. "I'm the Pumpkin Man."

"Excellent!" He yelped as he threw his head back and laughed, his mouth opening like one of those wooden nutcracker soldiers you see at Christmas. "The Pumpkin Man!"

I was confident this type of father-son bonding sealed my position in the front for the rest of the trip. But never underestimate the irrationality of adults. After a sound sleep in a respectable hotel somewhere east of Columbia, we were eating breakfast at a leisurely pace. I had five of those waffles you self-serve with the mix that you pour into a hot waffle iron that hinges close. We were chatting about the Yankees and politics, more specifically my dad's two idols: Jeeta and Obamer, as mix-pronounces them... not jokingly. Then we moved on to discuss why houses don't have exit signs like hotels, that profound question coming from Frizzy. "Good question," my dad said, his voice already tinged with a trace of sarcasm. "Maybe we should have them in homes so adulterers can find the door." I wondered if this had anything to do with the time my mother got stuck climbing in our small kitchen window one day before dawn when she claimed she forgot her key. We had to slice out the filling in her winter coat to get her unstuck. Not wanting to subject my kid sister to such iniquities, I brought the conversation about exit signs back down a little closer to her level. I was happy to entertain the topic as long as it meant steering clear of a grilling on the Lewis and Clark expedition. I'd had a few quickies from my dad as we were driving past St. Louis and then crossed the Missouri River, and I got the sense he was just warming himself back up after a bit of a welcomed overnight hiatus. Welcomed by me, maybe not by him. I tried to throw him off the trail by expounding upon the excitement the intrepid explorers felt when they hooked up with a guy named Injun Joe in St. Petersburg. I had my dad going for a while, until finally, scratching his head, he said, "Wait, isn't Injun Joe that guy from *Huck Finn?*" Darn.

In the hotel dining nook, I could see his brain beginning to smoke as he sat there spreading cream cheese on his onion bagel and peeking at his binder. It was a little strange that he didn't take the chance to dive right in then and there once again on the Lewis and Clark stuff, but maybe he felt we had a long ride ahead of us. The stranger thing about the morning was that Dale and Ashley—yikes, I said it again!—both showed up late, claiming the need to make "a call or two." Bugsy—that's right, I'm done with that Ashley crap—said this in a way that made me wonder if she had a drug deal going down or something. No matter. It left just the three of us for a while, which was nice. Just our little family. With Lewis and Clark, and Injun Joe, lurking in the shadows.

After Dale joined us he slurped down his strawberry yogurt, but not before taking ten minutes to methodically peel off the foil top as if he didn't want to disturb the balance of nature. It was about then I noticed the ski jump was smaller. Not a ski jump at all anymore, really. He'd reduced the size of his bandage to one thin layer of snow coating his nose, which is still long enough, mind you. He rubbed it, then leaned back and stretched his arms high over his head, which is very high. And that's when he said something very dangerous.

But first he said, with crisp, clean diction: "So, Doug, when do you think we'll be in Denver?"

"Eh, I figure in about two days, if we haul ass." My dad sounded cocky, which to me is just about when people set themselves up for the big fall. Several moments of silence passed, except for Bugsy—who had returned from her drug deal—crunching her granola like all those cows we'd been passing along the interstate.

"So..." Dale said, and then paused to flip a page in *USA Today*. "How far do you think Aspen is from Denver?" He asked this in a questioning tone that adults sometimes use when they already know the answer to a question they are asking you.

"Aspen?" my dad said. "Isn't that the ski place?" I knew he knew it was more than that.

"Yes," Dale said.

"Why do you ask?"

"Well, I don't know...I just happened to be talking to Corrine. I thought I'd give her a call and let her know I was hitching a little ride with you guys." My dad interrupted this comment with a quick snort, the kind where boogies sometimes mistakenly shoot out. But this time he was clean.

"...She happened to remind me," Dale continued, "that she is out in Aspen at Hubert's place."

"Yeah, so what of it?" my dad asked reproachfully. Oh, but I knew he could read the writing on the wall. Who couldn't?

"I told her we'd swing by," Dale said. Dangerously.

Swing by! Are you out of your goddamn mind? My dad didn't actually say that, but the quavering of his nostrils and the choking on his bagel were a sure clue as to what words I knew he was forming in his head. The gravity of his intentions was betrayed comically by the fleck of cream cheese gluing a crumb of onion bagel to his upper lip, right in that little strange canyon that forms under your nose.

I didn't actually witness the argument, as Dale and my dad had absconded to the far corner of the hotel parking lot after breakfast. I could see them in the distance, just their upper halves above the hoods of cars still moist from a morning drizzle that had taken a time-out. My dad's arms were flailing in all directions, and I could tell he was doing most of the talking. I could also tell he lost the debate when I saw Dale gently but authoritatively place his large hand on my dad's shoulder the way people do when they are comforting a loss. You ever watch the football coaches meet in the middle of a field after a game when the TV camera's on them? You don't even have to know who won the game. The guy putting his hand on the shoulder of the other guy: he's the winner. Belichick's got it down pat.

"Get in the car," my dad orders after stampeding back. He glances around and notices the shortage of people. "Where's Ashley?" he asks. I point in the other direction, where she's hiding behind a Suburban and talking covertly on her cell phone. To her drug dealer, probably. My dad whistles and nearly pierces my eardrum as I swing open the passenger door.

"In the back, Jame," he says with a finality that begs no further question.

"What for?" I ask anyway.

"Just get in." The irrationality!

"What's up?" The Snatcher asks perkily as she hops thievingly into the front seat. If I were behind it, I'd kick it.

"We're going to see Mommy!" Frizzy chimes in.

Great. I slip my headphones on and settle in for the painful ride. But not before my dad curses at the first car we pass coming out of the parking lot. "Ass! Watch where you're going!" I believe the guy's an ass because of what's on his license plate: *EAR DR*. Ooooh, my dad hates that: doctors with vanity plates. The ear doc does what any arrogant doctor would do:

ignore my plebeian dad's rebuke and continue to peck away at the keys on his cell phone. "Cell phones cause seventy-five percent of all accidents on the road," my dad lectures his audience in the car. "That and trucks."

That and trucks what? Does he mean cell phones and trucks together cause seventy-five percent of the accidents? Or just truckers talking on… ah, forget it. Speaking of cell phones, I have dozens of unanswered text messages and Facebook updates on mine to catch up on. I'd stored my phone away when I was riding shotgun, because I knew it could irritate my dad and jeopardize my status. If I'd only known how indiscriminately it could be snatched away from me. Most of my messages are inane things from my friends back home. Goofy jokes. Complaints about the boredom of summer. Bragging from my friend Randy about his new Wii to go along with his PS3 and Xbox 360. My dad hates all those games. He's forbidden me to get any of them, as he says they'll interfere with my intellectual development. He's convinced that nobody who's ever stepped foot in an Ivy League university has played a video game before in his life. That's like saying pro athletes don't cheat on their wives because it might throw them off their game. OK, I didn't make that last part up. I read it on some Web site recently.

I disregard most of the messages. Except one from Zach, where he tells me he's heading to a tournament in Chicago. *good luck*, I write back. Enough said. I hope the security people there have a sense of humor.

I notice nothing from Jessica since we last corresponded in Memphis. She was really down, as her mother had been sent back to the hospital. Her father thought it might be for good. A roller coaster, she called it.

wat do u think that crevasse is 4 betwn your upper lip & nose? I write in an e-mail, hoping she'll respond soon.

An hour passes and I think I may have actually dozed off. I awake to the smell of a fart and am ready to lash out at Frizzy, then realize it's not her texture. I glance at Dale and think, oh great, now I've got a double dose of bad air assaulting my intestinal equilibrium.

its like a flume ride at an amusement park for tiny microscopic bugs that crawl around your skin, I read from Jessica in response to my silly question.

haha. sounds like fun! I write, feeling giddy to have her back. *hows life?*

ok. i guess. just got back from the city. a photo shoot. the photog was this old creepy guy. i feel dirty. yuk. yuk. yuk. yuk…and…YUK!

hang in there :) I wonder if Jessica will continue modeling if her mother... well, I can't even think about that. A few years ago she won this contest in the mall her mom signed her up for and it snowballed from there. Jessica has confided to me many times how guilty she feels about hating it, because she knows it's helping to pay her mother's medical bills.

It rains most of the morning. It's a tepid, oily rain that convinces my dad to drive way under the speed limit, which thereby leads him to erupt about a dozen times with one of his favorite expressions on the road: "That guy's driving up my ass." Chicken, anyone?

Not quite. Barbecue ribs is what my dad insists we have for lunch in Kansas City. "They're famous there," he brags, as if he's the only one who watches Food Network. He orders a "half-slab of baby-backs" with his chest puffing out. And when The Snatcher orders the same thing, spicy southwestern sauce and all, I can tell my dad's got his testosterone up. He wolfs down the ribs with the determined look of a schoolkid not to be outdone by a girl. No doubt he was goaded on by her yodeling, "Mmmmm, these *are* zesty," after every other bite. In the end I think she kicked his ass, an opinion I'll keep to myself, thank you very much.

Outside in the parking lot, we're pleased to see the sun poking through some low, cindery stratus clouds. Dale lets out a huge belch, which just happens to occur at the same time as one from my dad in the same tenor. They both also have barbecue sauce stains on their shirts, despite wearing the bibs. This manly affiliation seems to whittle away at the lingering friction between the two, and my dad speaks to Dale for the first time since he learned we were going to visit my mother. "Hey, Dale," I hear him say perkily. He puts his hand out on Dale's shoulder, but it lacks the authority of the coach who has won the game. "Can you work with Jamie a little in the back there as we're driving this afternoon?"

I can see Dale's face turn blank, as he's a little hung up on the word *work*. When he asks for clarification, my dad pulls Dale a little more off to the side and begins whispering out of earshot, but I can hear him anyway. Indeed, I know just what he's saying. Especially the part about how the Asians are really getting a leg up in math and science. I can picture him declaring: "Just look at them with all these Internet companies they've started." The conversation ends fairly quickly. Dale punctuates it with a simple shoulder shrug like he'd just been told by Dawkins he had to take another pee in the bushes.

I'm ready for it when we get back in the car. Everyone's farting now from the barbecue and the windows are open, which makes it difficult to talk, so that's good. I slip on my headphones, which my dad notices in the mirror, and so he suggests Dale and I chat a bit. The windows all go up. Soon it stinks like the cheese section in a deli, and my stomach starts to do wicked spins like a pinwheel.

Or like a giant sprinkler shooting circular sprays of water over corn-fields that stretch to the horizon. "Those look like the skeleton of a giant pterodactyl," I declare, feeling quite proud of my creative simile. Why is it we're taught to always compare something to something else?

"That's a center-pivot irrigation system," Dale says pontifically. It's then I realize how much I miss his speech impediment. "The sprinklers are attached to these huge trusses that are mounted on those big towers with wheels," he continues. "The system moves in a big circle and then waters the crops…that's why they call it a pivot. You can see the circles sometimes when you fly over in an airplane. They really stand out. Big and green, where the crops have been watered. Quite nifty."

Nifty? That's a word I'll be sure not to use next time I'm hanging out with my friends. Soon I see another field growing in the distance. And another center-pivot. This one's at rest. "Don't the crops get crushed by those wheels?" I ask Dale, confident now he's an expert.

"Some do, but there are tracks, or furrows, the wheels move through," he explains. He goes on for several more minutes, throwing out some more lingo like *gooseneck pipes*, and *emitter flow rates* and *linear move systems*.

"How do you know all this?" I ask.

"I've done some investing in corn futures," he answers. "I always like to know as much as I can about something whenever I get involved in it."

This makes me think of my dad. He always likes to joke that Dale takes two hours to buy a pack of gum, or as Dale might say, "get involved in it." I've never quite gotten the joke before, but now I understand what my dad means. Or, you might say, I understand as much as we kids are *capable* of understanding adults. And maybe it's not that I didn't understand my grandfather's quirky habits, but my dad's quirky joking. Or quirkiness in general.

With this conundrum still lodged in my mind, I suddenly feel my dad's eyes on me through the rearview mirror. He quickly smiles ear to ear, which I can only assume is a reflection of his glee that Dale and I are "training." Whether he realizes we're talking about commodities and derivatives and the Chicago Merc and return on investment is highly questionable. Not that I really understand much of it. I do, however, grasp the concept of corn yields in bushels per acre. I wonder how he'll react when I tell him I might one day become a farmer instead of a CEO.

"Are all those hale bales supposed to be a certain size?" I ask Dale, returning the conversation to our classroom along the interstate. I point to a field littered with hundreds of giant round hay bales. We'd seen many like them in Virginia and Mississippi, but they've definitely multiplied as we've headed west, like a case of spreading poison ivy.

"Hmmm, I'm not sure about there being a standard size," Dale responds. "I'll have to do some research on that one."

"Why da heck do they leave them out dehhh?" Frizzy chimes in, negating my assumption that she's been glued to the TV. And wow, I think, she's really trying hard now to return her voice to its native Long Island twang. It was after she burglarized that house in Virginia and we fled like a bunch of convicts that I noticed her dropping the Southern drawl like a bad habit. Now she's gone hell-bent the other way. I'm hoping it eventually settles down somewhere in the middle.

"They're big and heavy, Frizzy," Dale says, "so they just leave them in the fields until they need them."

"For hay few-chizz?" she asks, quickly prompting me to pounce on her questions as an intrusion into my stimulating discussion with Dale.

"Why don't you just watch TV, dork," I growl. She sneers at me and sticks her tongue out.

Dale just laughs. The thin bandage on his nose wrinkles when he does. "Good question," he says, "but no, not for hay futures. To feed cattle."

"Can't somebody steal them out dehhh?" she asks.

Oh God, what a one-track mind. "You're stupid," I say, stupidly.

She sticks her tongue out at me again, across Dale's bandaged nose, as he says, "No, she's not stupid. That's another good question, Frizzy." I slink in my seat. Brat. "Unfortunately," he continues, "sometimes they do get stolen during droughts when there's a shortage of hay. Cattle still need to be fed. Some people get desperate. It's amazing what lengths people will go to sometimes."

That's for sure, I say to myself. I instinctively glance toward the guy in front again. There he is in the mirror, still smiling. I turn and watch the bales and pterodactyls slide by, content in my newly chastened state of ignorance to just chill for a bit.

The sun's slipping in the sky and we pass a sign that says two hundred and twenty miles to Burlington, Colorado. And my dad thought South Carolina was huge. I'm waiting for some kind of outburst from him, but he's mum. Like he's in some kind of zone. The car hums with a silent collision of blunt noises: the wind rattling past the windows, the cackling of the TV, Dale's snoring, The Snatcher humming a song that's off-key against the faint music piped from the car speakers. My dad reaches down and cranks up the volume, I assume to drown her out. And that's when I consider putting my own headphones on, but my eyes are heavy and I feel them clicking closed.

I awake to the sound of "Silent Night." Why she has that as her ringtone on her cell phone in the middle of the summer, I don't understand. Nor will I ever, because I frankly care to plumb her depths as little as possible. "Hi," she whispers into the phone, turning and ducking her head into the side of the door. I wonder if she's chewing on the lock. "Listen, can I call you back in a little while? We'll be stopping for the night soon." Shady.

As soon as she hangs up and turns back from chewing on the lock, my own cell phone goes off and I wonder if it's the same mysterious person that called her. But it's not. No "Silent Night" either. Mine's just a hum. I've cranked up the intensity on it because I'm *really* beginning to like how it feels in my lap. I just wish it wasn't my mother who was so often creating this nice sensation. This is the fifth time she's called since we left Memphis. That's when I last spoke to her, only to make Dale feel better. He seemed a little shaken when he saw me send one of her calls directly to voice mail somewhere on the road from Florida. It was as if I were planning to poison her wine or something.

"Hi, Mom," I say as cheerily as possible, even though Dale's still snoring. I think sometimes old people can hear in their sleep, just not so much when they're awake. I see my dad glance starkly in the rearview mirror, so

I make my own surreptitious turn toward the door and begin chewing on the lock.

"Where are you, honey?" she asks, and I notice her speech is slightly slurry. Maybe someone else has poisoned her wine.

"Kansas. We should be in Colorado tomorrow...that's what Dad says." I flabbergast myself with my candor. I glance at Dale: still snoring. The hale bales drift by in the distance like tawny Munchkins along the Yellow Brick Road. The music grows louder from the car speakers. A new song is on. I know just what it is. Uh-oh, I think, as my mother babbles in my ear something about catching a cold on the trip out from New York last week. Even though her voice is closest to my ear, it's my dad's I hear more clearly. He puts this song on from Dire Straits to psyche himself up any time he knows he has to see Uriah. That's what I call Hubert. Hubert Heap III. My mom calls him Trip, as do all his friends, which I can't attest to because I can't picture the weasel having any friends.

Here it comes. The part of the song my dad loves, something about a little faggot being a millionaire. My stomach does a pivot. My mom sneezes into the phone. Dale snores. Frizzy cuts one.

"Tell your father I heard that!" my mom orders in one of those wobbly voices between sneezes. After a few seconds she comes back and says, "Did you tell him?"

"Yes," I lie. "While you were sneezing."

"Well, tell him to turn down that song. It's rude and immature."

Coming from an expert. "Maybe I should just go, Mom." And I hang up before she can sneeze again.

We stop somewhere for the night. I don't know where. The Emerald City, maybe. The next morning, my dad wakes us before the sun's fully up. This is a rarity. He's got his act together early. "We'll be in Denver tonight, kiddos," he announces excitedly. I'm wondering if he's still deluding himself into thinking that once he gets there, we'll be turning north straight on toward Mount Rushmore.

Nobody warned me things wouldn't change much once we got into Colorado. I begin to really believe we're on the road to nowhere and that the road there is eternally flat. And for the first time I'm feeling deeply homesick. I get this sort of jiggling sensation pulsing through my veins, not like the nausea I'm completely accustomed to, but something entirely different, beyond description. I'm glad to be sitting or I'm afraid I'd fall over. Thankfully, I eventually notice the car going up and down a bit more, which I hope is a sign of some kind of change ahead. Far out in the distance on a brown hill, I watch the silhouette of a machine dipping toward the earth like a giant version of those birds I saw in Florida, pecking their pointy beaks into the muck for food. It's an oil pump, that I know. We've seen several of them along the way. Not as many as we've seen pivot systems. But enough. They're called pumpjacks actually. Dale's already educated me on them. It was somewhere back in Kansas, which feels like weeks ago. It was a conversation that meandered from the engineering minutia of an oil rig to the war in Iraq to the crash of some ship called the Valdez up in Alaska way before I was born. Then he started talking about the Toyota Prius. Jessica's mom drives one. Although, I guess not so much from her hospital bed. Dale was rambling on about how the car works and that's where he lost me.

But now as I see this pumpjack up on the hill, the conversation comes back to me, and I recall his saying how most people think the Prius is some new thing. But it's not. The Japanese first developed it in 1997. Which is the year I was born. Back at North Shore Hospital. A long, long, long way back.

I feel myself beginning to cry a bit and turn my head so no one notices. The door lock looks appetizing. That's when the car rounds a sloping curve in the road, and I spot in the distance a darkish hue that I think might be enormous storm clouds. Like those ugly things in Florida.

They seem to be growing as we drive on, and I'm ready for my dad to curse them, but instead he yelps, "The Rockies, kiddos!" My eyes quickly dry as I fix them on the mesmerizing panorama ahead. For several hours we seem in a race against the sun: Which will get to the mountains first? We lose, but not before an incandescent splash of colors paints the sky orange and red and pink, with some wispy cirrus clouds fading from white to silver. The mountains soon too disappear to nothing as the dark night explodes with stars that sit so low in the sky, I reach my hand out the window against the rush of air and try to grab them. Before long, the stars fade from the glow of big city lights winking in all directions. The air in Denver is mild and summery, not like the image I have from that game I watched on TV once, where the Broncos played in a blizzard so thick, you couldn't read the numbers on the field.

Just as thick possibly is the fog the next morning that obscures the world around us. As we all settle back into the car for the next defining leg of our trip, my dad stands by the open driver's side door and stares out into the opaqueness. I think of my math teacher, Mrs. Dagher. When we were starting a new lesson last year, she liked to say, "Now, this might seem a little opaque at first, but you'll eventually pick it up OK." My dad sucks in some gulps of the warm, misty air in a nervous gesture that makes me think he's preparing for the biggest lesson of his life. Or maybe he's just dreaming of playing against the Broncos at Mile High and thinking of a good game plan. Either way, I hope he eventually picks it up OK.

We drive for about an hour, sipping warm coffee from Starbucks. I slurp mine really loud to see if anyone notices, but they're all too busy slurping their own. I'm bored. Until the fog breaks. Or we rise above it. Not sure which. The blue sky bursts overhead and wraps its warm arms around dark peaks that jut upward in every direction. I stare out the window in awe, my neck growing stiff from craning it to trace the rocky slopes, twisting higher in strata of squares and rectangles and trapezoids. I begin to think maybe God made these mountains after he realized what a stupid mistake he made in all the flat places. The sun is out there, but I can't see it, its presence known only by the sharp shadows dancing on the granite faces. As we descend deeper into darker chasms, we sometimes lose the sky altogether, but I trust its return. Not like in New York City, where the cold steel skyscrapers box you in and stir fear that you might never again feel the sun on your face, just the whip of the weary wind buffeting you from all directions and shuddering with the faint cry of urban chaos.

There is no chaos in these mountains, only majestic order, from what I see. But I long to hear it too. The voice of the sublime. I tug at the window control, to no avail. I'm hot as hell as it is, having already peeled off my sweatshirt after noticing the heat oozing out of the car's air vents several miles back. I ask my dad to undo the locks so I can open my window. "Only a crack there, kiddo," he says. "Ashley's a little cold."

And we should care about that…because? The window goes down the whole way and the clean, chilly air rushes in. I feel the heater crank up overhead, so I reach and flip the vent closed. The road gradually plaits into a winding pattern, an observation hard to miss when my dad insists on shouting "Whoa!" every time he takes a curve, like he's saddled up on a rodeo horse or something. I can't help it, but each time we swing to the right I fall towards Dale, who subtly nudges me back into place without removing his eyes from the book he's reading. Which, by the way, I do my best to ignore, because the mere glance in his direction is enough to turn my stomach. The last time I tried to read on a winding road like this was back in Virginia, and it nearly made me barf. I haven't been much into reading at all lately, in fact, which I can't attribute to much except for a general malaise like you feel when you are recovering from the flu.

After stopping for lunch, we're back on the road, and my dad's driving even slower. I think it might be because of the increasing number of curves, but then I think maybe he just doesn't want to get where we're going. He doesn't even seem fazed by the other cars taking the turns at twice the speed he's driving. I'm just thankful it's not snowing, as it would probably take us three days to get to a place I was told we'd be at by mid-afternoon. Which it is clearly approaching, as I watch the shadows shift direction and become shorter and steeper along the rising cliffs. I also notice a river following our route. Its dark waters look cold and clean, and I crave a sip, the kind where you cup your hands and let the water dribble through the cracks in your fingers. I've never done it, but I've seen it on TV. "That's the Colorado," Dale says, his words surprising me a bit, as I had not realized he'd taken a break from his book to join my stare out the window, now only open halfway after repeated requests from my dad in his annoying concern for The Snatcher. "That's the same river that flows through the mighty Grand Canyon hundreds of miles from here," Dale continues. "We'll have to go there someday. You'd love it."

Right. Someday. The sun shifts so I can now see my reflection in the half-window. Or half my reflection, that is. From my nose down. My jaw is suspended like some eerie-looking head that's had its top half chomped off by a shark. Or an alligator.

My dad rounds a sweeping curve and slows to the point of stopping. The wind rushing in the window dies suddenly and the gurgle of the river floats up from below. Across the bank I spot a man fishing. In the brief moment my dad decelerates, the whole world seems to slow, as if it's passing by in a dream that really only lasts two seconds in your sleep but seems to go on for days. The man reaches back with his long rod and then in a fluid motion, he flicks his line forward. It loops and curls through the sky, arching, then dancing, suspending in the air for so long, I think it has stopped there, as if the man and his rod have been frozen in time on the edge of these cold mountain waters. Then, the line unfreezes and descends to the water as our car accelerates into the next straightaway.

"That's fly fishing," Dale says. "Ever been?"

"Never."

"Someday I'll teach you."

Someday, I remind myself.

"You know, I used to be pretty darn good at it years ago," Dale says without bravado. "I'd go up to Canada every autumn with some buddies. When I move to Sedona, I'll have you come out and I'll teach you. Or maybe I'll just move to Montana."

Someday. We head through a tunnel, and I try to pinch my ears for what's coming. "Yippee!" from The Snatcher. She's done it every time we've passed through a tunnel on this road, the first being the long one called the Eisenhower Tunnel. Bet she doesn't even know who he is. Retard.

"*A River Runs Through It*," Dale mumbles, and I wonder if he's talking to me or to himself.

"*A River Runs Through It*," he says again, this time louder as he turns to me. "By Norman Maclean. Ever read it?"

"No," I say.

"Best last line of a book ever," he declares.

OK. He turns away, and I begin to reach for my cell phone for want of something to do. That's when he says it. The last line...about how all things merge into one. I consider correcting him that, technically, that's not the last line (fine, I did read the book!); but I hold my tongue because, well, Dale's not my dad.

Instead, I watch him return to his reading, let a few seconds slip by, and then say, "Isn't that kinda like, *Everything That Rises Must Converge?*"

He slides his eyes away from his book and toward me without lifting his head and says, "Why, you devil. Flannery O'Connor, right?"

I nod my head with a subtlety that betrays a union of pride and self-consciousness.

"Technically, that's not the last line from a book, though…or any line. I don't think. That's just the title of one of her stories, right?"

Right, but who died and made you boss of this game?

"And I don't think she made that up, you know," Dale continues pensively. "I think she borrowed it…from some French priest, I think."

This reminds me of Father Kevin in my church, who likes to begin Mass by saying, "Bonjour, everyone," with a radiant smile on his face. Although, it's his frown that will always stick with me from that day I set off the fire alarm right before he was about to begin his homily.

My gaze wanders out the window again, and I assume Dale and I are done with the best-last-line-from-a-book game.

But then he says, "Mine's still better anyway." He follows this jibe with a soft elbow that I believe he intends for my ribs, but he's so tall, it catches my shoulder. I smile ingratiatingly as a way to signal that *now* we're done with this game.

But he presses on: "Of course Dawkins disagrees with me. About Maclean's being the best last line from a book, bar none. But he hasn't been able to refute it with any of his own. He comes up with a new one every time. But none of them have legs, if you ask me."

I wasn't asking. He decides to open his book again, which gives me hope, but then just as quickly he slams it shut and declares, "Yes, mine's definitely the best."

Now he sounds like some of my petty friends back home. Who I miss, by the way. Thus reminding me that I haven't been doing much smiling the past few days, as Dawkins had ordered me to do. And so I ask Dale, "Why are we doing this?"

"Doing what?"

"Going to see my mother?"

"When's the last time you saw her?"

"I asked you first."

"OK, then. Because you're angry." As he speaks, he leans in and lowers his voice to a whisper. I can smell the mustard on his breath from the sub he ate at lunch. My dad glances at us in the rearview mirror and stealthily turns down the radio so he can eavesdrop. Dale's not dumb, so he leans over and opens my window all the way to let the air whoosh in loudly as a distraction. He pushes his lanky torso against me as if he's thinking of shoving me out the door. Then he whispers, "You can't go through the rest of your life like that."

"Who says?"

"About what? The first thing or the second?"

"Ummm, the first, I think."

"Your being angry? I says it. I know you were supposed to see your mom the weekend before you left, and I know you cancelled. And I know you weren't sick."

"How do you know? You were all the way down in Florida." He doesn't answer my question, but releases his pressure against my body, dragging his mustard smell with him and returning to an upright position, his head scraping the roof. Several moments of silence pass in which I'm praying the conversation has ended. I search along the river for another fly fisherman, hoping we can discuss comparisons between religion and fly fishing. But no go. Dale leans in again, the mustard breath whipping by me and out into the canyon rushing past as my dad picks up the pace along a rare straight-away. I notice a little curl along the edge of Dale's nose bandage and some fine particles of dirt that have collected there.

"Sometimes in life," he begins in a whisper, "people say or do hurtful things to us. It's easy to take those things personally, like they're some fault of our own. But usually they're not. They're usually more of a reflection upon the person saying or doing the hurtful thing. Typically, those people are only acting out some hurt or anger they hold inside themselves."

OK.

"This is especially true with parents," he continues, undaunted, then pauses and rubs at the curled piece of his bandage to try to get it to stay in place. But it pops back up. "You know...in my long career, I had lots of challenges, lots of stress to deal with. I had to make some important deci-sions. But I got paid pretty decent money to do so. And none of those chal-lenges were anything like what I had to face as a parent. A job for which we don't get paid a red cent, obviously."

Never thought about it.

"Maybe I didn't always make the best decisions...as a parent. I've reminded myself of this a lot lately, as I've tried to figure out why my daughter did what she did to her family. I'm angry at her too, you know." He stops as I stare straight into the back of the tan driver's seat. I swallow and feel like there's a marble coated with sand going down my throat. He seems convinced I'm listening, so he continues, "But I know my anger isn't going to do any good. If anything, it will only make her feel worse about herself than I'm sure she already does. I know the best I can do is show her I still love her despite what she's done. Maybe we all can."

The Snatcher too? I try to laugh at my own cynicism, but it's not working. Not with tears flooding my eyes. I turn my head quickly toward the window and watch the watery shadows shift along the cliffs. I feel a hand on my knee. A big hand, a reassuring hand. I also feel Dale pull his body away and straighten up again. OK, maybe not all the way. As I peek in his direction with my eyes still soggy, I see his shoulders hunched. When Dale is walking, he always seems so upright, with his shoulders thrown stiffly back in a military march. I wonder if it's to compensate for all the hunching he has to do in cars. His head now hovers a few inches below the tan fabric roof of the car, and he begins to fumble with his book. Little wisps of his silver hair begin to rise as if they're being beckoned by the wand of a magician. They hover in the air momentarily, like the line from that man's fly rod. Then the hairs zip past some invisible threshold and rise quickly to cling at the tan fabric above. It's just a few, maybe four or five hairs, and I can't help but compare them to little boners on the top of his head. My shoulders begin to tremble a bit, as I feel a laugh swelling up from my gut like hot lava, the euphoric sensation mixing with the pain of my tears in that most remarkable combination of a half-laugh, half-cry. Dale doesn't even look at me, but just slips one hand inside the pages where his bookmark is and reaches up instinctively with the other hand to pat down the boners.

"Those are big," Frizzy says some time later. We've turned down another road, and I've seen several signs pointing to Aspen. We're getting close. "Are those the biggest mount-inz in the world?" she asks.

I try desperately to refrain from calling her an idiot for fear that she'll be told she's asked a good question again. But Dale just laughs, and I sniff silently for mustard. "Noooo," Dale says. "In other parts of the world there are mountains twice that size. But these are pretty big. Colorado generally has the biggest mountains of all the states, except Alaska, of course. Any mountains above fourteen-thousand feet in the lower forty-eight states are considered pretty big. Colorado has the most of these. They call them the fourteeners.

"Are those faw-teeners?" Frizzy asks, pointing out the window.

Dale says hesitantly, "I don't thhhhhink those are fourteeners, no. But there's a famous one down near Aspen we might see. It's two mountains, actually. They call them the Maroon Bells."

"What's ma-woon?" Frizzy asks.

"It's like reddish-purple," The Snatcher chimes in.

Shut up...I almost say.

"The Maroon Bells are spectacular," Dale adds.

"You've been there before?" I ask.

"Years ago I came to Aspen on a corporate junket."

"What's a junket?" Frizzy asks. I see my dad's eyes shift up to look into the rearview mirror.

"It's an event," Dale says, "where business executives go to junk their marriages." The car falls silent, except for some U2 murmuring on low volume. Frizzy turns to aim her camera out the window and clicks the button. All that comes out is *Puttt-fffff*. It's dying, thank God. Finally, Dale chuckles and we all follow along in the stilted way people do when they pretend to get the joke. "It's really just a fancy business trip," Dale clarifies, "paid for by the company. I hated them actually, but I saw some nice places."

Puttt-fffff.

As we get close to town, my heart begins to race and I try to calm it by searching for mountains that look maroon. Heck, they all do now that the sun has begun to sink and the world's palette is growing richer in the afternoon light. We turn off the main road and then cross a bridge over a small creek before climbing a steep hill that switches back and forth several times before leveling off. Then it climbs again, and I feel my ears pop. "Left here, Doug," Dale directs calmly. I can tell my father is wishing he was lost and contemplating turning right, but that decision would send us down a humungous canyon where you can only see the tops of the pine trees. So he turns left as directed.

"Number eleven, this must be the one," Dale says, consulting a rumpled piece of Holiday Inn paper cupped in his hand. My dad slows the car, but doesn't turn. There's no snake in the driveway, that's for certain. He just stares solemnly out the front window and waits. I feel like we're in church when it's just after communion and you're supposed to be praying, but your mind is racing elsewhere, like to the Giants game later that afternoon.

Then the silence is broken. The Snatcher shouts, "Whoa! This place looks cool." The car eventually edges into the driveway, crawling up a small incline. OK, she's right; it does look pretty cool. The house doesn't appear very big, but it's solid and is sunken into a hill that rises on three sides. The face of the house is made of huge boulders and thick timbers that look like they may have been cut from the forest encircling the property and towering from the slopes above the house.

As we step out onto the brick driveway, I feel the cool air on my face, tempered by a few rays from the descending sun just peeking through some grayish-white trees to the side of the property. "Those are aspen trees," Dale explains, with his uncanny ability to answer my questions without my even asking them. "This is a long way from Florida, huh?" he continues. "Just smell that fresh air perfumed from all the evergreens."

I inhale and close my eyes against the tears that suddenly seem to be seeping out. For a moment, I think it's the anxiety I feel about being here. But as I turn and watch Dale throw his shoulders back in rebellion against the suffocating car ride, I realize it's him. This is his exit. After our visit here, he is due to leave us on a flight back to Florida, now that the hurricane has blown out to sea. Without ten people dying.

My heart aches as I try to figure out whether I'd like to see this visit end as quickly as possible, or stretch on forever so that he never leaves us. Before I have a chance to resolve this dilemma, I realize we've scaled the steep stone steps to the front door. As we all stand there looking awkward, we hear a loud hum inside, as if there might be a jet readying for takeoff. I don't even hear the sound of a doorbell, but I know Dale's pushed it.

After several long agonizing seconds, my mother stands before us. "Hi, there," she says, I think, as I can't really hear her words over the jet engine sound that is now piercing as it bombards us through the open door. She gives Frizzy an awkward hug and then reaches for me. I offer her my left shoulder. Some more words are exchanged, but who knows what they are.

We step inside onto a dark stone floor matching the outside steps, and I gaze up at the lofty ceiling and the wide circular staircase winding up so high, I wonder if there might be clouds up there. Suddenly, the noise stops.

"Oh, thank God, I think they're done," my mother huffs, as she pulls a strand of hair back delicately over her ears. It's different, her hair, but I can't figure out how. Maybe I've just forgotten how it used to look. It's been nearly two months since I've seen her. It would only be one if I hadn't faked that illness. And the last time I did see her wasn't exactly "quality time." She came to my year-end choir concert at school, which was very considerate of her to support the one thing I hate more than anything else in this world.

"Tell me again what all that noise was," Dale says. But before my mother can answer, we all jump back at the scary sight of two figures clomping down the hallway. They look like astronauts, and one of them is pushing a square metal box with a tube coming out the side attached to a nozzle that looks like a vacuum.

"Dust mites," my mother says. "I'm cleaning the room where Frizzy's sleeping. These guys had to come all the way from Boulder. They're the best in the business." One of the guys nods enthusiastically with his helmeted head like Neil Armstrong. "I would have done it sooner," my mother continues, "but I didn't know you were coming, and, well, we just got here last week and it's been crazy ever since, what with Trip's operation and all." She flicks another strand of hair back between her ears. It's shorter, that's it. And a little darker. "This place is due for a good cleanup anyway. We've haven't been here since March," my mother concludes. Yes, getting around to all your houses can be difficult, I think, when you have four of them.

"And I threw out everything that has nuts in it," she continues, as she begins to walk down the hall, and we each obediently follow as her heels make a soldier's clicking on the wood-plank floor. At least she didn't have to throw away the pets. She doesn't have any, that I know. Frizzy acquired her animal allergies from my mother. The rest of the allergies, my dad always jokes, Frizzy got from the mailman. But I've never quite understood that one.

"And I took all the afghan blankets in the den and put them away..." What about the elephant figurines? "...I was afraid they might make her itchy." Or frizzy. My mom reaches for a tissue from a box concealed in a holder that looks like twigs woven together. She wipes her nose. "Sorry, I'm just getting over this cold." The Snatcher recoils and steps back on my toe. Ouch! Loser.

I almost forgot she was there. But it is impossible to forget she is there at dinnertime. She becomes the center of attention. But not before Uriah was. He'd come shuffling in just as we were getting ready to sit down. This was the first time we had seen him since our arrival. He was wearing a shiny red bathrobe with black fur around the neck. He pulled it up higher around his shoulders and coughed. As he did so, he stopped in his tracks, grabbed at his midsection, and winced like he'd been shot. His hair was combed but looked like it had been done so hurriedly, and a few stray pieces stuck up in the back. The blackness of his hair was dull, not shiny, and combed back in a wave like every other time I have been unfortunate to see him. He looked tired and his face had a yellowish tint. Greetings were exchanged. His hand felt cold and limp in mine, no different than usual.

"I'm really sorry about my appearance," he offered, but I didn't recognize any ounce of *sorry* in his voice at all. He coughed again, winced, and then said, "I am still a bit bloated from the surgery, and I can't get my pants on." Oh, that's nice to hear.

"What kind of surgery?" Dale asked.

"Hernia," Uriah said. "Double hernia."

"Like the pastor," my dad—who was off the side—said in a low whisper, as if he were talking to himself, like in a Shakespeare play.

"Come again," Uriah said. Don't you hate when people say that?

My dad does. So instead of coming again, he turned to my mother and said, "Brian's in Memphis. I saw him briefly on our way through."

My mother turned to Uriah and explained: "Doug's best friend from high school is a priest."

"Ah," Uriah said dully. That's when I remembered that he isn't Catholic. He's Lutheran. It's kinda like being Catholic, my mother once explained. That's good for her, because she's always been "kinda like a Catholic too," my dad once joked.

"The operation was tough on Trip," my mother said as we stood around the dining table awkwardly, getting ready to sit. My dad excused himself to go to the bathroom, and I wondered if he had reflux, despite the fact that we hadn't even started eating yet. As he walked away, my mother pressed her hands nervously down her side like she was trying to iron her hips under the black pants she wore. "We wanted it done out here," she continued to no one in particular, "because Trip has a college friend who's a top-notch surgeon. One of the best in the country, actually. He's down in Boulder." Where the dust-mite-killing astronauts are from.

As we settled into our seats, Uriah and my mother took the two ends of the table. I sat between Dale and Frizzy on one side. My dad returned from his reflux and was stuck across from us with The Snatcher, just the two of them like they were abandoned on a deserted island.

A door swung open from the kitchen, and a woman came through carrying drinks. She wore a pink polo shirt and tan pants just like those servers I've seen at Zach's country club. At least she wasn't black, thank God, like those other anachronistic places we've been to on this trip. But she wasn't really white either. She was in between. Hey, a tween! Kinda like me. Sort of.

She set the tray down on a serving table and then began placing the drinks in front of everyone. Water to start. Frizzy's came in a Styrofoam cup with a lid and straw. And then came mine, the same way. I threw up my arms in revulsion to this insult to my budding manhood, but no one noticed. Why my status jumped up a notch for dinner, I'll never know. Frizzy got served macaroni and cheese with garlic breadsticks. And I got what everyone else was served. And was it ever nasty-looking, whatever it was. The brussels sprouts I figured out, but the rest of it baffled me.

Until my mother spoke: "Since this is Trip's first real dinner since the operation, I hope you don't mind that we have his favorite meal. Lamb shanks with stewed pearl onions and brussels sprouts. Bon appetit."

Bless me, Father Kevin, I think I'm going to barf right now. Even The Snatcher is turning up her nose. I guess that means she and I are simpatico. Now don't think I'd really use that word seriously. It's the queerest word I've ever heard. I'm only imitating Uriah from a few moments earlier when he took his first bite and washed it down with a dainty sip of wine and said, "Mmmm, I find this cabernet is so simpatico with lamb shanks." I'm thinking I might shank his lambs under the table. He takes another sip and adds: "I haven't had a drop of wine since before my operation. It's been downright penal."

"You mean penis," Frizzy declares, her lisp miraculously cured.

"Frizzy!" my mother admonishes. This brief outburst somehow reminds Uriah that kids are actually at the table. He doesn't have kids of his own since his marriage to my mother is his first. And he's apparently never been a mailman. It's my impression that the hope of a long, kidless life together is what sealed the deal between the two of them. He looks at my mother and says, "Corrine, what about the…" he finishes his sentence with a gesture in which he cups his hand under his chin.

"Do you think it's really needed?" my mother asks with noticeable embarrassment.

"The rug, Corrine. The rug," Uriah says, nodding down at the floor, which is where rugs usually are. My mother excuses herself from the table and returns in a few moments. In her hand is a piece of scooped plastic like someone cut a lemonade pitcher in half. On each edge is a little rubber protector. My mother hesitantly walks behind Frizzy's chair. We all follow her with our eyes, including Frizzy who turns around frightened as if she's about to be murdered. By her own mother. "Let me just tie this on, Frizzy," my mother implores. "It's to prevent food from falling on the floor. This rug under the table is brand new and very expensive." Let me guess, it's one of the best there is. And you got it in Boulder.

When she's finished, Frizzy sits with the food catcher dangling from her chin. She looks like a hockey goalie that has that neck-guard thing on upside down. I'm about to bust out laughing, but I decide to do nothing. I don't want to draw any more attention to myself than is necessary, as I place a pearl onion in the napkin on my lap and then flick it onto the rug under the table. Score!

"A friend of mine from B-school invented that," Uriah says, gesturing toward my poor sister. "He's got it patented and thinks he can make a bundle."

"That's if he doesn't get picked up first for child abuse," my dad says under his breath, but loud enough for the whole table to hear.

Dale chuckles faintly.

Uriah says, "You mock, but they work."

"Can I try one?" That would be The Snatcher, and now I must say I can die and go to heaven. She puts on the thing, and now she has become The Food Catcher. She takes a bite of bread and a large crumb falls away, hits the food guard and bounces into her wine. So she reaches in with a finger and is attempting to dig it out as it squirms away and sinks deeper into the red sea.

I notice Uriah watching her scornfully. He has this nose where the nostrils point outward like the mouths of caves, instead of down like most people's. He frequently makes this scrunching face, which appears to be an effort to force the nostrils down to a more normal-looking disposition. The Food Catcher has now picked up a fork and is digging deeper into her wine for the crumb, saying, "Come on, you bugger." Uriah does the scrunching thing three quick times in agitated succession and then says to her: "So, I understand you went to Yale."

"Trip went to Yale," my mother squeaks.

"Yes," The Food Catcher says, giving up on her fishing expedition and setting the fork down on the table and staining the white cloth.

"What year did you graduate?" Uriah asks, glaring at the stain.

"O-Four," she says casually, the plastic thing jangling under her chin.

"Oh, to be so young," Uriah says like a dork. "What residential college were you in?"

"Pierson."

"Is *that* right. I was in Davenport. Neighbors. Sort of, if you forget about the fifteen years between us." He laughs without opening his mouth, but just sliding his top lip up so that it sticks to his big white teeth. "What was your major?" he continues with the grilling.

"Well, I was a philos—" But before she can finish, my hand reaches quickly for my water, overshoots it and whacks into Dale's wine glass. It is all so sudden and spontaneous, I don't know how it has happened. Like my arm has a mind of its own. Really, it was an accident!

"Shit!" Uriah squeals as the river of blood flows toward him. He pushes back his chair abruptly so the wine doesn't drip into his lap. This makes him wince in pain. He is half-standing as he reaches for his groin with one hand and for his napkin with the other to dam the flow. But it is too late; the river has edged to the side and drips in a thin stream onto the rug. The tween woman has appeared with a towel and is sopping it up. Uriah orders her to hurry.

I feel badly that I have sacrificed Dale's wine. He begins to lean toward me. When it comes to tall people, you can usually see their lean forming from a mile away. I'm thinking he is going to order me to apologize, which I have yet to do. Instead, he whispers in my ear, "Don't worry, we'll call the best rug cleaner. Down in Boulder."

u r BAD!!! Jessica writes to me later that evening when I describe how I spilled the wine. Although, I couldn't admit to her that, in doing so, I possibly just might have been compassionately diverting attention away

from The Snatcher…Food Catcher, whatever. Maybe I just couldn't bear to
see her become an unsuspecting victim of an attack by that jerk. Anyway,
I do tell Jessica about the food-catching invention itself, which gives her
a good laugh. *that'd be great for science fair,* she says. I'm glad to be making
her happy, because I know she's been very sad, spending a lot of time in the
hospital while her mother nears the end.

I'm up late e-mailing her back and forth, which might explain why I'm
a little bleary-eyed in the morning. It doesn't help to be up so early either,
but I couldn't sleep. This whole visit just has me feeling jittery. I stroll
out of my bedroom and enter a huge room with a high peaked ceiling and
timbers cutting across from one side to the other. There is a fireplace with
a chimney made out of stone and stretching up like a beanstalk for Jack
to climb. Opposite that is a huge window similar to the ones you see at
the front of a store in the mall. I gaze out. It's light but there's no sun yet.
The view stretches out over a valley that looks pink in the morning glow.
Mountains lurch up in the distance. I wonder if any are the Maroon Bells,
but they don't look impressive enough.

After finding some stairs I enter a whole new level of the house below.
This place is ten times bigger inside that it looks from the outside. I pass
through a large room with a pool table and a bunch of arcade games. I walk
by the pinball machine with a Batman theme and pull at the metal thing
that usually shoots the ball up, but all I hear is the thud of nothing. It's a
shame these games are not—and never will be—enjoyed by kids. I'm sure
of it.

Down a hall is a glass door. When I pull on the handle, I realize it's
locked. I cup my hands and peer in. In the darkness illuminated faintly by a
nightlight, I see hundreds of wine bottles lining the high walls. They'd all
look good spilled on that rug. As I pull away, I notice a splotch on the glass
left by my breath. So I etch my initials with the tip of my finger, slowly so
it squeaks on the glass.

The next door is not locked. When I open it, a whoosh of air hits me
like you feel when you go into the gym at school. Immediately I see it's not
a gym, but bigger. The splash of water echoes in my ears. In a pool, a figure
swims right toward me. I immediately recognize Dale, his arms and legs
shooting out like a giant frog as he does the breaststroke with his head out
of the water.

"Hey there, Jame," he says as he stops at the end of the pool and catches his breath. His silver hair is matted to his head and trickles of water meander down his cheeks. I notice right away his bandage is off. And for the first time in more than two years, I see Dale's nose. It's a little black and blue, maroon maybe, but otherwise looks fine. He stands up tall, and the top of the water barely comes above his hips. It's then I notice he's not wearing a bathing suit, and his thingie is flopping around. I avert my gaze quickly, not wanting to go *there* ever again.

"Watcha been doing?" he asks as he wipes his face with the palms of his hands and squints up like he's staring into the sun.

"Just lookin' around."

"This place really has the whole nine yards, doesn't it?"

"I guess so," I say, but I'm not sure that's too good, since it takes ten yards to make a first down.

"This pool's kind of nifty," he continues, "being indoors and all. I can see why. Even this morning, at the end of July, it's a little chilly out there. I just wish I'd brought my goggles from home." And a swimsuit maybe? "But we didn't exactly plan things out this way, did we?"

"No," I say, not really sure if I am supposed to answer. A few seconds tick by, and Dale pushes the water outward with his hands to make ripples.

"Grandpa," I say, then stop, surprised at myself for using that word.

"Yes?"

"Are you really…" I stop, feeling myself choke up, then force out: "Oh, never mind." He gives me a wet smile and says, "Just a few more laps," then turns and swims away.

I feel a pit in my stomach as I step up a flight of stairs, which I don't think are the same ones I came down. I push open another door, wondering what mystery lurks behind this one. It sticks a little when I push, so I push harder. The door's heavy as it opens, and I feel the chilly morning air from outside sting me, and then the sound of singing birds.

And then: "Hey there, kiddo!" Great, it's her. Immediately I begin to regret that I saved her from attack last night. "I'm doing some yoga," she says. Great. "This is the sphinx pose." Great, again. Unlike Dale, she has quite the knack for answering questions I never even considered asking. This irks me. But then I get to thinking: Hmmm, Sphinx? Now, that would be an appropriate name for her. Then I get to thinking some more: Sphinx kind of sounds like another word, doesn't it?

"It'll stretch me out for our hike later," The Sphincter says.

"*You're* going?" This question I definitely ask.

"Of course." Oh, this should be interesting.

Before you know it, we're on the mountain at one of the ski places nearby. We board a chairlift, which is a little scary at first. It's my first time on one of these things. I immediately think of Jessica, who skis all the time with her family in Vermont. I snap a picture of myself on my phone—one of those self-portraits where your head's cut off and your nose looks too big. I'd ask my dad to do it, but he looks spaced out as he stares off at the gray peaks around us, some of them still with speckles of snow at the top. I e-mail the picture and then lean over the bar in front of us and try to guess how far below us looms the steep slope littered with huge rocks among the long brownish-green grass that looks a little like the dunes at the beach. I turn around to awe myself with the vast world growing smaller behind us, hoping to maybe see some fourteeners. Unfortunately, all I catch sight of is The Sphincter. She's in the next chair alone talking on her cell phone. I'm just thankful I'm not in the chair ahead of us. The one with my mother, and Frizzy next to her, and poor Dale on the far end.

At the top, we gather near a bench while my mother unfolds a map that has no intention of cooperating in the wind. "I think we go this way for the easier trail," she says.

"You've never done this?" my dad asks bitterly.

"Well, no, this is only the second time I've been out here in the summer," she says. "And Trip's not much of an outdoorsy kind of person anyway."

"And yet, he's the one who suggested this," my dad says sarcastically.

"Well, he thought it would be a good idea to get everyone out of the way," my mother says, ending with that stark look adults get when they realize they've just said something they shouldn't have. So we send her to the rear. And leave her in the dust. And don't wait much for her. I do hear a couple of shrieks from her when we get to a part of the trail heavy with vegetation and then crossed by a stream. About an hour later at the bottom, she finally catches up about ten minutes behind us, her tennis shoes sloshing as she walks.

"Let's do that again!" The Sphincter coos. My mother shakes her head likes she's completely chafed, which is enough to make the rest of us shrug our shoulders in the silent code for: "What the hell, let's go for it."

Unfortunately, the second time doesn't go as well as the first. Frizzy is dragging a bit on a steep narrow trail, and somehow I'm stuck behind her. "Move it," I keep urging her on, but this only seems to slow her down.

Things are fine as we go up a little hill, but then we have to go down the other side, and I'm staring off to the side still trying to find a four-teener. Thus, what I fail to see is Frizzy stop to take a picture. *Puttt-fffff* is the last thing I hear before I bump her hard from behind. OK, I can't deny that I might have bumped her impulsively. Sometimes I can't help it, the impulses. Quickly I have visions of my dad in Publix. Fortunately, there is no stack of wine nearby, but there is a steep hill off to our right. "Jayyyy-aaaa-meeee!" she shouts, with a touch of her southern lilt returning and echoing around the valley as she tumbles down and finally comes to a stop with her camera next to her. Ouch.

The good thing about going to the hospital in Aspen is it's not like going to the hospital at all. Not like that time I had to get stitches on my chin when my dad was teaching me how to ride my bike without training wheels on the ice the afternoon of the Super Bowl. To this day I know I wouldn't have fallen if he hadn't slipped and tripped over my pedal first. He got stitches too. On his knee. Waiting in that hospital and watching the game on a crappy TV was gloomy, especially when that one guy came in with his clothes all dirty and ripped and his face bloody. He kept yelling crazy things at people in the waiting room like, "I am Jesus. You are healed! Go home!"

The only people doing the healing in the Aspen hospital are doctors. At least I think they are doctors. The one treating Frizzy is dressed more like a person who could have been hiking on the mountain with us. But she does have a stethoscope around her neck, so that's good. Her sweet flowery smell arrives before she does as she moves toward Frizzy sitting on the end of a metal-framed bed. We've all been allowed to sit with her while she's been waiting to be treated, and I've been offered a vitamin water and SunChips. It's me and my dad and my mother, who's very agitated. Dale has been taken to another room after he dropped a hint to a nice man behind a desk that he wouldn't mind having his nose checked out while he was waiting. My mother rudely told The Sphincter to stay outside.

"What happened to you, darling?" the doctor asks in a raspy, but caring, voice.

"I fell hiking."

"Ouch!" the doctor says. Her voice sounds so tender, I can't help but tear my attention away from digging at the last crumbs in my chip bag and staring at her. She has on a pale blue, long-sleeved North Face shirt that is very tight around her chest, which any fool can notice is quite ample. "Tell me what happened," she continues.

"Well, I was walking awong this path and I fell down a hill, because…" she stops and glances at my dad, then says, "my brother was driving up my ass."

"Frizzy!" my mom cries, then glowers at my dad.

The doctor laughs as she continues to feel around my sister's shoulder. After a few minutes, she says, "It's just a little sprain. You'll have to keep it in a sling for a few days. It may hurt for a while and it may turn a funny color. Sort of purplish-blue."

"Like ma-woon?" Frizzy asks.

"Yeah, like maroon," the doctor says with a smile. She turns and walks away leaving her sweet smell behind. My dad and I watch her go, mournfully.

Shattering the bliss, my mother says angrily to my dad: "This never would have happened if it wasn't for that girl wanting to go up again." My dad turns back to her halfway and responds silently with an evil smirk.

"I don't know how in the world she's going to sleep," my mother continues.

"Relax," my dad says, his gaze still off in the direction of the doctor with the big boobs, as she suddenly reappears to pick up her chart from the side of the bed, smiles at us and then leaves again. "It's not your problem… never is," my dad says. "We're leaving tomorrow anyway."

My mother continues to say something else, something about wondering when our odyssey is ever going to end. My dad pretends not to hear her in favor of the more pleasant experience of watching the woman doctor standing a little ways down the hall talking to a man doctor dressed like one in those mint-green surgical get-ups. My mother huffs and puffs, turns and then barges out the door.

Dale emerges from around the corner, rubbing gently at his naked nose. "Where's Corrine?" he asks.

"She left," Frizzy says.

"Why?"

"She was ang-wy."

"Why?" Dale asks again.

"I think," Frizzy starts then pauses. She briefly looks up at the ceiling for inspiration, then says, "because Daddy is obsessed wiff my doctor's fourteeners."

12

❖ ❖ ❖

COURT JESTER

Surreal. That's the word he was thinking of. The Kid uses it a lot. He'd
been trying to come up with it for an hour, ever since he'd awakened before
dawn with a case of the runs. It must have been the clams in the pasta sauce
at that little Italian place they went to for dinner. Without Corrine and the
weasel, thank God. *Uriah*, Jamie calls him, from that book. Doug chuckled
and took a sip of the flat club soda he'd dug out of the fridge. It had probably had been there since March. He gazed out a window and saw a huge
deer-looking animal munching on some flowers on the hill in back.

Surreal, for sure. That's what this visit had been. He was still kicking
himself for letting Dale talk him into it. So a mother could see her kids.
The ones she decided she didn't want. "This is just not for me," she had the
nerve to say that horrid night two years ago when she confessed to the affair
and her desire for another life. Like returning a new shirt you've decided
you don't want after you get it home and try it on in front of your *own* mirror. Without some pushy queer telling you how good it looks.

He'd wedged Corrine out of his mind over the past year, but spending
two nights in this house, this mansion on a hill, made the anger seep up,
like that damn cesspool that keeps overflowing in the front yard back on
Long Island. She had tried desperately that night so long ago to itemize all
the things he'd done wrong to drive her away. But he knew the only thing
he'd done wrong was believe in someone who was not what she originally
made herself out to be. He glanced at his watch: six-thirty. He'd wake the
kids at seven and be on the road. He dumped the rest of the flat soda into
the sink and then yanked at a handle to put the glass in the dishwasher.
But it opened instead to a huge bin—two bins actually—one for trash, one

for recycling. He thought for a moment about dropping it in the trash, but couldn't penalize the world just because of his hatred for her. So he dropped it in the recycling. It clinked loudly against the empty pearl onion jar.

"We actually like to save our glasses for future reuse." The sarcastic voice came from a few feet behind. He turned abruptly and stared at Corrine. She was dressed for the day in a pair of jeans with little swirly sparkling designs on them and a peach-colored silk blouse. She never used to dress this early. She liked to hang around ugly in her bathrobe until eight. She even had makeup on now. All in an effort to present a new image, perhaps. It wasn't working. Doug thought she looked terrible. Puffy under the eyes. Beefy in the hips. Even the new haircut was lame. It made her look like that famous Dorothy skater when he was a kid. He supposed in one respect he should feel fortunate that she had someone to remarry right after their divorce. Not like a lot of women who get divorced and, in an effort to enhance their new prospects as a swinging single, they go out and lose weight and get new boobs and really stylish haircuts. They look better nearing forty than they did at twenty. But not Corrine. Thank God for the weasel. Then again, if it weren't for him, maybe she never would have discovered that she wanted to return the shirt in the first place.

"You're up early," she said.

"Yeah, well, it's the new me," he said. "I'm thinking of getting a penis enlargement too. And a new haircut."

"You don't always have to rub it in, how much you hate my guts."

"But what if you forget?"

"Oh, I'm sure Jamie will be there to remind me." Her voice trailed off as she moved to the far side of the kitchen and began fiddling with the coffeemaker. "Are you going to want any?"

"Sure." He considered taking the opportunity to dart from the room as she poured in the water, but for some reason he felt his feet glued to the wood floor.

"So what's with this girl, Doug?" she said, as she moved in closer. He could tell she was trying to sound amicable, but her verbal skills always seemed to fail her in the way her words came out with the wrong tone. Like people who botch songs.

"Girl?" he asked, playing dumb.

"This little consultant." She made those goofy fake quotation marks in front of her face with her fingers when she said *consultant*.

"I already explained it all to you."

"Are you sleeping with her?"

"What? You're nuts! I'm not like you, thank you very much. And I never even met the woman until the day we left on the trip."

"How much is she costing?"

"That's none of your goddamn business." He had the urge to end things there. To just turn and storm out of the kitchen. But something compelled him to keep going. Maybe he felt he had the upper hand, like a team that confidently goes for it on fourth and two in their own end. "Look, you chose to opt out of our family. Like I've told you before, how I run it now is my business."

"But they're still my kids, and I'm just a little concerned, is all," she said, not looking at him, but staring out the window. "Damn, that elk's eating our flowers again," she muttered. "The poison's not working." Then she turned back to him and said, "I mean, this crazy trip you're on can't be cheap. And I take it you're not selling too many houses while you're gone."

"Yeah, well, I'm not going back to that crap anyway," he said, waving his hand boastfully as if he had something better up his sleeve.

"Oh, that's encouraging to know," she said cynically. She reached up into a cabinet and took down two coffee mugs. "Doug..." she paused and then shook something out of one of the mugs, like a dead bug, but nothing seemed to drop out. "...if you need some financial assistance, I have told you time and again I am willing to help."

He glowered at her and shook his head. "Never. I will never take a stinkin' dime from you. And I will never need to." Again, he considered walking out, but stopped and said weakly, "So just go to hell." This, he knew, was not a good way to finish things off. A woman could never let those stand as the final words. So he held his ground and waited for her to make the next move.

It was several moments. The coffeepot gurgled violently like it does when it's nearly done brewing. "That boy adores you," she said finally, again staring out the window with a blank look on her face. The elk must have run off. Or died.

"And? So?" he said, holding his palms up to underscore that he'd missed her point.

"That's where he's gifted," she said. "Not like all this other crap you always blabber on about. Being a genius."

"He is," Doug cut in. "All the testing says so."

"Testing" she said. "So he reads a lot. Pfff." As she made this noise, she quaked her body in an exaggerated fashion, like she'd just taken too big a bite of ice cream on a hot day. She poured a cup of coffee and handed it to him. He took it reluctantly. It was the cup she had shaken out earlier. He looked at it, wondering if he'd see the uncooperative dead bug floating on top.

"I suppose it's part of the reason why I've not made an issue of your keeping the kids," she continued. "I know I don't deserve them, but I'd simply be too scared to take that boy from you. He loves you too much. Despite all your flaws."

"*My* flaws!" He took a deep breath, but never had time to discharge his lode of accusations.

She cut him off, not to be derailed, and said, "I mean, let's face it, it's the one gift all kids are universally born with—an instinctive love for their parents. Not all parents want their kids right from the start, but all kids want their parents. Right?" He didn't answer. She took a sip of her coffee, the annoying, slurpy kind of sip you use when it's still too hot to drink. He looked again at his cup and just placed it on the counter, rebuffing the dead bug.

"His love definitely goes deeper." She paused, and as if to emphasize the validity of her theory, said, "*Definitely* deeper. I don't know why. Maybe it *does* have something to do with all that crap you're always boasting about. Maybe he can see things other kids can't. Or maybe it is all that reading he does. Books sometimes do put romantic notions into your head, don't they?" Again, no answer. He put his hands in his jeans pockets to affirm his pledge of silence to her onslaught of rhetorical questions. "But that doesn't mean his adoration can't be broken, Doug." As she spoke, she looked him straight in the eye and then paused, turned wistfully out the window one last time, and said, "Don't break the gift…not the way lots of us other parents somehow find a way to."

Who was she to give him advice? The one who wimped out on being a parent. Like these washed-up football players on TV who never made it on the field, but all of a sudden are critical experts up in the booth. His chagrin hadn't faded one bit when they finally loaded into the car an hour later. He made the last winding turn down from the mansion on the hill and headed for the road back to the interstate.

"Ahhhh, it's a left turn here, Doug," said the voice in the passenger seat diplomatically. Doug quickly jerked the steering wheel to correct his mistake, and said, "Thanks, Dale. I'm a little turned around this morning, I guess."

Dale gave him a knowing wink. Doug couldn't imagine how uncomfortable the guy must be riding in cars. But he insisted on coming. He canceled his flight out of Denver at the last minute and said he'd fly back from San Francisco. *Sure*, Doug thought. *Next thing you know, he'll be hitching a ride east and wanting us to drive him all the way back to Florida.* He wasn't sure exactly why the old man wanted to keep tagging along on the trip, always finding excuses to keep going. Maybe he just liked looking at Ashley. Men can get perverted as they age. Boredom does that. Or maybe Dale just couldn't take one more night in his daughter's house. Now that's understandable!

This thought drew Doug's anger back to Corrine. Spending time at that house was *definitely* a mistake. Or maybe it wasn't. Maybe it was just what he needed to inflame his passion some more. He'd show her. When Jamie's rich and successful and hopefully famous, he'd take all the credit. *Don't break the gift.* What the hell did that mean anyway? She has no idea what the hell she's talking about.

Fuck her, he mumbled to himself. There, he said it. He'd been thinking it ever since he fled from the kitchen earlier that morning with his heart pounding madly. He couldn't help saying it, as much as he hated using that word deliberately. He vowed when he was younger to stay away from it. Not after the way he hated his dad for using it when he'd come home drunk. "Where the fuck's this! Where the fuck's that!" It's hard to find things when you're drunk, and then you blame other fuckin' people for it. Like his mother. She'd greet his tirades with rapid-fire, panicked Hail Marys, like people must do when they're on a plane that's about to crash.

Like Flight 93. Or those people in the Towers. The faces of those he knew flashed by him: Matt from high school. Tony from down the street. The list goes on. September 11. It was supposed to change everything, but people are nastier to each now more than ever before. Aren't they?

"Why are you getting off here?" Dale asked, as Doug slowed the car on the interstate at an exit that wound down into a canyon with towering vermillion rock walls on each side.

"Shortcut," Doug said.

"Are you sure?" Dale asked. Doug just shrugged his shoulders in the face of doubt. Truth was, he didn't know if it'd be a shortcut at all. It sure looked that way on the map, instead of going all the way back through Denver again. Too close to Boulder.

"Well, I'm sure we'll be fine," Dale said after a few moments, as if he'd reconsidered his doubts. Doug nodded to show his gratitude for the old man's support and then accelerated out of the canyon up a winding, steep incline. He felt like he had the pedal to the metal and they were only going twenty. The road fell off on each side into oblivion. What if they broke down or got a flat? Nowhere to pull over. At least Dale would be there. He's smart. Doug couldn't deny that he felt a lot more secure having the guy along. And at least he didn't smell stale like most old people.

He peered in his mirror at the backseat. Ashley sat between the kids. If anything was buoying his mood, it was her request before they left to sit in back and go over some of the materials for the ELEGY program with The Kid, who hated the idea. But he'd live. She was flipping through them now to familiarize herself. Doug knew he'd made the right call bringing her along.

"Oooh," she said sensually, as Doug looked curiously in the rearview mirror and watched her eyebrows arching as if she were looking at smut. "Says here you're going to work on your leadership, teamwork, and critical thinking skills. That's good. Real good."

Was he even listening? "Jamie!" Doug yelled. "Jamie!" he yelled again louder.

"Yes?" he said, pulling one side of his headphones out.

"Ashley's talking to you."

"Oh." He turned to look at her, but she seemed in her own world, continuing to flip through the booklet like she was enjoying every moment without his help. So he put his headphones back in and returned his gaze out the window.

"Twenty-five hundred bucks?" she shrieked several minutes later. "You're *paying* to send him to this thing?"

Doug jumped. He flashed his eyes in the rearview mirror, then jerked the wheel of the car over the center line. Thank God no one was coming. Or that he didn't jerk it the other way into the canyon. His heart fluttered as he peered over the guardrail into nothingness. Then he looked again in the mirror and saw Jamie had his headphones back on. What a relief. Dale too didn't seem to hear. He was resting, but Doug didn't notice the old guy peek at him amusingly with one eye before snapping it shut like a sleeping dog in the corner.

"Ahh...that's none of your business," he finally said to Ashley irritably. "And it's beside the point. You have to be gifted to get asked to go in the first place. Just focus on going over the materials with The Kid, would ya."

So she elbowed Jamie in the guts. "Hey, Kid," she said. He jumped, then yanked off his headphones.

"What's the big idea?" he scowled.

"Says here," she pointed at the booklet, "you're going to learn how to design rockets."

"Oh, that sounds nifty," Dale said, suddenly perking up and turning his head. "I used to build rockets when I was a boy growing up in Massachusetts."

"Where in Massachusetts?" she asked.

"Springfield area."

"Get out! Me too!"

"Longmeadow, actually," Dale said. "Lived there until we moved in eighth grade."

"Get out! Me too! What street?"

"Tennyson Drive."

"Nooooo waaaaay!"

"Way."

"I lived on Longfellow. Did you go to Center Elementary?"

"You betcha," he said.

"Ooooh myyyyy God, what a small world!"

Dale shifted his whole body around in his seat to directly face Ashley. Doug wondered if the old man was getting a woody. Just as Dale was about to say something else, he was cut short.

"Enough already!" Doug screamed at the top of his lungs. Jamie jerked his headphones out, and Frizzy ripped her gaze away from the TV.

"What's wrong, Dad?" Jamie asked. Doug just shook his head. "I feel like I got a car full of little kids," he muttered to himself. Ashley snickered in the back.

They passed a sign for the next town, a small one just on the edge of a national forest. *Should be a beautiful ride ahead,* he thought. He rubbed his brow with his right hand as he steered with his left, trying to figure out the best seating arrangement that wouldn't drive him batty. Maybe he should put The Kid in front again. Naw, that's no good, next thing you know, the old man and the floozy will be groping each other in the back there. He should just put Frizzy in the front, with The Kid in back between the other two to keep them apart. The poor people do it all the time, don't they? Let their younguns ride up front against the law. *Hell, I'm virtually poor,* he thought. *Will be soon, at least.* He sighed deeply as he slowed around a sweeping curve. As the road straightened out, he saw the spinning red lights. At least not behind him this time. But what the hell was it up ahead?

A line of cars had formed that made him feel like he was back on the Long Island Expressway. They crept along and eventually could see a uniformed officer on the side of the road, directing each car as it rolled by. "Must be a bad accident," Doug said.

"Maybe someone got attacked by a bear," Ashley mused.

"Or a gorilla," Frizzy cried.

"There are no gorillas around here, you moron," Jamie said.

"How do you know?"

"This isn't Africa," he said.

"How do you know?" she said again. "Wiff Daddy driving, we could be anywhere." That quickly ended the debate.

"Hey, I think I know that guy!" Dale shouted as they rolled closer to the uniformed officer.

"He from Springfield too?" Doug asked sarcastically.

"No, no," Dale said. "That's my niece's husband! I forgot they live out here."

The car stopped and Doug put down his window. The officer was wearing a dark long-sleeved shirt with the word *POLICE* written in yellow lettering. He had on a heavy Kevlar vest with more yellow lettering that said DEA. It was unbuttoned in front, with several pockets stuffed with items indistinguishable under closed flaps. As he bent over to speak, Doug noticed he had slicked hair that appeared to be an attempt to keep an incorrigible cowlick in the back of his head from sticking up. But it was to no avail in the wind whipping off the high rock ledge behind him. Damned if he didn't look like Alfalfa from the *Little Rascals*, Doug thought. He even had a spray of freckles across the bridge of his nose, and they seemed to be multiplying right then and there in the beating sun. This guy's hair was red, though, different from Alfalfa's, but who could tell with that show in black and white. The man's jaw jutted out like it should have been supporting a lighthouse. It was about two sizes too big for his face and looked like he was packing a few Everlasting Gobstoppers in there.

"This road's—" the man began to say, stopping short when he saw Dale. "Well, I'll be…"

"Ricky! How the hell are you?" Dale said.

"Couldn't be better, Dale. What are you doing up here?"

"We're on a trip. This is Doug, my son-in-law…ex-son-in-law… whatever."

Doug shook the officer's hand.

"Corrine's husband," the man said. "I was at your wedding."

"Oh yeah, that's right, I remember," Doug lied.

"How's Corrine doing?" With that he leaned in some more to look in the backseat, presumably for Corrine.

"We're divorced," Doug said. "That's my son back there. And my daughter. And…a friend."

"Ma'am," the officer said, nodding coyly toward Ashley.

"Sorry ta hear about your wife, Dale," Ricky said. "I was over in Eyerack at the time, as you know…"

"Dale waved his hand. "I understand, thanks for the thought…"

"That musta been horrible and all," Ricky continued, "what with that alligator ripping her head…"

"Listen," Doug interrupted quickly. "We're in a bit of a rush. If you don't mind."

"Oh, of course, of course."

"What's the tie-up here?"

"Well, I'm really not suppose ta disclose. I'm suppose ta be sending everybody back down this road." He nodded behind them. "We gotta roadblock up ahead and no one's supposed ta get through. But you *are* family." He stopped and looked deep into the car again, nodding to Ashley the way he did the first time. "I'll let you all in on the inside scoop. We've nailed a big marijuana operation up ahead in the national forest."

"What!" Doug said. "Marijuana? In the national forest?"

"Yes, sir. Becoming a big problem. We found over ten thousand plants on this bust. They got a whole little village set up in there. See the thing is, the Mexicans are getting their chops busted a bit more back at the border, so they're steppin' up their internal operations, if you know what I mean. These forests here are immense. Thousands of acres. Some of the remote sections never see a human being for months on end. Great place to grow illegal crops. They recruited some local thugs from down in Denver, but they started fighting like idiots. One of them got shot in the ass, excuse the language, and then squealed like a little kid."

"Probably coulda found some better guys in Boulder," Doug said.

"Yes, sir, that's fine," the officer said, puzzled. They all stared off into the hills for several moments, as if looking for a gorilla. But not Doug. The phrase "shot in the ass" had finally settled into his mind and it drifted back to Dale's neighborhood. The woman on the ladder in the thong. Then the waffle woman in Publix with the thong. "Boy," he said, with the voice of someone far off in another land. "It's a long way back down from where we came. It'll really slow us down."

"Tell ya what I can do...for family," the man said, looking in back again. This time winking at Ashley, then self-consciously rubbing down his cowlick with the hand his wedding ring was on. "I'll let you pull on up there to that little picnic area where I been making all the cars turn around. We're trying to keep most people out for a while. But you wait there. It's right along the river. Real purty. I've been told they'll be opening the road back up in about thirty minutes, and I'll make sure you all get through."

At the picnic area, Doug stepped down a little trail to the edge of the river and sat on a rock. Something was gnawing at him. It had seized him right after he purged those fleeting thoughts about the thongs. He wasn't sure what this new distraction in his mind was, until Dale edged down the trail to join him on the rock.

"Nice boulder," Dale quipped.

"Funny," Doug said glumly. "Where are the kids?"

"Oh, they went for a little walk up that way a bit." Dale pointed in the other direction. "Ashley's with them."

"That's encouraging," Doug said.

"Boy, that sure was great running into Ricky like that," Dale said. "Huh. How do you like that? Really is a small world."

Doug picked at a piece of long grass and rubbed it between his fingers so it whistled. That's when it hit him and he said, "Sure hope someone's brother lives another day as a result of that pot bust up there."

"Ah-ha," Dale said with a bewildered rub of his sore nose. A big sneeze as they got out of the car a few moments back had sent pain rocketing through his whole body. But the doctor in Aspen had said it looked good. A Canuck, he was. Pronounced nose like *news*, and said "Moost hokey players would love to have a news like dat."

"Brothers in arms," Doug continued unprompted. "We played a song by that name all the time as our official theme song when we were in high school."

"Doug?"

"Yes?"

"What the hell are you talking about?"

"My brother, David. He was a year younger than me." Doug paused and flicked the piece of grass, watching it for several moments as it fluttered away in the breeze, then settled in the dust just short of the river's edge. "He was my best friend. I mean, we had our fights like all brothers do. But we were inseparable. It was our mutual disdain for our dad that drew us together. The yelling, the drinking, the craziness…almost every day, it seemed. Brothers in arms. In high school, we did everything together. Had the same friends, went to bars together. Chased the same girls. He usually won those contests." Doug stopped and pointed across the river. They were being stared at.

"Mule-deer," Dale said.

"You know," Doug continued, "sometimes when I see an animal staring at me like that, I think it's my brother. Like the rabbits in our back yard at home. They sit there like statues, sometimes letting you get real close. You think they're clueless, those dark eyes looking vacant. But they see you. It's like my brother staring at me. I know I'm not supposed to believe in reincarnation, you know as a Catholic and all, but sometimes, I don't know..."

"What happened? To your brother, Doug?"

"Corrine never told you?"

"No."

"Well, I suppose that would make sense. She knew. I told her, once. But I didn't like to talk about it, so we never discussed it again." He rubbed his hands over his cheeks like he was spreading on sunscreen. "It was the end of his junior year in high school. My senior year. He was riding in a van with some kids from a party. They were not even our friends, really. He was just hitching a ride home. I had left earlier with our car, an old Dodge we had scraped together to buy used. I had a girl with me. I don't even remember her name. She sure wasn't worth it." He stopped as the last word choked out of his mouth.

After wiping away a tear and taking a drink from his water bottle, he said, "They were smoking lots of dope in the van. There were six of them in there. I'm sure my brother was too. I mean, he wasn't into that stuff too much, but he had a weakness once in a while. The kid driving had enough dope in him to pay the daily wage of those sorry-ass Mexican henchmen back in that forest. At least that's what they found in the kid's blood, as much as they could tell it was his. After he tried to drive the van around the closed safety gates at a train crossing, and the van got pancaked by an express from Jamaica, there were body parts all over the place. Don't know how they could ever tell one from another." He stopped again, dry-eyed by now, and vacantly watched the mule-deer step gingerly away into the brambles. It had seen enough.

Dale put a hand on Doug's back. Big, like a first baseman's mitt. "I'm sorry, Doug. I'm really sorry."

"We talked about going into business together one day. I was set to go to college in the fall. St. John's. He would join me. After the accident, I decided to skip enrolling. Walked through life like a zombie for a year, then went to community college. Jeez. Waste of time. I often wonder what would have happened if my brother wasn't killed. I think I could have made something of myself and proved my father wrong."

"You have made something of yourself, Doug. Maybe you just don't realize it."

Doug snorted callously and shook his head. "I detest funerals now. How can you ever go to a funeral after burying a brother like that?"

"It tears your heart out," Dale said. "I know. I lost a brother too. The baby. Youngest of four. Killed in Vietnam."

"I'm sorry to hear that," Doug said. He closed his eyes and held his face up to the sun as it danced among the high scudding clouds. "You know," he continued, "this is the most I've ever talked about my brother to anyone."

"I'll take that as a compliment." Dale closed his eyes and shone his face up mimetically. He asked, "Do you think it would have helped…if maybe you'd talked to Corrine about it some more?"

"Helped? How?

"I don't know, your relationship."

"Pfff," Doug aspirated and quickly realized he'd just copied Corrine's queer expression. He opened his eyes and now watched the old man sun himself.

"In my marriage to Clara—Chip—we talked about everything," Dale said, eyes still closed, feeling Doug's stare on his face. "All our feelings. I quickly found it was a great trick for ensuring consistent sex up till the very end. We'd even done it on the floor of the living room just a few hours before the gator got her."

Doug winced and drew back with that ineffable sensation you get when you're forced to envision two regular, everyday people having sex. Older people do this to you, for sure. But the younger ones sometimes too. When they're ugly. Fat. Excessive tattoos. Oily skin. Nasty.

"Guys don't go much for sharing feelings, I know," Dale continued. "It's hard. Doesn't come natural. But it was a good lesson my dad taught me."

"Yeah, well," Doug said, "my dad didn't teach me very many good lessons."

"You'd be surprised, Doug." He opened his eyes, then slapped the baseball mitt on Doug's back again. This time the muffled thud echoed among the surrounding red cliffs. "You'd be surprised."

What Doug *was* surprised about was how good he felt talking to Dale. Cathartic it was. Lots of people, adults mostly, talked about catharsis after his brother's accident. But you don't buy it at that age, do you?

You can definitely appreciate things a lot more as you get older. *Bonding with Dale was nice,* Doug thought. But not so nice that he wanted to sleep with the guy. For Pete's sake.

They pulled into Laramie, Wyoming, just after 2 a.m. Some stinkin' shortcut, Doug admitted to himself. Dale asked if they could share a room. He had been getting his own room ever since they left Florida. Three rooms, everywhere they stopped for the group of them. What's with the change? Doug groused silently in the lobby of the hotel. He was too tired to debate it outright at 2 a.m. Who wouldn't be? Too bad he gave in before considering the sleeping arrangements. It would just have to be Dale with The Kid. That's that, he said to himself riding up in the elevator.

"No way, Dad, his farts stink, and I'm going to be thirteen soon," Jamie whispered in the bathroom as he and Doug brushed their teeth. "I can't sleep with my grandfather at that age."

"Then you sleep with me."

"Why can't Frizzy sleep on the floor and you and Dale sleep together?"

"I am not sleeping with that man, and I will never put your sister on the floor of a hotel room. It's gross down there."

"What about, you know...the Sphincter?"

"Sphincter?"

"The lady. Ashley." Jamie paused, amused at his unintended reference to Hemingway, then said, "Can't someone go sleep with her?"

"Who?" As Doug muttered the word, toothpaste dribbled out of his mouth down his chin. The Kid shrugged his shoulders at his question, and Doug reached for a tissue to wipe his face. Ashley had a room right across the hall. The logical person to send over there would be Dale, but there was no way he was doing that. No way, Jose. Not Mr. My-Sixty-Seven-Year-Old-Wife-and-I-Screwed-on-the-Living-Room-Floor-Before-She-Got-Eaten-By-an-Alligator. Not that guy. Mr. I-Don't-Need-Viagra. Pervert.

He could send Frizzy over there, but the two of them would probably stay up all night eating Twizzlers and watching *Friends* reruns on cable. The Kid would never go, so no point asking when he knew all he'd get was some caustic answer in return. Tweens. They're ripe. Then there was option D. Could he pull it off? The martyr, going over there?

He thought of Corrine's sarcastic question back in Aspen about his sleeping with the "consultant," and that settled it. No way he was going to give her the satisfaction of ever being right, that bitch. Even if she weren't exactly right. She'd think she was. She'd wake up in the middle of the night, sitting upright in her bed with a premonition. Women know. It's men who are clueless.

"It's either me or Dale," he said to Jamie as he jammed his toothbrush back into his toiletry kit.

"Dad!"

"Come on, Jamie, it's two stinkin' a.m. Me or Dale."

He should have known Dale and Frizzy together was a bad idea. What with his gangly arms flailing all over in his sleep, and her tender shoulder. She shrieked out in the middle of the night and started writhing in pain. A few minutes later, he had her settled down. But not with any measure of satisfaction, lying there in the double bed and all, with Dale at his side.

He was up as fast as he could in the morning. He wondered if he barely slept an hour. The good news was it got them on the road again early. They had a long drive and damned if he wasn't going to make it up to Mount Rushmore by nightfall. Their days were numbered.

What a flat colorless world it was driving up toward South Dakota. At least they made some good time. Doug juiced himself on Starbucks—he'd pick up a dozen in Laramie and chilled them on ice. Had them in the cooler stuffed in the way back, all the bags piled high so he could barely see out the window. Thank God Dale didn't have a lot of luggage. He'd left Florida with only a few days' supply of extra clothes. Good thing he had them washed in Aspen. But the guy might start smelling if they didn't get rid of him soon. He was in the backseat again. Doug had given up. "I don't give a crap where any of you sit," he'd said as they were loading up in Laramie. "Sit on the roof, for all I care."

Thankfully they all slept most of the morning. Peace and quiet. Neil Young most of the ride. After lunch everyone fell back to sleep again, no doubt tranquilized by the desolation all around them. The middle of nowhere. That sums up South Dakota, doesn't it? But don't judge a book by its cover, his mother always used to say...usually followed by a few devotions to St. Anthony. The roads began to curve sharply and flat terrain exploded into hills. Deep and green. He got a little nervous when they entered a national forest, but it looked like the Mexicans hadn't made it to this one. Or maybe they had, but they were all getting along OK in some remote corner.

They saw a sign for Mount Rushmore, and Doug's spirit's lifted through the haze of his exhaustion from a long day of driving. "Who's the fourth one again, kiddo?" he yelled into the backseat. No answer. "Hey, Jamie!"

"Whoa! What?" The Kid yanked out his headphones.

"Who's the fourth one?"

"Fourth one what?"

"On the mountain. Mount Rushmore."

"Which fourth one are you talking about?"

"Come on, don't be a wise-ass. There's Washington, Jefferson, Lincoln. Who's the fourth?"

"Roosevelt. Teddy."

"Such a cute name for a president," Ashley chimed in.

"I knew it," Doug said. "I thought it might have been the other one."

"Franklin?"

"Yeah, Franklin," Doug said. "FDR. *He* was cool. But Lincoln. Now he was *really* the man." He was hoping this comment might instigate some discussion. Maybe lead to some good quiz-work for The Kid. Damn, it had been too long. He glanced in his mirror and noticed Jamie starting to put his headphones back on. "Hey, Jame, do the Gettysburg Address, will ya."

"Dad, come on."

"Just one time, kiddo. Look, we're getting close. It'll get us all stoked."

"Dad."

"One time."

"Stop, Doug," Dale chimed in. "He doesn't want to do it."

"Yeah, you should back off," Ashley said.

Jamie glowered at the back of her head. That was enough to get him to say, "Fine, I'll do it. Four score and seventy years ago…"

"Seven. Come on, Jame," Doug admonished.

"Fine. Seven."

When he finished, Doug beamed. And Dale clapped. "Bravo," he said sincerely.

Doug took this as a sign of encouragement. Like a baby that claws its way to standing, drool dripping from its chin, before falling back on its diapered tush with a smile on its face and the adults all clapping with exaggerated élan. "The Kid can recite anything," Doug rejoiced. "Do some Shakespeare. Do some Shakespeare."

"Doug, come on, that's enough," Dale said. "He's not a dog performing tricks or..."

"Just one time. One time, then I'll stop."

"Fine," Jamie said. He cleared his throat, then recited, "How now? A rat? I'd goose a nun for a ducat!"

Dale wailed with laugher. But Doug was miffed. "Jamie! What's that all about? Come on, stop jerking my chain!"

"OK, Dad, sorry." He was sorry now. Feeling badly. So he began: "To be or not to be: that is the question..." As he recited, he found himself on a roll, pausing with a performer's exaggerated effect, before saying: "To die: to sleep." He paused again, unfortunately long enough to let Ashley yawn, loud and irritatingly. "Speaking of sleep," she interrupted.

It was enough to incite him onward:

"No more; and by a sleep to say we end

"The heart-ache and the thousand natural shocks

"That flesh is heir to."

Again, she cut in. "Fresh air, did you say?" She pumped down her window. "That's a great idea. I'd been thinking it was getting stuffy in here. Maybe then I won't feel so sleepy."

The Kid's blood was boiling. "'Tis a consummation," he continued. "Devoutly..."

"Enough!" That was Dale interrupting. "Enough. Enough. Enough. Doug, pull over."

"What?"

"Pull over."

"What? Why? Where? There's no place to pull over without going down a fifty-foot cliff."

"Then stop up there." Dale pointed. "There's an overlook up ahead."

Doug pulled in. "What's the deal, Dale?"

As the car stopped, Dale reached over Jamie's lap and opened the door. "We're getting out. Just me and Jamie."

"What the hell, Dale? What's the big idea?"

"No big idea at all, Doug," Dale said, as he shoved the boy out of the car. Dale got out himself, then said to Doug, "I just want some time

alone with Jamie. My back hurts from hunching over on this long ride."
He arched it back. "And we just need some…fresh air, as the young lady
suggested."

"And just what the hell are we supposed to do?"

"I don't know," Dale said. "Where are you planning on staying tonight?"

"Well, it's too late to go to Rushmore, obviously. It's been a long day. I
thought we'd get a hotel in Rapid City."

"We'll meet you there."

"What?"

"We'll meet you there, in Rapid City."

"But that's far. It's late. It's nearly dark."

"We'll be fine."

"What about the Mexicans?" Doug asked.

Dale chuckled. "We'll call you when we get there."

"Jeez, Dale, are you off your rocker? This is all kind of crazy." Doug
had been sitting in the car, talking out his open window. He began to open
the door.

"Stay in the car, Doug. Go. Go get some dinner, you and the girls.
We'll be fine."

"But he's a kid."

"And I'm a grown man. Served in Korea."

"What are you gonna do?"

"I don't know. Walk. Breathe in the piney air. Search out Calamity
Jane. Or Rocky Raccoon. Just have a nifty time, you know."

"You're nuts," Doug said, shaking his head and leering at Dale as he
threw the car in drive and pulled away. He dodged some motorcycles and
swung out onto the road. "*Rocky Raccoon?*" he thought as he sputtered down
a hill. From the *White Album*. Definitely a good album. And a great song.
Rex played it at his wedding. The first song he and his new wife danced to.
The darnedest thing. Everyone snickered at first, but it set the tone. It was
an amazing wedding. Best he'd ever been to. Rex. That bastard.

13

❖ ❖ ❖

WHENCE WE CAME

The first thing I do is reach for my cell phone. It's a natural reaction, I suppose. I notice an abundance of text messages waiting because, well, I am sufficiently popular. The messages must have arrived while I was delighting my eclectic audience in the Expedition, which I've creatively dubbed Ford's Theatre, much to my secret self-amusement. There's also an e-mail from Jessica, I'm sure, alerting me to the latest developments with her mother. But that is not really why I so eagerly reach for my cell phone. I believe I do so out of awkwardness. Here I am standing with Dale in a dusty little parking lot high atop a mountain in the Black Hills surrounded by woods. And a few gnarly-looking tourists who just arrived on Harleys. It's all sort of surreal and I'm still a little stunned at being shoved out of the car like I was being abducted. I'm not exactly sure what Dale and I are doing here. Alone. My dad having driven off, nearly colliding with one of the Harleys coming in as he floored the Expedition out of the lot. The bearded guy on the bike gave my dad the finger. I couldn't see enough to prove it, but I am sure my dad returned the favor. He was in some mood. He might be in a worse one if he finds Hells Angels chasing him down and shoving his middle finger up you-know-where. So, I grab my phone. Said that already, didn't I? What else is there to do but grab your cell phone when you are feeling awkward and don't know what to say to someone standing right next to you? It's what people do in this kind of situation, right? Check their e-mail, pretend they have an important voice mail. I've seen it enough. I even contemplate hitting a button to make my phone ring so I can hop on a fake call. I've seen that too. In fact, I'm convinced the whole world is populated with cell phones not so we can all talk to each other, but so we have an excuse not to.

"Why don't you put that thing away for a while, Jamie," Dale finally says.

"But I was thinking of calling my mom."

"Jamie, don't make me feel any worse about your mom than I already do. Put the phone away. Let's go for a little walk."

But there are Mexican drug dealers in these woods. And pissed-off Hells Angels hanging out, who know clearly I'm my father's son. And there might be gorillas up here, for Pete's sake. Who knows what lurks around these parts. These are the Black Hills after all, and black means dark, like evil, and sinister and full of bad things.

"Let's take a walk up this path," Dale says. Really bad things. Didn't he ever read *Where the Wild Things Are* to my mother? Maybe that's her problem. I follow his footsteps but don't feel his need to duck under several pine boughs along the way like he does. The path is a short one. We pass a guy with a huge camera around his neck that has a lens on it about two feet long. Darned if the guy doesn't look just like Ansel Adams. He doesn't seem to know or care that two people are walking past him. I say that not because he fails to look us in the eyes and smile like *hello* or something cordial, but because he stops and scratches so vigorously at his butt crack, I am sure his hand might get stuck up there.

"Beautiful, isn't it?" Dale says. He's now escaped several yards ahead and that's when I realize he didn't care about the butt-crack man. Which proves that old people are just like little kids in that scratching butt-crack is such routine business, it's not worthy of notation.

He's right. It is beautiful. I join him on a rock where he's perched. I can't tell which direction we're facing because a thin layer of clouds blanket the sky, which has turned orange and purple from the sun disappearing for the night somewhere. Out there. The distant hills don't quite seem big enough to be called mountains, certainly not compared to what we saw in Colorado, but they loom big enough after driving along all those flatlands in Wyoming. The lush forest covering the hillsides has turned a shade of olive in the gloaming (I think that's the first time I've ever used that word), but there are certain light spots where bare rocks stick out. One rounded slope reminds me of a human head that's suffered from the scissors of a blind barber: clumps of mussed hair spotted with several bald spots.

"If look you right over there," Dale says, pointing his incredibly long finger, "I think you can see Mount Rushmore."

"Oh, yeah." I say, trying to sound as genuinely pleased as possible. "Think this is the closest we'll get?"

"Ha, ha!" Dale laughs, the echo rebounding from the butchered haircut. "Your dad will get us there. Don't worry."

"You're too kind, Grandpa." I say. "Mind if I just call you *Grandpa* for now on?"

"Sure, why's that?"

"I don't know, sounds good," He puts his big hand on my shoulder, and it gives me enough of a jolt that I grab for the rock in fear of being catapulted down the slope. My heart skips a few beats, and then takes a jolt from a different type of shock when my cell phone buzzes in my pants pocket. Frankly, I'm getting jaded with that feeling down there, which I guess best describes the direction in which my mood is heading in general. It doesn't help that it's probably just my mother calling.

"Ever been to Rushmore, Da—I mean, Grandpa?" I ask in order to avoid any spell of silence.

"Nope, never have." OK, this is stimulating. I wish I had something to do, like take pictures with Frizzy's camera. Or scratch my butt. What next should I ask? Unavoidably, it's now quiet.

Then, "Do you think Jefferson's your favorite, being that, we're kind of descended from him and all?"

"What do you mean by that?" he asks.

"Well, my dad always says that your side of the family is distantly related to Thomas Jefferson, through some family connection in Virginia, or something like that. We went to see the people there on our way down to Florida. But it was the wrong family. I think."

Dale continues to stare admiringly at the vista, unfazed by my declaration. "It's not true, is it?" I finally ask, fazed by the silence. As if I really did believe it were true. Or wanted to, for the sake of my dad, I guess.

"Sometimes," Dale says, "Chip used to like when I pretended to be a reincarnation of Robin Hood, but that's another story. You're too young for that." He chuckles inwardly, then says. "But descendants of Jefferson... hmmm, that'd be hard to piece together. I suppose we all might be descended from one of those characters in some way or another: Jefferson, Washington, Franklin, Adams. Right?"

I shrug with disappointment. He continues: "I suppose I did like to tell your mother some stories when she was little. They were stories told to me by my father, and to him by his. Oral history is what you call it. Never proven by fact. But even if it were, Jamie, here's the thing..." He punctuates his pause by taking a huge breathe and blowing it out over the tip of the stubby pine tree growing out of the slope below us with gnarly branches that reach up like octopus arms. I suppose the tree got stubby like that from winds of all types harassing it every day in this wilderness.

"Here's the thing..." he says again. OK, here's the thing, I repeat to myself.

"Your mother is, well, Jamie, she's not my biological child." As I turn startled to look at him, wondering if he's going to tell me about the mailman, he quickly adds, "She's adopted."

Stunned, I absorb his words for several minutes. Seems like twenty. Then I collect myself and say, "So, I guess that means I don't get my smarts from you. How come my dad always says I do?"

"Oh, he doesn't know about your mother being adopted, Jamie." He pauses briefly and makes a guttural sound like when you're trying to get mucus to come up your throat. Then he says, "Your mother doesn't know either."

"You never told her?" I ask with a little too much scorn, so much so that I try to compensate by asking more diplomatically, "How come?"

"Back then it was not as accepted as it is today. There was more stigma attached, and we were embarrassed about not being able to conceive our own child. Time just went on. The longer it went, the harder it became to tell her. It's a terrible burden I've carried with me my whole life." He puts his hands up in front of his lips, as if in prayer, and squints like he's trying to read something enlightening in the distant sky. "You know," he says, "just telling *you* makes me feel a little better."

"Will you ever tell her?"

"I don't know. I sometimes wonder if it's too late."

"It's never too late for anything, Grandpa, is it?"

He chuckles, stops squinting and praying, and slaps my back. "It doesn't matter that I didn't give you all those brains you got, right? I mean, I love you just the same, you know that."

"Of course." Here's where I begin to choke up a little, so I turn away.

"You know what Isaac Newton's famous for, don't you?" he asks.

"He was a famous football player, right?" I quip.

But Dale just ignores the dig at my dad and says, "Lots of people think Newton discovered gravity by just standing under that stupid apple tree. Just like that, the apple fell and he was famous." He snaps his fingers, and it echoes through the valley. "Nothing comes that easy. It took him years and years of hard work to discover gravity and help the world to understand it. Hard work, lots and lots of hard work. Don't ever think that just because you're standing under the tree, you've got it made." He pauses as he hears a humming sound, looking around confused.

"That's my phone," I say.

He nods and seems undeterred from finishing his thought. "At the same time, if you're standing under the tree, don't put incredible pressure on yourself to discover gravity. You know what I mean?" Well, sure, I guess. But he doesn't wait for my timid answer. "Maybe, all you are able to do is just enjoy the tree. And if that's all you can do, to the best of your ability, well then, so be it, enjoy it. Nothing more."

We stare out at the sliver of a quarter moon beginning to slice through the clouds. "Now your dad..." he begins, then pauses.

That's when my phone hums again. This time it registers to him.

"You better get that, in case it's your mother calling."

It's not. "Hey, Dad," I say.

"You guys alive?"

"Yeah, we're fine."

"Where are you?"

"Still in that place where you dropped us off."

"What are you doing?"

"Nothing. Talking."

"Well, it's dark, we're coming to get you. We're just at the next parking area down the road. It's about a mile."

"Dad, we're fine. We'll be fine." There's silence on the other end for a few seconds.

"All right," he finally says. "But I'm going to call you back in a few minutes." I hang up.

"He's concerned about his investment, huh?" Dale asks.

"Guess so."

"Where are they?"

"Almost in Rapid City."

"That so?" Dale says. "Well, we better get walking." OK. We make our way out to the road just as the roar of a hulking RV passes us. It says *Leprechaun* on the side, which to me seems like a name better suited for a tricycle. Then three motorcycles pass. Another RV with bikes hooked to the back. Then another RV that has pictures of busty women painted all over the side, making it look more like a tour bus for a rock band. Then more motorcycles. I'm beginning to wonder if anyone drives regular cars around here. The next RV that passes, one of those half-ones attached to a pick-up, nearly knocks us off the road down a steep hill. It's not his fault really, it's just that the road has begun to curve sharply and then narrow to a width no wider than the RV itself, leaving not an inch to spare for two people out on a nice evening stroll. I watch Dale as he slides slowly backward in the dirt, grabbing the limb of a nearby pine tree to keep his balance. A small avalanche of gravel tumbles down the slope behind us.

Maybe it's the spooked look on his face, I don't know. But the next vehicle that approaches stops. Two, actually. Motorcycles. They idle with a sputtering throb that sounds like rockets launching.

"You OK?" the first man asks loudly above the roar. The first thing I notice is his mustache, which swoops out to each side and does about two or three loops before ending so far away from the side of his skinny cheekbones, I wonder if he risks snagging the hair on passing branches, what with a road like this so tight.

"We're fine," Dale yells. Speak for yourself. "We were just out on a stroll. We're going to find my son-in-law."

"Where's he at?" the second man asks. He doesn't have a mustache, and as I look closer at his short, wavy silver hair, I realize it's not a he at all. I don't think. As I stare, he/she nods at me, then winks. I turn away. Just then my cell phone rings. I'm too worried to answer it for fear it will throw me off balance and send me cart-wheeling down the hill where the gravel avalanche was. I'm sure it's just my dad anyway. In the meantime, Dale's answered to the motorcycle people that my dad's down in Rapid City.

"Whoa!" says the mustache man. "You can't walk that far!"

"Oh, we'll be fine," Dale says again with amazing confidence.

"You sure you don't want a ride?" the he/she says, again winking at me.

"Yeah," says the mustache man. "We's give people rides all the time. Me and Billy here," he nods back at the he/she. Billy? "We been ridin' round the country for two years straight. Forty-eight thousand miles. Been to every national park in the land. We've come back this way for a second go-round. Badlands, then Yellowstone, Glacier, then back to Alaska. It's the life."

By now I notice a line of vehicles waiting patiently behind the mustache man and his boyfriend/girlfriend, Billy. There's actually a car right behind them. A simple little car. What a novelty. Then, of course, another RV. No one honks like they would in New York. That's a relief. My phone gives two quick buzzes to indicate a new voice mail has arrived. My dad's probably about ready to have a heart attack.

I don't hear the last words that eventually convince the motorcycle people not to abduct us. The man driving the car that slides by us next merely nods nervously, while a lady in the front seat looks at a map that I swear is upside down. The RV is next. It rolls to a stop. "Y'all want a lift?" says a woman leaning out a window on the passenger side. She's beefy and has curlers in her hair.

"No, we're fine," Dale says. I'm wondering when he's going to ask for my input on this topic. "Suit yourself," the woman says, not rudely but effortlessly, as if she utters this statement a hundred times a day. As the RV chugs by us, filling our lungs with fumes, two more motorcycles appear in its wake. Sitting astride the bikes are two nuns. *That* it doesn't take a fool to see. They wear black habits and brown scapulas. We only have a few nuns left in our school, enough for me to know what I'm talking about. What I'm not sure about is their nationality. They're Asian, for sure. Both in age somewhere between my dad and my grandfather. The first one stares with wide, unblinking eyes that give the appearance of perpetual surprise. Her pupils look lost in a sea of whiteness.

"You two need ride," she says. This I take as a divine command, not a question.

"Well, OK." Dale says compliantly, as if he realizes he might get struck by lightning should he be stubborn enough to decline.

"Boy get on back there." She nods to the nun behind her. "He need helmet. It law for minor in Dakota." At least she's not making me drink from a cup with a top and straw.

The nun on the second motorcycle hands me the helmet. I plop it on my head just like I do my bike helmet, but it weighs much more than I expect, causing me to momentarily lose my balance. That's when the thought occurs to me: What if these women are ax murderers dressed like nuns? So I begin to ask: "Are you ax murderers?" But I stop myself for fear it may be true, or for fear that it might be a sin to accuse a nun of being an ax murderer. So I try this instead: "Where are you from?"

"Philippine," the holy mother answers. Fine. Good enough. I hop on back. "Grab hold," she says. So I grab hold, which I assume means around her waist. And no higher. My arms barely reach the distance, and they sink into such a soft blanket of vestment and flab that I wonder if I'll ever be able to extricate them.

The nuns drive slowly. This is good news, because I can't imagine ax murderers don't drive like maniacs. We round a sharp curve. Then another. That's when I see the turn-off. I don't see my dad's car, since it's dark and several trees cover the entrance. I wonder if we'll go right by, but Dale has evidently told his nun, the lead driver with the wide eyes, to turn off. Either he needs to take a pee, or he no way believed me when I told him my dad was in Rapid City and knew intuitively all along that he'd been waiting down at the next scenic area.

We get off the motorcycles and thank our escorts. My dad steps out of the Expedition parked in a corner and is eyeing the nuns suspiciously. "It's about time," he says to us while still looking at the nuns as they pull away. "I was just about to call again."

"Sorry I didn't answer last time you called," I say meekly. "I was in a bit of a tricky position."

"What do you mean?" he says.

"Well, I was about to fall down…oh, never mind."

"No," he says, "I mean I only called you that one time that we talked." That's when I pull out my phone and look at my voice mail list. One message. From Jessica. My heart sinks. I feel sick.

"Let's get going," my dad says impatiently.

"Wait, I've got to pee," Dale says. My dad groans. OK, maybe he did think my dad was in Rapid City after all. I follow him. Not because I'm eager to clarify any confusion on this matter. Or because I have to pee. But because I feel like he's become a magnet to me, and I have a metal head that's forever pulled toward him. I follow him deep into the bushes and whip it out for effect. Nothing happens, because I really truly don't have to pee. But his I can hear like it's coming from a garden hose.

"Dale? Grandpa?"

"Ahhhh," he says. "That feels good." Then, finally, "Yes, Jame?"

"How does it feel when someone close to you dies?"

"Well," he says, then stops and grunts as he apparently pushes hard on his bladder. "Are you talking about what it was like when Chip died?"

"Well…" I stop, I guess I really wasn't thinking that because I've never had a wife. Obviously.

"That was the hardest," he says without waiting for me to clarify. "She was my best friend. Next to that, it was losing our babies. Miscarriages." He stops again as he finishes his chore and packs it back in his pants. "Chip had three miscarriages before we finally gave up and adopted your mom. The third one was the most devastating. A little boy. Nearly nine months along. Tore my heart out to think what could've been."

OK. But I've never had kids either. Obviously. So, that's not really what I was thinking about. "What about a parent?" I ask.

"Oh," he says, "Losing my dad was the worst I'd experienced up to that point." He turns and we begin to pick our way out of the woods.

"Ah…Grandpa," I say, nodding at his fly.

"Oh, thanks." He zips slowly, deliberately, as if not to pinch anything in haste, which I suppose is just not a word in his vocabulary. "My dad was my idol," he continues. "He died of a heart attack when I was doing grad work up at Dartmouth in New Hampshire. We'd just had a huge blizzard. The lines were all down. I didn't learn the news until two days later. I sped home in the snow and ice as fast as I could. Lucky I didn't kill myself in the process."

We can see the car now through the thinning pine bowers. Dale stops. "Why do you ask, Jame?"

I shrug my shoulders and feel my tears begin to flow. For Jessica.

"Hey, you all right?" As he asks the question, he crouches low, like he's about ready to get into a football stance, so he can look directly into my teary eyes.

"My best friend Jessica's mom just died," I mumble softly, as I taste a salty tear trickle into my mouth. Then I add, "I think."

"What do you mean *you think*?" he asks.

"She left me a message on my phone. I haven't listened to it. I'm afraid to. I just know what it's about." I explain to him about the cancer and how Jessica and I have been exchanging e-mails about her mom's illness during my trip. We're standing on the edge of the woods. The Expedition's about fifty feet away. My dad honks. "Hey, how 'bout it!" he shouts out the window. "Didn't you have enough time already to talk! It's late. I'm hungry!"

Dale waves him off like a pesky fly. He asks me if I intend to go back to the funeral.

"Like back to New York!" I shout in surprise, so loud, it makes my dad tilt his head and perk his ears like a dog that's suddenly heard the distant rumble of thunder that no human can hear.

"Why, sure," Dale says. "She's your best friend, right?"

"Right."

"It'd mean the world to her."

"But..." But. But. I can't finish.

He cuts off my lame attempts with the big hand to the shoulder, and says, "We'll figure it out."

Does he realize "figuring it out" will significantly, if not entirely, involve my dad? I ponder this the whole way down to Rapid City as the car winds through the darkness. We decide on Chili's for dinner. We all enter quietly. Everyone's tired. I, additionally, am extremely anxious. I'm praying this goes well, assuming Dale is fearless enough to bring up the subject. Why he waits until my dad has stuffed his mouth with two huge bites of chimichanga is an interesting strategy. I suppose it could have worked as a gag, but that theory quickly flies out the window when my dad just as quickly spits out the masticated chimichanga onto his plate.

"No way!" is his response. Six times I believe he says it. I don't think I've ever seen him so irate. Ever. Not even at my mom. Dale alertly recognizes that this forum maybe isn't the greatest idea after all. What with half-chewed chimichanga staring up at us, and The Sphincter snapping her fingers at the waiter and asking if we can get more chips and salsa. Dale suggests to my dad they go outside for a few minutes into the parking lot. Like men who are about to brawl with each other?

Not quite. My dad goes compliantly. Some might call him a wimp. A sucker. But I see the huge heart that lurks down there under the agitation. The heart that's convincing him to go out there in the parking lot where he knows he's doomed to lose a battle against Dale, once the big hand goes on his shoulder. The Belichick Pat.

As my dad is getting ready for bed later in the bathroom, Dale fills me in. It's Tuesday night. The funeral will be Friday morning. This I know from having finally gotten the nerve to call Jessica before we went into dinner. She was surprisingly calm, which made it all the more embarrassing when I cried.

Anyway, Dale tells me that tomorrow morning he'll book and pay for plane tickets for me and my dad and Frizzy to fly back to New York. He'll stay in Rapid City with The Sphincter until we get back, which hopefully will be Saturday afternoon. This will give us almost four days to get to San Francisco for the start of the program...or camp...whatever it is. Plenty of time, Dale assures me, with another slap on my shoulder, this one stinging smartly on my bare skin as I change into my PJs.

While this incredible gesture of generosity amazes me, I can't help to feel angst over the stress I know it's causing my dad. Nor can I minimize the gesture enough to argue against sleeping with Dale. So he batters me all night with his long arms, but I have to admit, I'm feeling on the further side of giddy as we make our way up to Mount Rushmore the next afternoon. Dale's worked on a computer in the hotel all morning to get us flights. We'll fly out the next day, which gives us a free day today. I've been waiting all summer for Rushmore. As we march frantically up the Avenue of Flags, however, I quickly realize my dad is not fueled by the same excitement. He is dragged behind by a heavy mood. It's not anger. It's not irritation. It's something else. Something more like a malaise. Like what you see from a football team at the two minute warning when they're down by twenty-four points. The malaise lingers the next morning as we head to the airport in Rapid City. He even lets Dale drive us in the Expedition. Grandpa's taken command. With my dad in the passenger seat. Never thought I'd see that.

After we get out of the car, I hug Dale. Real tight. I feel myself start to cry. He pulls away from me and says, "Hey, remember the other night, we were talking about, you know, life and stuff?"

"You mean the apple tree," I say.

He laughs, "Yeah, the apple tree. There was something else I wanted to say, but I couldn't find the words. Sometimes that happens to us. We fail to find the right words. So we look to others to express the right words for us."

OK. My dad's getting impatient. He's hovering on the curb with the bags.

"There's a poem I've always loved. It's a classic. Even Dawkins agrees with me." Ah, Dawkins, wonder how his peeing problem is these days. "Stick this in your pocket," Dale orders. "Read it when you have a chance." He hands me a piece of white paper. It's folded neatly into a perfect square about the size of a Wheat Thin. "I love you, Jamie," he says, as he scrubs his big hand roughly through my hair.

I'm tearful as I enter the airport, but it slackens as I think about my first airplane ride ever. It excites me more than scares me. What I find really cool is that we have to first fly through Denver to connect to another plane back to New York. I comment to my dad how coincidental it is that we're flying right back over several of the places we just drove through, but he's not amused.

In Denver, I decide to give Zach a call to tell him I just had my first plane ride. I'd rather share the news with Jessica first, but I figure it's not the best time for her, so Zach's next on my list. He texted me the day before that he thought he'd be home for the funeral, so I'm excited about that too.

He's been in Chicago at a tournament. He won his first game that morning ten-zero. He scored eight of the goals. This I only know after prompting him several times to confess how many he scored. He isn't happy about it.

"What's wrong?" I ask.

"So…my dad," he starts, "after the game, he comes in and starts giving me high fives, calling me Gretzky, and just generally making a schmuck of himself in front of my entire team. He coulda congratulated our goalie for having a shut-out. Kid's sitting right next to me. But no…Gretzky this, Gretzky that."

"That stinks," I say. Is there anything else you can say?

"There's more," he adds. Uh-oh. Not Spider Man again. "So...during the next game, apparently, my mom called and told him I wanted to fly home to Jessica's mom's funeral and just skip the next tournament in Milwaukee. So...we play the next game. We won again, the championship for the tournament. I scored five of the six goals. And instead of being Great Gretzky, I'm a jerk. A loser. A pussy. That's what he calls me in the locker room after the game. A pussy. In front of my entire team. Just because I want to skip Milwaukee."

"Jeez, Zach, that stinks." There's silence on the phone, and all I hear is a woman on a loudspeaker in the airport announcing Flight #1702 to West Palm boarding at Gate C32. I begin to wonder if the call's been dropped. I do have AT&T after all.

"Sometimes I wish I'd rather be dead," Zach finally says.

"Don't say that," I say lamely, feeling too much like an adult. More silence follows.

"He's such a dingleberry," Zach eventually adds, as if he's already said this in his head a hundred times.

"So what are you going to do?" I ask.

"What can I do? I can't just leave here without him. He's such a dingleberry," he says again in despair, then quickly chirps: "Hey, how's that lady? Is she still with you?"

I think about mentioning that I call her Sphincter, but realize there've been enough anal allusions for now. "Yeah, she's still around, but she's staying in South Dakota while we go back to New York."

"She get you into Harvard yet?" I allow him to chuckle to himself. Who can begrudge that to a friend whose dad's a dingleberry?

"She's all right," I finally say. "Just a little wacky."

"That's cool."

"Gotta go, Zach. Good luck in Milwaukee."

"Yeah. Whatever."

Our conversation bothers me as we take off from Denver. Lots of kids at school these days talk about killing themselves, like it's some kind of hip thing to say. But I've never heard Zack say anything like it before. I stare out the window through the cloudless sky at the circles below dotting the farm land. My thoughts shift to Dale and his intricate description of the central pivot irrigation systems. I miss him already. That's when I remember the Wheat Thin in my pocket. I pull out the paper and slowly unfold it, turning toward the window as I read the title of Dale's poem, by William Wordsworth: "My Heart Leaps Up When I Behold."

The title is also the first line: "...when I behold / A rainbow in the sky." It only takes a few seconds to read through the short poem. "So was it when my life began; / So is it now I am a man." I re-read it several times, lingering on the last three lines: "The Child is father of the Man; / And I could wish my days to be / Bound each to each by natural piety." After the last time through, I glance up, seeking answers in the face of my dad, his eyes fluttering in restless sleep. Finally satisfied, I refold the paper and put it back in my pocket. That's about all the reading I do on the plane. I brought a few of my books, but have not been able to concentrate. Too many distractions with people constantly walking by to use the bathroom. And I feel cooped up, claustrophobic. I've ultimately concluded that reading and traveling—by car, by plane, whatever—don't go together well at all. So I close my own eyes and dream of apple trees. I feel like Dale has been with me forever, and not just the past few weeks of our trip. It's empty and strange not having him with us now.

But not as strange as being back in New York. We get a cab from LaGuardia Airport. Other than the short trip to the airport in Rapid City this morning, I realize I have never been in a car with my dad when he's not driving. I wonder if this might relax him a bit, but I wonder wrong. He's more uptight than ever, not at the cars around us, but the car we're in. The guy's driving like a lunatic, weaving in and out of traffic. My dad asks him to slow down a bit. "Two small kids in the car, you know," he squawks at the driver. Who's he calling small?

The driver either doesn't understand English, or conveniently pretends not to understand. Fortunately, his manic driving habits are soon hampered by a traffic jam on the Grand Central Parkway. What else is new? Like things may have changed since we drove three-quarters of the way across the country. Only to fly right back. Any calm my dad welcomes from slowing down is offset by his disdain for sitting still in traffic. I wonder if some deep breathing might do him some good. Instead he starts seeking out cars where parents are smoking while their kids are stuffed in the back inhaling secondhand smoke and growing cancerous tumors as he watches. This really pisses him off. As if he needs any more help.

Being back in my own room is eerie after being away for so long and not expecting to be back for another month, which is what it will be once the program in San Francisco ends and we drive back. That will be interesting. I can't say I have time to dwell on much. We're home just around dinnertime. We all eat a bowl of Rice Krispies. Then my dad takes me to the wake. He drops me off. Then does the same thing the next morning at the funeral. He claims he can't attend because Frizzy's too young for it, and he needs to stay with her. But there's something else, isn't there?

I can't say much about the funeral strikes me. I sit with a few of my friends from school and their parents. What I will never forget is Jessica. She wears a black velvety dress with sort of an oval scoop around her neck, showing just a hint of her white bony shoulders. As she exits the church, a warm breeze brushes at the dress, and she grabs at it to keep it under control. Her eyes are moist, and I see in them a deep blue mountain lake sparkling with infinite glory. Her smile, as I search it, conquers the pain that hides deep in her soul and turns my world into a prism for tomorrow's destiny. She is beautiful. A sight that makes your skin tingle. The way a fresh snowfall does, early in the morning, as the sun glitters up on the horizon, a world pure and white and resolute against any sounds that seek to defy its quest to wake us with just the quiet hum of power lines encased in ice.

When she hugs me good-bye that evening as I leave her house where a small get-together has been gathered, I hold on tight. I don't want to let go. And I silently pray she never models again. She is too perfect to ruin. I don't want get on a plane again back to South Dakota. Then off to San Francisco. I want to stay home, but as I watch my dad lock the house quickly so we can load up the cab, I begin to wonder if this is really his home anymore. I will always go where he does.

I try to read on the plane ride back, but I can't. Eventually my eyes close. For how long I don't know. I am awakened by a voice over the plane's intercom announcing that they have closed Denver's airport temporarily due to bad thunderstorms. We will divert to Minneapolis, the closest airport where the weather is fair. Fair *is* foul, isn't it?

14

✤ ✤ ✤

MERRILY, MERRILY, MERRILY, MERRILY...

At least it's not Dallas. Or someplace farther. That was Dale's response when Doug called him from the airport in Minneapolis. They had sat on the plane on the tarmac for over two hours waiting for the airport in Denver to open. It was like an oven inside the plane. Doug's head was throbbing, his throat parched, and his temper short. Which may have been the reason why he snapped at the woman across the aisle when she ripped open a bag of peanuts. "Nooo!" Doug shouted so loud every single person on the plane in front of them—which was everyone, since they were in the last row—snapped their heads around. One of the flight attendants stiffened with shock and grabbed at the two seats on either side with white knuckles, her eyes wide with fear. She had to be thinking: *Shoe bomber!* But Doug quickly quelled the anxiety by saying, "The peanuts, the peanuts! Please, no. My daughter's hyper allergic." The peanut-woman, who looked like she'd had her fill already from the surplus of candy bars that clearly figured into her daily diet, just shook her head scornfully.

Doug wanted to call her a rude name, *fatso* maybe, but his ire was quickly distracted when the pilot came over the intercom and said Denver was clear. But the plane wouldn't budge. One of the engines died, and they couldn't revive it. After trying for more than a half-hour, they finally wheeled the plane to a gate and let everyone off.

"You're pretty darn close to Rapid City," Dale had said over the phone. "You can drive from there. You didn't check bags, did you?"

"No way, not at fifty bucks a bag!" Doug said.

"Then just tell them at the gate you're driving to your destination. You can be here by noon tomorrow, unless you want to drive all night," Dale declared. "It's better than taking the risk flying. You never know when they'll get you here."

The old man was right. But that didn't appease Doug's utter aggravation. By the time they rented a car and hit the road, they should have been about landing in Rapid City, according to their original schedule. There was no way he was stopping for the night. They had to be in San Francisco in four days. What seemed from the beginning like it would be an easy target to reach at their leisure, had now become a fretful quest.

"Hey, Jame," Doug yelled, at the same time poking his son in the arm to get his attention. Jamie pulled out his earphones. "Call Dale and tell him we'll be there by sunup tomorrow."

"OK," Jamie said. He hit the speed-dial for Dale's number on his cell.

"Hey, Grandpa," he said, after several seconds. "We're on our way. Dad says we'll be there by early morning." Pause. "Hold on." He lifted the phone from his ear and said to Doug, "We driving all night?"

"Yep."

"Yep," Jamie echoed back into the phone. Over the next several minutes of the conversation, he did most of the listening, only saying: "OK." Then, "Sure." Then, "Really?" Then, "That's cool." Followed by, "OK." And finally, another, "OK, sure."

Doug glanced over several times throughout the conversation, wondering what they were talking about. What was the old man filling The Kid's mind with? And did he call him *Grandpa*? When Jamie hung up, he had started to put his headphones right back in at about the same time Doug asked, "What was he saying?"

But The Kid ignored him. Until about a minute later when he took the headphones back out, as if he had second thoughts. He stared out the front window momentarily, then he said, "Dad? Did Dale sound weird when you talked to him on the phone when we were in the airport?"

"Weird? What do you mean *weird*?"

"I don't know…his voice was scratchy, and he was pronouncing words funny" Jamie said. "Like he had the bandage back on his nose. I guess…he just sounded really tired."

"Well, what did he say?" Doug asked.

"He told me you were nuts for driving all night."

"After that."

"He said they went to Badlands National Park yesterday."

"Who's *they*? He and Ashley?"

"Of course, Dad, who else do you think?" He paused long enough for Doug to snicker, and then said, "He told me it was really awesome there. That we should go there someday. Maybe on the way back from San Francisco."

Doug snickered again, then snarled, "I thought he was flying home from there. I knew it."

"I don't know, Dad. Whatever. But he said it was awesome. Like when you make sand castles at the beach and dribble wet sand from your hands into big piles. Like that, only these are real piles. Real mountains made of dribbled sand. He didn't actually say it was awesome. He said it was... nifty."

I bet, Doug thought. Real nifty with Ashley there. He probably let her lead the way all the time like a gentleman so he could watch from behind. He snickered again.

"He said it was real hot, though," Jamie continued. "Over a hundred degrees." Jamie stopped and stared out into the darkness, the lights in the distance dancing in and out of the trees as the car sped along Interstate 90. "He said the heat really wiped him out...that he stayed in the hotel all day and just rested in bed. It just didn't sound like him, Dad."

"He's fine, Jame, don't worry about it. He's old. Maybe he just pushed himself a bit too hard." *Following Ashley around*, Doug added to himself. *Serves him right.* "Did he say what Ashley was doing today?"

"No, he didn't say. We didn't talk that long."

All day by herself. Doug could only imagine what she was doing. He had a mind to call her right now. Catch her whooping it up late at some cowboy bar, probably. He pushed out a hot, stale breath. "Get some sleep, Jame. It's late."

Jamie closed his eyes. The next time he opened them was to the sound of Doug's voice as the car slowed. It was just west of Sioux Falls, where the road narrowed to one lane.

"Damn construction, on a Saturday night of all times," Doug groused. "Look at that, they have one lane completely torn up. I guess out here these roads don't last too long. Winter must play a number on them."

At least they were actually working. Stimulus must have made it all the way out here. Go figure. In several spots, bright lights illuminated the highway while front loaders jerked and rolled in their effort to move earth. All in all they cruised along fine since there were so few cars on the road. For a while at least. Until Doug spotted ahead the dreaded curse of red tail-lights in lock mode.

"Ahhh, for Pete's sake!" he grunted.

"What's wong?" Frizzy asked, neither Doug nor Jamie realizing she was awake.

"Must be an accident," Doug said. "Or maybe it's just part of the construction or something."

The car rolled to a complete stop. *The Mexicans can't be growing drugs out here too, can they? It's just open prairie for miles around.* They didn't move an inch for several minutes. Doug threw the car into park, then sat and seethed. Rubbing his face with his hands. Scratching his hair. Clenching and unclenching his fists. Nothing assuaged his impatience.

They could see the emergency lights ahead. Maybe twenty-five cars or so were in front of them. None of them moving. Several doors started to open. People got out in the darkness, thinned a bit by the early gesture of dawn. They were stretching, smoking. One guy was eating a banana. Another was walking his dog. He headed straight for the Expedition. As he drew closer, his dog stopped to poop. Doug opened his window.

"Any idea what the holdup is?" Doug asked the man as he stared at the pooping dog, its back arched into a furry *U*. Doug's gaze then slipped over to the man's legs. He was wearing shorts, exposing extremely hairy toothpick thighs. On his feet he wore topsiders and white tube socks pulled up high and sporting red stripes around the tops. *Maybe he hadn't intended to get out of his car,* Doug thought. But the dog had to poop.

"Well, 'parently..." the man began as he stepped closer, showing no signs of insecurity over his appearance, "...a man got flattened by a Mack truck while using one of them Porta-Potty jobbers on the side of the road."

"What?" Doug yelped.

"That's what I was told. By some guy up there near the front of the line." The man nodded toward the flashing lights.

"What do you mean, he got flattened by a Mack truck?"

"Nature was callin'," the man said. "He had to pee, I guess." One of his front teeth was twisted so that it seemed like you were looking at the back of the tooth instead of the front. He had a wheezy voice like he smoked. There are more smokers out there still than you think. "So he pulled over to use the Porta-Potty they got out here for them construction men," the man continued. "His friend who was traveling with him said he couldn't no longer hold it. He was in there a few moments, and this eighteen-wheeler comes zippin' by and flattens the dag-garn thing. I guess."

"Jeez," Doug said.

"Yeah, jeez," the man echoed, staring off toward the accident. "Tough way to go."

"Sure is. At least he wasn't, you know, doing the other thing, number two. Sitting, you know?"

"Yeah, I s'pose standing's better. A man ain't got much dignity when he's sittin' on the crapper."

"Yeah. Jeez," Doug said again. "He coulda just gone in a bush, for Pete's sake. Would've saved his life."

"Bush?" the man said, casting quick glances over each shoulder. "Ain't see many of those out here, do ya?"

"Guess not," Doug answered.

It was an hour before they finally opened the road and let traffic through. The sun had lifted into the sky behind them. They were closing in on Rapid City. Just past the turnoff for Badlands National Park. Jamie pointed it out excitedly, but Doug was too exhausted to care. Back when the trip started, he might have used the opportunity to enrich The Kid's knowledge. Not now. His focus was completely on getting there, to San Francisco. He couldn't even dwell on the fact that they had no more time to see the sights. Nor could he worry anymore that The Kid was not reading much, like he was at the beginning.

Doug felt the car drifting under him. His speed ebbed and flowed. The people behind him must have thought he was senile. Or drunk. Or both. Instead, he was just plain dead from lack of sleep. A quick nap in the hotel would do the trick, before checking out and getting the hell out of Dodge. He'd load up on coffee. That would keep him going from there.

He was about to order Jamie to call Dale again. Let him know they were close. But instead his own phone rang and rattled from its perch in the cupholder. He picked it up and glanced at the ID: Elite Schools R Us.

"Hello," Doug said tentatively.

"Mr. Shoop?"

"Yes?"

"Mr. Shoop. This is Juddy Hildenberger. From Elite Schools R Us."

"Yes?"

"Mr. Shoop. I'm sorry for calling you on a Sunday. So early, at that, especially knowing too you must be in Los Angeles already, with a three-hour time difference. Isn't that where you were going?"

"San Francisco," Doug corrected peevishly. "We're not quite there. Yet."

"Oh, well, OK," said Juddy Hildenberger. "Listen, Mr. Shoop…"

"You don't have to keep calling me Mr. Shoop," Doug cut in. People use your name a lot as a preface when they're nervous about something. Just get to the point, would ya.

"OK, OK," Hildenberger said, reading the vibes. "I have a little problem I'm calling about…and I am really sorry about it."

"Yes?" Doug said, jogging his mind, wondering if the credit card that he was using to pay for the consultant had maxed out.

"It's about Ms. Weiner," Hildenberger continued. "She is, well, not quite who we thought she was."

"What do you mean?"

"Well, we've discovered that she lied on her employment application. She never went to Yale."

"What! Well, where the hell she'd go?"

"Some pathetic community college, Mr. Shoop. I'm sorry."

"What's wrong with that?" Doug carped.

"Nothing. Nothing. It's just not Yale. Anyway, it's beside the point. I'm just letting you know that I'm going to have to terminate her employment with Elite Schools R Us. I wanted to give you the courtesy of a heads-up. After this conversation, I'll be attempting to contact her to give her the news."

"What about my money?" Doug asked, in a voice close to a shout.

"Well, I thought you'd be concerned about that. Since this was our mistake, we'll refund your money, Mr. Shoop. Like I said, I am greatly sorry.

This kind of situation has never happened before at Elite Schools R Us, and we're really embarrassed by it. Not sure how it happened, but it did, and we're taking steps to rectify it as quickly as we can."

When Doug finally clicked off the call, he muttered, "Damn it, Hildenberger, you moron. Nice job. What the hell kind of name is Juddy anyway?"

Next, he heard Jamie yell, "Dad, what the heck!" The Kid was pointing to the speedometer. It was down to forty-five. In his funk, Doug had lightened up on the accelerator. It wasn't surprise he felt. No way, how could it be? He'd had his suspicions all along about the girl, didn't he? He knew he did. It was just a kick in the gut, that's all. In his fury, he slammed his foot down and the car sped forward.

"Whoa, Dad!" Jamie shouted. "Take it easy. You all right? What was that call about?"

"Ashley's fired," Doug said, quickly glancing in the mirror back at Frizzy for fear she might hear. But she was watching TV, this time with headphones on. Still, as a precaution he whispered to Jamie: "She won't be with us anymore."

His rage swelled the closer they got to Rapid City. The first thing he wanted to do was track her down and tell her off. How she wasted his time and jeopardized his kid's chances of being successful. It's all he thought about the whole way, and if the hotel wasn't right along the highway, they might have zipped right passed it and gone into Wyoming. Except that Jamie saw it coming and navigated them back safely.

"Hey, Dad," he said as they stepped out of the rental car. "Can we go get something to eat? I'm starved."

"Not now, Jamie," Doug growled. "I'm spent. I need to go up and find Dale so we can return this rental car as soon as possible. Then I need a nap so we can head on our way. Time is dwindling."

"Can I go? By myself, over there to the McDonald's?"

"I don't know, Jamie…"

"Come on, Dad, I'm going to be thirteen. I can handle myself. It's just across the parking lot."

"Fine, go ahead, but make it quick and come right back to the room." Jamie started to walk away.

"I want to go!" Frizzy shrieked. Jamie stopped, turned around and frowned. Doug sighed deeply.

"Just take her, Jamie. I need some space." He nudged Frizzy toward her brother. "And hold her hand! And Jamie..." he waited for his son to stop and turn around. Staring at the half dozen or so motorcycles lined up in the McDonald's parking lot, with their long handlebars and front forks, Doug thought to himself, *what's with this city and all the motorcycles?* "Stay away from the bikers," he finally ordered to Jamie.

"They're probably just nuns, Dad."

"Very funny."

When Doug got to the room, the plastic *Do Not Disturb* sign was hanging on the handle. He slid his key card into the door. From the entryway you could see only the foot of each double bed. That's all. On the closest one, he spotted Dale's feet hanging off the end, splayed in opposite directions. Doug ducked in the bathroom, and when he came out a few minutes later, he walked into the main part of the room. Dale was crashed. He considered waking him, sending him down to find the kids at McDonald's and having them go somewhere for a while. So he could take a nap. He sat on the edge of the bed and put his elbows on his knees, then let his head fall into his hands. He rubbed his eyes, seeking answers. He was so tired, he just wanted to lie back. As he began to swing his feet onto the bed, he glanced again at Dale. He had on a pair of yellow shorts and a blue polo shirt, the same clothes he was wearing the day they left Florida. Nothing strange there, but something else caught Doug's attention, in a way things do when a fleeting pulse in your brain counsels further measurement of the natural state. He leaned in more closely to Dale. He was perfectly still. His face pointed to the ceiling. One hand was on his stomach. The other at his side. Doug stared again. His heart skipped a few beats. He immediately felt a shooting pain in his head. A wave of nausea through his stomach. He reached over tentatively and touched Dale's hand. The one that lay at his side. It was cold.

"Holy shit," Doug said softly, with disbelief. He stood up, now noticing Dale's sunken face, white as a ghost. His lips were slightly spread. Doug peered into the darkness between them, then lowered his ear, hoping to hear and feel Dale's hot breath. Nothing. He put his hand on his chest. Nothing.

"Holy shit," he said again, louder, this time raising his right hand disquietingly to his face and pinching his temples with his thumb and middle finger as if they were a vise.

"Oh my God!" he shouted, and as the words came out, he felt his breath sucked in, which caused him to teeter as he walked toward the other end of the room. He veered around the foot of his bed, cutting the corner too quickly. He caught a leg and fell over. He sat on the floor. "Jesus, Mary, and Joseph," he said with utter despondence. Tears began to fall from his eyes, for what he didn't know. For Dale? Or for himself?

Suddenly he heard a soft knock at the door. The kids! Doug jumped and raced over. He couldn't let them see Dale. He had to think. "Just a minute," he ordered, as he ducked into the bathroom, splashed cold water on his face, and dried it vigorously with a hand towel that smelled like bleach.

He took several deep breaths and moved toward the door. He would tell them they couldn't come in. They should go downstairs. He'd tell them about Dale down there. Jamie, at least. Not Frizzy, no way. She'd freak.

He cracked the door. It wasn't them. It was Ashley.

"Oh, you're back," she said pleasantly. Doug stood mute. He couldn't force a word out. "I just came to check on Dale." As she spoke the words, she hoisted herself up on tiptoes to see over Doug's shoulders into the room. But it was impossible. He had the door wedged open only a few inches.

"What's going on?" she asked. "Everything all right?" A second of silence passed, then, "You look terrible. You OK?"

"Yeah, yeah, I'm fine," he whispered, so as not to wake the dead. "Why were you checking on Dale?"

"Oh, he seemed really tired yesterday. We went to that Badlands place on Friday. It was sooo wicked. But he was bushed. It was so hot there. I felt badly for him." She stopped and gave a sudden look of surprise. "What's going on, why won't you open the door?"

"Oh," he said. "Dale's, ah, sleeping. Keep your voice down."

"Oh. OK. I hope he's fine. We had dinner together last night, but he didn't eat a thing. He just didn't seem right, but I thought a good night's rest would do him good. So I came to check on him."

"Yeah, well, he's fine. He's, ahhh, sleeping."

"You said that already."

"Right, of course." He wanted desperately to get rid of her. Suddenly, his mind cleared from the shock of the past few minutes, and he remembered Juddy Hildenberger. "Say, ah, have you gotten a call from Mr. Hildenberger today?"

"Mr. Hildenberger?"

"Yeah, your boss."

"I know who he is. Why would he call me on Sunday morning? I just talked to him a few days ago."

"Oh, nothing. Nothing."

"You sure you're OK? You look terrible."

"You said that already."

"I know. But you do."

"Just tired. We had a rough trip."

"I heard. Bummer about the plane pooping out on you like that and…"

"Listen," he cut her off sharply, "the kids are over at that McDonald's across the parking lot. Could you go find them for me? And keep them busy for a little while. I'll be down. I don't want them to come up and wake Dale.

"Oh, sure, you bet. I could use an Egg McMuffin myself."

He clicked the door closed quietly as she left. He let his back slide down the metal face. How long he sat there, he couldn't guess. He stared into space. Just thinking. Thoughts that swirled into a stew of doubt and confusion. A plan. He needed a plan. He couldn't let this new problem stop him now.

Eventually, he wandered downstairs. Mechanically, he walked outside, across the parking lot toward McDonald's, with his mind miles away. He passed his rental car and kicked a rear tire in frustration.

"What's wrong, Dad?" It was Jamie, he now saw, heading towards him with Frizzy and Ashley.

"Oh, nothing." Doug stood and stared off into the distance for several moments. Finally he turned to Ashley and said, "Can you take Frizzy for a few moments? I need to talk to Jamie."

"Where?"

"I don't know where. Take her to your room or something and watch cartoons."

She skipped away with Frizzy in tow. She still hadn't gotten the call, had she? Doug guided Jamie down the sidewalk. They turned into the pool area. It was a small pool, maybe fifteen feet long. An old woman wearing a purple bathing cap with two plastic flowers on each side was doing laps, taking short strokes so she wouldn't get to the end too quickly. Doug sat Jamie down on a lounge chair and then squatted on another across from him.

"Look, Jame," he said, trying to establish a calm tone. "There's been a...little problem."

"What kind of little problem?"

Doug squinted into the distance, took a deep breath, then said, "Dale's dead."

"Dead!"

"Shhhh! Keep your voice down." Doug glanced at the woman in the pool. She was still stroking.

"What do you mean dead, Dad?"

"What do you mean 'what do you mean'? He's dead, I said."

"How? Why? Where?"

"Upstairs in the hotel room. I don't know exactly how. I found him lying on the bed when we got back. I think he may have had a heart attack, or a stroke or something. Maybe it was the heat from that visit to the Badlands place."

"The Sphincter killed him!" Jamie said angrily.

"Who's the Sphincter?"

"That moron you hired. She killed him."

"She's not a moron, Jamie," he said, surprising himself at the words that came out. "And she didn't kill him. I don't think. Not like murder or anything. But maybe she pushed him too hard, I don't know." He paused and all they could hear was the burble of an old lady pushing water aside as she daintily executed the breaststroke. It was suddenly shattered by the roar of the motorcycles starting up over at McDonald's. Doug looked at Jamie. "Hey, don't cry. It will be all right."

Jamie just stared into the pool, stunned, mute. He wiped his tears with his T-shirt, but it couldn't staunch their flow.

"Anyway," Doug finally said. "I've got to think about what to do."

"What do you...mean?" Jamie asked while sniffling.

"Well, we've got just about three days to get to San Francisco for the start of ELEGY. This little wrinkle here makes things a little challenging, so I've got to figure out a plan."

"We're still going to go?"

"Of course we are. We've come this far, Jame. But if I report that Dale's died, we'll never get there on time."

Jamie now scowled at his dad. Baffled. Too numb to form any words. Perhaps too short on experience, he thought, to understand. Dale, dead? He felt sick to his stomach.

"I'll think of something," Doug finally said, as the old woman climbed up the steps of the pool, the flabby skin on her thighs blue from the tight elastic on her bathing suit. "Let's go," Doug continued. "We've got to dump this rental car."

They went upstairs to Ashley's room. She'd need to help with returning the car. *There had to be no way she'd received the call yet,* Doug thought. She was chipper as can be. He kept an eye on her in the rental car as she tailed behind him. No phone conversations, best he could tell. What the hell's that Hildenberger guy waiting for, the cows to come home to roost?

"That car was nifty," she said twenty minutes later, as they left the agency after the drop-off.

Nifty? "Yeah, well, I certainly preferred not to rent a Cadillac," he muttered. "It was all they had left. Cost me an arm and a leg."

"Awww, you need to lighten up a bit." As she finished the words, her phone rang in her purse. It wasn't "Silent Night" anymore. It was set to one of those old-fashioned rings like you used to hear on a rotary phone. It was muffled like it was buried deep. She fished it out and glanced at the display screen. Doug had pulled to a red light, giving him plenty of time to observe her motions and reactions. Her natural blitheness quickly drained from her face as she clicked a button without answering and immediately shoved the phone back in her purse. She was quiet the rest of the way, as if her mind had been transported somewhere far away.

Doug glanced at her several times, but she'd angled her stare out the side window. That *had* to be Hildenberger calling her. His throat felt dry and his head began to throb again, despite the two Tylenol he gulped down before returning the car. He had been so eager for her to get the call. His anger at her, his complete fatigue, his feelings of failure, all boiled together into a raging vortex of disdain for her. But now that she'd presumably received it, something changed. The only thing he felt now was regret. Not regret for hiring her, but regret for seeing her go.

When he pulled into the hotel parking lot, she flung her door open immediately and mumbled something about needing to get to her room, barely acknowledging anyone in the car as she slid away. He watched her stride to the front of the hotel, knowing it would be the last he'd probably see of her. He pulled his key out of the ignition. The kids had gotten out of the car. That's when he glanced down and saw her purse. He reached for it and immediately succumbed to his burning curiosity. He dug out her phone and scanned her list of recent calls. Right on top was Juddy Hildenberger. His hand shook. He felt like crying. He began to put the phone back, but couldn't help seeing the list of calls below that. All from the same person. He scrolled down. At least ten of them over the past several days. The name just said *Lola*. Who's Lola? he wondered.

A sudden knock at his window sent him nearly jumping through the roof. It was her. She had her hand out and a sneer on her face that said, "Caught you, dickwad. Turn it over."

He slid the phone back into the purse, popped open the door, and shamefully slipped it to her through a small opening. "You forgot this," he said lamely.

She snatched it in a huff and disappeared inside. *Who is she to be mad at me?* he thought. Oh well. It was definitely the last he'd see of her. He got out of the car and told the kids to go wait in the lobby a few minutes. He needed to think, a process he stoked by leaning against the hood of the Expedition and staring out across the parking lot. The sun baked off the blacktop. Motorcycles zoomed along the road out front. He heard little kids playing in the hotel pool around the corner. He knew that reporting Dale's death meant the end of the trip. All the paperwork and hoops he'd have to jump through. It would take days, it would have to. He had to find a way to get the body to San Francisco as soon as possible. He'd report the death there. Make up a story about how the guy died in the car, and how he was too worried to stop somewhere out in the boondocks. How he wanted to get to a *real* city where they could care for him the right way. That all sounded believable, right? But how to get him there? He couldn't just prop a dead guy up in the backseat. Not with the kids in the car. They'd be tormented for life. And what if he got pulled over? After all, he'd need to drive pretty darn fast to get to San Fran on time.

He sighed deeply as he watched a car across the parking lot back out of its space. Something about the car suddenly caught Doug's eye. It was what was tied to the roof. His eyes lit up with delight, just like the Grinch when he realizes he's concocted a plan to ruin Christmas in Whoville.

Doug dashed into the hotel to ask directions for the nearest outdoor sporting goods store.

"Why are we go-wing shopping?" Frizzy asked in the car.

"To buy something fun," Doug said.

Are we going to a toy staww?" she asked.

"Kinda like that," Doug answered as he swung the front door open. They made a loop of the store before they finally found what he was seeking: rows and rows of kayaks and canoes stacked on shelves floor to ceiling. "Dad, why are we getting a kayak?" Jamie asked.

"We're not, we're getting a canoe."

"We're getting a canoe!" Frizzy shouted. Doug ignored her and walked back and forth, examining the boats, growing frustrated with what he saw.

"Where the hell are the canoes?" he groused.

"Up there." Jamie pointed to the highest shelves.

"What are they doing up there?"

"Most people want kayaks, Dad, not canoes."

"Well, we need a canoe."

"Yippee, we're getting a canoe! Where are we go-wing canoe-wing, Daddy?"

"We're not going canoeing."

"Then why are we buying a canoe, Dad?"

"I'll explain later."

"We should just get a kayak, they're lower."

"That won't work."

"Work for what?"

"I told you, I'll explain later. Isn't there any help in this store?"

"I saw a guy over by the tents."

"Can you go find him for me? I need to look these over."

"You're not going to climb up there, Dad, are you?"

"No, for Pete's sake. Just go."

Jamie returned about ten minutes later with a salesperson. He sighed with relief when he saw his dad still on the ground.

"What can I do for you?" the salesperson asked. He was a kid, Doug noticed. Barely older than Jamie. Skin white as milk. Dark peach fuzz over his upper lip. Jet black hair, long in front and hooked toward one side, so that it appeared to be poking him in the eye. He blew on it to get it away, but it was too heavy with grease to move.

"I don't see any prices on those canoes up there," Doug said. "How come?'

"Hmmm." the milky kid said, with a slight tug at his crotch. "Maybe someone forgot to mark them."

"Well, which one is the cheapest?" Doug asked. "I need to know."

"Hmmm, I'm not…too…sure," the milky kid said. "I don't work this section normally."

"Well, where's the person who does?"

"She got fired yesterday. Apparently she caught a case of the crabs, you see, and she kept itching—like down there, you know?" He nodded toward Doug's crotch and then tugged again slightly at his own. "Felix, our manager, said it was bad for business."

"OK," Doug snapped. "Then who can help me with the canoes?"

"I'll do my best." He blew his sickle hair again nervously, to no avail.

"How much is that silver-looking one up there?" Doug asked. "And can you lay in it? A big person. Maybe someone six inches taller than me?"

"Lay in it?" the milky kid asked.

"Yeah, like if someone wanted to lay down, like on the bottom, flat. Could they fit?"

"Gee. I don't know. I'll have to go find Felix." They waited for what seemed like forever. Store waiting swells time. Ten minutes later, maybe more, the milky kid returned. "You can't really lay in that one, Felix said. It has seats attached to the bottom."

"Well, what about that other one, the red one? Or the green one?"

"Hold on, I'll go ask Felix." Ten minutes later he returned. "You could lay OK in either one."

"What do you mean OK?"

"Yeah, you can lay in it. I guess."

"How much are they?"

The kid blew his cheeks out like a balloon. His eyes grew wide. He turned silently on his heels, bowing slightly, then holding his pointer finger in the air to signal "one minute."

But it was ten minutes until he got back. "Fifteen hundred for the green one. A grand for the red one."

"A thousand bucks!" Doug moaned. "Jeez, I'll take the red one." Another ten minutes passed while the milky kid recruited two fat guys in dirty white T-shirts from the back to help lift the canoe down.

"Don't you want paddles?" the milky kid asked as they began to follow in behind the guys lugging the canoe.

"Paddles? How much?" Doug asked.

"I don't know," the milky kid said, picking up the first one he saw and reading the price. "Forty bucks for a pair."

"I have paddles," Doug said.

"We have paddles?" Jamie asked.

"Hush!" Doug barked, then turned to the milky kid. "But I do need locks. A couple of them."

"What kind of locks?"

"To lock it to the roof of my car."

"You need a special transport system for that," one of the guys carrying the canoe yelled back over his shoulder. "You gotta roof rack?"

"Yes."

"Ninety-nine bucks for the transport system."

"Ninety-nine bucks!"

"Otherwise this puppy'll never stay on the roof. It'll be flying off like a bride's pajamas." He and the other fat guy hacked in unison.

Fortunately, they both offered to help install the transport system and lift the canoe onto the roof.

"How much does that thing weigh?" Doug asked as he watched them hoist it.

"About eighty pounds."

"Jeez," Doug muttered, as he felt his skin tingle with fear that his plan might be a little harder to execute than he first thought.

"Dad?" No response. "Dad!"

"Oh, what?" Doug finally said as they got ready to get in the car.

"Tell me. Please tell me this canoe doesn't have something to do with Dale."

Frizzy heard the question and said, "Where *is* Dale?"

"He's back in the hotel resting. Now get in the car, Frizzy." Doug closed the door on her, then turned to Jamie. "Look," he said with a forced whisper, while making a politician-like slicing gesture with his hands. "Here's the plan. We just need to get Dale to San Francisco so we can get you to the program on time. Then I will deal with reporting him dead. In the meantime, I don't want Frizzy to know. And we can't very well stick the guy in the car. So, I'll put him on the roof."

"On the roof?"

"Yeah. Under the canoe." He glanced up at the canoe. "It'll be fine."

Jamie grew suddenly pale. Like he might get sick. "That's nuts, Dad."

"I know it's nuts. But we've got to get to San Francisco."

"With Dale dead, riding under a canoe on the roof?"

"Look, Jamie, come on, work with me here. Otherwise, we'll never get to ELEGY on time."

"I don't know, Dad. Can't we get in trouble for this or something? Hiding a dead body under a canoe and driving him across the country. Isn't there a law against that?"

"We're not breaking any laws. I don't think. Three states. That's all we have to get across until we're in northern California. We'll leave before sunup tomorrow. We'll drive straight through. I'll have us there by Tuesday night. No sweat. We'll say he died in the car along the way."

"Won't he start to smell?"

"He'll be on the roof! I don't know. Maybe he will. I'll drive fast. I'll park away from people wherever we stop. No one will notice. The whole world smells."

"When are you going to sleep?"

"I'll catch some sleep tonight. A few hours, maybe. I'll pull off the road occasionally for some catnaps. Otherwise, I'll make it. With lots of coffee."

"What are you going to tell Frizzy?"

"Jeez, this is a lot of questions, Jame. I guess I'll make up a story or something. I don't know. Maybe I'll tell her that Dale and Ashley decided to fly to San Francisco. That they're sick of driving. Then I'll tell her the truth when we get there. But not now. No way. She'll be hysterical. You know girls."

They stood there silently for several moments. A family walked by in the parking lot. A mom. A dad. Two little kids holding hands. Jamie's eyes followed them.

"Come on, Jame," his dad said with forced enthusiasm. "We've got to get rockin'."

Jamie stood still. "I don't know, Dad."

"Don't know what?"

"About this whole idea you have. Why don't we just bag it?"

"Bag it? Bag what?"

"San Francisco."

"Bag it?"

Jamie shrugged his shoulders. It was like friction from the movement sparked some dynamite.

"Bag it?" Doug said again with a razor-sharp voice. "You want to bag it?"

Jamie hung his head and shrugged again.

Doug glanced away. Then back. "I've schlepped across the entire country for this! I've spent a fortune. Some of it I'm getting back only because of some loser who lied and said she went to Yale. I've put up with delays and excuses. With an old leech who wouldn't leave us alone and then had the nerve to die on us. Oh, no sirree. I'm not bagging it." His agitated voice grew louder and higher pitched, as if he were just getting rolling. "I've dealt with snobs in Virginia who aren't even Virginians. With Mexican drug lords. Morons who pee in the wrong places. And crazy old ladies in Florida with their fuuu—gerring Tyson chickens!"

"Perdue."

"What?"

"Perdue. She wanted Perdue chickens."

"Peeerddddduue!!" he screamed at the top of his lungs, his fists clenched, his face turning the same shade as his hair so that his entire head looked like a tomato.

"Are you all right?" an old woman asked as she walked behind the car and stopped, with a concerned look on her face.

"I'm fine," Jamie assured her.

"No, I was talking about him," she said, pointing at Doug.

"He's fine," Jamie said. "He's just my dad."

She passed. Doug ripped open his door and said angrily to Jamie: "Get in."

Ain't no stoppin' now, he said to himself through clenched teeth as he drove back toward the hotel. No way. No how. This ELEGY program was not the be-all-end-all, that's for sure. He knew that. It's not like it was *the* ticket to fame and fortune. But missing it would be missing the chance at opportunity. Kids who miss opportunity wind up losers. And then have to lie about going to Yale. If they didn't go to ELEGY, he'd be forever plagued by "What if?" What if there is someone important there for The Kid to impress? What if The Kid is the star of the program? They won't know these things if they don't go, will they? And he'll never be able to stick it in the face of all those privileged kids there. Or that stinkin' Rex back home with his elite private school and his estate and his horses in the back field crapping all over the place. And then there's Corrine. He'd stick it to her good. And the weasel too. Even Brian seemed to doubt him. Father Brian with his Gospel according to John Lennon. Jeez.

His mind was still storming when they pulled back into the hotel. But it wasn't enough to make him forget Ashley. He wondered if she'd left by now. He wasn't sure why he wondered about it. On the way in, he asked the clerk at the front desk if Ms. Weiner had checked out of Room 123. "No," he was told. Maybe she was hanging around to say good-bye to Frizzy. That wouldn't surprise him. Maybe he should go looking for her. Interrogate her about why she did what she did. He was in that frame of mind. Why not keep rolling? But perhaps he'd just let bygones be bygones and say good-bye.

But then he remembered he needed to book another room. No way they could go near the room Dale was in. "Why is it twenty-five bucks more than the other room I've had?" he asked the clerk when she told him the rate.

"We've filled up. Supply and demand, you know?"

This guy's really costing me money, Doug thought. *But what can you do? He's dead.*

By the time they headed to their new room, he'd purged Ashley from his mind. He had to. Too much to do. First, it entailed going up to the next floor where their other room was. Doug's heart sank into his stomach as he got off the elevator and wondered if he remembered to put the *Do Not Disturb* sign on the door. He was relieved when he raced down the hall and saw the white piece of plastic hanging there. OK. Things were going to be fine. He moved all their clothes. They went across the parking lot to McDonald's for dinner. He hated fast food with all the germs from those teenagers putting their hands on everything. But no time to go elsewhere.

"Where's Dale and Ashley?" Frizzy asked.

"Dale's resting," Doug said impatiently. "I told you, that's why we needed a second room, so he can rest. I don't know where Ashley is." Heck, it's not all lies.

He settled the kids into bed just after dark and lay down himself, setting his alarm on his watch for 2 a.m. The dead of night. No one would be up, would they?

Just philanderers. And boozers. The former he saw as soon as he cracked the door of the room. He'd wrapped Dale in a sheet. Two it took. He'd figure out later what to tell the hotel. He'd probably have to pay for them. Add that to the growing expense. Anyway, after wrapping him and tying the sheets tight with some string he had in the car, he'd flung the big guy over his shoulder. Staggering, he reached for the door and wedged it open. That's when he heard the laughing and giggling down the hall. He could barely see the guy, or his wench; but he observed enough of their stumbling to tell that they qualified as boozers too.

After waiting for them to disappear, he stumbled with Dale to the stairway. Thank God the room was near the end of the hall. Once out in the parking lot, he gently set Dale on the hood of the Expedition. That's when he heard the next boozer. The guy must have been sitting, or sleeping, in his car a few spots down. He staggered out and closed the door. Then he stood there wavering like he was being knocked around by a stiff breeze. He pointed his keyless remote at the car and pushed the button. Not satisfied, he did it again, with more deliberateness. Still nothing. No car honk, or beep that signals the remote had worked. Again, he did it. Doug stared impatiently. "Godddd-stammit!" the man slurred, then pressed the button again. Nothing.

Quickly out of patience, Doug darted over and grabbed the keyless remote from the guy's hand, pushing the correct button. The horn tooted.

He gave the remote back to the drunk. "Why, frank you…very muck…my young flend," the drunk drooled. As he spoke, he wavered again and then tried to peer over Doug's shoulder toward the Expedition. Is that a dead body on the trunk? But before the guy could slur it out, Doug stepped in front of his vision, spun him toward the front door to the hotel, and said, "Have a nice rest."

Now free of meddling derelicts, he took off his shoes—so as not to dent the car—stepped up onto the hood, and dragged Dale up to the roof. This was the tricky part. There was no way he could take the canoe down and expect to get it back up with Dale inside. He figured the total weight would be about three hundred pounds. So he unhooked the canoe, and holding it up with one hand, he pushed and wedged Dale under, like he was stuffing a piece of baloney into a sandwich. His knees were on fire from bending and crouching, and sweat had soon drenched his shirt. His heart beat so fast he felt like it might burst through his chest. Several times he had to stop and crouch low as cars entered and left the parking lot. So much for the dead of night. He was just glad none of them were cop cars. Probably all eating donuts somewhere. Or baloney sandwiches.

When he'd finally wrapped up, satisfied that Dale was tucked under and tied in tight, he rubbed his hands together in satisfaction. "Worked like a charm," he said smugly as he stood in front of the Expedition. Even though it took about twice as long as he expected, he still had time for some sleep. Just an hour was all he needed. Back in the room, he splashed warm water on his face, changed into clean boxer shorts, set the alarm on his watch for 5 a.m., and sunk his weary head into the soft pillow. Life is but a dream.

15

HOLY GROUND

As the time crawls past midnight, I suspect this might become the worst day of my life. To begin, I can't stop crying over the loss of Dale. I stare up at the ceiling of the room through my watery eyes and follow a crack across the white surface that has soaked to gray in the darkness, its pocked surface like a picture of the moon. A month ago, Dale's death would have been a distant mirage to me, stitched together by faint memories of two or three visits he and Chip made to New York before my mother and dad divorced. For the last visit, Chip was packed in an urn after being cremated, and we had a private service for her in that church in Massapequa where she was born. It now ironically occurs to me that her ashes must have been pretty scant, given the large helping of her poached by that alligator. But that's a little off point, isn't it? My current sadness swells only from the dramatic change of events that has occurred in the past several weeks. The fact that such a fleeting time with Dale on our journey will forever translate into a belief that he's an inextricable part of my life. The mirage has morphed into a tangible permanence. His face crystal-clear and forever real. Like's he always been there, and always would be. Yet now he's gone. It is only at this moment, I realize, that I know how Jessica must feel.

It seems like several hours before my tears recede and I begin to doze. Only to be awakened by my dad as he stumbles around in the darkness. After he sneaks out the door, I begin again to cry. This time for him. I wonder if he has slipped off the deep end. And as I lie in bed with Frizzy kicking me—he insisted I sleep with her tonight—I can't help but fear that he will not return. I mean, what are the odds of dragging a dead body out of a hotel and not being caught and thrown in jail? It seems like hours have passed, during which time I've contemplated several times getting up and checking on him outside, if not for the distaste I have for leaving my little sister unattended in a dank hotel room in Rapid City.

I feel a surge of relief when he finally returns. He collapses into bed, and I wonder if he'll toss restlessly, unlike the few hours he slept soundly before getting up to do the deed. But he doesn't toss restlessly. Within moments he is once again snoring away, which I judge to be a symptom of sheer exhaustion in favor of calculating callousness. I cannot deny that the deepest hope dwelling within me claws against the notion that he has really tied Dale to the underside of that canoe. That instead, he did the decent thing and drove him down to the local morgue. That we will get up sometime later this morning, make sure everything is in order for Dale to be sent home with dignity, and then we—my Dad, Frizzy and I; no Sphincter!—will get back into the Expedition with me permanently affixed in the shotgun slot. We will drive directly east, home to Long Island. Where I will hug Jessica comfortingly for a long, long time.

It is this vision I cling to when my Dad's alarm on his watch begins dinging. He doesn't budge, so I contemplate reaching over and turning the alarm off and trying to get some sleep. But I can't do it. I wake him excitedly under the delusional spell that he will tell me all about his change of plans. He rubs his eyes and moans deeply, glances at his watch, and says, "We've got to hit the road."

Like, with Dale on the roof? The answer to this question grows more and more evident as my dad nervously gathers our things in the room and hustles us out the door with Frizzy in tow, I believe nearly walking in her sleep.

"But I haven't bwushed my teeth," she pleads groggily.

"That's OK, you'll be fine," he says curtly.

"But I haff to pee," she says. This he knows is a potential impediment, so he points to the bathroom and says: "Go!"

When she comes out, she asks, "What about Dale and Ashley?"

"What about them?" he asks back, his patience near empty.

"Are they coming?"

"I'll explain later," he says, as he pushes her forward and yanks the bags behind him, catching one in the closing door and spewing a mumbled curse word that sounds to me like: "Shhhhack-it-snot."

Downstairs in the lobby he heads directly to the complimentary coffee cart and begins to fill a tall cup. I notice his hand shaking wildly, which I can't necessarily attribute to nervousness in favor of agitation over Frizzy's fart that has overwhelmed the scent of Arabian roast with the stench of molded cheese. We check out and then storm to the parking lot. It's blistering hot for so early in the morning.

He has the lead on us by several paces as we all soldier down the sidewalk toward the car. I stop to wait for Frizzy, urging her forward. It's when I resume my steps that I literally smack into my dad from behind. He's stopped. Still as a statue.

"What the...?" he stammers with the horrified look of someone walking to get his car and then noticing it's gone.

"It's gone," he says. Told you.

"What's gone?" I ask anyway, my heart sinking quickly to my stomach, which is not so bad compared to my dad's heart, which I think might have fallen all the way through his rectum to the sidewalk.

"The goddamn's car's gone."

"Does that mean Dale's gone?" I asked cautiously, grasping the last vestige of hope that my dad did indeed go with the alternative plan and take Dale to the morgue.

"Everything's gone," he says.

"Where's Dale gone?" Frizzy asks innocently.

"Nowhere, hush," I say, as my dad's proxy, because clearly, by the looks of him, he's crossed the threshold into a world of utter speechlessness. The three of us stand immovable for several moments, staring at the vacant spot where the Expedition had been parked.

That's when I come up with a bright idea. "Dad, are you sure you didn't move it?"

"No" he says adamantly.

"No, you're not sure? Or no, you didn't move it?" He answers me with chilling silence and then begins to shake his head, which I accept as the conclusive statement that he just plain means *no*—there's no hope of this not being a monumental disaster. As if any doubt remains, he continues to shake his head, which I'm beginning to find quite nettlesome to the point where I crave the urge to reach over and subdue it, like you might do to a flopping fish you've just hooked with your fly rod. In Montana. With Dale. 'Cept he's dead. And gone.

"Please tell me, Dad, that you moved the car," I plead, as my anger begins to rise at the notion of Dale being stolen.

"No, Jamie, I did not move the damn car. It was right there when I was out here just a few hours ago."

When you were tying Dale to the roof. Great. I watch him as he shuffles back a few steps and plunks down onto the edge of a two-foot brick wall around some landscaping that includes a leafless bush and some wilted marigolds. "Who would steal our car?" I finally ask, trying to get all the uncomfortable facts out in the open. Why not?

He begins to shake his head again. But I don't feel the need to stop it this time, because he stops it on his own, then looks up with a startled expression. As if maybe he just realized he *did* drive Dale to the morgue last night and parked the car on the other side of the building when he returned. Hurray!

"That bitch!" he says through clenched teeth. OK, maybe my theory's a bit off, wouldn't you say? He leaps to his feet and marches back to the hotel. Frizzy and I hustle behind and catch up in time to hear him ask the front desk clerk if Ms. Weiner has checked out of Room 123. "Yes," the woman answers. "About an hour ago. Right when I came on duty."

"That bitch!" my dad mutters again. It's loud enough for the fat woman behind the counter to hear, and she reacts by raising her eyebrows at me. At *me*! What are you looking at me for?

My dad walks out the door. This time his stride is slow and deliberate. The stride of someone who has just suffered the worst defeat of his life. Beyond worthy of the Belichick Pat. We follow behind. Frizzy attempts to ask several more questions, but I cut her off abruptly each time. My dad sits back on the same wall near the marigolds in a trance. After several moments, he hangs his head and lets it settle into the palms of his hands. I fight back tears. After what seems like an eternity, he pulls out his cell phone and despondently taps away at a few numbers. He waits several moments, then says, "Yes, I'd like to report a stolen car…please." And what about a dead body?

The police arrive quicker than I expect. After the third squad car pulls in, my dad turns to me and says, "Jamie, please take Frizzy over to McDonald's for a little while."

I say, "But I'm not hungry." Actually, I'm starved, but who can eat at a time like this?

He says forlornly, "Don't give me a hard time. I don't need you two around to hear this."

I assume that means the part about how my dead grandfather was tucked inside the canoe on the roof of the car that was stolen. By a crazy lady who he might describe to the police as someone who runs like a bug-catching marionette that didn't go to Yale, but did grow up in Longshadow, or Longmeadow, whatever the hell it's called. Is there anything else he could possibly add that he knows about this person?

So Frizzy and I stroll over to McDonald's with twenty dollars that my dad has given me. I'm sick of this place by now. I order hotcakes with syrup for Frizzy and a Coke. Just what she needs at 5:30 in the morning. I position myself so I can see out the window toward the scene of the crime. I suppose its OK to call it that. Through the dusty haze of a sultry dawn, I can make out the reddish hue of my dad's head a few times, ducking in and out of the tops of cars in the parking lot. After about forty-five minutes, I call him and ask if it's OK to come back. "Not yet," he answers abruptly.

So I order another Coke for Frizzy, which keeps her complacent and innocent of the trauma that is now decimating her family. I play a few games on my phone to distract myself, but nothing is working. As with last night in bed, my initial emotions have focused on the loss of Dale. Literally, the loss of him this time. But they now give way to fear over the potential loss of my dad. Literally, the loss of him. I begin to cry as I worry that he will be thrown in jail and taken from me. Frizzy asks me why I am crying. I tell her to "Just shut up," and then hide my face in my hands. I am still sobbing when my phone rings. "You can come back now," he says. I am about to ask whether he is going to be arrested, but he cuts me off when he says, "Your mother's on her way." Great…and I thought things were bad already.

It is when I arrive back at the scene that I feel I am stepping into a netherworld of blurry images and distorted sounds. The only words from my dad that register to me are: "They're looking for her." At first I assume *her* to be the Expedition, the basis of which is the recollection I have of my dad saying, "Isn't she a beauty?" back when he bought the car right before our trip. Yet somehow I'm not so sure that what he's now talking about. They're looking for *her*? I repeat to myself. What about *him*? As in Dale.

But then it dawns on me he means *her* as in The Sphincter, who has stolen our car, my grandfather, and, I am now convinced, my father's life. So I keep my mouth shut and succumb to the numbness assailing me. After a short while, I realize we are riding in the back of a police car. My dad, Frizzy, and me. But I have no pulse on the details. It might as well be a basset hound driving the car, for all I can tell. The eerie cackle from the radio only stokes my catalepsy. After a short ride, we are taken inside the police station, where the world is like a psychedelic painting, spinning and whirling with iridescence, with me in the center and the passing faces a gang of schizoid artists mocking me with maniacal laughter as they splash watercolor in my eyes.

I am aware enough to know my dad has been separated from us, and Frizzy and I are left to sit on cold metal chairs across from a woman typing on a computer at a desk. She is not a police officer, of that I am sure. First, she looks like she could be someone's grandmother. I suppose there's no rule against grandmothers serving as police officers. But I can't imagine there's not a rule against blind people serving as police officers. Or blind grand-mothers. And she's definitely blind. This I realize after several moments when she takes out the headphones I now see she's been wearing, gets up and nudges across the room with the aid of a stick that blind people use for navigation—blind sticks, I suppose they're called—fills up her coffee, then nudges back to her desk, sits down gingerly, and begins typing again. Maybe she can't be a police officer, but I think it's pretty darn cool that she can type the way she does.

In a very short time my mother arrives with...you guessed it. It's amaz-ing how traveling by private jet can get you places where you want to go so much faster. Heck, I'd be at home right now, getting ready to fly to San Francisco tomorrow, and the past four weeks of my life would have been filled with the mundane summer pastimes of youth, instead of the calamity of affairs that have eventually led to my sitting in this dingy police station across from a blind typist. With a coffee stain on her blouse. Thanks a lot, Uriah...for offering me your plane.

My mother barely acknowledges her two children, which I suppose is no deviation from her normal predilection. Certainly not when she can't brag about spending a fortune to clean dust mites. She's whisked back to join my dad, which I am sure is bound to make his interrogation by the police just a whole heap more pleasurable. Did I just say *heap*? Wouldn't you know it, Uriah is now standing in front of me with a smarmy grin. I'm thankful there are no more metal chairs for him to sit on—Frizzy and I occupying the only two—and that the blind lady is in no condition to see that he needs one. But never underestimate the disabled. She senses he's there. Maybe she can smell a rat. So she asks if she can help, which he unctuously answers by saying, "No, thank you, I'm just here to retrieve the children." Retrieve? My day just got worse.

We drive silently around for a while and eventually pull into a Barnes and Noble. *This* has my mother written all over it. I can only imagine she told him to take us here to keep me happy, otherwise she might quickly become a widow. It's fine, though, because this allows me to ditch Uriah. I find Frizzy a few children's books to keep her happy and then grab the latest Grisham novel and plunk down in a cushy peach chair with a kaleidoscope of stains.

Several hours pass, during which time I take Frizzy to the bathroom four times, each one coinciding within moments of the coffee and scone I purchase for her at the mini-Starbucks in the bookstore. It's all on Uriah. I had flagged him down in the self-help section (at least he knows he needs it!) and begged forty bucks from him, every penny of which I have spent on Frizzy, as well as a little something here and there for myself. Sitting back in my chair, I just turn past page one hundred in the book, when I catch a glimpse of Uriah out of the corner of my eye. I pretend he's not there, even after he issues a gnarly cough to get my attention. When that doesn't work, he says, "Ah, Jamie, we need to get going." I glance up at him, but say nothing and don't move. That's when he steps closer and whispers with hot breath, "They've found the, ah, canoe."

"What? What do you mean?"

"They've found the canoe. Abandoned in a park."

"Was Dale in it?" I ask, loudly enough to draw the gaze of a teenage girl sitting in the stained chair across from me. She has a diamond fleck piercing her nose, and, I now notice, emerald eyes like a cat's. She smiles at me and I smile back, my attention distracted enough that I barely hear Uriah speaking.

"They found him?" I ask as I slowly pull my gaze away from the girl.

"Yes, that's what I said," he whines.

As we drive back to the police station, I try to imagine the reaction of The Sphincter when she pulled into a park to dump the canoe and saw my dead grandfather bundled up inside. As much as I want to enjoy this image, it hurts too much to think of Dale getting discarded like he was a piece of stale meat. Stale Dale. While this development does not necessarily absolve my dad of his transgressions, it does help tremendously that a body has been discovered and he can no longer be accused of killing my grandfather and ditching the body, which is what my worse nightmare had convinced me of.

I don't bother to verify his criminal status with him, as I can clearly tell he is in no mood to discuss his experience with the police. Perhaps ever. We ride silently in the back of Uriah's rented Cadillac. My dad and I are dropped back at the rental-car place where we had just yesterday returned our own rented Cadillac. We won't be renting one of *those* again. That I'm sure of. I am waiting for Frizzy to climb out of the back, when my mother orders her to stay in the car. Frizzy's told she is going to return with my mother to Colorado and then a few days later go back home with her to New York for the rest of the summer. Well, you'd think my mother just stabbed the child in the back with a dagger. Frizzy emits a bloodcurdling shriek that makes the employee across the parking lot with one of those wireless credit card thingamajigs drop it onto the pavement.

Frizzy declares that she is absolutely not going with my mother back to Colorado. Or *Colowado*, as she says. When my mother insists that she is indeed going with her to Colowado, Frizzy shrieks again and glares at Uriah as if he's the one who should be worried about the dagger. He leans over to my mother and whispers something. Whatever it was seems to summarily settle things, and Frizzy stays with us. Wow, he really loves kids.

While waiting in line inside the car-rental place, I ask my dad what's going to happen to Dale.

"Your mother's taking care of it. They will get him sent back East, do an autopsy to confirm the cause of death. He'll be cremated like Chip. That's what he wanted, apparently." Ah, yes, but he could have done without the canoe ride first.

So, here we are back in Chili's eating dinner. I'm not sure why we've come back here. Maybe my dad wants to reminisce. After all, it's the same place where nearly a week ago Dale convinced my dad to take me home to New York for the funeral. Maybe if my dad had stood up to Dale and said "Screw you," Dale would still be alive, and we'd be in San Francisco right now.

Which reminds me. "Ah, Dad, are we, ah, still going to Sand Fwansicko?" I ask casually before biting into a chip loaded with cheese, beans, and hot chilies. I've steered the bowl away from Frizzy lest she ingest more farting fuel.

"Well," my dad says, "I don't think it makes sense anymore. We'd be late."

Late? I'm certain the threat of tardiness has *never* deterred him from anything in his whole life. And I'm more certain he's already run the calculations in his head on the distance remaining and the time available to get there, including a few all-night drives if necessary. So, I just stare at him waiting for an amended answer.

But instead, he says, "Plus..." then pauses and curls his right hand, puts it to his mouth, and blows into it like a pitcher moistening his fingers as he prepares to throw a curveball. Here it comes: "Your mother has demanded we not go. So, I guess we'll have to...bag it, as you would say."

"She's *demanded* we not go?" I ask incredulously.

"Yes, that's what I said. Demanded." He surveys the huge chimichanga, which has now been placed in front of him. "Unfortunately, the tables have suddenly been turned on the situation between me and your mother." Situation? I don't say anything, but arch my eyebrows fiercely with the "do tell" sign.

"Let's just say..." he pauses and puts down the chimichanga, which he was just about to bite into. "Let's just say, your mother now has a bit of the upper hand."

"Upper hand?"

"Yes. Upper hand. I was banking on being able to push her around the rest of my life. You know, forever using her...misconduct...as leverage against her. But now..."

"You've trumped her misconduct?"

"Welllll...I wouldn't go that far," he says, now with a mouthful of chimichanga. "Mine's just a little more recent. Give it time, though."

I chew on this assertion a moment. Then bite my burrito. "Maybe it's not a bad thing," I mutter with a full mouth, since I'm getting the impression manners are not required here.

"What's that?" he asks, then suddenly reaches out next to him and grabs Frizzy's hand. "Don't pick the salsa off the table and eat it! That's gross!"

"The tables being turned," I say.

"Huh?"

"Maybe it's not a bad thing…for the tables to be turned."

"How's that?"

"Well, I was thinking, maybe it would be good for us to no longer be mad at Mom."

He looks up at me guardedly. "Dale really got into your head, didn't he?"

I shrug my shoulders and pick at my food. My dad takes another bite and says, "Maybe you're right."

Really? We'll see. We eat the rest of our meals in near silence. My dad grows strangely distracted. He doesn't even notice Frizzy spilling beans on her shirt and then sticking the shirt in her mouth to suck the beans off. He stares up at the TV at the far end of the room near the bar. There's a baseball game on, but it's impossible to tell who's playing. Finally, he looks back at me and says, "Listen, Jame. I'm really sorry."

I shrug. As much as I know it annoys him. But it's about all I can do except mumble nervously, "That's OK."

"I mean," he continues, "I know how important this ELEGY program was and all."

"Oh," I say and consider stopping there, but the next words come out despite myself: "I thought you were saying you were sorry about Dale."

"About Dale?"

"Yeah."

"What do you mean? Why should I be sorry about him? It's not like I killed the guy."

"No, but you stuffed him in a canoe. Like a…ravioli."

"Like a ravioli?"

"It's all I could think of. Mexican would have been too easy."

He leans back as the waitress deposits the check on the table. Then he props his elbows on the surface, with one of them landing in a spot of salsa, and says, "OK, you're right. That wasn't the brightest idea."

"Or the kindest."

"I didn't think you could be unkind to a dead person," he quips.

"Daaaad," I plead.

"OK. Or the kindest," he concedes, then pauses. "I'm sorry." He stares again over to the TV, this time keeping his eyes there as he says, "I just really didn't want you to miss this program. It was important."

The words hang in the air for several seconds, then I ask, "To who?"

He shifts his gaze slowly toward me, looks me in the eye, and twists up his mouth like a kid who's been caught stealing Oreos from the pantry. In fact, I can't help visualize him shrinking before me across the table to the stature of Frizzy. Two little kids with freckles sitting next to each other with dinner slop on their shirts. Who's going to drive?

I take a couple of deep breaths to shake this unsettling image from my brain and then search desperately for something to say to bring reality back to our table. "So, Dad. What's next?"

"What do you mean?" he asks, in a deep voice that's truly the possession of an adult male, not some little kid I had imagined. He signs the credit card receipt, which offers added comfort.

"If we're not going to San Francisco, what are we going to do?"

Guess what he does? Shrugs his shoulders. How do you like that?

"I want to go see the wok men again," Frizzy chimes in.

"Wok men?" my dad asks.

"Rock men," I clarify. "I think she means Mount Rushmore."

Whether this suggestion has any bearing on our choice of hotels for the night is hard to say. I'm just relieved it's not the same one we'd used for the past week. Bad memories of Dale dying there? Sure. But nearly as bad is the fact that when we were checking out very early this morning—which seems like days ago—my dad told the desk clerk he would need to pay for the sheets from Room 234 because his son puked all over them and they had to be tossed out. Kids are so easy to blame.

Anyway, we head out the highway toward Mount Rushmore. It's very late, and we're lucky to get the last room in a Best Western that is designed like a rustic lodge. My dad doesn't flinch when he's told the price, which is about double the rate of the other place, even after they hiked it twenty-five bucks.

We're all sound asleep before you know it, and I'm pleased to have my own bed. We're also up in the morning before you know it. My dad has set the alarm for 7 a.m., and while it's not 5 a.m., I still can't help but wonder what mischief he's up to now.

When I ask why we're up so early, he responds, "Frizzy's right. We need to go back and see the Rock Men. I think I missed it last time we were there."

This early? But who's stopping him? He's on a roll. He doesn't even bat an eye when we trundle up the steep roads toward Mount Rushmore behind an RV going about seven miles per hour. Nor does it roil him when several cars and a half-dozen motorcycles roar by us in the passing lane.

It's so early, we're among the first people into the facility. I don't think my dad's ever been first anywhere. Rather than viewing the presidents from the amphitheater like we did last time, which I guess he missed, I suggest we hike up the path—steps mostly—that allows you to get closer. Nearly right underneath them. So close you can see the detail of the nosepiece on Teddy's glasses.

My dad stops at the platform and closes his eyes, breathing in the fresh air. Frizzy takes a few pictures with her broken camera, or at least pretends. We stand around for a long time, long enough for several groups of visitors to cycle through, including a family from Europe who asks me to take their picture. All four of them—mother, father, and a boy and a girl around my age—are wearing tight athletic shorts and equally tight Adidas shirts. For the fun of it, I ask them to hold still so I can take their picture with my sister's camera too. They're all smiles. Ripe.

After they leave, my dad says out of the blue, "Hey, Jame, remember that word I used the other day when I yelled at you outside the sporting goods store?'

"What word?" I ask, honestly confused.

"The 'f' word."

"Oh, you mean *fuggering*?"

"Yes," he says. "I, ah, just want to ask that you never use that word."

"*Fuggering*?"

"Nooooo. The real 'f' word."

"Dad, it's not like I've never heard it before. I hear kids use it at school all the time. And it's in most of the books I read. And Eminem's songs."

"Who's that?"

"A rapper."

"Great. Well, I don't care whether M&M says it...or Reese's Pieces...or whoever. Whomever. Whatever. Don't use the damn word." He turns away emphatically and begins to walk down the steps. We wander through some of the exhibits showing how Mount Rushmore was made, and then we wind up back at the amphitheater, staring off one last time at the majestic faces in the granite.

I realize our time here has run its course, so I ask, "What the fuggering do we do now, Dad?" OK, I didn't say *fuggering*.

"I don't know," he says.

"Are we just going to...drive back home?"

He looks up behind him, staring off pensively likes he's searching for home. He's looking east, I'm pretty sure, given the morning glow radiating off the presidents' faces in the other direction. He stares for several more moments, then turns west and says again, "I don't know."

After several minutes, an idea pops into my head randomly, the way things do when you're my age. "Why don't we go to Yellowstone?" I say.

"Yellowstone?"

"Yeah, Yellowstone National Park. I don't think it's too far from here."

"It's not toward home," he says, surprising me by his awareness. As he speaks the words, he again shifts his gaze east, still searching.

"Dawkins says it's spectacular," I say cajolingly.

"Dawkins? Who's Dawkins?"

"Dale's friend. From Florida. He was telling me all about the best national parks when we were in Costco."

"Costco?"

"Yeah, waiting for Dale to clean the bird poop off his head."

"Bird poop?"

"It's not that important, Dad. The question is, wouldn't it be cool to go to Yellowstone?"

The answer is: "Ah, what the hell." We hustle back to the car. My dad starts the engine and then tells me to wait a moment. He gets out and goes to the trunk and is rummaging around back there for a little while. Finally he marches away from the car and walks toward a trash can. He's holding something in his hand. It's the white binder, the one with all of his research for the trip. He slams it into the trash like he's LeBron. He gets back into the car and says, "Let's go." OK then. I smile.

Riding shotgun, I have been confidently delegated navigation duties. With the road atlas in hand and the GPS tucked away in the glove box, I guide us through the Black Hills again. We pass familiar territory, and I briefly envision me and Dale out walking along the road talking about apple trees. Soon we descend through Custer State Park. The first time we had passed through here, a week ago, my dad had made some comment like, "Ooooh, Custer," which I took to be a suggestion in my direction. One I chose to completely ignore.

This time, he makes no suggestions. After several minutes, in which we slow to let a few deer cross the road, I say, "Custer first made a name for himself in the Civil War, you know?"

"Really?" my dad says.

"Yes," I continue with an amazing renewal of vigor and enthusiasm. It is a relief to remember how much I really do love this, especially when I am not being poked and prodded like a mule. "He fought in a lot of the big ones. Bull Run. Chancellorsville. Gettysburg."

"Cool," my dad says enthusiastically. Yeah, cool.

We roar across eastern Wyoming, flat as can be. But I don't despair this time. I know from experience what we'll soon see. Out West, the land can only remain flat for so long. Sure enough, by late afternoon, mountains soar in the distance. We curve along the foot of them and bend north on Interstate 90 toward Sheridan. I am in full control of our route. But not my sister. Alas, I'm sure I never will be. She's bored. Or "bawd," as she pronounces it in authentic Long Island diction, making every effort to bury her southern pidgin for good. We were in such a rush to head west in our rental car, my dad and I never gave a second's thought to how we'd keep her occupied without a TV.

"When are we going to get our other car back?" she asks finally. I look at my dad and laugh. He laughs too.

"Seriously, Dad," I say, "Do you think they'll ever find it...find her?"

"Who knows. Maybe it's in Canada by now," he answers, as I duly note his substitution of the gender-neutral pronoun. "Let's just not talk about it," he concludes.

OK then. My dad's feeling calm. Not a forced fake calm. But a genuine insouciance. That's a word I'll never use around my friends. Anyway, this is good. The insouciance. The new dad. Or maybe, I hope, it's just the *real* dad.

Frizzy grumbles one more time about being bawd. I turn around and tell her she'll live, that TV is crap anyway. She sticks her tongue out at me, and I'm glad to see she's still my *real* sister. I'd tell her to just look out the window, but I notice there's not much to look at. A thick layer of clouds has plopped onto the highway, and an oily mist coats the windshield. We turn off the interstate and head for the mountains. The Big Horns. At least that's what the map says. Any doubt is quickly allayed when we begin to rise in elevation and my ears begin to pop. The rain falls harder, and the car slithers back and forth up the snaking road. My dad's going about four miles per hour. Even an RV is "riding up his ass." But he's none the wiser, and life is good. The real dad. We continue to ascend for well over an hour, and I'm wondering if there is ever going to be a peak to these mountains. The air in the car grows noticeably chillier, and then we hear a pelting sound on the windshield. It sounds like ice crystals, because, well, it is. The rain has turned to sleet and then, several moments later, we see flurries mixed in. Snow in July! This is cool. Even Frizzy thinks so. Who needs TV?

Finally, the car makes its first decent, slowly, deliberately, at times my dad bringing it almost to a complete stop as we inch around the sharp, slick curves. The rain, sleet, and snow concoction has eased up a bit, but the visibility is still no more than five feet in front of us. My dad pulls over and lets three RVs pass. Then we proceed. As we inch down, I notice the clouds begin to lift as if God were sucking them up with a vacuum cleaner. It seems like it would be the perfect conditions for a rainbow, and my heart leaps. I search the sky, but unfortunately I behold no arc of color. We continue down a broad sweep of road. There is a wide dirt shoulder, and my dad pulls off as if drawn by his own curiosity. We step out, the cold air whipping at our bare legs, all of us in shorts. Why not? We left a place this morning where the temperature was near ninety. As the road twists below us, two sharp slopes on either side form a giant *V*, between and beyond which a valley floor stretches out for what seems like eternity. It's a tawny color in the late afternoon sunlight that has now edged its way through the clouds departing toward the other side of the Big Horns.

A giant blue splotch in the distance appears to be a lake or a river. I glance at the map I have in my hand to determine what might be the nearest peak. The best I can determine, it's Bald Mountain, just over ten thousand feet. One of many that size in the Big Horn range. Bald's no fourteener, for sure, but that's OK. Because I have no doubt this is the highest I have ever been in my life. Not as high as being in that airplane last week, of course, but this is different. More tangible. The view sweeps majestically and is unlike anything we saw in Colorado where we always seemed to be wedging up and down through shaded canyons. Or maybe my anger there, as Dale suggested, wouldn't allow me to see broadly enough.

Frizzy snaps a few silent pictures, and then we hop back in the car and continue our descent. I glance back at one point and see a towering peak receding below the tops of the pine trees. Bald Mountain. I am certain beyond doubt we left something behind that peak when we passed it. I don't know what. But I do know it is something we might never need, or want, again.

The blue splotch we saw from above grows larger and larger before us. It is a lake, a reservoir actually. And a river. The Bighorn, cutting through it. I think of Dale's favorite line from the book. My dad makes a quip about the ubiquitous name out here. Bighorn. So I decide to amuse him by telling him what I know about the Battle of the Little Bighorn. Which isn't much. What do you want from me?

Nor do I know much about Buffalo Bill. But I promise to get up to speed on him too. After all, we spend the night in his town: Cody. A huge sign advertises the Cody Nite Rodeo, but my dad says that might not be a good place for three people from Long Island.

"From *where?*" I ask him playfully. He smiles the way people do when they understand your hidden meaning. Still, we skip the rodeo. Someday, maybe. We also skip the Buffalo Bill Historical Center the next morning. But we do drive right through Buffalo Bill State Park as we zoom toward Yellowstone. The morning is cool and bright, a deep blue sky enveloping the jagged hills, some with dabs of snow near their peaks. I wonder what it's like in San Francisco. That's where we're supposed to be this morning. I have no doubt it is on my dad's mind, but I keep silent and enjoy the ride.

In about an hour we officially enter Yellowstone National Park. To our left, Yellowstone Lake sprawls out forever like a large sea. We come to an intersection, and my dad asks which way. "Left," I command. I want to see more of the lake. There is an overlook a few miles down. We stop and get out. We stare. Silently.

After several moments, my dad breaks the silence when he says, pausing with wonderment between each word: "Jesus. Mary. And Joseph."

"Wow," I say more simply. "This is better than San Francisco."

"I don't know," he mutters, his gaze still fixed on the shimmering lake below us. "I've never been to San Francisco."

"Well," I say. "It's definitely better than Fort Sumter."

"And a helluva lot better than Disney." He smiles and sits back on a rock. The view is like a painting, it's so pristine in its beauty, framed with pine trees in the foreground and a bulwark of mountains that seem shrunken by their impressive distance on the far side of the lake. In fact, I now recall that Dawkins told me if I ever came out here, to Yellowstone, to the Western parks in general, I'd feel like I was standing in an Albert Bierstadt painting. I thought at the time he said "Beerspot," which he might have, so I had looked it up on the computer when I got back to Dale's place. Yes, his paintings look like this. But being here is way better.

"You're a moron if you don't see God in this view," my dad says, jarring my thoughts.

Actually, I was just in the process of seeing Jessica in this view. The lake is the color of her eyes. I snap a picture with my phone and e-mail it to her. I haven't been a good friend lately, what with all the distractions I had over Dale in the canoe and my dad going to jail. OK, maybe he wasn't actually going to jail, but the story will always work better that way. Especially when I tell it to my kids. Someday.

We stop about five more times to view the lake from different vantage points. And then we follow the road toward Old Faithful, first crossing over the Continental Divide. After we watch the geyser erupt, we push on farther, knowing and expecting there are more tantalizing sites to see. After all, this is a place where you don't have to lie.

That's why my dad doesn't hesitate to pull over when Frizzy screams that she sees buffalo. We hop out and discover a whole herd of bison grazing along a river. "Take that, Rex," I hear my dad mumble at one point as he stares in awe.

We search long and hard all afternoon to see a grizzly, but no luck. My dad declares at one point that we need a place to stay for the night; otherwise we'll be sleeping out with the bears ourselves. We stop at a lodge and are told they are booked up for the evening. All the lodges in the park are; it's the busiest time of the year. Of course, we knew that! But there is a cancellation tomorrow night. I'm about to beg and plead with my dad, but he has already taken out his credit card. When he asks the woman where we could stay tonight, she suggests Cody, or down in Jackson. "Oh, we've done Cody," he drawls like a cool customer.

So we head for Jackson. "I wonder when school starts out here?" he asks to no one in particular as we're getting back in the car.

"School?" I ask perplexed. "Why do you ask that, Dad?"

"Just wondering," he says, with a shrug of his shoulders.

By the time we drift out of the southern entrance to the park, it's dark. I look at the map and explain we're going right past Grand Teton National Park. I explain to my dad that I read somewhere how the mountains got their name from early French explorers who thought they looked like *tetons*, which is the French word for *breasts*. He laughs and I say, "Maybe we can stop there in the morning and see the breasts on the way back to Yellowstone."

And that's exactly what we do. We pull off into a parking area where some signs alert visitors to several hiking trails. Dawkins was right again when he told me you haven't lived until you stood at the foot of the Tetons. My dad steps out and looks up. "This just keeps getting better and better," he says in awe. I assume he means that not even breasts are this captivating.

"That one right there," I explain, pointing to one of the jagged peaks capped with snow, "is Grand Teton. It's the tallest one in the range." Not quite a fourteener either, but the way it juts up so sharply, it appears to me the tallest mountain in the world. It has rained lightly this morning, and a curtain of clouds momentarily moves over the face of the peaks. So I close my eyes and seal the image of these mountains in my mind. Will I ever again see anything more beautiful in all my life? The air is cool and the peace enhanced not by silence but by the sound of whispering pines and birds singing their morning melodies.

I hear a car pull in behind us, knowing it is unrealistic to expect us to be alone for too long. How could this majestic place possibly keep other people away?

I open my eyes and see my dad gazing around, at peace. Content. Frizzy has bent over and is picking wildflowers at the base of a fence. I hear soft footsteps behind us. I turn and see someone. "Oh, my God," I say in as subdued a tone as I can muster, but I have no doubt the words sounded soaked with fright.

"What?" my dad asks, suddenly jarred from his hypnotic trance. He turns and sees the person too. His eyes stare wide. The person stares back. It is a moment suspended in time. I flit my eyes back and forth from him to her. From her to him. It's like watching tennis, without the grunting. I see his fists clench. His face bleeds crimson with fury. He breathes sharply several times. "You bitch!" he finally screams. The old dad is back, the one I thought we may have left in Rapid City. The one I was certain we'd left on the other side of the Big Horn Mountains.

He takes a step toward The Sphincter. She steps back. He takes another step. She retreats some more, defensively. Suddenly, he accelerates into an all-out sprint. She turns and runs. I stare helplessly. Frizzy has scampered to my side, holding her wildflowers, just staring.

He chases The Sphincter around the parking lot. She evades him with a serpentine orbit that is downright remarkable, given her stiff-legged gait. I am afraid if he catches her, he might strangle her, but I stand helpless, stupefied, numb with horror. Then just as quickly, my horror gives way to a fleeting chuckle as I compare the chase to the recollection of some clip I saw once on YouTube of some old TV show. In the video, two people were chasing each other in fast motion to the sound of quirky big-band music. Around and around in circles they ran, soon joined by others, whose legs also fluttered wildly in fast motion.

I am afraid if I step into this chase, I will become like one of those absurd characters in the video. So I stand there and just yell, "Dad!" But I know it's a feckless effort, as they have now skittered to the other side of the parking area. It is amazing how fast she is for someone who runs without bending her knees. He'll never catch her.

Oops, change that. She slips and falls, and he pounces on her. That's my cue to run over there. To do what, I am still not sure. I hear Frizzy huffing behind me. When we arrive, my dad is grabbing The Sphincter by the shoulders and screaming, "You stole my car! You stole my car!"

And my grandfather, I consider adding, but who needs to make this quandary any more complex than it is.

"Stop! Stop!" she exhorts.

"You stole my car!"

And my grandfather.

"Stop!" Her voice is breathless, but somehow she squeaks out, "You're mad…"

Oh, yes, he's mad all right.

"You stole my car!" He shakes harder.

I am wondering if he has anything else to say. Or how long this could possibly go on. "Dad," I implore, lamely.

He ignores me and screams again, "You stole my car!"

"Shut uuuup! For Pizza's sake! Get awff her and shut up!"

Now, that would be Frizzy. Her voice is still echoing among the mountains, the wildlife presumably ducking for cover, when we all turn to stare at her.

My dad has stopped shaking The Sphincter.

"It's Pete's sake," he says to Frizzy calmly.

"Who's Pete?" she asks, as if this question has been weighing on her mind for several years.

"I don't know," he says in defeat and rolls off The Sphincter, sitting with his knees pulled up to his chest and his hands clasped around them. The Sphincter slowly sits up herself and brushes pine needles from her shirt.

"What are you doing here?" my dad asks, his voice tinged with resignation.

She looks at him, her eyes betraying a fear that if she speaks, he may pounce on her again. He stares out at the parking lot. An RV has just pulled in. Other than that, it is just our rental car, and parked several spaces away, a small blue car. "So, where's my car?" he asks petulantly.

She begins to shake her head slowly and mutters, "I don't know what in the world you're talking about."

"You stole my car." Oh no, not this again.

"What?" she says with obvious affront and clearly much more cogency than when she used that word near the beginning of our trip. "You're a jerk," she adds. "I didn't steal your car."

"Then who did?" he asks.

"I don't know! I may have lied about going to Yale. But I didn't steal your car."

"Then what are you doing here?" he asks again, this time with a little more force.

"I guess...I came to see you. All of you." She hangs her head and stares at the ground as she speaks. "I felt horrible about what I did. Lying."

"Why did you lie?" he asks.

"About going to Yale?"

"Well, that, and everything. You basically lied to us the entire way... by not telling us the truth." Good one, Dad.

She takes a deep breath. A cloud passes over. "I lied about going to Yale so I could get a good job to...to help my mom."

"Help your mom?"

"Yes. Help my mom." She pauses. "Maybe I should just start at the beginning."

"Please do," he says. Frizzy and I take this as a cue to sit, Frizzy preferring to nestle in close to The Sphincter, who drapes an arm warmly around my sister's shoulder.

"My dad died when I was very young," she begins. "My mom worked hard to bring me up. Me and my two younger sisters. But she, my mom, didn't always seem to have the best luck with work. One time she got a job at a place and the building burned down the day after she started. That kind of stuff. Just bad luck. But she never gave up. Always worked hard. Always stayed positive. Then about a year ago, she made a big mistake. She got caught writing bad checks. She had to get a lawyer and all that. It was expensive. My two younger sisters are still trying to finish college." She stops for a minute and collects her breath, wiping a tiny tear from the edge of her left eye.

"I didn't lie about working in the admissions office at Harvard. I worked there as an assistant, a secretary, I suppose they used to call it. I saw enough to fudge it a bit when I spotted this job opening at Toys R Us."

"You mean Elite Schools R Us?" my dad tries to clarify.

"You know what I mean," she says with a wry grin forced through the trickle of more tears. "And I had a boyfriend who went to Yale, so I knew enough to fudge that part too."

"You had a boyfriend who went to Yale?" my dad asks, a little heavy on the incredulity in my book.

"He was a jerk," she adds.

"But he did take you to Mory's?" I can't help asking.

She chuckles. "Yes, he took me to Mory's."

"What's Mory's?" my dad asks.

"Never mind, Dad. Just listen," I command.

"So I took the job," she continues. "But I only expected to do it for a month or so. Just to get a few nice paychecks to give to my mom, to help her pay her bills. But then I got sent on this trip with you guys." She stops again and wipes her nose. Then laughs.

"What's so funny?" my dad asks, impatiently.

"You are," she says, looking at my dad. "You're all funny. Well, except for your driving...and that quizzing, of course." I laugh, and he scrunches his brow as if he has no clue what she's talking about. "Anyway," she continues, "I was having a good time. And I thought, maybe I could actually be of assistance to you after all...by somehow making you think twice about prep school or Yale or Harvard or whatever..."

"What do you mean?" my dad asks, as if he's been unduly insulted.

"Well, not necessarily not sending him there," she backtracks quickly. "I don't mean that. But *how* it is you're *trying* to send him there." She impulsively pulls Frizzy tighter to her, as if to shield herself from being pounced on again, then says, "Let's just say, I've seen enough. I've seen enough to know how manufactured some of those kids are by their parents. It's like these kids grow up according to some strict formula their parents force on them for fear they'll all be complete failures. The parents especially. It doesn't take a genius to recognize this. Even a dunce like me can see it. I mean, what fun is it for kids to grow up that way? I used to stay late at my job in the Harvard admissions office and read through some of those applications for laughs. But then I realized it wasn't funny at all. It made me sad. One kid, you should have seen it...his application. He wrote this thoroughly depressing essay about tart reform..."

"Like Pop-Tarts?" Frizzy asks.

"No, that's not what he was blabbering on about. I couldn't even tell..."

"I think it was probably tort reform," I clarify. "A tort has to do with civil law."

"Borrrrr-ring," she declares, making a thumbs-down sign with both hands. "Tarts would have been better. I betcha ninety-five percent of Americans would rather hear about tarts than torts."

"Yeah…" my dad says with a sarcastic look in his eyes, "the other five percent of course being all the rich people."

"Why are you so obsessed with rich people?" The Sphincter asks.

"They have it all…" he begins.

But she cuts him off. "That's what you think," she says. "Maybe you should just let the rich be rich, Doug. And you just be…the Shoops."

My dad purses his lips and scrunches his brow like he does when he's trying to figure out the puzzle on *Wheel of Fortune*.

"Anyway," The Sphincter continues, "I just read a lot of those applications wondering where the fun was in those kids' lives, rich or not. Maybe a kid thinks torts—whatever they are—are fun. If so, good for him, but I hope it's him deciding it and not his parents. Hey, like I said, I'm not saying going to Yale and all is not what Jamie, The Kid, should do…" She hesitates, wondering perhaps if she's wandered too deep into territory where she shouldn't be. She stares at the ground for several moments, shifts herself and then says, "I'm sorry. I shoulda left after the first day. I knew I shoulda. But I couldn't, and the farther we got, the harder it was to leave. After a few days, I knew I couldn't tell you the truth, or you'd be so angry."

"Not my dad," I interject. She laughs at my joke, which I have to admit is kind of cool.

"It tore me up inside," she continues. "So I called my mom and told her what I'd done and asked what to do. She told me to tell the truth, of course. But I just couldn't do it. It was like I was sinking in quicksand and couldn't get out. I was calling my mom several times a day just for her to comfort me."

"Lola?" my dad asks.

"Yes, Lola. Finally, after the call came from Mr. Hildenberger, I was stunned. Not by him finding me out. I knew that would happen sooner or later. I didn't even have to answer the phone to know what was going on. No, I was stunned by the realization that I let you all down. I was like… embarrassed. So I left."

"But not in my car?"

"No, not in your car. I rented my own car. I was just going to drive around for a while, but I still felt so badly about all of you. So I went to church and prayed."

"You're not Lutheran, are you?" I ask, thinking of Uriah. Unfortunately.

"No, I'm Catholic," she says.

Now, I know it shouldn't matter whether she's a Catholic, Lutheran, Jew, Muslim...or Scientologist—that weird stuff the celebrities do. But there was something fateful in her words. After all, religion draws us together—I'd like to hope—more than it wedges us apart. So I smile at her welcomingly, and my dad winks my way. So too does my grandmother in heaven I think. Both of them, actually. Best of all, Dale winks too, and that means everything to me.

"But," she continues, "I didn't exactly get anywhere...with my prayers, I mean. Then, I was having coffee in Dunkin' Donuts, about ready to leave town, when I saw you pull up across the street to Walgreens."

Ah, yes, we had stopped there on our way out to that hotel by Mount Rushmore to reload on Frizzy's antihistamines since her supply had been stolen. Along with Dale's body.

"At first, I was a little confused," she says. "I saw all of you get out, but it wasn't your car. Then I thought, well, maybe your car had been repossessed."

"Gee, thanks," my dad murmurs.

"When you came out," she says, "I followed you."

"You followed us?" he asks.

"Yes, I wasn't sure why, but I just figured it had something to do with my prayers. I watched you go to Mount Rushmore."

"What did you do?" my dad asks.

"Waited in the car?"

"Waited in the car!"

"Yes, I waited in the car everywhere you stopped. The gas stations, that lake...like ten times! What was up with that? And then at Old Yeller."

Old Yeller? "That's a dog," I clarify. "You mean Old Faithful."

"Whatever. I also slept in my car for two nights and waited for you to come out of your hotel both mornings.

"You slept in your car!" my dad says with building astonishment.

"Yeah, my back aches. And it didn't help with you pouncing on me like that."

"Sorry," he says bashfully. There is a slight pause. Frizzy is quietly picking at the pine needles, and it clearly pleases her to have her friend back. "You've followed us for three days," my dad finally says, more to himself as a way to wade through his disbelief.

"Yep."

"Why here?" he asks. "Why now?"

"I don't know…maybe I was too sore to sleep in my car again tonight." She chirps at her own joke, then continues, "I guess I just realized I wanted to be with all of you. And when I followed you from your hotel and we could see the mountains glowing in the morning light, I thought, this is it. Now or never. This is the most beautiful place I have ever seen. It must be God telling me what to do."

My dad stares off in the distance, as I've noticed him prone to do lately when he's seeking answers. "I guess I should start praying some more myself," he says. "Or start going back to church…or reading the Bible…or something like that."

"I think all that might just help you," she says.

"Help me!" he squawks. "What the heck does that mean?"

"Well, what I mean," she says confidently, "is that first of all you need to let go, once and for all. You're pretty uptight about your son becoming a big shot. If that's meant to happen, it will on its own and not because of you. And secondly…I realize I haven't known you very long and stuff, but it's not difficult to see that maybe you've misplaced something in your life…something you learned along the way from somebody…I don't know who. But you've lost it. And I think you might benefit from finding it again. Better yet, I think your kids…*both* of them…might benefit."

He looks a little miffed, maligned maybe, and begins to speak, then stops. He lets out a big sigh, perhaps it's the pride he's bottled up inside. It takes several moments to fade out under the sound of the wind in the pine trees.

After a few more moments, she says, "This might not be a bad place to start."

"How's that?" he says, his gaze again fixed far up on the mountains.

"Well, I was just thinking that it's kinda like going to church out here. It's certainly more beautiful than any church people could build."

"You know, Dad," I butt in, "they do call this group of mountains the Cathedrals."

"Yeah," she says, pointing up to one of the peaks. "There's the spire. All these trees are the parishioners. And those rocks are the altar. "

"Upon this rock I will build my church," I say.

"And the gates of hell shall not prevail against it," she finishes.

My dad chuckles, I think because he has drawn his gaze down from the mountains in time to catch me smiling at her again.

She's smiling back at me, but it quickly turns to a frown, and she does this quick whip of her head as if some sharp pain went through it. Or a lightbulb came on. "Hey, where the heck's Dale?" she says.

This causes my dad to suck in a big gulp of air, and before he can squeeze a word out, Frizzy says, "My daddy killed him."

"I didn't kill him!" he scowls.

"That's not what Mommy told me," she says.

I erupt with a huge laugh but I'm really not sure what's so funny. Then my dad says quickly, "Jamie, why don't you take Frizzy for a walk up there... to that altar, as you call it."

OK, fine, I concede silently. This might be her only chance in life to get walked up to the altar. "Does she need her inhaler?" I ask.

"No, she'll be OK." But she does want her camera.

So we stop by the car, and then I take her hand and guide her along a trail leading up to a low bluff, minuscule beneath the towering peak above us. Peace has returned. Except when she tells me she has to pee. I point to the bushes, then wait while she crouches and hums "Old McDonald" as she's going.

We hike up a little farther, stepping cautiously up a gravelly shoot between two outcroppings. We are up high enough that we can now look down to the parking area, where everything is reduced in size. But not so small that I can't see a man and a woman walking toward the head of the trail. Are they holding hands? It sure looks that way as she pulls him gently forward up the first few steps of the path. I wonder if I'll still be allowed to call her Sphincter. OK. Lady Ashley it is. With a nod of respect to Hemingway. "Look, Frizzy," I say, pointing to them.

"They're coming," she squeals. "And she's holding his hand!"

"Good for him," I say in a normal voice, and then more softly, to myself, "Good for you, Dad. Hold her hand. And let go. Once and for all."

I guess this means I'll have to give up shotgun again. But that's OK. We sit on a rock—on Peter—and wait. Faint contours begin to form around us as the soft fog that has been drifting by in spurts begins to fade for good. Frizzy clicks her camera, but the only sound is silence. We can again hear the evergreens whispering in the wind. A hawk soars overhead, warning us with its hoarse scream. My father and Lady Ashley have momentarily disappeared from view as they approach the steepest part of the slope below us.

I glance up and notice that blue sky is spreading out like a huge blanket for miles. The clouds blow off and colors splash across the sky in a half-arc. "See the rainbow, Frizzy?" She looks up and says nothing, just clicking her camera again and again.

"It's broken, Frizzy," I say.

"No kidding," she snaps, then adds: "You tart," before turning the camera up to the mountains and clicking away, as she has done so hundreds of times on this trip. Not one of those clicks will translate into a real lasting picture from that piece of crap. But the images might forever be etched in her little mind...I hope. I glance up and behold that the rainbow has now stretched to completion, its newly formed descending arc landing out in the valley below at a distance that seems a hundred miles away, but close enough to touch. I reach down and pinch the pocket where the piece of paper is with the poem. The Wheat Thin. I have carried it there every day since Dale gave it to me. "The Child is father of the Man."

A granite pinnacle punctures the final wisp of cloud cover and scrapes at the deep blue sky. Everything that's hidden must emerge. Into a shape. The world is all about shapes, isn't it? The Bermuda Triangle. The Oval Office. The Pentagon. Pandora's Box. A square peg in a round hole. The circle of life. Even Florida has its shape. And the Great Plains, I suppose. Flat like a pancake. And never changing, no matter which way you turn. But now I see how these mountains captivate so easily. How they change you. And why they've always drawn people here for generations to challenge their awesomeness and leave everything of inconsequence behind. In each direction different shapes greet you. They seem to beckon your mind to accept new ideas. And to make you venture to places where you've never been and never thought you'd go. Nifty.

I will miss Jessica.

www.ingramcontent.com/pod-product-compliance
Lightning Source LLC
Chambersburg PA
CBHW070551130626
46556CB00001B/109